THE WOLVES OF GOD

THE WOLVES OF GOD

And Other Fey Stories

BY

ALGERNON BLACKWOOD

Author of "The Wave," "The Promise of Air," etc

AND

WILFRED WILSON

BORGO PRESS / WILDSIDE PRESS

www.wildsidepress.com

TO THE MEMORY

OF

OUR CAMP-FIRES IN THE WILDERNESS

CONTENTS

THE WOLVES OF GOD

THE WOLVES OF GOD

I

THE WOLVES OF GOD

1

AS the little steamer entered the bay of Kettletoft in the
Orkneys the beach at Sanday appeared so low that
the houses almost seemed to be standing in the water; and
to the big, dark man leaning over the rail of the upper
deck the sight of them came with a pang of mingled
pain and pleasure. The scene, to his eyes, had not changed.
The houses, the low shore, the flat treeless country beyond, the vast open sky, all looked exactly the same as
when he left the island thirty years ago to work for the
Hudson Bay Company in distant N. W. Canada. A lad
of eighteen then, he was now a man of forty-eight, old
for his years, and this was the home-coming he had so
often dreamed about in the lonely wilderness of trees where
he had spent his life. Yet his grim face wore an anxious
rather than a tender expression. The return was perhaps not quite as he had pictured it.

Jim Peace had not done too badly, however, in the
Company's service. For an islander, he would be a rich
man now; he had not married, he had saved the greater
part of his salary, and even in the far-away Post where
he had spent so many years there had been occasional
opportunities of the kind common to new, wild countries

where life and law are in the making. He had not hesitated to take them. None of the big Company Posts, it
was true, had come his way, nor had he risen very high
in the service; in another two years his turn would have
come, yet he had left of his own accord before those two
years were up. His decision, judging by the strength
in the features, was not due to impulse; the move had
been deliberately weighed and calculated; he had renounced
his opportunity after full reflection. A man with those
steady eyes, with that square jaw and determined mouth,
certainly did not act without good reason.

A curious expression now flickered over his weather-
hardened face as he saw again his childhood's home, and
the return, so often dreamed about, actually took place at
last. An uneasy light flashed for a moment in the deep-
set grey eyes, but was quickly gone again, and the tanned
visage recovered its accustomed look of stern compo-
sure. His keen sight took in a dark knot of figures on
the landing-pier—his brother, he knew, among them. A
wave of home-sickness swept over him. He longed to see
his brother again, the old farm, the sweep of open country, the sand-dunes, and the breaking seas. The smell
of long-forgotten days came to his nostrils with its sweet,
painful pang of youthful memories.

How fine, he thought, to be back there in the old
familiar fields of childhood, with sea and sand about him
instead of the smother of endless woods that ran a thousand miles without a break. He was glad in particular
that no trees were visible, and that rabbits scampering
among the dunes were the only wild animals he need ever
meet. . . .

Those thirty years in the woods, it seemed, oppressed
his mind; the forests, the countless multitudes of trees,
had wearied him. His nerves, perhaps, had suffered
finally. Snow, frost and sun, stars, and the wind had
been his companions during the long days and endless
nights in his lonely Post, but chiefly—trees. Trees, trees,

trees! On the whole, he had preferred them in stormy weather, though, in another way, their rigid hosts, 'mid the deep silence of still days, had been equally oppressive. In the clear sunlight of a windless day they assumed a waiting, listening, watching aspect that had something spectral in it, but when in motion—well, he preferred a moving animal to one that stood stock-still and stared. Wind, moreover, in a million trees, even the lightest breeze, drowned all other sounds—the howling of the wolves, for instance, in winter, or the ceaseless harsh barking of the husky dogs he so disliked.

Even on this warm September afternoon a slight shiver ran over him as the background of dead years loomed up behind the present scene. He thrust the picture back, deep down inside himself. The self-control, the strong, even violent will that the face betrayed, came into operation instantly. The background was background; it belonged to what was past, and the past was over and done with. It was dead. Jim meant it to stay dead.

The figure waving to him from the pier was his brother. He knew Tom instantly; the years had dealt easily with him in this quiet island; there was no startling, no unkindly change, and a deep emotion, though unexpressed, rose in his heart. It was good to be home again, he realized, as he sat presently in the cart, Tom holding the reins, driving slowly back to the farm at the north end of the island. Everything he found familiar, yet at the same time strange. They passed the school where he used to go as a little bare-legged boy; other boys were now learning their lessons exactly as he used to do. Through the open window he could hear the droning voice of the schoolmaster, who, though invisible, wore the face of Mr. Lovibond, his own teacher.

"Lovibond?" said Tom, in reply to his question. "Oh, he's been dead these twenty years. He went south, you know—Glasgow, I think it was, or Edinburgh. He got typhoid."

Stands of golden plover were to be seen as of old in the fields, or flashing overhead in swift flight with a whir of wings, wheeling and turning together like one huge bird. Down on the empty shore a curlew cried. Its piercing note rose clear above the noisy clamour of the gulls. The sun played softly on the quiet sea, the air was keen but pleasant, the tang of salt mixed sweetly with the clean smells of open country that he knew so well. Nothing of essentials had changed, even the low clouds beyond the heaving uplands were the clouds of childhood.

They came presently to the sand-dunes, where rabbits sat at their burrow-mouths, or ran helter-skelter across the road in front of the slow cart.

"They're safe till the colder weather comes and trapping begins," he mentioned. It all came back to him in detail.

"And they know it, too—the canny little beggars," replied Tom. "Any rabbits out where you've been?" he asked casually.

"Not to hurt you," returned his brother shortly.

Nothing seemed changed, although everything seemed different. He looked upon the old, familiar things, but with other eyes. There were, of course, changes, alterations, yet so slight, in a way so odd and curious, that they evaded him; not being of the physical order, they reported to his soul, not to his mind. But his soul, being troubled, sought to deny the changes; to admit them meant to admit a change in himself he had determined to conceal even if he could not entirely deny it.

"Same old place, Tom," came one of his rare remarks. "The years ain't done much to it." He looked into his brother's face a moment squarely. "Nor to you, either, Tom," he added, affection and tenderness just touching his voice and breaking through a natural reserve that was almost taciturnity.

His brother returned the look; and something in that instant passed between the two men, something of under-

standing that no words had hinted at, much less expressed.
The tie was real, they loved each other, they were loyal,
true, steadfast fellows. In youth they had known no
secrets. The shadow that now passed and vanished left
a vague trouble in both hearts.

"The forests," said Tom slowly, "have made a silent
man of you, Jim. You'll miss them here, I'm thinking."

"Maybe," was the curt reply, "but I guess not."

His lips snapped to as though they were of steel and
could never open again, while the tone he used made Tom
realize that the subject was not one his brother cared to
talk about particularly. He was surprised, therefore, when,
after a pause, Jim returned to it of his own accord. He
was sitting a little sideways as he spoke, taking in the
scene with hungry eyes. "It's a queer thing," he observed, "to look round and see nothing but clean empty
land, and not a single tree in sight. You see, it don't
look natural quite."

Again his brother was struck by the tone of voice, but
this time by something else as well he could not name.
Jim was excusing himself, explaining. The manner, too,
arrested him. And thirty years disappeared as though
they had not been, for it was thus Jim acted as a boy when
there was something unpleasant he had to say and wished
to get it over. The tone, the gesture, the manner, all were
there. He was edging up to something he wished to say,
yet dared not utter.

"You've had enough of trees then?" Tom said sympathetically, trying to help, "and things?"

The instant the last two words were out he realized
that they had been drawn from him instinctively, and that
it was the anxiety of deep affection which had prompted
them. He had guessed without knowing he had guessed,
or rather, without intention or attempt to guess. Jim had
a secret. Love's clairvoyance had discovered it, though not
yet its hidden terms.

"I have——" began the other, then paused, evidently

to choose his words with care. "I've had enough of trees."
He was about to speak of something that his brother had
unwittingly touched upon in his chance phrase, but instead of finding the words he sought, he gave a sudden
start, his breath caught sharply. "What's that?" he exclaimed, jerking his body round so abruptly that Tom automatically pulled the reins. "What is it?"

"A dog barking," Tom answered, much surprised. "A
farm dog barking. Why? What did you think it was?"
he asked, as he flicked the horse to go on again. "You
made me jump," he added, with a laugh. "You're used to
huskies, ain't you?"

"It sounded so—not like a dog, I mean," came the slow
explanation. "It's long since I heard a sheep-dog bark, I
suppose it startled me."

"Oh, it's a dog all right," Tom assured him comfort-
ingly, for his heart told him infallibly the kind of tone to
use. And presently, too, he changed the subject in his
blunt, honest fashion, knowing that, also, was the right
and kindly thing to do. He pointed out the old farms
as they drove along, his brother silent again, sitting stiff
and rigid at his side. "And it's good to have you back,
Jim, from those outlandish places. There are not too
many of the family left now—just you and I, as a matter
of fact."

"Just you and I," the other repeated gruffly, but in
a sweetened tone that proved he appreciated the ready
sympathy and tact. "We'll stick together, Tom, eh?
Blood's thicker than water, ain't it? I've learnt that
much, anyhow."

The voice had something gentle and appealing in it,
something his brother heard now for the first time. An
elbow nudged into his side, and Tom knew the gesture
was 'not solely a sign of affection, but grew partly also
from the comfort born of physical contact when the heart
is anxious. The touch, like the last words, conveyed an

appeal for help. Tom was so surprised he couldn't believe it quite.

Scared! Jim scared! The thought puzzled and afflicted him who knew his brother's character inside out, his courage, his presence of mind in danger, his resolution. Jim frightened seemed an impossibility, a contradiction in terms; he was the kind of man who did not know the meaning of fear, who shrank from nothing, whose spirits rose highest when things appeared most hopeless. It must, indeed, be an uncommon, even a terrible danger that could shake such nerves; yet Tom saw the signs and read them clearly. Explain them he could not, nor did he try. All he knew with certainty was that his brother, sitting now beside him in the cart, hid a secret terror in his heart. Sooner or later, in his own good time, he would share it with him.

He ascribed it, this simple Orkney farmer, to those thirty years of loneliness and exile in wild desolate places, without companionship, without the society of women, with only Indians, husky dogs, a few trappers or fur-dealers like himself, but none of the wholesome, natural influences that sweeten life within reach. Thirty years was a long, long time. He began planning schemes to help. Jim must see people as much as possible, and his mind ran quickly over the men and women available. In women the neighbourhood was not rich, but there were several men of the right sort who might be useful, good fellows all. There was John Rossiter, another old Hudson Bay man, who had been factor at Cartwright, Labrador, for many years, and had returned long ago to spend his last days in civilization. There was Sandy McKay, also back from a long spell of rubber-planting in Malay. . . . . Tom was still busy making plans when they reached the old farm and presently sat down to their first meal together since that early breakfast thirty years ago before Jim caught the steamer that bore him off to exile—an exile

that now returned him with nerves unstrung and a secret
terror hidden in his heart.

"I'll ask no questions," he decided. "Jim will tell
me in his own good time. And meanwhile, I'll get him
to see as many folks as possible." He meant it too; yet
not only for his brother's sake. Jim's terror was so vivid
it had touched his own heart too.

"Ah, a man can open his lungs here and breathe!" exclaimed Jim, as the two came out after supper and stood
before the house, gazing across the open country. He drew
a deep breath as though to prove his assertion, exhaling
with slow satisfaction again. "It's good to see a clear
horizon and to know there's all that water between—
between me and where I've been." He turned his face
to watch the plover in the sky, then looked towards the
distant shore-line where the sea was just visible in the
long evening light. "There can't be too much water for
me," he added, half to himself. "I guess they can't cross
water—not that much water at any rate."

Tom stared, wondering uneasily what to make of it.

"At the trees again, Jim?" he said laughingly. He
had overheard the last words, though spoken low, and
thought it best not to ignore them altogether. To be
natural was the right way, he believed, natural and cheery.
To make a joke of anything unpleasant, he felt, was to
make it less serious. "I've never seen a tree come across
the Atlantic yet, except as a mast—dead," he added.

"I wasn't thinking of the trees just then," was the
blunt reply, "but of—something else. The damned trees
are nothing, though I hate the sight of 'em. Not of much
account, anyway"—as though he compared them mentally
with another thing. He puffed at his pipe, a moment.

"They certainly can't move," put in his brother, "nor
swim either."

"Nor another thing," said Jim, his voice thick suddenly, but not with smoke, and his speech confused, though

the idea in his mind was certainly clear as daylight. "Things can't hide behind 'em—can they?"

"Not much cover hereabouts, I admit," laughed Tom, though the look in his brother's eyes made his laughter as short as it sounded unnatural.

"That's so," agreed the other. "But what I meant was" —he threw out his chest, looked about him with an air of intense relief, drew in another deep breath, and again exhaled with satisfaction—"if there are no trees, there's no hiding."

It was the expression on the rugged, weathered face that sent the blood in a sudden gulping rush from his brother's heart. He had seen men frightened, seen men afraid before they were actually frightened; he had also seen men stiff with terror in the face both of natural and so-called supernatural things; but never in his life before had he seen the look of unearthly dread that now turned his brother's face as white as chalk and yet put the glow of fire in two haunted burning eyes.

Across the darkening landscape the sound of distant barking had floated to them on the evening wind.

"It's only a farm-dog barking." Yet it was Jim's deep, quiet voice that said it, one hand upon his brother's arm.

"That's all," replied Tom, ashamed that he had betrayed himself, and realizing with a shock of surprise that it was Jim who now played the rôle of comforter—a startling change in their relations. "Why, what did you think it was?"

He tried hard to speak naturally and easily, but his voice shook. So deep was the brothers' love and intimacy that they could not help but share.

Jim lowered his great head. "I thought," he whispered, his grey beard touching the other's cheek, "maybe it was the wolves"—an agony of terror made both voice and body tremble—"the Wolves of God!"

2

The interval of thirty years had been bridged easily enough; it was the secret that left the open gap neither of them cared or dared to cross. Jim's reason for hesitation lay within reach of guesswork, but Tom's silence was more complicated.

With strong, simple men, strangers to affectation or pretence, reserve is a real, almost a sacred thing. Jim offered nothing more; Tom asked no single question. In the latter's mind lay, for one thing, a singular intuitive certainty: that if he knew the truth he would lose his brother. How, why, wherefore, he had no notion; whether by death, or because, having told an awful thing, Jim would hide—physically or mentally—he knew not, nor even asked himself. No subtlety lay in Tom, the Orkney farmer. He merely felt that a knowledge of the truth involved separation which was death.

Day and night, however, that extraordinary phrase which, at its first hearing, had frozen his blood, ran on beating in his mind. With it came always the original, nameless horror that had held him motionless where he stood, his brother's bearded lips against his ear: *The Wolves of God*. In some dim way, he sometimes felt—tried to persuade himself, rather—the horror did not belong to the phrase alone, but was a sympathetic echo of what Jim felt himself. It had entered his own mind and heart. They had always shared in this same strange, intimate way. The deep brotherly tie accounted for it. Of the possible transference of thought and emotion he knew nothing, but this was what he meant perhaps.

At the same time he fought and strove to keep it out, not because it brought uneasy and distressing feelings to him, but because he did not wish to pry, to ascertain, to discover his brother's secret as by some kind of subterfuge that seemed too near to eavesdropping almost. Also, he wished most earnestly to protect him. Meanwhile, in spite of himself, or perhaps because of himself, he watched his brother as a wild animal watches its young. Jim was the only tie he had on earth. He loved him with a brother's love, and Jim, similarly, he knew, loved him. His job was difficult. Love alone could guide him.

He gave openings, but he never questioned:

"Your letter did surprise me, Jim. I was never so delighted in my life. You had still two years to run."

"I'd had enough," was the short reply. "God, man, it was good to get home again!"

This, and the blunt talk that followed their first meeting, was all Tom had to go upon, while those eyes that refused to shut watched ceaselessly always. There was improvement, unless, which never occurred to Tom, it was self-control; there was no more talk of trees and water, the barking of the dogs passed unnoticed, no reference to the loneliness of the backwoods life passed his lips; he spent his days fishing, shooting, helping with the work of the farm, his evenings smoking over a glass—he was more than temperate—and talking over the days of long ago.

The signs of uneasiness still were there, but they were negative, far more suggestive, therefore, than if open and direct. He desired no company, for instance—an unnatural thing, thought Tom, after so many years of loneliness.

It was this and the awkward fact that he had given up two years before his time was finished, renouncing, therefore, a comfortable pension—it was these two big details that stuck with such unkind persistence in his brother's thoughts. Behind both, moreover, ran ever the strange whispered phrase. What the words meant, or whence they were derived, Tom had no possible inkling. Like the wicked refrain of some forbidden song, they haunted him day and night, even his sleep not free from them entirely. All of which, to the simple Orkney farmer, was so new an experience that he knew not how to deal

with it at all. Too strong to be flustered, he was at any
rate bewildered. And it was for Jim, his brother, he
suffered most.

What perplexed him chiefly, however, was the attitude his brother showed towards old John Rossiter. He
could almost have imagined that the two men had met
and known each other out in Canada, though Rossiter
showed him how impossible that was, both in point of
time and of geography as well. He had brought them
together within the first few days, and Jim, silent, gloomy,
morose, even surly, had eyed him like an enemy. Old
Rossiter, the milk of human kindness as thick in his veins
as cream, had taken no offence. Grizzled veteran of the
wilds, he had served his full term with the Company and
now enjoyed his well-earned pension. He was full of
stories, reminiscences, adventures of every sort and kind;
he knew men and values, had seen strange things that
only the true wilderness delivers, and he loved nothing
better than to tell them over a glass. He talked with Jim
so genially and affably that little response was called for
luckily, for Jim was glum and unresponsive almost to
rudeness. Old Rossiter noticed nothing. What Tom noticed was, chiefly perhaps, his brother's acute uneasiness.
Between his desire to help, his attachment to Rossiter,
and his keen personal distress, he knew not what to do or
say. The situation was becoming too much for him.

The two families, besides—Peace and Rossiter—had
been neighbours for generations, had intermarried freely,
and were related in various degrees. He was too fond of
his brother to feel ashamed, but he was glad when the
visit was over and they were out of their host's house.
Jim had even declined to drink with him.

"They're good fellows on the island," said Tom on
their way home, "but not specially entertaining, perhaps.
We all stick together though. You can trust 'em mostly."

"I never was a talker, Tom," came the gruff reply.
"You know that." And Tom, understanding more than

he understood, accepted the apology and made generous allowances.

"John likes to talk," he helped him. "He appreciates a good listener."

"It's the kind of talk I'm finished with," was the rejoinder. "The Company and their goings-on don't interest me any more. I've had enough."

Tom noticed other things as well with those affectionate eyes of his that did not want to see yet would not close. As the days drew in, for instance, Jim seemed reluctant to leave the house towards evening. Once the full light of day had passed, he kept indoors. He was eager and ready enough to shoot in the early morning, no matter at what hour he had to get up, but he refused point blank to go with his brother to the lake for an evening flight. No excuse was offered; he simply declined to go.

The gap between them thus widened and deepened, while yet in another sense it grew less formidable. Both knew, that is, that a secret lay between them for the first time in their lives, yet both knew also that at the right and proper moment it would be revealed. Jim only waited till the proper moment came. And Tom understood. His deep, simple love was equal to all emergencies. He respected his brother's reserve. The obvious desire of John Rossiter to talk and ask questions, for instance, he resisted staunchly as far as he was able. Only when he could help and protect his brother did he yield a little. The talk was brief, even monosyllabic; neither the old Hudson Bay fellow nor the Orkney farmer ran to many words:

"He ain't right with himself," offered John, taking his pipe out of his mouth and leaning forward. "That's what I don't like to see." He put a skinny hand on Tom's knee, and looked earnestly into his face as he said it.

"Jim!" replied the other. "Jim ill, you mean!" It sounded ridiculous.

"His mind is sick."

"I don't understand," Tom said, though the truth bit like rough-edged steel into the brother's heart.

"His soul, then, if you like that better."

Tom fought with himself a moment, then asked him to be more explicit.

"More'n I can say," rejoined the laconic old backwoodsman. "I don't know myself. The woods heal some men and make others sick."

"Maybe, John, maybe." Tom fought back his resentment. "You've lived, like him, in lonely places. You ought to know." His mouth shut with a snap, as though he had said too much. Loyalty to his suffering brother caught him strongly. Already his heart ached for Jim. He felt angry with Rossiter for his divination, but perceived, too, that the old fellow meant well and was trying to help him. If he lost Jim, he lost the world—his all.

A considerable pause followed, during which both men puffed their pipes with reckless energy. Both, that is, were a bit excited. Yet both had their code, a code they would not exceed for worlds.

"Jim," added Tom presently, making an effort to meet the sympathy half way, "ain't quite up to the mark, I'll admit that."

There was another long pause, while Rossiter kept his eyes on his companion steadily, though without a trace of expression in them—a habit that the woods had taught him.

"Jim," he said at length, with an obvious effort, "is skeered. And it's the soul in him that's skeered."

Tom wavered dreadfully then. He saw that old Rossiter, experienced backwoodsman and taught by the Company as he was, knew where the secret lay, if he did not yet know its exact terms. It was easy enough to put the question, yet he hesitated, because loyalty forbade.

"It's a dirty outfit somewheres," the old man mumbled to himself.

Tom sprang to his feet. "If you talk that way," he exclaimed angrily, "you're no friend of mine—or his." His anger gained upon him as he said it. "Say that again," he cried, "and I'll knock your teeth——"

He sat back, stunned a moment.

"Forgive me, John," he faltered, shamed yet still angry. "It's pain to me, it's pain. Jim," he went on, after a long breath and a pull at his glass, "Jim *is* scared, I know it." He waited a moment, hunting for the words that he could use without disloyalty. "But it's nothing he's done himself," he said, "nothing to his discredit. I know *that*."

Old Rossiter looked up, a strange light in his eyes.

"No offence," he said quietly.

"Tell me what you know," cried Tom suddenly, standing up again.

The old factor met his eye squarely, steadfastly. He laid his pipe aside.

"D'ye really want to hear?" he asked in a lowered voice. "Because, if you don't—why, say so right now. I'm all for justice," he added, "and always was."

"Tell me," said Tom, his heart in his mouth. "Maybe, if I knew—I might help him." The old man's words woke fear in him. He well knew his passionate, remorseless sense of justice.

"Help him," repeated the other. "For a man skeered in his soul there ain't no help. But—if you want to hear—I'll tell you."

"Tell me," cried Tom. "I *will* help him," while rising anger fought back rising fear.

John took another pull at his glass.

"Jest between you and me like."

"Between you and me," said Tom. "Get on with it."

There was a deep silence in the little room. Only the sound of the sea came in, the wind behind it.

"The Wolves," whispered old Rossiter. "The Wolves of God."

Tom sat still in his chair, as though struck in the

face. He shivered. He kept silent and the silence seemed
to him long and curious. His heart was throbbing, the
blood in his veins played strange tricks. All he remembered was that old Rossiter had gone on talking. The
voice, however, sounded far away and distant. It was
all unreal, he felt, as he went homewards across the bleak,
wind-swept upland, the sound of the sea for ever in his
ears. . . .

Yes, old John Rossiter, damned be his soul, had gone
on talking. He had said wild, incredible things. Damned
be his soul! His teeth should be smashed for that. It
was outrageous, it was cowardly, it was not true.

"Jim," he thought, "my brother, Jim!" as he ploughed
his way wearily against the wind. "I'll teach him. I'll
teach him to spread such wicked tales!" He referred to
Rossiter. "God blast these fellows! They come home
from their outlandish places and think they can say anything! I'll knock his yellow dog's teeth. . . . !"

While, inside, his heart went quailing, crying for help,
afraid.

He tried hard to remember exactly what old John had
said. Round Garden Lake—that's where Jim was located
in his lonely Post—there was a tribe of Redskins. They
were of unusual type. Malefactors among them—thieves,
criminals, murderers—were not punished. They were
merely turned out by the Tribe to die.

But how?

The Wolves of God took care of them. What were
the Wolves of God?

A pack of wolves the Redskins held in awe, a sacred
pack, a spirit pack—God curse the man! Absurd, outlandish nonsense! Superstitious humbug! A pack of
wolves that punished malefactors, killing but never eating
them. "Torn but not eaten," the words came back to
him, "white men as well as red. They could even cross
the sea. . . ."

"He ought to be strung up for telling such wild yarns. By God—I'll teach him!"

"Jim! My brother, Jim! It's monstrous."

But the old man, in his passionate cold justice, had said a yet more terrible thing, a thing that Tom would never forget, as he never could forgive it: "You mustn't keep him here; you must send him away. We cannot have him on the island." And for that, though he could scarcely believe his ears, wondering afterwards whether he heard aright, for that, the proper answer to which was a blow in the mouth, Tom knew that his old friendship and affection had turned to bitter hatred.

"If I don't kill him, for that cursed lie, may God—and Jim—forgive me!"

3

It was a few days later that the storm caught the islands, making them tremble in their sea-born bed. The wind tearing over the treeless expanse was terrible, the lightning lit the skies. No such rain had ever been known. The building shook and trembled. It almost seemed the sea had burst her limits, and the waves poured in. Its fury and the noises that the wind made affected both the brothers, but Jim disliked the uproar most. It made him gloomy, silent, morose. It made him—Tom perceived it at once—uneasy. "Scared in his soul"—the ugly phrase came back to him.

"God save anyone who's out to-night," said Jim anxiously, as the old farm rattled about his head. Whereupon the door opened as of itself. There was no knock. It flew wide, as if the wind had burst it. Two drenched and beaten figures showed in the gap against the lurid sky—old John Rossiter and Sandy. They laid their fowling pieces down and took off their capes; they had been up at the lake for the evening flight and six birds were in the game bag. So suddenly had the storm come up that they had been caught before they could get home.

And, while Tom welcomed them, looked after their creature wants, and made them feel at home as in duty bound, no visit, he felt at the same time, could have been less opportune. Sandy did not matter—Sandy never did matter anywhere, his personality being negligible—but John Rossiter was the last man Tom wished to see just then. He hated the man; hated that sense of implacable justice that he knew was in him; with the slightest excuse he would have turned him out and sent him on to his own home, storm or no storm. But Rossiter provided no excuse; he was all gratitude and easy politeness, more pleasant and friendly to Jim even than to his brother. Tom set out the whisky and sugar, sliced the lemon, put the kettle on, and furnished dry coats while the soaked garments hung up before the roaring fire that Orkney makes customary even when days are warm.

"It might be the equinoctials," observed Sandy, "if it wasn't late October." He shivered, for the tropics had thinned his blood.

"This ain't no ordinary storm," put in Rossiter, drying his drenched boots. "It reminds me a bit"—he jerked his head to the window that gave seawards, the rush of rain against the panes half drowning his voice—"reminds me a bit of yonder." He looked up, as though to find someone to agree with him, only one such person being in the room.

"Sure, it ain't," agreed Jim at once, but speaking slowly, "no ordinary storm." His voice was quiet as a child's. Tom, stooping over the kettle, felt something cold go trickling down his back. "It's from acrost the Atlantic too."

"All our big storms come from the sea," offered Sandy, saying just what Sandy was expected to say. His lank red hair lay matted on his forehead, making him look like an unhappy collie dog.

"There's no hospitality," Rossiter changed the talk, "like an islander's," as Tom mixed and filled the glasses.

"He don't even ask 'Say when?'" He chuckled in his beard and turned to Sandy, well pleased with the compliment to his host. "Now, in Malay," he added dryly, "it's probably different, I guess." And the two men, one from Labrador, the other from the tropics, fell to bantering one another with heavy humour, while Tom made things comfortable and Jim stood silent with his back to the fire. At each blow of the wind that shook the building, a suitable remark was made, generally by Sandy: "Did you hear that now?" "Ninety miles an hour at least." "Good thing you build solid in this country!" while Rossiter occasionally repeated that it was an "uncommon storm" and that "it reminded" him of the northern tempests he had known "out yonder."

Tom said little, one thought and one thought only in his heart—the wish that the storm would abate and his guests depart. He felt uneasy about Jim. He hated Rossiter. In the kitchen he had steadied himself already with a good stiff drink, and was now half-way through a second; the feeling was in him that he would need their help before the evening was out. Jim, he noticed, had left his glass untouched. His attention, clearly, went to the wind and the outer night; he added little to the conversation.

"Hark!" cried Sandy's shrill voice. "Did you hear that? That wasn't wind, I'll swear." He sat up, looking for all the world like a dog pricking its ears to something no one else could hear.

"The sea coming over the dunes," said Rossiter. "There'll be an awful tide to-night and a terrible sea off the Swarf. Moon at the full, too." He cocked his head sideways to listen. The roaring was tremendous, waves and wind combining with a result that almost shook the ground. Rain hit the glass with incessant volleys like duck shot.

It was then that Jim spoke, having said no word for a long time.

"It's good there's no trees," he mentioned quietly. "I'm glad of that."

"There'd be fearful damage, wouldn't there?" remarked Sandy. "They might fall on the house too."

But it was the tone Jim used that made Rossiter turn stiffly in his chair, looking first at the speaker, then at his brother. Tom caught both glances and saw the hard keen glitter in the eyes. This kind of talk, he decided, had got to stop, yet how to stop it he hardly knew, for his were not subtle methods, and rudeness to his guests ran too strong against the island customs. He refilled the glasses, thinking in his blunt fashion how best to achieve his object, when Sandy helped the situation without knowing it.

"That's my first," he observed, and all burst out laughing. For Sandy's tenth glass was equally his "first," and he absorbed his liquor like a sponge, yet showed no effects of it until the moment when he would suddenly collapse and sink helpless to the ground. The glass in question, however, was only his third, the final moment still far away.

"Three in one and one in three," said Rossiter, amid the general laughter, while Sandy, grave as a judge, half emptied it at a single gulp. Good-natured, obtuse as a cart-horse, the tropics, it seemed, had first worn out his nerves, then removed them entirely from his body. "That's Malay theology, I guess," finished Rossiter. And the laugh broke out again. Whereupon, setting his glass down, Sandy offered his usual explanation that the hot lands had thinned his blood, that he felt the cold in these "arctic islands," and that alcohol was a necessity of life with him. Tom, grateful for the unexpected help, encouraged him to talk, and Sandy, accustomed to neglect as a rule, responded readily. Having saved the situation, however, he now unwittingly led it back into the danger zone.

"A night for tales, eh?" he remarked, as the wind came howling with a burst of strangest noises against the house. "Down there in the States," he went on, "they'd say the evil spirits were out. They're a superstitious crowd, the natives. I remember once——" And he told a tale, half foolish, half interesting, of a mysterious track he had seen when following buffalo in the jungle. It ran close to the spoor of a wounded buffalo for miles, a track unlike that of any known animal, and the natives, though unable to name it, regarded it with awe. It was a good sign, a kill was certain. They said it was a spirit track.

"You got your buffalo?" asked Tom.

"Found him two miles away, lying dead. The mysterious spoor came to an end close beside the carcass. It didn't continue."

"And that reminds me——" began old Rossiter, ignoring Tom's attempt to introduce another subject. He told them of the haunted island at Eagle River, and a tale of the man who would not stay buried on another island off the coast. From that he went on to describe the strange man-beast that hides in the deep forests of Labrador, manifesting but rarely, and dangerous to men who stray too far from camp, men with a passion for wild life overstrong in their blood—the great mythical Wendigo. And while he talked, Tom noticed that Sandy used each pause as a good moment for a drink, but that Jim's glass still remained untouched.

The atmosphere of incredible things, thus, grew in the little room, much as it gathers among the shadows round a forest camp-fire when men who have seen strange places of the world give tongue about them, knowing they will not be laughed at—an atmosphere, once established, it is vain to fight against. The ingrained superstition that hides in every mother's son comes up at such times to breathe. It came up now. Sandy, closer by several glasses to the moment, Tom saw, when he would be suddenly drunk, gave birth again, a tale this time of a Scottish planter who had brutally dismissed a native servant for no other reason than that he disliked him. The man dis-

appeared completely, but the villagers hinted that he would
—soon indeed that he had—come back, though "not quite
as he went." The planter armed, knowing that vengeance
might be violent. A black panther, meanwhile, was seen
prowling about the bungalow. One night a noise outside
his door on the veranda roused him. Just in time to see
the black brute leaping over the railings into the com-
pound, he fired, and the beast fell with a savage growl
of pain. Help arrived and more shots were fired into
the animal, as it lay, mortally wounded already, lashing
its tail upon the grass. The lanterns, however, showed
that instead of a panther, it was the servant they had shot
to shreds.

Sandy told the story well, a certain odd conviction in
his tone and manner, neither of them at all to the liking
of his host. Uneasiness and annoyance had been growing
in Tom for some time already, his inability to control the
situation adding to his anger. Emotion was accumulat-
ing in him dangerously; it was directed chiefly against
Rossiter, who, though saying nothing definite, somehow
deliberately encouraged both talk and atmosphere. Given
the conditions, it was natural enough the talk should take
the turn it did take, but what made Tom more and more
angry was that, if Rossiter had not been present, he could
have stopped it easily enough. It was the presence of the
old Hudson Bay man that prevented his taking decided
action. He was afraid of Rossiter, afraid of putting his
back up. That was the truth. His recognition of it made
him furious.

"Tell us another, Sandy McKay," said the veteran.
"There's a lot in such tales. They're found the world over
—men turning into animals and the like."

And Sandy, yet nearer to his moment of collapse, but
still showing no effects, obeyed willingly. He noticed
nothing; the whisky was good, his tales were appreciated,
and that sufficed him. He thanked Tom, who just then
refilled his glass, and went on with his tale. But Tom,

hatred and fury in his heart, had reached the point where he could no longer contain himself, and Rossiter's last words inflamed him. He went over, under cover of a tremendous clap of wind, to fill the old man's glass. The latter refused, covering the tumbler with his big, lean hand. Tom stood over him a moment, lowering his face. "You keep still," he whispered ferociously, but so that no one else heard it. He glared into his eyes with an intensity that held danger, and Rossiter, without answering, flung back that glare with equal, but with a calmer, anger.

The wind, meanwhile, had a trick of veering, and each time it shifted, Jim shifted his seat too. Apparently, he preferred to face the sound, rather than have his back to it.

"Your turn now for a tale," said Rossiter with purpose, when Sandy finished. He looked across at him, just as Jim, hearing the burst of wind at the walls behind him, was in the act of moving his chair again. The same moment the attack rattled the door and windows facing him. Jim, without answering, stood for a moment still as death, not knowing which way to turn.

"It's beatin' up from all sides," remarked Rossiter, "like it was goin' round the building."

There was a moment's pause, the four men listening with awe to the roar and power of the terrific wind. Tom listened too, but at the same time watched, wondering vaguely why he didn't cross the room and crash his fist into the old man's chattering mouth. Jim put out his hand and took his glass, but did not raise it to his lips. And a lull came abruptly in the storm, the wind sinking into a moment's dreadful silence. Tom and Rossiter turned their heads in the same instant and stared into each other's eyes. For Tom the instant seemed enormously prolonged. He realized the challenge in the other and that his rudeness had roused it into action. It had become a contest of wills—Justice battling against Love.

Jim's glass had now reached his lips, and the chattering of his teeth against its rim was audible.

But the lull passed quickly and the wind began again, though so gently at first, it had the sound of innumerable swift footsteps treading lightly, of countless hands fingering the doors and windows, but then suddenly with a mighty shout as it swept against the walls, rushed across the roof and descended like a battering-ram against the farther side.

"God, did you hear that?" cried Sandy. "It's trying to get in!" and having said it, he sank in a heap beside his chair, all of a sudden completely drunk. "It's wolves or panthersh," he mumbled in his stupor on the floor, "but whatsh's happened to Malay?" It was the last thing he said before unconsciousness took him, and apparently he was insensible to the kick on the head from a heavy farmer's boot. For Jim's glass had fallen with a crash and the second kick was stopped midway. Tom stood spellbound, unable to move or speak, as he watched his brother suddenly cross the room and open a window into the very teeth of the gale.

"Let be! Let be!" came the voice of Rossiter, an authority in it, a curious gentleness too, both of them new. He had risen, his lips were still moving, but the words that issued from them were inaudible, as the wind and rain leaped with a galloping violence into the room, smashing the glass to atoms and dashing a dozen loose objects helter-skelter on to the floor.

"I saw it!" cried Jim, in a voice that rose above the din and clamour of the elements. He turned and faced the others, but it was at Rossiter he looked. "I saw the leader." He shouted to make himself heard, although the tone was quiet. "A splash of white on his great chest. I saw them all!"

At the words, and at the expression in Jim's eyes, old Rossiter, white to the lips, dropped back into his chair as if a blow had struck him. Tom, petrified, felt his own

heart stop. For through the broken window, above yet
within the wind, came the sound of a wolf-pack running,
howling in deep, full-throated chorus, mad for blood. It
passed like a whirlwind and was gone. And, of the three
men so close together, one sitting and two standing, Jim
alone was in that terrible moment wholly master of himself.

Before the others could move or speak, he turned and
looked full into the eyes of each in succession. His speech
went back to his wilderness days:

"I done it," he said calmly. "I killed him—and I got
ter go."

With a look of mystical horror on his face, he took
one stride, flung the door wide, and vanished into the
darkness.

So quick were both words and action, that Tom's
paralysis passed only as the draught from the broken window banged the door behind him. He seemed to leap
across the room, old Rossiter, tears on his cheeks and
his lips mumbling foolish words, so close upon his heels
that the backward blow of fury Tom aimed at his face
caught him only in the neck and sent him reeling sideways
to the floor instead of flat upon his back.

"Murderer! My brother's death upon you!" he shouted
as he tore the door open again and plunged out into the
night.

And the odd thing that happened then, the thing that
touched old John Rossiter's reason, leaving him from that
moment till his death a foolish man of uncertain mind
and memory, happened when he and the unconscious,
drink-sodden Sandy lay alone together on the stone floor
of that farm-house room.

Rossiter, dazed by the blow and his fall, but in full
possession of his senses, and the anger gone out of him
owing to what he had brought about, this same John Rossiter sat up and saw Sandy also sitting up and staring at

him hard. And Sandy was sober as a judge, his eyes and speech both clear, even his face unflushed.

"John Rossiter," he said, "it was not God who appointed you executioner. It was the devil." And his eyes, thought Rossiter, were like the eyes of an angel.

"Sandy McKay," he stammered, his teeth chattering and breath failing him. "Sandy McKay!" It was all the words .that he could find. But Sandy, already sunk back into his stupor again, was stretched drunk and incapable upon the farm-house floor, and remained in that condition till the dawn.

Jim's body lay hidden among the dunes for many months and in spite of the most careful and prolonged searching. It was another storm that laid it bare. The sand had covered it. The clothes were gone, and the flesh, torn but not eaten, was naked to the December sun and wind,

II

CHINESE MAGIC

1

D R. OWEN FRANCIS felt a sudden wave of pleasure and admiration sweep over him as he saw her enter the room. He was in the act of going out; in fact, he had already said good-bye to his hostess, glad to make his escape from the chattering throng, when the tall and graceful young woman glided past him. Her carriage was superb; she had black eyes with a twinkling happiness in them; her mouth was exquisite. Round her neck, in spite of the warm afternoon, she wore a soft thing of fur or feathers; and as she brushed by to shake the hand he had just shaken himself, the tail of this touched his very cheek. Their eyes met fair and square. He felt as though her eyes also touched him.

Changing his mind, he lingered another ten minutes, chatting with various ladies he did not in the least remember, but who remembered him. He did not, of course, desire to exchange banalities with these other ladies, yet did so gallantly enough. If they found him absent-minded they excused him since he was the famous mental specialist whom everybody was proud to know. And all the time his eyes never left the tall graceful figure that allured him almost to the point of casting a spell upon him.

His first impression deepened as he watched. He was aware of excitement, curiosity, longing; there was a touch even of exaltation in him; yet he took no steps to seek the introduction which was easily enough procurable. He checked himself, if with an effort. Several times their eyes

met across the crowded room; he dared to believe—he felt
instinctively—that his interest was returned. Indeed, it
was more than instinct, for she was certainly aware of his
presence, and he even caught her indicating him to a
woman she spoke with, and evidently asking who he was.
Once he half bowed, and once, in spite of himself, he went
so far as to smile, and there came, he was sure, a faint,
delicious brightening of the eyes in answer. There was, he
fancied, a look of yearning in the face. The young woman
charmed him inexpressibly; the very way she moved delighted him. Yet at last he slipped out of the room without a word, without an introduction, without even knowing
her name. He chose his moment when her back was
turned. It was characteristic of him.

For Owen Francis had ever regarded marriage, for
himself at least, as a disaster that could be avoided. He
was in love with his work, and his work was necessary to
humanity. Others might perpetuate the race, but he must
heal it. He had come to regard love as the bait where-
with Nature lays her trap to fulfill her own ends. A man
in love was a man enjoying a delusion, a deluded man.
In his case, and he was nearing forty-five, the theory had
worked admirably, and the dangerous exception that proved
it had as yet not troubled him.

"It's come at last—I do believe," he thought to himself, as he walked home, a new tumultuous emotion in his
blood; "the exception, quite possibly, has come at last.
I wonder . . ."

And it seemed he said it to the tall graceful figure by
his side, who turned up dark eyes smilingly to meet his
own, and whose lips repeated softly his last two words "I
wonder . . . "

The experience, being new to him, was baffling. A
part of his nature, long dormant, received the authentic
thrill that pertains actually to youth. He was a man of
chaste, abstemious custom. The reaction was vehement.
That dormant part of him became obstreperous. He

thought of his age, his appearance, his prospects; he looked thirty-eight, he was not unhandsome, his position was secure, even remarkable. That gorgeous young woman—he called her gorgeous—haunted him. Never could he forget that face, those eyes. It was extraordinary—he had left her there unspoken to, unknown, when an introduction would have been the simplest thing in the world.

"But it still is," he replied. And the reflection filled his being with a flood of joy.

He checked himself again. Not so easily is established habit routed. He felt instinctively that, at last, he had met his mate; if he followed it up he was a man in love, a lost man enjoying a delusion, a deluded man. But the way she had looked at him! That air of intuitive invitation which not even the sweetest modesty could conceal! He felt an immense confidence in himself; also he felt oddly sure of her.

The presence of that following figure, already precious, came with him into his house, even into his study at the back where he sat over a number of letters by the open window. The pathetic little London garden showed its pitiful patch. The lilac had faded, but a smell of roses entered. The sun was just behind the buildings opposite, and the garden lay soft and warm in summer shadows.

He read and tossed aside the letters; one only interested him, from Edward Farque, whose journey to China had interrupted a friendship of long standing. Edward Farque's work on eastern art and philosophy, on Chinese painting and Chinese thought in particular, had made its mark. He was an authority. He was to be back about this time, and his friend smiled with pleasure. "Dear old unpractical dreamer, as I used to call him," he mused. "He's a success, anyhow!" And as he mused, the presence that sat beside him came a little closer, yet at the same time faded. Not that he forgot her—that was impossible—but that just before opening the letter from his friend, he

had come to a decision. He had definitely made up his
mind to seek acquaintance. The reality replaced the remembered substitute.

"As the newspapers may have warned you," ran the
familiar and kinky writing, "I am back in England after
what the scribes term my ten years of exile in Cathay.
I have taken a little house in Hampstead for six months,
and am just settling in. Come to us to-morrow night and
let me prove it to you. Come to dinner. We shall have
much to say; we both are ten years wiser. You know
how glad I shall be to see my old-time critic and dis-
parager, but let me add frankly that I want to ask you
a few professional, or, rather, technical, questions. So
prepare yourself to come as doctor and as friend. I am
writing, as the papers said truthfully, a treatise on Chinese
thought. But—don't shy!—it is about Chinese Magic
that I want your technical advice [the last two words were
substituted for "professional wisdom," which had been
crossed out] and the benefit of your vast experience. So
come, old friend, come quickly, and come hungry! I'll
feed your body as you shall feed my mind.—Yours,
                              "EDWARD FARQUE."

"P.S.—'The coming of a friend from a far-off land
—is not this true joy?'"

Dr. Francis laid down the letter with a pleased anticipatory chuckle, and it was the touch in the final sentence
that amused him. In spite of being an authority, Farque
was clearly the same fanciful, poetic dreamer as of old.
He quoted Confucius as in other days. The firm but
kinky writing had not altered either. The only sign of
novelty he noticed was the use of scented paper, for a
faint and pungent aroma clung to the big quarto sheet.
"A Chinese habit, doubtless," he decided, sniffing it
with a puzzled air of disapproval. Yet it had nothing in
common with the scented sachets some ladies use too

lavishly, so that even the air of the street is polluted by their passing for a dozen yards. He was familiar with every kind of perfumed note-paper used in London, Paris, and Constantinople. This one was difficult. It was delicate and penetrating for all its faintness, pleasurable too. He rather liked it, and while annoyed that he could not name it, he sniffed at the letter several times, as though it were a flower.

"I'll go," he decided at once, and wrote an acceptance then and there. He went out and posted it. He meant to prolong his walk into the Park, taking his chief preoccupation, the face, the eyes, the figure, with him. Already he was composing the note of inquiry to Mrs. Malleson, his hostess of the tea-party, the note whose willing answer should give him the name, the address, the means of introduction he had now determined to secure. He visualized that note of inquiry, seeing it in his mind's eye ; only, for some odd reason, he saw the kinky writing of Farque instead of his own more elegant script. Association of ideas and emotions readily explained this. Two new and unexpected interests had entered his life on the same day, and within half an hour of each other. What he could not so readily explain, however, was that two words in his friend's ridiculous letter, and in that kinky writing, stood out sharply from the rest. As he slipped his envelope into the mouth of the red pillar-box they shone vividly in his mind. These two words were "Chinese Magic."

2

It was the warmth of his friend's invitation as much as his own state of inward excitement that decided him suddenly to anticipate his visit by twenty-four hours. It would clear his judgment and help his mind, if he spent the evening at Hampstead rather than alone with his own thoughts. "A dose of China," he thought, with a smile, "will do me good. Edward won't mind. I'll telephone."

He left the Park soon after six o'clock and acted upon his impulse. The connexion was bad, the wire buzzed and popped and crackled; talk was difficult; he did not hear properly. The Professor had not yet come in, apparently. Francis said he would come up anyhow on the chance.

"Velly pleased," said the voice in his ear, as he rang off.

Going into his study, he drafted the note that should result in the introduction that was now, it appeared, the chief object of his life. The way this woman with the black, twinkling eyes obsessed him was—he admitted it with joy—extraordinary. The draft he put in his pocket, intending to re-write it next morning, and all the way up to Hampstead Heath the gracious figure glided silently beside him, the eyes were ever present, his cheek still glowed where the feather boa had touched his skin. Edward Farque remained in the background. In fact, it was on the very door-step, having rung the bell, that Francis realized he must pull himself together. "I've come to see old Farque," he reminded himself, with a smile. "I've got to be interested in him and his, and, probably, for an hour or two, to talk Chinese——" when the door opened noiselessly, and he saw facing him, with a grin of celestial welcome on his yellow face, a Chinaman.

"Oh!" he said, with a start. He had not expected a Chinese servant.

"Velly pleased," the man bowed him in.

Dr. Francis stared round him with astonishment he could not conceal. A great golden idol faced him in the hall, its gleaming visage blazing out of a sort of miniature golden palanquin, with a grin, half dignified, half cruel. Fully double human size, it blocked the way, looking so life-like that it might have moved to meet him without too great a shock to what seemed possible. It rested on a throne with four massive legs, carved, the doctor saw, with serpents, dragons, and mythical monsters generally.

Round it on every side were other things in keeping.
Name them he could not, describe them he did not try.
He summed them up in one word—China: pictures,
weapons, cloths and tapestries, bells, gongs, and figures of
every sort and kind imaginable.

Being ignorant of Chinese matters, Dr. Francis stood
and looked about him in a mental state of some confusion. He had the feeling that he had entered a Chinese
temple, for there was a faint smell of incense hanging
about the house that was, to say the least, un-English.
Nothing English, in fact, was visible at all. The matting
on the floor, the swinging curtains of bamboo beads that
replaced the customary doors, the silk draperies and pictured cushions, the bronze and ivory, the screens hung with
fantastic embroideries, everything was Chinese. Hampstead vanished from his thoughts. The very lamps were
in keeping, the ancient lacquered furniture as well. The
value of what he saw, an expert could have told him, was
considerable.

"You likee?" queried the voice at his side.

He had forgotten the servant. He turned sharply.

"Very much; it's wonderfully done," he said. "Makes
you feel at home, John, eh?" he added tactfully, with a
smile, and was going to ask how long all this preparation
had taken, when a voice sounded on the stairs beyond. It
was a voice he knew, a note of hearty welcome in its deep
notes.

"The coming of a friend from a far-off land, even from
Harley Street—is not this true joy?" he heard, and the
next minute was shaking the hand of his old and valued
friend. The intimacy between them had always been of
the truest.

"I almost expected a pigtail," observed Francis, looking him affectionately up and down, "but, really—why,
you've hardly changed at all!"

"Outwardly, not as much, perhaps, as Time expects,"
was the happy reply, "but inwardly——!" He scanned

appreciatively the burly figure of the doctor in his turn.
"And I can say the same of you," he declared, still holding his hand tight. "This is a real pleasure, Owen," he
went on in his deep voice, "to see you again is a joy
to me. Old friends meeting again—there's nothing like
it in life, I believe, nothing." He gave the hand another
squeeze before he let it go. "And we," he added, leading
the way into a room across the hall, "neither of us is
a fugitive from life. We take what we can, I mean."

The doctor smiled as he noted the un-English turn of
language, and together they entered a sitting-room that
was, again, more like some inner chamber of a Chinese
temple than a back room in a rented Hampstead house.

"I only knew ten minutes ago that you were coming,
my dear fellow," the scholar was saying, as his friend
gazed round him with increased astonishment, "or I would
have prepared more suitably for your reception. I was out
till late. All this"—he waved his hand—"surprises you,
of course, but the fact is I have been home some days
already, and most of what you see was arranged for me
in advance of my arrival. Hence its apparent completion.
I say 'apparent,' because, actually, it is far from faithfully carried out. Yet to exceed," he added, "is as bad as
to fall short."

The doctor watched him while he listened to a somewhat lengthy explanation of the various articles surrounding them. The speaker—he confirmed his first impression
—had changed little during the long interval; the same
enthusiasm was in him as before, the same fire and dreami-
ness alternately in the fine grey eyes, the same humour
and passion about the mouth, the same free gestures, and
the same big voice. Only the lines had deepened on the
forehead, and on the fine face the air of thoughtfulness
was also deeper. It was Edward Farque as of old, scholar,
poet, dreamer and enthusiast, despiser of western civilization, contemptuous of money, generous and upright, a type
of value, an individual.

"You've done well, done splendidly, Edward, old man," said his friend presently, after hearing of Chinese wonders that took him somewhat beyond his depth perhaps. "No one is more pleased than I. I've watched your books. You haven't regretted England, I'll be bound?" he asked.

"The philosopher has no country, in any case," was the reply, steadily given. "But out there, I confess, I've found my home." He leaned forward, a deeper earnestness in his tone and expression. And into his face, as he spoke, came a glow of happiness. "My heart," he said, "is in China."

"I see it is, I see it is," put in the other, conscious that he could not honestly share his friend's enthusiasm. "And you're fortunate to be free to live where your treasure is," he added after a moment's pause. "You must be a happy man. Your passion amounts to nostalgia, I suspect. Already yearning to get back there, probably?"

Farque gazed at him for some seconds with shining eyes. "You remember the Persian saying, I'm sure," he said. " 'You see a man drink, but you do not see his thirst.' Well," he added, laughing happily, "you may see me off in six months' time, but you will not see my happiness."

While he went on talking, the doctor glanced round the room, marvelling still at the exquisite taste of everything, the neat arrangement, the perfect matching of form and colour. A woman might have done this thing, occurred to him, as the haunting figure shifted deliciously into the foreground of his mind again. The thought of her had been momentarily replaced by all he heard and saw. She now returned, filling him with joy, anticipation and enthusiasm. Presently, when it was his turn to talk, he would tell his friend about this new, unimagined happiness that had burst upon him like a sunrise. Presently, but not just yet. He remembered, too, with a passing twinge of possible boredom to come, that there must be some delay before his own heart could unburden itself in its turn. Farque wanted to ask some professional questions, of course. He had for the moment forgotten that part of the letter in his general interest and astonishment.

"Happiness, yes . . ." he murmured, aware that his thoughts had wandered, and catching at the last word he remembered hearing. "As you said just now in your own queer way—you haven't changed a bit, let me tell you, in your picturesqueness of quotation, Edward—one must not be fugitive from life; one must seize happiness when and where it offers."

He said it lightly enough, hugging internally his own sweet secret; but he was a little surprised at the earnestness of his friend's rejoinder: "Both of us, I see," came the deep voice, backed by the flash of the far-seeing grey eyes, "have made some progress in the doctrine of life and death." He paused, gazing at the other with sight that was obviously turned inwards upon his own thoughts. "Beauty," he went on presently, his tone even more serious, "has been my lure; yours, Reality. . . ."

"You don't flatter either of us, Edward. That's too exclusive a statement," put in the doctor. He was becoming every minute more and more interested in the workings of his friend's mind. Something about the signs offered eluded his understanding. "Explain yourself, old scholar-poet. I'm a dull, practical mind, remember, and can't keep pace with Chinese subtleties."

"*You've* left out Beauty," was the quiet rejoinder, "while *I* left out Reality. That's neither Chinese nor subtle. It is simply true."

"A bit wholesale, isn't it?" laughed Francis. "A big generalization, rather."

A bright light seemed to illuminate the scholar's face. It was as though an inner lamp was suddenly lit. At the same moment the sound of a soft gong floated in from the hall outside, so soft that the actual strokes were not distinguishable in the wave of musical vibration that reached the ear.

Farque rose to lead the way in to dinner.

"What if I——" he whispered, "have combined the two?" And upon his face was a look of joy that reached down into the other's own full heart with its unexpectedness and wonder. It was the last remark in the world he had looked for. He wondered for a moment whether he interpreted it correctly.

"By Jove . . . !" he exclaimed. "Edward, what d'you mean?"

"You shall hear—after dinner," said Farque, his voice mysterious, his eyes still shining with his inner joy. "I told you I have some questions to ask you—professionally." And they took their seats round an ancient, marvellous table, lit by two swinging lamps of soft green jade, while the Chinese servant waited on them with the silent movements and deft neatness of his imperturbable celestial race.

3

To say that he was bored during the meal were an over-statement of Dr. Francis's mental condition, but to say that he was half-bored seemed the literal truth; for one-half of him, while he ate his steak and savoury and watched Farque manipulating *chou chop suey* and *chou om dong* most cleverly with chop-sticks, was too pre-occupied with his own romance to allow the other half to give its full attention to the conversation.

He had entered the room, however, with a distinct quickening of what may be termed his instinctive and infallible sense of diagnosis. That last remark of his friend's had stimulated him. He was aware of surprise, curiosity, and impatience. Willy-nilly, he began automatically to study him with a profounder interest. Something, he gathered, was not quite as it should be in Edward Farque's mental composition. There was what might be called an

elusive emotional disturbance. He began to wonder and
to watch.

They talked, naturally, of China and of things Chinese,
for the scholar responded to little else, and Francis listened
with what sympathy and patience he could muster. Of art
and beauty he had hitherto known little, his mind was
practical and utilitarian. He now learned that all art was
derived from China, where a high, fine, subtle culture had
reigned since time immemorial. Older than Egypt was
their wisdom. When the western races were eating one
another, before Greece was even heard of, the Chinese had
reached a level of knowledge and achievement that few
realized. Never had they, even in earliest times, been deluded by anthropomorphic conceptions of the Deity, but
perceived in everything the expressions of a single whole
whose giant activities they reverently worshipped. Their
contempt for the western scurry after knowledge, wealth,
machinery, was justified, if Farque was worthy of belief.
He seemed saturated with Chinese thought, art, philosophy, and his natural bias towards the celestial race had
hardened into an attitude to life that had now become
ineradicable.

"They deal, as it were, in essences," he declared;
"they discern the essence of everything, leaving out the
superfluous, the unessential, the trivial. Their pictures
alone prove it. Come with me," he concluded, "and see
the 'Earthly Paradise,' now in the British Museum. It
is like Botticelli, but better than anything Botticelli ever
did. It was painted"—he paused for emphasis—"600
years B.C."

The wonder of this quiet, ancient civilization, a sense
of its depth, its wisdom, grew upon his listener as the
enthusiastic poet described its charm and influence upon
himself. He willingly allowed the enchantment of the
other's Paradise to steal upon his own awakened heart.
There was a good deal Francis might have offered by way
of criticism and objection, but he preferred on the whole

to keep his own views to himself, and to let his friend
wander unhindered through the mazes of his passionate
evocation. All men, he well knew, needed a dream to
carry them through life's disappointments, a dream that
they could enter at will and find peace, contentment, happiness. Farque's dream was China. Why not? It was
as good as another, and a man like Farque was entitled
to what dream he pleasel.

"And their women?" he inquired at last, letting both
halves of his mind speak together for the first time.

But he was not prepared for the expression that leaped
upon his friend's face at the simple question. Nor for
his method of reply. It was no reply, in point of fact.
It was simply an attack upon all other types of woman,
and upon the white, the English, in particular—their emptiness, their triviality, their want of intuitive imagination,
of spiritual grace, of everything, in a word, that should
constitute woman a meet companion for man, and a little
higher than the angels into the bargain. The doctor
listened spellbound. Too humorous to be shocked, he was,
at any rate, disturbed by what he heard, displeased a little,
too. It threatened too directly his own new tender dream.

Only with the utmost self-restraint did he keep his
temper under, and prevent hot words he would have regretted later from tearing his friend's absurd claim into
ragged shreds. He was wounded personally as well. Never
now could he bring himself to tell his own secret to him.
The outburst chilled and disappointed him. But it had
another effect—it cooled his judgment. His sense of diagnosis quickened. He divined an *idée fixe,* a mania possibly. His interest deepened abruptly. He watched. He
began to look about him with more wary eyes, and a sense
of uneasiness, once the anger passed, stirred in his friendly
and affectionate heart.

They had been sitting alone over their port for scme
considerable time, the servant having long since left the
room. The doctor had sought to change the subject many

times without much success, when suddenly Farque
changed it for him.

"Now," he announced, "I'll tell you something," and
Francis guessed that the professional questions were on
the way at last. "We must pity the living, remember, and
part with the dead. Have you forgotten old Shan-Yu?"

The forgotten name came back to him, the picturesque
East End dealer of many years ago. "The old merchant
who taught you your first Chinese? I do recall him dimly,
now you mention it. You made quite a friend of him,
didn't you? He thought very highly of you—ah, it comes
back to me now—he offered something or other very wonderful in his gratitude, unless my memory fails me?"

"His most valuable possession," Farque went on, a
strange look deepening on his face, an expression of
mysterious rapture, as it were, and one that Francis recognized and swiftly pigeon-holed in his now attentive mind.

"Which was?" he asked sympathetically. "You told
me once, but so long ago that really it's slipped my mind.
Something magical, wasn't it?" He watched closely for
his friend's reply.

Farque lowered his voice to a whisper almost devotional:

"The Perfume of the Garden of Happiness," he murmured, with an expression in his eyes as though the mere
recollection gave him joy. " 'Burn it,' he told me, 'in a
brazier; then inhale. You will enter the Valley of a
Thousand Temples wherein lies the Garden of Happiness,
and there you will meet your Love. You will have seven
years of happiness with your Love before the Waters of
Separation flow between you. I give this to you who
alone of men here have appreciated the wisdom of my land.
Follow my body towards the Sunrise. You, an eastern
soul in a barbarian body, will meet your Destiny.' "

The doctor's attention, such is the power of self-inter-
est, quickened amazingly as he heard. His own romance

flamed up with power. His friend—it dawned upon him suddenly—loved a woman.

"Come," said Farque, rising quietly, "we will go into the other room, and I will show you what I have shown to but one other in the world before. You are a doctor," he continued, as he led the way to the silk-covered divan where golden dragons swallowed crimson suns, and wonderful jade horses hovered near. "You understand the mind and nerves. States of consciousness you also can explain, and the effect of drugs is, doubtless, known to you." He swung to the heavy curtains that took the place of door, handed a lacquered box of cigarettes to his friend, and lit one himself. "Perfumes, too," he added, "you probably have studied, with their extraordinary evocative power." He stood in the middle of the room, the green light falling on his interesting and thoughtful face, and for a passing second Francis, watching keenly, observed a change flit over it and vanish. The eyes grew narrow and slid tilted upwards, the skin wore a shade of yellow underneath the green from the lamp of jade, the nose slipped back a little, the cheek-bones forward.

"Perfumes," said the doctor, "no. Of perfumes I know nothing, beyond their interesting effect upon the memory. I cannot help you there. But, you, I suspect,' and he looked up with an inviting sympathy that concealed the close observation underneath, "you yourself, I feel sure, can tell me something of value about them?"

"Perhaps," was the calm reply, "perhaps, for I have smelt the perfume of the Garden of Happiness, and I have been in the Valley of a Thousand Temples." He spoke with a glow of joy and reverence almost devotional.

The doctor waited in some suspense, while his friend moved towards an inlaid cabinet across the room. More than broad-minded, he was that much rarer thing, an open-minded man, ready at a moment's notice to discard all preconceived ideas, provided new knowledge that necessitated the holocaust were shown to him. At present, none the less, he held very definite views of his own. "Please ask me any questions you like," he added. "All I know is entirely yours, as always." He was aware of suppressed excitement in his friend that betrayed itself in every word and look and gesture, an excitement intense, and not as yet explained by anything he had seen or heard.

The scholar, meanwhile, had opened a drawer in the cabinet and taken from it a neat little packet tied up with purple silk. He held it with tender, almost loving care, as he came and sat down on the divan beside his friend.

"This," he said, in a tone, again, of something between reverence and worship, "contains what I have to show you first." He slowly unrolled it, disclosing a yet smaller silken bag within, coloured a deep rich orange. There were two vertical columns of writing on it, painted in Chinese characters. The doctor leaned forward to examine them. His friend translated:

"The Perfume of the Garden of Happiness," he read aloud, tracing the letters of the first column with his finger. "The Destroyer of Honourable Homes," he finished, passing to the second, and then proceeded to unwrap the little silken bag. Before it was actually open, however, and the pale shredded material resembling coloured chaff visible to the eyes, the doctor's nostrils had recognized the strange aroma he had first noticed about his friend's letter received earlier in the day. The same soft, penetrating odour, sharply piercing, sweet and delicate, rose to his brain. It stirred at once a deep emotional pleasure in him. Having come to him first when he was aglow with his own unexpected romance, his mind and heart full of the woman he had just left, that delicious, torturing state revived in him quite naturally. The evocative power of perfume with regard to memory is compelling. A livelier sympathy towards his friend, and towards what he was about to hear, awoke in him spontaneously.

He did not mention the letter, however. He merely leaned over to smell the fragrant perfume more easily.

Farque drew back the open packet instantly, at the same time holding out a warning hand. "Careful," he said gravely, "be careful, my old friend—unless you desire to share the rapture and the risk that have been mine. To enjoy its full effect, true, this dust must be burned in a brazier and its smoke inhaled; but even sniffed, as you now would sniff it, and you are in danger——"

"Of what?" asked Francis, impressed by the other's extraordinary intensity of voice and manner.

"Of Heaven; but, possibly, of Heaven before your time."

4

The tale that Farque unfolded then had certainly a strange celestial flavour, a glory not of this dull world; and as his friend listened, his interest deepened with every minute, while his bewilderment increased. He watched closely, expert that he was, for clues that might guide his deductions aright, but for all his keen observation and experience he could detect no inconsistency, no weakness, nothing that betrayed the smallest mental aberration. The origin and nature of what he already decided was an *idée fixe,* a mania, evaded him entirely. This evasion piqued and vexed him; he had heard a thousand tales of similar type before; that this one in particular should baffle his unusual skill touched his pride. Yet he faced the position honestly, he confessed himself baffled until the end of the evening. When he went away, however, he went away satisfied, even forgetful—because a new problem of yet more poignant interest had replaced the first.

"It was after three years out there," said Farque, "that a sense of my loneliness first came upon me. It came upon me bitterly. My work had not then been recognized; obstacles and difficulties had increased; I felt a failure; I had accomplished nothing. And it seemed to me I had mis-

judged my capacities, taken a wrong direction, and wasted
my life accordingly. For my move to China, remember,
was a radical move, and my boats were burnt behind me.
This sense of loneliness was really devastating."

Francis, already fidgeting, put up his hand.

"One question, if I may," he said, "and I'll not inter-
rupt again."

"By all means," said the other patiently, "what is it?"

"Were you—we are such old friends"—he apologized
—"were you still celibate as ever?"

Farque looked surprised, then smiled. "My habits had
not changed," he replied, "I was, as always, celibate."

"Ah!" murmured the doctor, and settled down to listen.

"And I think now," his friend went on, "that it was
the lack of companionship that first turned my thoughts
towards conscious disappointment. However that may be,
it was one evening, as I walked homewards to my little
house, that I caught my imagination lingering upon English memories, though chiefly, I admit, upon my old
Chinese tutor, the dead Shan-Yu.

"It was dusk, the stars were coming out in the pale
evening air, and the orchards, as I passed them, stood
like wavering ghosts of unbelievable beauty. The effect
of thousands upon thousands of these trees, flooding the
twilight of a spring evening with their sea of blossom, is
almost unearthly. They seem transparencies, their colour
hangs sheets upon the very sky. I crossed a small wooden
bridge that joined two of these orchards above a stream,
and in the dark water I watched a moment the mingled
reflection of stars and flowering branches on the quiet surface. It seemed too exquisite to belong to earth, this
fairy garden of stars and blossoms, shining faintly in the
crystal depths, and my thought, as I gazed, dived suddenly
down the little avenue that memory opened into former
days. I remembered Shan-Yu's present, given to me when
he died. His very words came back to me: The Garden
of Happiness in the Valley of the Thousand Temples,

with its promise of love, of seven years of happiness, and the prophecy that I should follow his body towards the Sunrise and meet my destiny.

"This memory I took home with me into my lonely little one-storey house upon the hill. My servants did not sleep there. There was no one near. I sat by the open window with my thoughts, and you may easily guess that before very long I had unearthed the long-forgotten packet from among my things, spread a portion of its contents on a metal tray above a lighted brazier, and was comfortably seated before it, inhaling the light blue smoke with its exquisite and fragrant perfume.

"A light air entered through the window, the distant orchards below me trembled, rose and floated through the dusk, and I found myself, almost at once, in a pavilion of flowers; a blue river lay shining in the sun before me, as it wandered through a lovely valley where I saw groves of flowering trees among a thousand scattered temples. Drenched in light and colour, the Valley lay dreaming amid a peaceful loveliness that woke what seemed impossible, unrealizable, longings in my heart. I yearned towards its groves and temples, I would bathe my soul in that flood of tender light, and my body in the blue coolness of that winding river. In a thousand temples must I worship. Yet these impossible yearnings instantly were satisfied. I found myself there at once . . . and the time that passed over my head you may reckon in centuries, if not in ages. I was in the Garden of Happiness and its marvellous perfume banished time and sorrow, there was no end to chill the soul, nor any beginning, which is its foolish counterpart.

"Nor was there loneliness." The speaker clasped his thin hands, and closed his eyes a moment in what was evidently an ecstasy of the sweetest memory man may ever know. A slight trembling ran through his frame, communicating itself to his friend upon the divan beside him —this understanding, listening, sympathetic friend, whose eyes had never once yet withdrawn their attentive gaze from the narrator's face.

"I was not alone," the scholar resumed, opening his eyes again, and smiling out of some deep inner joy. "Shan-Yu came down the steps of the first temple and took my hand, while the great golden figures in the dim interior turned their splendid shining heads to watch. Then, breathing the soul of his ancient wisdom in my ear, he led me through all the perfumed ways of that enchanted garden, worshipping with me at a hundred deathless shrines, led me, I tell you, to the sound of soft gongs and gentle bells, by fragrant groves and sparkling streams, mid a million gorgeous flowers, until, beneath that unsetting sun, we reached the heart of the Valley, where the source of the river gushed forth beneath the lighted mountains. He stopped and pointed across the narrow waters. I saw the woman——"

"*The* woman," his listener murmured beneath his breath, though Farque seemed unaware of interruption.

"She smiled at me and held her hands out, and while she did so, even before I could express my joy and wonder in response, Shan-Yu, I saw, had crossed the narrow stream and stood beside her. I made to follow then, my heart burning with inexpressible delight. But Shan-Yu held up his hand, as they began to move down the flowered bank together, making a sign that I should keep pace with them, though on my own side.

"Thus, side by side, yet with the blue sparkling stream between us, we followed back along its winding course, through the heart of that enchanted valley, my hands stretched out towards the radiant figure of my Love, and hers stretched out towards me. They did not touch, but our eyes, our smiles, our thoughts, these met and mingled in a sweet union of unimagined bliss, so that the absence of physical contact was unnoticed and laid no injury on our marvellous joy. It was a spirit union, and our kiss a spirit kiss. Therein lay the subtlety and glory of the

Chinese wonder, for it was our *essences* that met, and for such union there is no satiety and, equally, no possible end. The Perfume of the Garden of Happiness is an essence. We were in Eternity.

"The stream, meanwhile, widened between us, and as it widened, my Love grew farther from me in space, smaller, less visibly defined, yet ever essentially more perfect, and never once with a sense of distance that made our union less divinely close. Across the widening reaches of blue, sunlit water I still knew her smile, her eyes, the gestures of her radiant being; I saw her exquisite reflection in the stream; and, mid the music of those soft gongs and gentle bells, the voice of Shan-Yu came like a melody to my ears:

" 'You have followed me into the sunrise, and have found your destiny. Behold now your Love. In this Valley of a Thousand Temples you have known the Garden of Happiness, and its Perfume your soul now inhales.'

" 'I am bathed,' I answered, 'in a happiness divine. It is forever.'

" 'The Waters of Separation,' his answer floated like a bell, 'lie widening between you.'

"I moved nearer to the bank, impelled by the pain in his words to take my Love and hold her to my breast.

" 'But I would cross to her,' I cried, and saw that, as I moved, Shan-Yu and my Love came likewise closer to the water's edge across the widening river. They both obeyed, I was aware, my slightest wish.

" 'Seven years of Happiness you may know,' sang his gentle tones across the brimming flood, 'if you would cross to her. Yet the Destroyer of Honourable Homes lies in the shadows that you must cast outside.'

"I heard his words, I noticed for the first time that in the blaze of this radiant sunshine we cast no shadows on the sea of flowers at our feet, and—I stretched out my arms towards my Love across the river.

" 'I accept my destiny,' I cried, 'I will have my seven

years of bliss,' and stepped forward into the running flood.
As the cool water took my feet, my Love's hands stretched
out both to hold me and to bid me stay. There was acceptance in her gesture, but there was warning too.

"I did not falter. I advanced until the water bathed
my knees, and my Love, too, came to meet me, the stream
already to her waist, while our arms stretched forth above
the running flood towards each other.

"The change came suddenly. Shan-Yu first faded behind her advancing figure into air; there stole a chill upon
the sunlight; a cool mist rose from the water, hiding the
Garden and the hills beyond; our fingers touched, I gazed
into her eyes, our lips lay level with the water—and the
room was dark and cold about me. The brazier stood
extinguished at my side. The dust had burnt out, and no
smoke rose. I slowly left my chair and closed the window, for the air was chill."

5

It was difficult at first to return to Hampstead and the
details of ordinary life about him. Francis looked round
him slowly, freeing himself gradually from the spell his
friend's words had laid even upon his analytical temperament. The transition was helped, however, by the details
that everywhere met his eye. The Chinese atmosphere
remained. More, its effect had gained, if anything. The
embroideries of yellow gold, the pictures, the lacquered
stools and inlaid cabinets, above all, the exquisite figures
in green jade upon the shelf beside him, all this, in the
shimmering pale olive light the lamps shed everywhere,
helped his puzzled mind to bridge the gulf from the Garden of Happiness into the decorated villa upon Hampstead
Heath.

There was silence between the two men for several
minutes. Far was it from the doctor's desire to injure his
old friend's delightful fantasy. For he called it fantasy,

although something in him trembled. He remained, therefore, silent. Truth to tell, perhaps, he knew not exactly what to say.

Farque broke the silence himself. He had not moved since the story ended; he sat motionless, his hands tightly clasped, his eyes alight with the memory of his strange imagined joy, his face rapt and almost luminous, as though he still wandered through the groves of the Enchanted Garden and inhaled the perfume of its perfect happiness in the Valley of the Thousand Temples.

"It was two days later," he went on suddenly in his quiet voice, "only two days afterwards, that I met her."

"You met her? You met the woman of your dream?" Francis's eyes opened very wide.

"In that little harbour town," repeated Farque calmly, "I met her in the flesh. She had just landed in a steamer from up the coast. The details are of no particular interest. She knew me, of course, at once. And, naturally, I knew her."

The doctor's tongue refused to act as he heard. It dawned upon him suddenly that his friend was married. He remembered the woman's touch about the house; he recalled, too, for the first time that the letter of invitation to dinner had said "come to *us*." He was full of a bewildered astonishment.

The reaction upon himself was odd, perhaps, yet wholly natural. His heart warmed towards his imaginative friend. He could now tell him his own new strange romance. The woman who haunted him crept back into the room and sat between them. He found his tongue.

"You married her, Edward?" he exclaimed.

"She is my wife," was the reply, in a gentle, happy voice.

"A Ch——" he could not bring himself to say the word. "A foreigner?"

"My wife is a Chinese woman," Farque helped him easily, with a delighted smile.

So great was the other's absorption in the actual moment, that he had not heard the step in the passage that
his host had heard. The latter stood up suddenly.

"I hear her now," he said. "I'm glad she's come
back before you left." He stepped towards the door.

But before he reached it, the door was opened and in
came the woman herself. Francis tried to rise, but something had happened to him. His heart missed a beat.
Something, it seemed, broke in him. He faced a tall,
graceful young English woman with black eyes of sparkling
happiness, the woman of his own romance. She still wore
the feather boa round her neck. She was no more Chinese
than he was.

"My wife," he heard Farque introducing them, as he
struggled to his feet, searching feverishly for words of
congratulation, normal, everyday words he ought to use,
"I'm so pleased, oh, so pleased," Farque was saying—
he heard the sound from a distance, his sight was blurred
as well—"my two best friends in the world, my English
comrade and my Chinese wife." His voice was absolutely
sincere with conviction and belief.

"But we have already met," came the woman's delightful voice, her eyes full upon his face with smiling pleasure,
"I saw you at Mrs. Malleson's tea only this afternoon."

And Francis remembered suddenly that the Mallesons
were old acquaintances of Farque's as well as of himself.
"And I even dared to ask who you were," the voice went
on, floating from some other space, it seemed, to his ears,
"I had you pointed out to me. I had heard of you from
Edward, of course. But you vanished before I could be
introduced."

The doctor mumbled something or other polite and, he
hoped, adequate. But the truth had flashed upon him with
remorseless suddenness. She had "heard of" him—the
famous mental specialist. Her interest in him was cruelly
explained, cruelly both for himself and for his friend.
Farque's delusion lay clear before his eyes. An awaken-

ing to reality might involve dislocation of the mind. *She,* too, moreover, knew the truth. She was involved as well. And her interest in himself was—consultation.

"Seven years we've been married, just seven years to-day," Farque was saying thoughtfully, as he looked at them. "Curious, rather, isn't it?"

"Very," said Francis, turning his regard from the black eyes to the grey.

Thus it was that Owen Francis left the house a little later with a mind in a measure satisfied, yet in a measure forgetful too—forgetful of his own deep problem, because another of even greater interest had replaced it.

"Why undeceive him?" ran his thought. "He need never know. It's harmless anyhow—I can tell her that."

But, side by side with this reflection, ran another that was oddly haunting, considering his type of mind: "Destroyer of Honourable Homes," was the form of words it took. And with a sigh he added "Chinese Magic."

III

RUNNING WOLF

THE man who enjoys an adventure outside the general experience of the race, and imparts it to others, must not be surprised if he is taken for either a liar or a fool, as Malcolm Hyde, hotel clerk on a holiday, discovered in due course. Nor is "enjoy" the right word to use in describing his emotions; the word he chose was probably "survive."

When he first set eyes on Medicine Lake he was struck by its still, sparkling beauty, lying there in the vast Canadian backwoods; next, by its extreme loneliness; and, lastly—a good deal later, this—by its combination of beauty, loneliness, and singular atmosphere, due to the fact that it was the scene of his adventure.

"It's fairly stiff with big fish," said Morton of the Montreal Sporting Club. "Spend your holiday there—up Mattawa way, some fifteen miles west of Stony Creek. You'll have it all to yourself except for an old Indian who's got a shack there. Camp on the east side—if you'll take a tip from me." He then talked for half an hour about the wonderful sport; yet he was not otherwise very communicative, and did not suffer questions gladly, Hyde noticed. Nor had he stayed there very long himself. If it was such a paradise as Morton, its discoverer and the most experienced rod in the province, claimed, why had he himself spent only three days there?

"Ran short of grub," was the explanation offered; but to another friend he had mentioned briefly, "flies," and to a third, so Hyde learned later, he gave the excuse that his half-breed "took sick," necessitating a quick return to civilization.

Hyde, however, cared little for the explanations; his interest in these came later. "Stiff with fish" was the phrase he liked. He took the Canadian Pacific train to Mattawa, laid in his outfit at Stony Creek, and set off thence for the fifteen-mile canoe-trip without a care in the world.

Travelling light, the portages did not trouble him; the water was swift and easy, the rapids negotiable; everything came his way, as the saying is. Occasionally he saw big fish making for the deeper pools, and was sorely tempted to stop; but he resisted. He pushed on between the immense world of forests that stretched for hundreds of miles, known to deer, bear, moose, and wolf, but strange to any echo of human tread, a deserted and primeval wilderness. The autumn day was calm, the water sang and sparkled, the blue sky hung cloudless over all, ablaze with light. Toward evening he passed an old beaver-dam, rounded a little point, and had his first sight of Medicine Lake. He lifted his dripping paddle; the canoe shot with silent glide into calm water. He gave an exclamation of delight, for the loveliness caught his breath away.

Though primarily a sportsman, he was not insensible to beauty. The lake formed a crescent, perhaps four miles long, its width between a mile and half a mile. The slanting gold of sunset flooded it. No wind stirred its crystal surface. Here it had lain since the redskin's god first made it; here it would lie until he dried it up again. Towering spruce and hemlock trooped to its very edge, majestic cedars leaned down as if to drink, crimson sumachs shone in fiery patches, and maples gleamed orange and red beyond belief. The air was like wine, with the silence of a dream.

It was here the red men formerly "made medicine," with all the wild ritual and tribal ceremony of an ancient day. But it was of Morton, rather than of Indians, that

Hyde thought. If this lonely, hidden paradise was really stiff with big fish, he owed a lot to Morton for the information. Peace invaded him, but the excitement of the hunter lay below.

He looked about him with quick, practised eye for a camping-place before the sun sank below the forests and the half-lights came. The Indian's shack, lying in full sunshine on the eastern shore, he found at once; but the trees lay too thick about it for comfort, nor did he wish to be so close to its inhabitant. Upon the opposite side, however, an ideal clearing offered. This lay already in shadow, the huge forest darkening it toward evening; but the open space attracted. He paddled over quickly and examined it. The ground was hard and dry, he found, and a little brook ran tinkling down one side of it into the lake. This outfall, too, would be a good fishing spot. Also it was sheltered. A few low willows marked the mouth.

An experienced camper soon makes up his mind. It was a perfect site, and some charred logs, with traces of former fires, proved that he was not the first to think so. Hyde was delighted. Then, suddenly, disappointment came to tinge his pleasure. His kit was landed, and preparations for putting up the tent were begun, when he recalled a detail that excitement had so far kept in the background of his mind—Morton's advice. But not Morton's only, for the storekeeper at Stony Creek had reinforced it. The big fellow with straggling moustache and stooping shoulders, dressed in shirt and trousers, had handed him out a final sentence with the bacon, flour, condensed milk, and sugar. He had repeated Morton's half-forgotten words:

"Put yer tent on the east shore. I should," he had said at parting.

He remembered Morton, too, apparently. "A shortish fellow, brown as an Indian and fairly smelling of the woods. Travelling with Jake, the half-breed." That assuredly was Morton. "Didn't stay long, now, did he?" he added in a reflective tone.

"Going Windy Lake way, are yer? Or Ten Mile Water, maybe?" he had first inquired of Hyde.

"Medicine Lake."

"Is that so?" the man said, as though he doubted it for some obscure reason. He pulled at his ragged moustache a moment. "Is that so, now?" he repeated. And the final words followed him down-stream after a considerable pause—the advice about the best shore on which to put his tent.

All this now suddenly flashed back upon Hyde's mind with a tinge of disappointment and annoyance, for when two experienced men agreed, their opinion was not to be lightly disregarded. He wished he had asked the storekeeper for more details. He looked about him, he reflected, he hesitated. His ideal camping-ground lay certainly on the forbidden shore. What in the world, he wondered, could be the objection to it?

But the light was fading; he must decide quickly one way or the other. After staring at his unpacked dunnage and the tent, already half erected, he made up his mind with a muttered expression that consigned both Morton and the storekeeper to less pleasant places. "They must have *some* reason," he growled to himself; "fellows like that usually know what they're talking about. I guess I'd better shift over to the other side—for to-night, at any rate."

He glanced across the water before actually reloading. No smoke rose from the Indian's shack. He had seen no sign of a canoe. The man, he decided, was away. Reluctantly, then, he left the good camping-ground and paddled across the lake, and half an hour later his tent was up, firewood collected, and two small trout were already caught for supper. But the bigger fish, he knew, lay waiting for him on the other side by the little outfall, and he fell asleep at length on his bed of balsam boughs, annoyed and disappointed, yet wondering how a mere sentence could have persuaded him so easily against his own better judgment. He slept like the dead; the sun was well up before he stirred.

But his morning mood was a very different one. The brilliant light, the peace, the intoxicating air, all this was too exhilarating for the mind to harbour foolish fancies, and he marvelled that he could have been so weak the night before. No hesitation lay in him anywhere. He struck camp immediately after breakfast, paddled back across the strip of shining water, and quickly settled in upon the forbidden shore, as he now called it, with a contemptuous grin. And the more he saw of the spot, the better he liked it. There was plenty of wood, running water to drink, an open space about the tent, and there were no flies. The fishing, moreover, was magnificent. Morton's description was fully justified, and "stiff with big fish" for once was not an exaggeration.

The useless hours of the early afternoon he passed dozing in the sun, or wandering through the underbrush beyond the camp. He found no sign of anything unusual. He bathed in a cool, deep pool; he revelled in the lonely little paradise. Lonely it certainly was, but the loneliness was part of its charm; the stillness, the peace, the isolation of this beautiful backwoods lake delighted him. The silence was divine. He was entirely satisfied.

After a brew of tea, he strolled toward evening along the shore, looking for the first sign of a rising fish. A faint ripple on the water, with the lengthening shadows, made good conditions. *Plop* followed *plop,* as the big fellows rose, snatched at their food, and vanished into the depths. He hurried back. Ten minutes later he had taken his rods and was gliding cautiously in the canoe through the quiet water.

So good was the sport, indeed, and so quickly did the big trout pile up in the bottom of the canoe that, despite the growing lateness, he found it hard to tear himself

away. "One more," he said, "and then I really will go."
He landed that "one more," and was in act of taking it
off the hook, when the deep silence of the evening was
curiously disturbed. He became abruptly aware that
someone watched him. A pair of eyes, it seemed, were
fixed upon him from some point in the surrounding
shadows.

Thus, at least, he interpreted the odd disturbance in
his happy mood; for thus he felt it. The feeling stole
over him without the slightest warning. He was not alone.
The slippery big trout dropped from his fingers. He sat
motionless, and stared about him.

Nothing stirred; the ripple on the lake had died away;
there was no wind; the forest lay a single purple mass
of shadow; the yellow sky, fast fading, threw reflections
that troubled the eye and made distances uncertain. But
there was no sound, no movement; he saw no figure anywhere. Yet he knew that someone watched him, and a
wave of quite unreasoning terror gripped him. The nose
of the canoe was against the bank. In a moment, and
instinctively, he shoved it off and paddled into deeper
water. The watcher, it came to him also instinctively, was
quite close to him upon that bank. But where? And
who? Was it the Indian?

Here, in deeper water, and some twenty yards from
the shore, he paused and strained both sight and hearing
to find some possible clue. He felt half ashamed, now,
that the first strange feeling passed a little. But the certainty remained. Absurd as it was, he felt positive that
someone watched him with concentrated and intent regard.
Every fibre in his being told him so; and though he could
discover no figure, no new outline on the shore, he could
even have sworn in which clump of willow bushes the
hidden person crouched and stared. His attention seemed
drawn to that particular clump.

The water dripped slowly from his paddle, now lying
across the thwarts. There was no other sound. The can-

vas of his tent gleamed dimly. A star or two were out.
He waited. Nothing happened.

Then, as suddenly as it had come, the feeling passed,
and he knew that the person who had been watching him
intently had gone. It was as if a current had been turned
off; the normal world flowed back; the landscape emptied
as if someone had left a room. The disagreeable feeling
left him at the same time, so that he instantly turned the
canoe in to the shore again, landed, and, paddle in hand,
went over to examine the clump of willows he had singled
out as the place of concealment. There was no one there,
of course, nor any trace of recent human occupancy. No
leaves, no branches stirred, nor was a single twig displaced; his keen and practised sight detected no sign of
tracks upon the ground. Yet, for all that, he felt positive that a little time ago someone had crouched among
these very leaves and watched him. He remained absolutely convinced of it. The watcher, whether Indian,
hunter, stray lumberman, or wandering half-breed, had
now withdrawn, a search was useless, and dusk was falling. He returned to his little camp, more disturbed perhaps than he cared to acknowledge. He cooked his supper,
hung up his catch on a string, so that no prowling animal
could get at it during the night, and prepared to make
himself comfortable until bedtime. Unconsciously, he built
a bigger fire than usual, and found himself peering over
his pipe into the deep shadows beyond the firelight, straining his ears to catch the slightest sound. He remained
generally on the alert in a way that was new to him.

A man under such conditions and in such a place need
not know discomfort until the sense of loneliness strikes
him as too vivid a reality. Loneliness in a backwoods
camp brings charm, pleasure, and a happy sense of calm
until, and unless, it comes too near. It should remain an
ingredient only among other conditions; it should not be
directly, vividly noticed. Once it has crept within short
range, however, it may easily cross the narrow line be-

tween comfort and discomfort, and darkness is an undesirable time for the transition. A curious dread may easily follow—the dread lest the loneliness suddenly be disturbed, and the solitary human feel himself open to attack.

For Hyde, now, this transition had been already accomplished; the too intimate sense of his loneliness had shifted abruptly into the worse condition of no longer being quite alone. It was an awkward moment, and the hotel clerk realized his position exactly. He did not quite like it. He sat there, with his back to the blazing logs, a very visible object in the light, while all about him the darkness of the forest lay like an impenetrable wall. He could not see a foot beyond the small circle of his campfire; the silence about him was like the silence of the dead. No leaf rustled, no wave lapped; he himself sat motionless as a log.

Then again he became suddenly aware that the person who watched him had returned, and that same intent and concentrated gaze as before was fixed upon him where he lay. There was no warning; he heard no stealthy tread or snapping of dry twigs, yet the owner of those steady eyes was very close to him, probably not a dozen feet away. This sense of proximity was overwhelming.

It is unquestionable that a shiver ran down his spine. This time, moreover, he felt positive that the man crouched just beyond the firelight, the distance he himself could see being nicely calculated, and straight in front of him. For some minutes he sat without stirring a single muscle, yet with each muscle ready and alert, straining his eyes in vain to pierce the darkness, but only succeeding in dazzling his sight with the reflected light. Then, as he shifted his position slowly, cautiously, to obtain another angle of vision, his heart gave two big thumps against his ribs and the hair seemed to rise on his scalp with the sense of cold that shot horribly up his spine. In the darkness facing him he saw two small and greenish circles that were certainly a pair of eyes, yet not the eyes of Indian,

hunter, or of any human being. It was a pair of animal
eyes that stared so fixedly at him out of the night. And
this certainly had an immediate and natural effect upon
him.

For, at the menace of those eyes, the fears of millions
of long dead hunters since the dawn of time woke in him.
Hotel clerk though he was, heredity surged through him
in an automatic wave of instinct. His hand groped for
a weapon. His fingers fell on the iron head of his small
camp axe, and at once he was himself again. Confidence
returned; the vague, superstitious dread was gone. This
was a bear or wolf that smelt his catch and came to steal
it. With beings of that sort he knew instinctively how
to deal, yet admitting, by this very instinct, that his original dread had been of quite another kind.

"I'll damned quick find out what it is," he exclaimed
aloud, and snatching a burning brand from the fire, he
hurled it with good aim straight at the eyes of the beast
before him.

The bit of pitch-pine fell in a shower of sparks that lit
the dry grass this side of the animal, flared up a moment,
then died quickly down again. But in that instant of
bright illumination he saw clearly what his unwelcome visitor was. A big timber wolf sat on its hindquarters, staring
steadily at him through the firelight. He saw its legs
and shoulders, he saw its hair, he saw also the big hemlock trunks lit up behind it, and the willow scrub on each
side. It formed a vivid, clear-cut picture shown in clear
detail by the momentary blaze. To his amazement, however, the wolf did not turn and bolt away from the burning log, but withdrew a few yards only, and sat there
again on its haunches, staring, staring as before. Heavens,
how it stared! He "shoo-ed" it, but without effect; it
did not budge. He did not waste another good log on it,
for his fear was dissipated now; a timber wolf was a timber wolf, and it might sit there as long as it pleased, provided it did not try to steal his catch. No alarm was in

him any more. He knew that wolves were harmless in the summer and autumn, and even when "packed" in the winter, they would attack a man only when suffering desperate hunger. So he lay and watched the beast, threw bits of stick in its direction, even talked to it, wondering only that it never moved. "You can stay there for ever, if you like," he remarked to it aloud, "for you cannot get at my fish, and the rest of the grub I shall take into the tent with me!"

The creature blinked its bright green eyes, but made no move.

Why, then, if his fear was gone, did he think of certain things as he rolled himself in the Hudson Bay blankets before going to sleep? The immobility of the animal was strange, its refusal to turn and bolt was still stranger. Never before had he known a wild creature that was not afraid of fire. Why did it sit and watch him, as with purpose in its dreadful eyes? How had he felt its presence earlier and instantly? A timber wolf, especially a solitary timber wolf, was a timid thing, yet this one feared neither man nor fire. Now, as he lay there wrapped in his blankets inside the cosy tent, it sat outside beneath the stars, beside the fading embers, the wind chilly in its fur, the ground cooling beneath its planted paws, watching him, steadily watching him, perhaps until the dawn.

It was unusual, it was strange. Having neither imagination nor tradition, he called upon no store of racial visions. Matter of fact, a hotel clerk on a fishing holiday, he lay there in his blankets, merely wondering and puzzled. A timber wolf was a timber wolf and nothing more. Yet this timber wolf—the idea haunted him—was different. In a word, the deeper part of his original uneasiness remained. He tossed about, he shivered sometimes in his broken sleep; he did not go out to see, but he woke early and unrefreshed.

Again, with the sunshine and the morning wind, how-

ever, the incident of the night before was forgotten, almost
unreal. His hunting zeal was uppermost. The tea and
fish were delicious, his pipe had never tasted so good, the
glory of this lonely lake amid primeval forests went to
his head a little; he was a hunter before the Lord, and
nothing else. He tried the edge of the lake, and in the
excitement of playing a big fish, knew suddenly that *it,*
the wolf, was there. He paused with the rod, exactly as
if struck. He looked about him, he looked in a definite
direction. The brilliant sunshine made every smallest
detail clear and sharp—boulders of granite, burned stems,
crimson sumach, pebbles along the shore in neat, separate
detail—without revealing where the watcher hid. Then,
his sight wandering farther inshore among the tangled
undergrowth, he suddenly picked up the familiar, half-
expected outline. The wolf was lying behind a granite
boulder, so that only the head, the muzzle, and the eyes
were visible. It merged in its background. Had he not
known it was a wolf, he could never have separated it
from the landscape. The eyes shone in the sunlight.

There it lay. He looked straight at it. Their eyes, in
fact, actually met full and square. "Great Scott!" he exclaimed aloud, "why, it's like looking at a human being!"
From that moment, unwittingly, he established a singular personal relation with the beast. And what followed
confirmed this undesirable impression, for the animal rose
instantly and came down in leisurely fashion to the shore,
where it stood looking back at him. It stood and stared
into his eyes like some great wild dog, so that he was aware
of a new and almost incredible sensation—that it courted
recognition.

"Well! well!" he exclaimed again, relieving his feelings by addressing it aloud, "if this doesn't beat everything I ever saw! What d'you want, anyway?"

He examined it now more carefully. He had never
seen a wolf so big before; it was a tremendous beast, a
nasty customer to tackle, he reflected, if it ever came to

that. It stood there absolutely fearless and full of confidence. In the clear sunlight he took in every detail of it—a huge, shaggy, lean-flanked timber wolf, its wicked eyes staring straight into his own, almost with a kind of purpose in them. He saw its great jaws, its teeth, and its tongue, hung out, dropping saliva a little. And yet the idea of its savagery, its fierceness, was very little in him.

He was amazed and puzzled beyond belief. He wished the Indian would come back. He did not understand this strange behaviour in an animal. Its eyes, the odd expression in them, gave him a queer, unusual, difficult feeling. Had his nerves gone wrong, he almost wondered.

The beast stood on the shore and looked at him. He wished for the first time that he had brought a rifle. With a resounding smack he brought his paddle down flat upon the water, using all his strength, till the echoes rang as from a pistol-shot that was audible from one end of the lake to the other. The wolf never stirred. He shouted, but the beast remained unmoved. He blinked his eyes, speaking as to a dog, a domestic animal, a creature accustomed to human ways. It blinked its eyes in return.

At length, increasing his distance from the shore, he continued fishing, and the excitement of the marvellous sport held his attention—his surface attention, at any rate. At times he almost forgot the attendant beast; yet whenever he looked up, he saw it there. And worse; when he slowly paddled home again, he observed it trotting along the shore as though to keep him company. Crossing a little bay, he spurted, hoping to reach the other point before his undesired and undesirable attendant. Instantly the brute broke into that rapid, tireless lope that, except on ice, can run down anything on four legs in the woods. When he reached the distant point, the wolf was waiting for him. He raised his paddle from the water, pausing a moment for reflection; for this very close attention—there were dusk and night yet to come—he certainly did not relish. His camp was near; he had to land; he felt uncomfortable even in the sunshine of broad day, when, to his keen relief, about half a mile from the tent, he saw the creature suddenly stop and sit down in the open. He waited a moment, then paddled on. It did not follow. There was no attempt to move; it merely sat and watched him. After a few hundred yards, he looked back. It was still sitting where he left it. And the absurd, yet significant, feeling came to him that the beast divined his thought, his anxiety, his dread, and was now showing him, as well as it could, that it entertained no hostile feeling and did not meditate attack.

He turned the canoe toward the shore; he landed; he cooked his supper in the dusk; the animal made no sign. Not far away it certainly lay and watched, but it did not advance. And to Hyde, observant now in a new way, came one sharp, vivid reminder of the strange atmosphere into which his commonplace personality had strayed: he suddenly recalled that his relations with the beast, already established, had progressed distinctly a stage further. This startled him, yet without the accompanying alarm he must certainly have felt twenty-four hours before. He had an understanding with the wolf. He was aware of friendly thoughts toward it. He even went so far as to set out a few big fish on the spot where he had first seen it sitting the previous night. "If he comes," he thought, "he is welcome to them. I've got plenty, anyway." He thought of it now as "he."

Yet the wolf made no appearance until he was in the act of entering his tent a good deal later. It was close on ten o'clock, whereas nine was his hour, and late at that, for turning in. He had, therefore, unconsciously been waiting for him. Then, as he was closing the flap, he saw the eyes close to where he had placed the fish. He waited, hiding himself, and expecting to hear sounds of munching jaws; but all was silence. Only the eyes glowed steadily out of the background of pitch darkness.

He closed the flap. He had no slightest fear. In ten minutes he was sound asleep.

He could not have slept very long, for when he woke up he could see the shine of a faint red light through the canvas, and the fire had not died down completely. He rose and cautiously peeped out. The air was very cold; he saw his breath. But he also saw the wolf, for it had come in, and was sitting by the dying embers, not two yards away from where he crouched behind the flap. And this time, at these very close quarters, there was something in the attitude of the big wild thing that caught his attention with a vivid thrill of startled surprise and a sudden shock of cold that held him spellbound. He stared, unable to believe his eyes; for the wolf's attitude conveyed to him something familiar that at first he was unable to explain. Its pose reached him in the terms of another thing with which he was entirely at home. What was it? Did his senses betray him? Was he still asleep and dreaming?

Then, suddenly, with a start of uncanny recognition, he knew. Its attitude was that of a dog. Having found the clue, his mind then made an awful leap. For it was, after all, no dog its appearance aped, but something nearer to himself, and more familiar still. Good heavens! It sat there with the pose, the attitude, the gesture in repose of something almost human. And then, with a second shock of biting wonder, it came to him like a revelation. The wolf sat beside that camp-fire as a man might sit.

Before he could weigh his extraordinary discovery, before he could examine it in detail or with care, the animal, sitting in this ghastly fashion, seemed to feel his eyes fixed on it. It slowly turned and looked him in the face, and for the first time Hyde felt a full-blooded, superstitious fear flood through his entire being. He seemed transfixed with that nameless terror that is said to attack human beings who suddenly face the dead, finding themselves bereft of speech and movement. This moment of paralysis certainly occurred. Its passing, however, was as singular as its advent. For almost at once he was aware of something beyond and above this mockery of human attitude and pose, something that ran along unaccustomed nerves and reached his feeling, even perhaps his heart. The revulsion was extraordinary, its result still more extraordinary and unexpected. Yet the fact remains. He was aware of another thing that had the effect of stilling his terror as soon as it was born. He was aware of appeal, silent, half expressed, yet vastly pathetic. He saw in the savage eyes a beseeching, even a yearning, expression that changed his mood as by magic from dread to natural sympathy. The great grey brute, symbol of cruel ferocity, sat there beside his dying fire and appealed for help.

This gulf betwixt animal and human seemed in that instant bridged. It was, of course, incredible. Hyde, sleep still possibly clinging to his inner being with the shades and half shapes of dream yet about his soul, acknowledged, how he knew not, the amazing fact. He found himself nodding to the brute in half consent, and instantly, without more ado, the lean grey shape rose like a wraith and trotted off swiftly, but with stealthy tread, into the background of the night.

When Hyde woke in the morning his first impression was that he must have dreamed the entire incident. His practical nature asserted itself. There was a bite in the fresh autumn air; the bright sun allowed no half lights anywhere; he felt brisk in mind and body. Reviewing what had happened, he came to the conclusion that it was utterly vain to speculate; no possible explanation of the animal's behaviour occurred to him; he was dealing with something entirely outside his experience. His fear, however, had completely left him. The odd sense of friendliness remained. The beast had a definite purpose, and he himself was included in that purpose. His sympathy held good.

But with the sympathy there was also an intense curiosity. "If it shows itself again," he told himself, "I'll go up close and find out what it wants." The fish laid out the night before had not been touched.

It must have been a full hour after breakfast when he next saw the brute; it was standing on the edge of the clearing, looking at him in the way now become familiar. Hyde immediately picked up his axe and advanced toward it boldly, keeping his eyes fixed straight upon its own. There was nervousness in him, but kept well under; nothing betrayed it; step by step he drew nearer until some ten yards separated them. The wolf had not stirred a muscle as yet. Its jaws hung open, its eyes observed him intently; it allowed him to approach without a sign of what its mood might be. Then, with these ten yards between them, it turned abruptly and moved slowly off, looking back first over one shoulder and then over the other, exactly as a dog might do, to see if he was following.

A singular journey it was they then made together, animal and man. The trees surrounded them at once, for they left the lake behind them, entering the tangled bush beyond. The beast, Hyde noticed, obviously picked the easiest track for him to follow; for obstacles that meant nothing to the four-legged expert, yet were difficult for a man, were carefully avoided with an almost uncanny skill, while yet the general direction was accurately kept. Occasionally there were windfalls to be surmounted; but though the wolf bounded over these with ease, it was always waiting for the man on the other side after he had laboriously climbed over. Deeper and deeper into the heart of the lonely forest they penetrated in this singular fashion, cutting across the arc of the lake's crescent, it seemed to Hyde; for after two miles or so, he recognized the big rocky bluff that overhung the water at its northern end. This outstanding bluff he had seen from his camp, one side of it falling sheer into the water; it was probably the spot, he imagined, where the Indians held their medicine-making ceremonies, for it stood out in isolated fashion, and its top formed a private plateau not easy of access. And it was here, close to a big spruce at the foot of the bluff upon the forest side, that the wolf stopped suddenly and for the first time since its appearance gave audible expression to its feelings. It sat down on its haunches, lifted its muzzle with open jaws, and gave vent to a subdued and long-drawn howl that was more like the wail of a dog than the fierce barking cry associated with a wolf.

By this time Hyde had lost not only fear, but caution too; nor, oddly enough, did this warning howl revive a sign of unwelcome emotion in him. In that curious sound he detected the same message that the eyes conveyed— appeal for help. He paused, nevertheless, a little startled, and while the wolf sat waiting for him, he looked about him quickly. There was young timber here; it had once been a small clearing, evidently. Axe and fire had done their work, but there was evidence to an experienced eye that it was Indians and not white men who had once been busy here. Some part of the medicine ritual, doubtless, took place in the little clearing, thought the man, as he advanced again towards his patient leader. The end of their queer journey, he felt, was close at hand.

He had not taken two steps before the animal got up and moved very slowly in the direction of some low bushes that formed a clump just beyond. It entered these, first looking back to make sure that its companion watched. The bushes hid it; a moment later it emerged again. Twice it performed this pantomime, each time, as it reappeared, standing still and staring at the man with as distinct an expression of appeal in the eyes as an animal may compass, probably. Its excitement, meanwhile, certainly increased, and this excitement was, with equal certainty, communicated to the man. Hyde made up his mind quickly. Gripping his axe tightly, and ready to use it at the first hint of malice, he moved slowly nearer to the bushes, wondering with something of a tremor what would happen.

If he expected to be startled, his expectation was at once fulfilled; but it was the behaviour of the beast that made him jump. It positively frisked about him like a happy dog. It frisked for joy. Its excitement was intense, yet from its open mouth no sound was audible. With a sudden leap, then, it bounded past him into the clump of bushes, against whose very edge he stood, and began scraping vigorously at the ground. Hyde stood and stared, amazement and interest now banishing all his nervousness, even when the beast, in its violent scraping, actually touched his body with its own. He had, perhaps, the feeling that he was in a dream, one of those fantastic dreams in which things may happen without involving an adequate surprise; for otherwise the manner of scraping and scratching at the ground must have seemed an impossible phenomenon. No wolf, no dog certainly, used its paws in the way those paws were working. Hyde had the odd, distressing sensation that it was hands, not paws, he watched. And yet, somehow, the natural, adequate surprise he should have felt was absent. The strange action seemed not entirely unnatural. In his heart some deep hidden spring of sympathy and pity stirred instead. He was aware of pathos.

The wolf stopped in its task and looked up into his face. Hyde acted without hesitation then. Afterwards he was wholly at a loss to explain his own conduct. It seemed he knew what to do, divined what was asked, expected of him. Between his mind and the dumb desire yearning through the savage animal there was intelligent and intelligible communication. He cut a stake and sharpened it, for the stones would blunt his axe-edge. He entered the clump of bushes to complete the digging his four-legged companion had begun. And while he worked, though he did not forget the close proximity of the wolf, he paid no attention to it; often his back was turned as he

stooped over the laborious clearing away of the hard earth;
no uneasiness or sense of danger was in him any more.
The wolf sat outside the clump and watched the operations. Its concentrated attention, its patience, its intense
eagerness, the gentleness and docility of the grey, fierce,
and probably hungry brute, its obvious pleasure and satisfaction, too, at having won the human to its mysterious
purpose—these were colours in the strange picture that
Hyde thought of later when dealing with the human herd
in his hotel again. At the moment he was aware chiefly
of pathos and affection. The whole business was, of
course, not to be believed, but that discovery came later,
too, when telling it to others.

The digging continued for fully half an hour before
his labour was rewarded by the discovery of a small
whitish object. He picked it up and examined it—the
finger-bone of a man. Other discoveries then followed
quickly and in quantity. The *cache* was laid bare. He
collected nearly the complete skeleton. The skull, however, he found last, and might not have found at all but
for the guidance of his strangely alert companion. It lay
some few yards away from the central hole now dug, and
the wolf stood nuzzling the ground with its nose before
Hyde understood that he was meant to dig exactly in that
spot for it. Between the beast's very paws his stake
struck hard upon it. He scraped the earth from the bone
and examined it carefully. It was perfect, save for the
fact that some wild animal had gnawed it, the teeth-marks
being still plainly visible. Close beside it lay the rusty
iron head of a tomahawk. This and the smallness of the
bones confirmed him in his judgment that it was the skeleton not of a white man, but of an Indian.

During the excitement of the discovery of the bones
one by one, and finally of the skull, but, more especially,
during the period of intense interest while Hyde was
examining them, he had paid little, if any, attention to the
wolf. He was aware that it sat and watched him, never

moving its keen eyes for a single moment from the actual
operations, but of sign or movement it made none at all.
He knew that it was pleased and satisfied, he knew also
that he had now fulfilled its purpose in a great measure.
The further intuition that now came to him, derived, he
felt positive, from his companion's dumb desire, was perhaps the cream of the entire experience to him. Gathering the bones together in his coat, he carried them, together with the tomahawk, to the foot of the big spruce
where the animal had first stopped. His leg actually
touched the creature's muzzle as he passed. It turned its
head to watch, but did not follow, nor did it move a
muscle while he prepared the platform of boughs upon
which he then laid the poor worn bones of an Indian who
had been killed, doubtless, in sudden attack or ambush,
and to whose remains had been denied the last grace of
proper tribal burial. He wrapped the bones in bark; he
laid the tomahawk beside the skull; he lit the circular fire
round the pyre, and the blue smoke rose upward into the
clear bright sunshine of the Canadian autumn morning till
it was lost among the mighty trees far overhead.

In the moment before actually lighting the little fire
he had turned to note what his companion did. It sat
five yards away, he saw, gazing intently, and one of its
front paws was raised a little from the ground. It made
no sign of any kind. He finished the work, becoming so
absorbed in it that he had eyes for nothing but the tend-
ing and guarding of his careful ceremonial fire. It was
only when the platform of boughs collapsed, laying their
charred burden gently on the fragrant earth among the
soft wood ashes, that he turned again, as though to show
the wolf what he had done, and seek, perhaps, some look
of satisfaction in its curiously expressive eyes. But the
place he searched was empty. The wolf had gone.

He did not see it again; it gave no sign of its presence
anywhere; he was not watched. He fished as before, wandered through the bush about his camp, sat smoking round

his fire after dark, and slept peacefully in his cosy little tent. He was not disturbed. No howl was ever audible in the distant forest, no twig snapped beneath a stealthy tread, he saw no eyes. The wolf that behaved like a man had gone for ever.

It was the day before he left that Hyde, noticing smoke rising from the shack across the lake, paddled over to exchange a word or two with the Indian, who had evidently now returned. The Redskin came down to meet him as he landed, but it was soon plain that he spoke very little English. He emitted the familiar grunts at first; then bit by bit Hyde stirred his limited vocabulary into action. The net result, however, was slight enough, though it was certainly direct:

"You camp there?" the man asked, pointing to the other side.

"Yes."

"Wolf come?"

"Yes."

"You see wolf?"

"Yes."

The Indian stared at him fixedly a moment, a keen, wondering look upon his coppery, creased face.

"You 'fraid wolf?" he asked after a moment's pause.

"No," replied Hyde, truthfully. He knew it was useless to ask questions of his own, though he was eager for information. The other would have told him nothing. It was sheer luck that the man had touched on the subject at all, and Hyde realized that his own best rôle was merely to answer, but to ask no questions. Then, suddenly, the Indian became comparatively voluble. There was awe in his voice and manner.

"Him no wolf. Him big medicine wolf. Him spirit wolf."

Whereupon he drank the tea the other had brewed for him, closed his lips tightly, and said no more. His outline was discernible on the shore, rigid and motionless, an hour later, when Hyde's canoe turned the corner of the lake three miles away, and landed to make the portages up the first rapid of his homeward stream.

It was Morton who, after some persuasion, supplied further details of what he called the legend. Some hundred years before, the tribe that lived in the territory beyond the lake began their annual medicine-making ceremonies on the big rocky bluff at the northern end; but no medicine could be made. The spirits, declared the chief medicine man, would not answer. They were offended. An investigation followed. It was discovered that a young brave had recently killed a wolf, a thing strictly forbidden, since the wolf was the totem animal of the tribe. To make matters worse, the name of the guilty man was Running Wolf. The offence being unpardonable, the man was cursed and driven from the tribe:

"Go out. Wander alone among the woods, and if we see you we slay you. Your bones shall be scattered in the forest, and your spirit shall not enter the Happy Hunting Grounds till one of another race shall find and bury them."

"Which meant," explained Morton laconically, his only comment on the story, "probably for ever."

IV

FIRST HATE

THEY had been shooting all day; the weather had been perfect and the powder straight, so that when they assembled in the smoking-room after dinner they were well pleased with themselves. From discussing the day's sport and the weather outlook, the conversation drifted to other, though still cognate, fields. Lawson, the crack shot of the party, mentioned the instinctive recognition all animals feel for their natural enemies, and gave several instances in which he had tested it—tame rats with a ferret, birds with a snake, and so forth.

"Even after being domesticated for generations," he said, "they recognize their natural enemy at once by instinct, an enemy they can never even have seen before. It's infallible. They know instantly."

"Undoubtedly," said a voice from the corner chair; "and so do we."

The speaker was Ericssen, their host, a great hunter before the Lord, generally uncommunicative but a good listener, leaving the talk to others. For this latter reason, as well as for a certain note of challenge in his voice, his abrupt statement gained attention.

"What do you mean exactly by 'so do we'?" asked three men together, after waiting some seconds to see whether he meant to elaborate, which he evidently did not.

"We belong to the animal kingdom, of course," put in a fourth, for behind the challenge there obviously lay a story, though a story that might be difficult to drag out of him. It was.

Ericssen, who had leaned forward a moment so that

74

his strong, humorous face was in clear light, now sank back again into his chair, his expression concealed by the red lampshade at his side. The light played tricks, obliterating the humorous, almost tender lines, while emphasizing the strength of the jaw and nose. The red glare lent to the whole a rather grim expression.

Lawson, man of authority among them, broke the little pause.

"You're dead right," he observed, "but how do you know it?"—for John Ericssen never made a positive statement without a good reason for it. That good reason, he felt sure, involved a personal proof, but a story Ericssen would never tell before a general audience. He would tell it later, however, when the others had left. "There's such a thing as instinctive antipathy, of course," he added, with a laugh, looking around him. "That's what you mean probably."

"I meant exactly what I said," replied the host bluntly. "There's first love. There's first hate, too."

"Hate's a strong word," remarked Lawson.

"So is love," put in another.

"Hate's strongest," said Ericssen grimly. "In the animal kingdom, at least," he added suggestively, and then kept his lips closed, except to sip his liquor, for the rest of the evening—until the party at length broke up, leaving Lawson and one other man, both old trusted friends of many years' standing.

"It's not a tale I'd tell to everybody," he began, when they were alone. "It's true, for one thing; for another, you see, some of those good fellows"—he indicated the empty chairs with an expressive nod of his great head—"some of 'em knew him. You both knew him too, probably."

"The man you hated," said the understanding Lawson.

"And who hated me," came the quiet confirmation. "My other reason," he went on, "for keeping quiet was that the tale involves my wife."

The two listeners said nothing, but each remembered the curiously long courtship that had been the prelude to his marriage. No engagement had been announced, the pair were devoted to one another, there was no known rival on either side; yet the courtship continued without coming to its expected conclusion. Many stories were afloat in consequence. It was a social mystery that intrigued the gossips.

"I may tell you two," Ericssen continued, "the reason my wife refused for so long to marry me. It is hard to believe, perhaps, but it is true. Another man wished to make her his wife, and she would not consent to marry me until that other man was dead. Quixotic, absurd, unreasonable? If you like. I'll tell you what she said." He looked up with a significant expression in his face which proved that he, at least, did not now judge her reason foolish. "'Because it would be murder,' she told me. 'Another man who wants to marry me would kill you.'"

"She had some proof for the assertion, no doubt?" suggested Lawson.

"None whatever," was the reply. "Merely her woman's instinct. Moreover, *I* did not know who the other man was, nor would she ever tell me."

"Otherwise you might have murdered him instead?" said Baynes, the second listener.

"I did," said Ericssen grimly. "But without knowing he was the man." He sipped his whisky and relit his pipe. The others waited.

"Our marriage took place two months later—just after Hazel's disappearance."

"Hazel?" exclaimed Lawson and Baynes in a single breath. "Hazel! Member of the Hunters!" His mysterious disappearance had been a nine days' wonder some ten years ago. It had never been explained. They had all been members of the Hunters' Club together.

"That's the chap," Ericssen said. "Now I'll tell you

the tale, if you care to hear it." They settled back in their chairs to listen, and Ericssen, who had evidently never told the affair to another living soul except his own wife, doubtless, seemed glad this time to tell it to two men.

"It began some dozen years ago when my brother Jack and I came home from a shooting trip in China. I've often told you about our adventures there, and you see the heads hanging up here in the smoking-room—some of 'em." He glanced round proudly at the walls. "We were glad to be in town again after two years' roughing it, and we looked forward to our first good dinner at the club, to make up for the rotten cooking we had endured so long. We had ordered that dinner in anticipatory detail many a time together. Well, we had it and enjoyed it up to a point—the point of the *entrée,* to be exact.

"Up to that point it was delicious, and we let ourselves go, I can tell you. We had ordered the very wine we had planned months before when we were snow-bound and half starving in the mountains." He smacked his lips as he mentioned it. "I was just starting on a beautifully cooked grouse," he went on, "when a figure went by our table, and Jack looked up and nodded. The two exchanged a brief word of greeting and explanation, and the other man passed on. Evidently they knew each other just enough to make a word or two necessary, but enough.

" 'Who's that?' I asked.

" 'A new member, named Hazel,' Jack told me. 'A great shot.' He knew him slightly, he explained; he had once been a client of his—Jack was a barrister, you remember—and had defended him in some financial case or other. Rather an unpleasant case, he added. Jack did not 'care about' the fellow, he told me, as he went on with his tender wing of grouse."

Ericssen paused to relight his pipe a moment.

"Not care about him!" he continued. "It didn't surprise me, for my own feeling, the instant I set eyes on

the fellow, was one of violent, instinctive dislike that
amounted to loathing. Loathing! No. I'll give it the
right word—hatred. I simply couldn't help myself; I
hated the man from the very first go off. A wave of
repulsion swept over me as I followed him down the room
a moment with my eyes, till he took his seat at a distant
table and was out of sight. Ugh! He was a big, fat-
faced man, with an eyeglass glued into one of his pale-
blue cod-like eyes—out of condition, ugly as a toad, with
a smug expression of intense self-satisfaction on his jowl
that made me long to——

"I leave it to you to guess what I would have liked
to do to him. But the instinctive loathing he inspired
in me had another aspect, too. Jack had not introduced
us during the momentary pause beside our table, but as
I looked up I caught the fellow's eye on mine—he was
glaring at me instead of at Jack, to whom he was talking
—with an expression of malignant dislike, as keen evidently as my own. That's the other aspect I meant. He
hated me as violently as I hated him. We were instinctive
enemies, just as the rat and ferret are instinctive enemies.
Each recognized a mortal foe. It was a case—I swear it—
of whoever got first chance."

"Bad as that!" exclaimed Baynes. "I knew him by
sight. He wasn't pretty, I'll admit."

"I knew him to nod to," Lawson mentioned. "I never
heard anything particular against him." He shrugged
his shoulders.

Ericssen went on. "It was not his character or qualities I hated," he said. "I didn't even know them. That's
the whole point. There's no reason you fellows should
have disliked him. *My* hatred—our mutual hatred—was
instinctive, as instinctive as first love. A man knows his
natural mate; also he knows his natural enemy. I did,
at any rate, both with him and with my wife. Given the
chance, Hazel would have done me in; just as surely,

given the chance, I would have done him in. No blame
to either of us, what's more, in my opinion."

"I've felt dislike, but never hatred like that," Baynes
mentioned. "I came across it in a book once, though.
The writer did not mention the instinctive fear of the
human animal for its natural enemy, or anything of that
sort. He thought it was a continuance of a bitter feud
begun in an earlier existence. He called it memory."

"Possibly," said Ericssen briefly. "My mind is not
speculative. But I'm glad you spoke of fear. I left that
out. The truth is, I feared the fellow, too, in a way;
and had we ever met face to face in some wild country
without witnesses I should have felt justified in drawing
on him at sight, and he would have felt the same. Murder?
If you like. I should call it self-defence. Anyhow, the
fellow polluted the room for me. He spoilt the enjoyment of that dinner we had ordered months before in
China."

"But you saw him again, of course, later?"

"Lots of times. Not that night, because we went on
to a theatre. But in the club we were always running
across one another—in the houses of friends at lunch or
dinner; at race meetings; all over the place; in fact, I
even had some trouble to avoid being introduced to him.
And every time we met our eyes betrayed us. He felt in
his heart what I felt in mine. Ugh! He was as loath-
some to me as leprosy, and as dangerous. Odd, isn't it?
The most intense feeling, except love, I've ever known.
I remember"—he laughed gruffly—"I used to feel quite
sorry for him. If he felt what I felt, and I'm convinced
he did, he must have suffered. His one object—to get
me out of the way for good—was so impossible. Then
Fate played a hand in the game. I'll tell you how.

"My brother died a year or two later, and I went
abroad to try and forget it. I went salmon fishing in
Canada. But, though the sport was good, it was not
like the old times with Jack. The camp never felt the

same without him. I missed him badly. But I forgot
Hazel for the time; hating did not seem worth while,
somehow.

"When the best of the fishing was over on the Atlantic
side, I took a run back to Vancouver and fished there for
a bit. I went up the Campbell River, which was not so
crowded then as it is now, and had some rattling sport.
Then I grew tired of the rod and decided to go after
wapiti for a change. I came back to Victoria and learned
what I could about the best places, and decided finally to
go up the west coast of the island. By luck I happened
to pick up a good guide, who was in the town at the
moment on business, and we started off together in one
of the little Canadian Pacific Railway boats that ply along
that coast.

"Outfitting two days later at a small place the steamer
stopped at, the guide said we needed another man to help
pack our kit over portages, and so forth, but the only
fellow available was a Siwash of whom he disapproved.
My guide would not have him at any price; he was lazy,
a drunkard, a liar, and even worse, for on one occasion
he came back without the sportsman he had taken up
country on a shooting trip, and his story was not convincing, to say the least. These disappearances are always
awkward, of course, as you both know. We preferred,
anyhow, to go without the Siwash, and off we started.

"At first our luck was bad. I saw many wapiti, but
no good heads; only after a fortnight's hunting did I
manage to get a decent head, though even that was not so
good as I should have liked.

"We were then near the head waters of a little river
that ran down into the Inlet; heavy rains had made the
river rise; running downstream was a risky job, what
with old log-jams shifting and new ones forming; and,
after many narrow escapes, we upset one afternoon and
had the misfortune to lose a lot of our kit, amongst it
most of our cartridges. We could only muster a few be-

tween us. The guide had a dozen; I had two—just
enough, we considered, to take us out all right. Still, it
was an infernal nuisance. We camped at once to dry out
our soaked things in front of a big fire, and while this
laundry work was going on, the guide suggested my filling
in the time by taking a look at the next little valley, which
ran parallel to ours. He had seen some good heads over
there a few weeks ago. Possibly I might come upon the
herd. I started at once, taking my two cartridges with
me.

"It was the devil of a job getting over the divide, for
it was a badly bushed-up place, and where there were no
bushes there were boulders and fallen trees, and the going
was slow and tiring. But I got across at last and came
out upon another stream at the bottom of the new valley.
Signs of wapiti were plentiful, though I never came up
with a single beast all the afternoon. Blacktail deer were
everywhere, but the wapiti remained invisible. Provi-
dence, or whatever you like to call that which there is
no escaping in our lives, made me save my two cartridges."

Ericssen stopped a minute then. It was not to light
his pipe or sip his whisky. Nor was it because the remainder of his story failed in the recollection of any vivid
detail. He paused a moment to think.

"Tell us the lot," pleaded Lawson. "Don't leave out
anything."

Ericssen looked up. His friend's remark had helped
him to make up his mind apparently. He *had* hesitated
about something or other, but the hesitation passed. He
glanced at both his listeners.

"Right," he said. "I'll tell you everything. I'm not
imaginative, as you know, and my amount of superstition,
I should judge, is microscopic." He took a longer breath,
then lowered his voice a trifle. "Anyhow," he went on,
"it's true, so I don't see why I should feel shy about
admitting it—but as I stood there in that lonely valley,
where only the noises of wind and water were audible,

and no human being, except my guide, some miles away, was within reach, a curious feeling came over me I find difficult to describe. I felt"—obviously he made an effort to get the word out—"I felt creepy."

"You," murmured Lawson, with an incredulous smile —"you creepy?" he repeated under his breath.

"I felt creepy and afraid," continued the other, with conviction. "I had the sensation of being seen by some-one—as if someone, I mean, was watching me. It was so unlikely that anyone was near me in that God-forsaken bit of wilderness, that I simply couldn't believe it at first. But the feeling persisted. I felt absolutely positive some-body was not far away among the red maples, behind a boulder, across the little stream, perhaps, somewhere, at any rate, so near that I was plainly visible to him. It was not an animal. It was human. Also, it was hostile.

"I was in danger.

"You may laugh, both of you, but I assure you the feeling was so positive that I crouched down instinctively to hide myself behind a rock. My first thought, that the guide had followed me for some reason or other, I at once discarded. It was not the guide. It was an enemy.

"No, no, I thought of no one in particular. No name, no face occurred to me. Merely that an enemy was on my trail, that he saw me, and I did not see him, and that he was near enough to me to—well, to take instant action. This deep instinctive feeling of danger, of fear, of any-thing you like to call it, was simply overwhelming.

"Another curious detail I must also mention. About half an hour before, having given up all hope of seeing wapiti, I had decided to kill a blacktail deer for meat. A good shot offered itself, not thirty yards away. I aimed. But just as I was going to pull the trigger a queer emo-tion touched me, and I lowered the rifle. It was exactly as though a voice said, 'Don't!' I heard no voice, mind you; it was an emotion only, a feeling, a sudden inexplicable change of mind—a warning, if you like. I didn't fire, anyhow.

"But now, as I crouched behind that rock, I remembered this curious little incident, and was glad I had not used up my last two cartridges. More than that I cannot tell you. Things of that kind are new to me. They're difficult enough to tell, let alone to explain. But they were *real*.

"I crouched there, wondering what on earth was happening to me, and, feeling a bit of a fool, if you want to know, when suddenly, over the top of the boulder, I saw something moving. It was a man's hat. I peered cautiously. Some sixty yards away the bushes parted, and two men came out on to the river's bank, and I knew them both. One was the Siwash I had seen at the store. The other was Hazel. Before I had time to think I cocked my rifle."

"Hazel. Good Lord!" exclaimed the listeners.

"For a moment I was too surprised to do anything but cock that rifle. I waited for what puzzled me was that, after all, Hazel had *not* seen me. It was only the feeling of his beastly proximity that had made me feel I was seen and watched by him. There was something else, too, that made me pause before—er—doing anything. Two other things, in fact. One was that I was so intensely interested in watching the fellow's actions. Obviously he had the same uneasy sensation that I had. He shared with me the nasty feeling that danger was about. His rifle, I saw, was cocked and ready; he kept looking behind him, over his shoulder, peering this way and that, and sometimes addressing a remark to the Siwash at his side. I caught the laughter of the latter. The Siwash evidently did not think there was danger anywhere. It was, of course, unlikely enough——"

"And the other thing that stopped you?" urged Lawson, impatiently interrupting.

Ericssen turned with a look of grim humour on his face.

"Some confounded or perverted sense of chivalry in me, I suppose," he said, "that made it impossible to shoot him down in cold blood, or, rather, without letting him have a chance. For my blood, as a matter of fact, was far from cold at the moment. Perhaps, too, I wanted the added satisfaction of letting him know who fired the shot that was to end his vile existence."

He laughed again. "It was rat and ferret in the human kingdom," he went on, "but I wanted my rat to have a chance, I suppose. Anyhow, though I had a perfect shot in front of me at easy distance, I did not fire. Instead I got up, holding my cocked rifle ready, finger on trigger, and came out of my hiding place. I called to him. 'Hazel, you beast! So there you are—at last!'

"He turned, but turned away from me, offering his horrid back. The direction of the voice he misjudged. He pointed down stream, and the Siwash turned to look. Neither of them had seen me yet. There was a big log-jam below them. The roar of the water in their ears concealed my footsteps. I was, perhaps, twenty paces from them when Hazel, with a jerk of his whole body, abruptly turned clean round and faced me. We stared into each other's eyes.

"The amazement on his face changed instantly to hatred and resolve. He acted with incredible rapidity. I think the unexpected suddenness of his turn made me lose a precious second or two. Anyhow he was ahead of me. He flung his rifle to his shoulder. 'You devil!' I heard his voice. 'I've got you at last!' His rifle cracked, for he let drive the same instant. The hair stirred just above my ear.

"He had missed!

"Before he could draw back his bolt for another shot I had acted.

"'You're not fit to live!' I shouted, as my bullet

crashed into his temple. I had the satisfaction, too, of knowing that he heard my words. I saw the swift expression of frustrated loathing in his eyes.

"He fell like an ox, his face splashing in the stream. I shoved the body out. I saw it sucked beneath the log-jam instantly. It disappeared. There could be no inquest on him, I reflected comfortably. Hazel was gone—gone from this earth, from my life, our mutual hatred over at last."

The speaker paused a moment. "Odd," he continued presently—"very odd indeed." He turned to the others. "I felt quite sorry for him suddenly. I suppose," he added, "the philosophers are right when they gas about hate being very close to love."

His friends contributed no remark.

"Then I came away," he resumed shortly. "My wife —well, you know the rest, don't you? I told her the whole thing. She—she said nothing. But she married me, you see."

There was a moment's silence. Baynes was the first to break it. "But—the Siwash?" he asked. "The witness?"

Lawson turned upon him with something of contemptuous impatience.

"He told you he had *two* cartridges."

Ericssen, smiling grimly, said nothing at all.

V

THE TARN OF SACRIFICE

JOHN HOLT, a vague excitement in him, stood at the door of the little inn, listening to the landlord's directions as to the best way of reaching Scarsdale. He was on a walking tour through the Lake District, exploring the smaller dales that lie away from the beaten track and are accessible only on foot.

The landlord, a hard-featured north countryman, half innkeeper, half sheep farmer, pointed up the valley. His deep voice had a friendly burr in it.

"You go straight on till you reach the head," he said, "then take to the fell. Follow the 'sheep-trod' past the Crag. Directly you're over the top you'll strike the road."

"A road up there!" exclaimed his customer incredulously.

"Aye," was the steady reply. "The old Roman road. The same road," he added, "the savages came down when they burst through the Wall and burnt everything right up to Lancaster——"

"They were held—weren't they—at Lancaster?" asked the other, yet not knowing quite why he asked it.

"I don't rightly know," came the answer slowly. "Some say they were. But the old town has been that built over since, it's hard to tell." He paused a moment. "At Ambleside," he went on presently, "you can still see the marks of the burning, and at the little fort on the way to Ravenglass."

Holt strained his eyes into the sunlit distance, for he would soon have to walk that road and he was anxious to

86

be off. But the landlord was communicative and interesting. "You can't miss it," he told him. "It runs
straight as a spear along the fell top till it meets the Wall.
You must hold to it for about eight miles. Then you'll
come to the Standing Stone on the left of the track——"

"The Standing Stone, yes?" broke in the other a little
eagerly.

"You'll see the Stone right enough. It was where the
Romans came. Then bear to the left down another 'trod'
that comes into the road there. They say it was the war-
trail of the folk that set up the Stone."

"And what did they use the Stone for?" Holt inquired,
more as though he asked it of himself than of his companion.

The old man paused to reflect. He spoke at length.

"I mind an old fellow who seemed to know about such
things called it a Sighting Stone. He reckoned the sun
shone over it at dawn on the longest day right on to the
little holm in Blood Tarn. He said they held sacrifices in
a stone circle there." He stopped a moment to puff at his
black pipe. "Maybe he was right. I have seen stones
lying about that may well be that."

The man was pleased and willing to talk to so good
a listener. Either he had not noticed the curious gesture
the other made, or he read it as a sign of eagerness to
start. The sun was warm, but a sharp wind from the
bare hills went between them with a sighing sound. Holt
buttoned his coat about him. "An odd name for a mountain lake—Blood Tarn," he remarked, watching the landlord's face expectantly.

"Aye, but a good one," was the measured reply. "When
I was a boy the old folk had a tale that the savages flung
three Roman captives from that crag into the water.
There's a book been written about it; they say it was a
sacrifice, but most likely they were tired of dragging them
along, I say. Anyway, that's what the writer said. One,
I mind, now you ask me, was a priest of some heathen

temple that stood near the Wall, and the other two were his daughter and her lover." He guffawed. At least he made a strange noise in his throat. Evidently, thought Holt, he was sceptical yet superstitious. "It's just an old tale handed down, whatever the learned folk may say," the old man added.

"A lonely place," began Holt, aware that a fleeting touch of awe was added suddenly to his interest.

"Aye," said the other, "and a bad spot too. Every year the Crag takes its toll of sheep, and sometimes a man goes over in the mist. It's right beside the track and very slippery. Ninety foot of a drop before you hit the water. Best keep round the tarn and leave the Crag alone if there's any mist about. Fishing? Yes, there's some quite fair trout in the tarn, but it's not much fished. Happen one of the shepherd lads from Tyson's farm may give it a turn with an 'otter,'" he went on, "once in a while, but he won't stay for the evening. He'll clear out before sunset."

"Ah! Superstitious, I suppose?"

"It's a gloomy, chancy spot—and with the dusk falling," agreed the innkeeper eventually. "None of our folk care to be caught up there with night coming on. Most handy for a shepherd, too—but Tyson can't get a man to bide there." He paused again, then added significantly: "Strangers don't seem to mind it though. It's only our own folk——"

"Strangers!" repeated the other sharply, as though he had been waiting all along for this special bit of information. "You don't mean to say there are people living up there?" A curious thrill ran over him.

"Aye," replied the landlord, "but they're daft folk—a man and his daughter. They come every spring. It's early in the year yet, but I mind Jim Backhouse, one of Tyson's men, talking about them last week." He stopped to think. "So they've come back," he went on decidedly. "They get milk from the farm."

"And what on earth are they doing up there?" Holt asked.

He asked many other questions as well, but the answers were poor, the information not forthcoming. The landlord would talk for hours about the Crag, the tarn, the legends and the Romans, but concerning the two strangers he was uncommunicative. Either he knew little, or he did not want to discuss them; Holt felt it was probably the former. They were educated town-folk, he gathered with difficulty, rich apparently, and they spent their time wandering about the fell, or fishing. The man was often seen upon the Crag, his girl beside him, bare-legged, dressed as a peasant. "Happen they come for their health, happen the father is a learned man studying the Wall"— exact information was not forthcoming.

The landlord "minded his own business," and inhabitants were too few and far between for gossip. All Holt could extract amounted to this: the couple had been in a motor accident some years before, and as a result they came every spring to spend a month or two in absolute solitude, away from cities and the excitement of modern life. They troubled no one and no one troubled them.

"Perhaps I may see them as I go by the tarn," remarked the walker finally, making ready to go. He gave up questioning in despair. The morning hours were passing.

"Happen you may," was the reply, "for your track goes past their door and leads straight down to Scarsdale. The other way over the Crag saves half a mile, but it's rough going along the scree." He stopped dead. Then he added, in reply to Holt's good-bye: "In my opinion it's not worth it," yet what he meant exactly by "it" was not quite clear.

*   *   *   *   *

The walker shouldered his knapsack. Instinctively he gave the little hitch to settle it on his shoulders—much as he used to give to his pack in France. The pain that

shot through him as he did so was another reminder of
France. The bullet he had stopped on the Somme still
made its presence felt at times. . . . Yet he knew, as
he walked off briskly, that he was one of the lucky ones.
How many of his old pals would never walk again, con-
demned to hobble on crutches for the rest of their lives!
How many, again, would never even hobble! More terrible still, he remembered, were the blind. . . . The dead,
it seemed to him, had been more fortunate. . . .

He swung up the narrowing valley at a good pace
and was soon climbing the fell. It proved far steeper
than it had appeared from the door of the inn, and he
was glad enough to reach the top and fling himself down
on the coarse springy turf to admire the view below.

The spring day was delicious. It stirred his blood. The
world beneath looked young and stainless. Emotion rose
through him in a wave of optimistic happiness. The bare
hills were half hidden by a soft blue haze that made them
look bigger, vaster, less earthly than they really were.
He saw silver streaks in the valleys that he knew were
distant streams and lakes. Birds soared between. The
dazzling air seemed painted with exhilarating light and
colour. The very clouds were floating gossamer that he
could touch. There were bees and dragon-flies and fluttering thistle-down. Heat vibrated. His body, his physical sensations, so-called, retired into almost nothing. He
felt himself, like his surroundings, made of air and sunlight. A delicious sense of resignation poured upon him.
He, too, like his surroundings, was composed of air and
sunshine, of insect wings, of soft, fluttering vibrations that
the gorgeous spring day produced. . . . It seemed that
he renounced the heavy dues of bodily life, and enjoyed
the delights, momentarily at any rate, of a more ethereal
consciousness.

Near at hand, the hills were covered with the faded
gold of last year's bracken, which ran down in a brimming
flood till it was lost in the fresh green of the familiar

woods below. Far in the hazy distance swam the sea of
ash and hazel. The silver birch sprinkled that lower world
with fairy light.

Yes, it was all natural enough. He could see the road
quite clearly now, only a hundred yards away from where
he lay. How straight it ran along the top of the hill!
The landlord's expression recurred to him: "Straight as
a spear." Somehow, the phrase seemed to describe exactly
the Romans and all their works. . . . The Romans, yes,
and all their works. . . .

He became aware of a sudden sympathy with these
long dead conquerors of the world. With them, he felt
sure, there had been no useless, foolish talk. They had
known no empty words, no bandying of foolish phrases.
"War to end war," and "Regeneration of the race"—no
hypocritical nonsense of that sort had troubled their minds
and purposes. They had not attempted to cover up the
horrible in words. With them had been no childish, vain
pretence. They had gone straight to their ends.

Other thoughts, too, stole over him, as he sat gazing
down upon the track of that ancient road; strange
thoughts, not wholly welcome. New, yet old, emotions
rose in a tide upon him. He began to wonder. . . . Had
he, after all, become brutalized by the War? He knew
quite well that the little "Christianity" he inherited had
soon fallen from him like a garment in France. In his
attitude to Life and Death he had become, frankly, pagan.
He now realized, abruptly, another thing as well: in
reality he had never been a "Christian" at any time.
Given to him with his mother's milk, he had never accepted,
felt at home with Christian dogmas. To him they had
always been an alien creed. Christianity met none of his
requirements. . . ."

But what were his "requirements"? He found it difficult to answer.

Something, at any rate, different and more primitive,
he thought. . . .

Even up here, alone on the mountain-top, it was hard to be absolutely frank with himself. With a kind of savage, honest determination, he bent himself to the task. It became suddenly important for him. He must know exactly where he stood. It seemed he had reached a turning point in his life. The War, in the objective world, had been one such turning point; now he had reached another, in the subjective life, and it was more important than the first.

As he lay there in the pleasant sunshine, his thoughts went back to the fighting. A friend, he recalled, had divided people into those who enjoyed the War and those who didn't. He was obliged to admit that he had been one of the former—he had thoroughly enjoyed it. Brought up from a youth as an engineer, he had taken to a soldier's life as a duck takes to water. There had been plenty of misery, discomfort, wretchedness; but there had been compensations that, for him, outweighed them. The fierce excitement, the primitive, naked passions, the wild fury, the reckless indifference to pain and death, with the loss of the normal, cautious, pettifogging little daily self all these involved, had satisfied him. Even the actual killing. . . .

He started. A slight shudder ran down his back as the cool wind from the open moorlands came sighing across the soft spring sunshine. Sitting up straight, he looked behind him a moment, as with an effort to turn away from something he disliked and dreaded because it was, he knew, too strong for him. But the same instant he turned round again. He faced the vile and dreadful thing in himself he had hitherto sought to deny, evade. Pretence fell away. He could not disguise from himself, that he had thoroughly enjoyed the killing; or, at any rate, had not been shocked by it as by an unnatural and ghastly duty. The shooting and bombing he performed with an effort always, but the rarer moments when he

had been able to use the bayonet . . . the joy of feeling
the steel go home . . .

He started again, hiding his face a moment in his
hands, but he did not try to evade the hideous memories
that surged. At times, he knew, he had gone quite mad
with the lust of slaughter; he had gone on long after he
should have stopped. Once an officer had pulled him up
sharply for it, but the next instant had been killed by a
bullet. He thought he had gone on killing, but he did
not know. It was all a red mist before his eyes and he
could only remember the sticky feeling of the blood on
his hands when he gripped his rifle. . . .

And now, at this moment of painful honesty with himself, he realized that his creed, whatever it was, must cover
all that; it must provide some sort of a philosophy for it;
must neither apologize nor ignore it. The heaven that
it promised must be a man's heaven. The Christian heaven
made no appeal to him, he could not believe in it. The
ritual must be simple and direct. He felt that in some
dim way he understood why those old people had thrown
their captives from the Crag. The sacrifice of an animal
victim that could be eaten afterwards with due ceremonial
did not shock him. Such methods seemed simple, natural,
effective. Yet would it not have been better—the horrid
thought rose unbidden in his inmost mind—better to have
cut their throats with a flint knife . . . slowly?

Horror-stricken, he sprang to his feet. These terrible
thoughts he could not recognize as his own. Had he slept
a moment in the sunlight, dreaming them? Was it some
hideous nightmare flash that touched him as he dozed a
second? Something of fear and awe stole over him. He
stared round for some minutes into the emptiness of the
desolate landscape, then hurriedly ran down to the road,
hoping to exorcize the strange sudden horror by vigorous
movement. Yet when he reached the track he knew that
he had not succeeded. The awful pictures were gone perhaps, but the mood remained. It was as though some new

attitude began to take definite form and harden within him.

He walked on, trying to pretend to himself that he was some forgotten legionary marching up with his fellows to defend the Wall. Half unconsciously he fell into the steady tramping pace of his old regiment: the words of the ribald songs they had sung going to the front came pouring into his mind. Steadily and almost mechanically he swung along till he saw the Stone as a black speck on the left of the track, and the instant he saw it there rose in him the feeling that he stood upon the edge of an adventure that he feared yet longed for. He approached the great granite monolith with a curious thrill of anticipatory excitement, born he knew not whence.

But, of course, there was nothing. Common sense, still operating strongly, had warned him there would be, could be, nothing. In the waste the great Stone stood upright, solitary, forbidding, as it had stood for thousands of years. It dominated the landscape somewhat ominously. The sheep and cattle had used it as a rubbing-stone, and bits of hair and wool clung to its rough, weather-eaten edges; the feet of generations had worn a cup-shaped hollow at its base. The wind sighed round it plaintively. Its bulk glistened as it took the sun.

A short mile away the Blood Tarn was now plainly visible; he could see the little holm lying in a direct line with the Stone, while, overhanging the water as a dark shadow on one side, rose the cliff-like rock they called "the Crag." Of the house the landlord had mentioned, however, he could see no trace, as he relieved his shoulders of the knapsack and sat down to enjoy his lunch. The tarn, he reflected, was certainly a gloomy place; he could understand that the simple superstitious shepherds did not dare to live there, for even on this bright spring day it wore a dismal and forbidding look. With failing light, when the Crag sprawled its big lengthening shadow across the water, he could well imagine they would give it the

widest possible berth. He strolled down to the shore after
lunch, smoking his pipe lazily—then suddenly stood still.
At the far end, hidden hitherto by a fold in the ground,
he saw the little house, a faint column of blue smoke rising from the chimney, and at the same moment a woman
came out of the low door and began to walk towards the
tarn. She had seen him, she was moving evidently in his
direction; a few minutes later she stopped and stood waiting on the path—waiting, he well knew, for him.

And his earlier mood, the mood he dreaded yet had
forced himself to recognize, came back upon him with
sudden redoubled power. As in some vivid dream that
dominates and paralyses the will, or as in the first stages
of an imposed hypnotic spell, all question, hesitation,
refusal sank away. He felt a pleasurable resignation steal
upon him with soft, numbing effect. Denial and criticism
ceased to operate, and common sense died with them. He
yielded his being automatically to the deeps of an adventure he did not understand. He began to walk towards the
woman.

It was, he saw as he drew nearer, the figure of a young
girl, nineteen or twenty years of age, who stood there
motionless with her eyes fixed steadily on his own. She
looked as wild and picturesque as the scene that framed
her. Thick black hair hung loose over her back and
shoulders; about her head was bound a green ribbon; her
clothes consisted of a jersey and a very short skirt which
showed her bare legs browned by exposure to the sun and
wind. A pair of rough sandals covered her feet. Whether
the face was beautiful or not he could not tell; he only
knew that it attracted him immensely and with a strength
of appeal that he at once felt curiously irresistible. She
remained motionless against the boulder, staring fixedly
at him till he was close before her. Then she spoke:

"I am glad that you have come at last," she said
in a clear, strong voice that yet was soft and even tender.
"We have been expecting you."

"You have been expecting me!" he repeated, astonished beyond words, yet finding the language natural, right and true. A stream of sweet feeling invaded him, his heart beat faster, he felt happy and at home in some extraordinary way he could not understand yet did not question.

"Of course," she answered, looking straight into his eyes with welcome unashamed. Her next words thrilled him to the core of his being. "I have made the room ready for you."

Quick upon her own, however, flashed back the landlord's words, while common sense made a last faint effort in his thought. He was the victim of some absurd mistake evidently. The lonely life, the forbidding surroundings, the associations of the desolate hills had affected her mind. He remembered the accident.

"I am afraid," he offered, lamely enough, "there is some mistake. I am not the friend you were expecting. I——" He stopped. A thin slight sound as of distant laughter seemed to echo behind the unconvincing words.

"There is no mistake," the girl answered firmly, with a quiet smile, moving a step nearer to him, so that he caught the subtle perfume of her vigorous youth. "I saw you clearly in the Mystery Stone. I recognized you at once."

"The Mystery Stone," he heard himself saying, bewilderment increasing, a sense of wild happiness growing with it.

Laughing, she took his hand in hers. "Come," she said, drawing him along with her, "come home with me. My father will be waiting for us; he will tell you everything, and better far than I can."

He went with her, feeling that he was made of sunlight and that he walked on air, for at her touch his own hand responded as with a sudden fierceness of pleasure that he failed utterly to understand, yet did not question for an instant. Wildly, absurdly, madly it flashed across his mind: "This is the woman I shall marry—*my* woman. I am her man."

They walked in silence for a little, for no words of any sort offered themselves to his mind, nor did the girl attempt to speak. The total absence of embarrassment between them occurred to him once or twice as curious, though the very idea of embarrassment then disappeared entirely. It all seemed natural and unforced, the sudden intercourse as familiar and effortless as though they had known one another always.

"The Mystery Stone," he heard himself saying presently, as the idea rose again to the surface of his mind. "I should like to know more about it. Tell me, dear."

"I bought it with the other things," she replied softly.

"What other things?"

She turned and looked up into his face with a slight expression of surprise; their shoulders touched as they swung along; her hair blew in the wind across his coat. "The bronze collar," she answered in the low voice that pleased him so, "and this ornament that I wear in my hair."

He glanced down to examine it. Instead of a ribbon, as he had first supposed, he saw that it was a circlet of bronze, covered with a beautiful green patina and evidently very old. In front, above the forehead, was a small disk bearing an inscription he could not decipher at the moment. He bent down and kissed her hair, the girl smiling with happy contentment, but offering no sign of resistance or annoyance.

"And," she added suddenly, "the dagger."

Holt started visibly. This time there was a thrill in her voice that seemed to pierce down straight into his heart. He said nothing, however. The unexpectedness of the word she used, together with the note in her voice that moved him so strangely, had a disconcerting effect that kept him silent for a time. He did not ask about

the dagger. Something prevented his curiosity finding
expression in speech, though the word, with the marked
accent she placed upon it, had struck into him like the
shock of sudden steel itself, causing him an indecipherable
emotion of both joy and pain. He asked instead, presently,
another question, and a very commonplace one: he asked
where she and her father had lived before they came to
these lonely hills. And the form of his question—his
voice shook a little as he said it—was, again, an effort
of his normal self to maintain its already precarious
balance.

The effect of his simple query, the girl's reply above
all, increased in him the mingled sensations of sweetness
and menace, of joy and dread, that half alarmed, half
satisfied him. For a moment she wore a puzzled expression, as though making an effort to remember.

"Down by the sea," she answered slowly, thoughtfully,
her voice very low. "Somewhere by a big harbour with
great ships coming in and out. It was there we had the
break—the shock—an accident that broke us, shattering
the dream we share To-day." Her face cleared a little.
"We were in a chariot," she went on more easily and
rapidly, "and father—my father was injured, so that I
went with him to a palace beyond the Wall till he grew
well."

"You were in a chariot?" Holt repeated. "Surely
not."

"Did I say chariot?" the girl replied. "How foolish
of me!" She shook her hair back as though the gesture
helped to clear her mind and memory. "That belongs,
of course, to the other dream. No, not a chariot; it was
a car. But it had wheels like a chariot—the old war-
chariots. You know."

"Disk-wheels," thought Holt to himself. He did not
ask about the palace. He asked instead where she had
bought the Mystery Stone, as she called it, and the other
things. Her reply bemused and enticed him farther, for

he could not unravel it. His whole inner attitude was shifting with uncanny rapidity and completeness. They walked together, he now realized, with linked arms, moving slowly in step, their bodies touching. He felt the blood run hot and almost savage in his veins. He was aware how amazingly precious she was to him, how deeply, absolutely necessary to his life and happiness. Her words went past him in the mountain wind like flying birds.

"My father was fishing," she went on, "and I was on my way to join him, when the old woman called me into her dwelling and showed me the things. She wished to give them to me, but I refused the present and paid for them in gold. I put the fillet on my head to see if it would fit, and took the Mystery Stone in my hand. Then, as I looked deep into the stone, this present dream died all away. It faded out. I saw the older dreams again—*our* dreams."

"The older dreams!" interrupted Holt. "Ours!" But instead of saying the words aloud, they issued from his lips in a quiet whisper, as though control of his voice had passed a little from him. The sweetness in him became more wonderful, unmanageable; his astonishment had vanished; he walked and talked with his old familiar happy Love, the woman he had sought so long and waited for, the woman who was his mate, as he was hers, she who alone could satisfy his inmost soul.

"The old dream," she replied, "the very old—the oldest of all perhaps—when we committed the terrible sacrilege. I saw the High Priest lying dead—whom my father slew —and the other whom *you* destroyed. I saw you prise out the jewel from the image of the god—with your short bloody spear. I saw, too, our flight to the galley through the hot, awful night beneath the stars—and our escape. . . ."

Her voice died away and she fell silent.

"Tell me more," he whispered, drawing her closer against his side. "What had *you* done?" His heart was racing now. Some fighting blood surged uppermost. He felt that he could kill, and the joy of violence and slaughter rose in him.

"Have you forgotten so completely?" she asked very low, as he pressed her more tightly still against his heart. And almost beneath her breath she whispered into his ear, which he bent to catch the little sound: "I had broken my vows with you."

"What else, my lovely one—my best beloved—what more did you see?" he whispered in return, yet wondering why the fierce pain and anger that he felt behind still lay hidden from betrayal.

"Dream after dream, and always we were punished. But the last time was the clearest, for it was here—here where we now walk together in the sunlight and the wind —it was here the savages hurled us from the rock."

A shiver ran through him, making him tremble with an unaccountable touch of cold that communicated itself to her as well. Her arm went instantly about his shoulder, as he stooped and kissed her passionately. "Fasten your coat about you," she said tenderly, but with troubled breath, when he released her, "for this wind is chill although the sun shines brightly. We were glad, you remember, when they stopped to kill us, for we were tired and our feet were cut to pieces by the long, rough journey from the Wall." Then suddenly her voice grew louder again and the smile of happy confidence came back into her eyes. There was the deep earnestness of love in it, of love that cannot end or die. She looked up into his face. "But soon now," she said, "we shall be free. For you have come, and it is nearly finished—this weary little present dream."

"How," he asked, "shall we get free?" A red mist swam momentarily before his eyes.

"My father," she replied at once, "will tell you all. It is quite easy."

"Your father, too, remembers?"

"The moment the collar touches him," she said, "he is a priest again. See! Here he comes forth already to meet us, and to bid you welcome."

Holt looked up, startled. He had hardly noticed, so absorbed had he been in the words that half intoxicated him, the distance they had covered. The cottage was now close at hand, and a tall, powerfully built man, wearing a shepherd's rough clothing, stood a few feet in front of him. His stature, breadth of shoulder and thick black beard made up a striking figure. The dark eyes, with fire in them, gazed straight into his own, and a kindly smile played round the stern and vigorous mouth.

"Greeting, my son," said a deep, booming voice, "for I shall call you my son as I did of old. The bond of the spirit is stronger than that of the flesh, and with us three the tie is indeed of triple strength. You come, too, at an auspicious hour, for the omens are favourable and the time of our liberation is at hand." He took the other's hand in a grip that might have killed an ox and yet was warm with gentle kindliness, while Holt, now caught wholly into the spirit of some deep reality he could not master yet accepted, saw that the wrist was small, the fingers shapely, the gesture itself one of dignity and refinement.

"Greeting, my father," he replied, as naturally as though he said more modern words.

"Come in with me, I pray," pursued the other, leading the way, "and let me show you the poor accommodation we have provided, yet the best that we can offer."

He stooped to pass the threshold, and as Holt stooped likewise the girl took his hand and he knew that his bewitchment was complete. Entering the low doorway, he passed through a kitchen, where only the roughest, scantiest furniture was visible, into another room that was completely bare. A heap of dried bracken had been spread on the floor in one corner to form a bed. Beside it lay two cheap, coloured blankets. There was nothing else.

"Our place is poor," said the man, smiling courteously, but with that dignity and air of welcome which made the hovel seem a palace. "Yet it may serve, perhaps, for the short time that you will need it. Our little dream here is wellnigh over, now that you have come. The long weary pilgrimage at last draws to a close." The girl had left them alone a moment, and the man stepped closer to his guest. His face grew solemn, his voice deeper and more earnest suddenly, the light in his eyes seemed actually to flame with the enthusiasm of a great belief. "Why have you tarried thus so long, and where?" he asked in a lowered tone that vibrated in the little space. "We have sought you with prayer and fasting, and she has spent her nights for you in tears. You lost the way, it must be. The lesser dreams entangled your feet, I see." A touch of sadness entered the voice, the eyes held pity in them. "It is, alas, too easy, I well know," he murmured. "It is too easy."

"I lost the way," the other replied. It seemed suddenly that his heart was filled with fire. "But now," he cried aloud, "now that I have found her, I will never, never let her go again. My feet are steady and my way is sure."

"For ever and ever, my son," boomed the happy, yet almost solemn answer, "she is yours. Our freedom is at hand."

He turned and crossed the little kitchen again, making a sign that his guest should follow him. They stood together by the door, looking out across the tarn in silence. The afternoon sunshine fell in a golden blaze across the bare hills that seemed to smoke with the glory of the fiery light. But the Crag loomed dark in shadow overhead, and the little lake lay deep and black beneath it.

"Acella, Acella!" called the man, the name breaking upon his companion as with a shock of sweet delicious fire that filled his entire being, as the girl came the same instant from behind the cottage. "The Gods call me," said her father. "I go now to the hill. Protect our guest and comfort him in my absence."

Without another word, he strode away up the hillside and presently was visible standing on the summit of the Crag, his arms stretched out above his head to heaven, his great head thrown back, his bearded face turned upwards. An impressive, even a majestic figure he looked, as his bulk and stature rose in dark silhouette against the brilliant evening sky. Holt stood motionless, watching him for several minutes, his heart swelling in his breast, his pulses thumping before some great nameless pressure that rose from the depths of his being. That inner attitude which seemed a new and yet more satisfying attitude to life than he had known hitherto, had crystallized. Define it he could not, he only knew that he accepted it as natural. It satisfied him. The sight of that dignified, gaunt figure worshipping upon the hill-top enflamed him. . . .

"I have brought the stone," a voice interrupted his reflections, and turning, he saw the girl beside him. She held out for his inspection a dark square object that looked to him at first like a black stone lying against the brown skin of her hand. "The Mystery Stone," the girl added, as their faces bent down together to examine it. "It is there I see the dreams I told you of."

He took it from her and found that it was heavy, composed apparently of something like black quartz, with a brilliant polished surface that revealed clear depths within. Once, evidently, it had been set in a stand or frame, for the marks where it had been attached still showed, and it was obviously of great age. He felt confused, the mind in him troubled yet excited, as he gazed. The effect upon him was as though a wind rose suddenly and passed across his inmost subjective life, setting its entire contents in rushing motion.

"And here," the girl said, "is the dagger."

He took from her the short bronze weapon, feeling at once instinctively its ragged edge, its keen point, sharp and effective still. The handle had long since rotted away, but the bronze tongue, and the holes where the rivets had been, remained, and, as he touched it, the confusion and trouble in his mind increased to a kind of turmoil, in which violence, linked to something tameless, wild and almost savage, was the dominating emotion. He turned to seize the girl and crush her to him in a passionate embrace, but she held away, throwing back her lovely head, her eyes shining, her lips parted, yet one hand stretched out to stop him.

"First look into it with me," she said quietly. "Let us see together."

She sat down on the turf beside the cottage door, and Holt, obeying, took his place beside her. She remained very still for some minutes, covering the stone with both hands as though to warm it. Her lips moved. She seemed to be repeating some kind of invocation beneath her breath, though no actual words were audible. Presently her hands parted. They sat together gazing at the polished surface. They looked within.

"There comes a white mist in the heart of the stone," the girl whispered. "It will soon open. The pictures will then grow. Look!" she exclaimed after a brief pause, "they are forming now."

"I see only mist," her companion murmured, gazing intently. "Only mist I see."

She took his hand and instantly the mist parted. He found himself peering into another landscape which opened before his eyes as though it were a photograph. Hills covered with heather stretched away on every side.

"Hills, I see," he whispered. "The ancient hills——"

"Watch closely," she replied, holding his hand firmly.

At first the landscape was devoid of any sign of life; then suddenly it surged and swarmed with moving figures. Torrents of men poured over the hill-crests and down their

heathery sides in columns. He could see them clearly—
great hairy men, clad in skins, with thick shields on their
left arms or slung over their backs, and short stabbing
spears in their hands. Thousands upon thousands poured
over in an endless stream. In the distance he could see
other columns sweeping in a turning movement. A few
of the men rode rough ponies and seemed to be directing
the march, and these, he knew, were the chiefs. . . .

The scene grew dimmer, faded, died away completely.
Another took its place:

By the faint light he knew that it was dawn. The
undulating country, less hilly than before, was still wild
and uncultivated. A great wall, with towers at intervals,
stretched away till it was lost in shadowy distance. On
the nearest of these towers he saw a sentinel clad in
armour, gazing out across the rolling country. The
armour gleamed faintly in the pale glimmering light, as
the man suddenly snatched up a bugle and blew upon it.
From a brazier burning beside him he next seized a brand
and fired a great heap of brushwood. The smoke rose in
a dense column into the air almost immediately, and from
all directions, with incredible rapidity, figures came pouring up to man the wall. Hurriedly they strung their
bows, and laid spare arrows close beside them on the cop-
ing. The light grew brighter. The whole country was
alive with savages; like the waves of the sea they came
rolling in enormous numbers. For several minutes the
wall held. Then, in an impetuous, fearful torrent, they
poured over. . . .

It faded, died away, was gone again, and a moment
later yet another took its place:

But this time the landscape was familiar, and he recognized the tarn. He saw the savages upon the ledge that
flanked the dominating Crag; they had three captives with
them. He saw two men. The other was a woman. But
the woman had fallen exhausted to the ground, and a
chief on a rough pony rode back to see what had delayed

the march. Glancing at the captives, he made a fierce gesture with his arm towards the water far below. Instantly the woman was jerked cruelly to her feet and forced onwards till the summit of the Crag was reached. A man snatched something from her hand. A second later she was hurled over the brink.

The two men were next dragged on to the dizzy spot where she had stood. Dead with fatigue, bleeding from numerous wounds, yet at this awful moment they straightened themselves, casting contemptuous glances at the fierce savages surrounding them. They were Romans and would die like Romans. Holt saw their faces clearly for the first time.

He sprang up with a cry of anguished fury.

"The second man!" he exclaimed. "You saw the second man!"

The girl, releasing his hand, turned her eyes slowly up to his, so that he met the flame of her ancient and undying love shining like stars upon him out of the night of time.

"Ever since that moment," she said in a low voice that trembled, "I have been looking, waiting for you——"

He took her in his arms and smothered her words with kisses, holding her fiercely to him as though he would never let her go. "I, too," he said, his whole being burning with his love, "I have been looking, waiting for you. Now I have found you. We have found each other.... !"

The dusk fell slowly, imperceptibly. As twilight slowly draped the gaunt hills, blotting out familiar details, so the strong dream, veil upon veil, drew closer over the soul of the wanderer, obliterating finally the last reminder of To-day. The little wind had dropped and the desolate moors lay silent, but for the hum of distant water falling to its valley bed. His life, too, and the life of the girl, he knew, were similarly falling, falling into some deep shadowed bed where rest would come at last. No details troubled him, he asked himself no questions. A profound sense of happy peace numbed every nerve and stilled his beating heart.

He felt no fear, no anxiety, no hint of alarm or uneasiness vexed his singular contentment. He realized one thing only—that the girl lay in his arms, he held her fast, her breath mingled with his own. They had found each other. What else mattered?

From time to time, as the daylight faded and the sun went down behind the moors, she spoke. She uttered words he vaguely heard, listening, though with a certain curious effort, before he closed the thing she said with kisses. Even the fierceness of his blood was gone. The world lay still, life almost ceased to flow. Lapped in the deeps of his great love, he was redeemed, perhaps, of violence and savagery. . . .

"Three dark birds," she whispered, "pass across the sky . . . they fall beyond the ridge. The omens are favourable. A hawk now follows them, cleaving the sky with pointed wings."

"A hawk," he murmured. "The badge of my old Legion."

"My father will peform the sacrifice," he heard again, though it seemed a long interval had passed, and the man's figure was now invisible on the Crag amid the gathering darkness. "Already he prepares the fire. Look, the sacred island is alight. He has the black cock ready for the knife."

Holt roused himself with difficulty, lifting his face from the garden of her hair. A faint light, he saw, gleamed fitfully on the holm within the tarn. Her father, then, had descended from the Crag, and had lit the sacrificial fire upon the stones. But what did the doings of the father matter now to him?

"The dark bird," he repeated dully, "the black victim the Gods of the Underworld alone accept. It is good, Acella, it is good!" He was about to sink back again, taking her against his breast as before, when she resisted and sat up suddenly.

"It is time," she said aloud. "The hour has come. My father climbs, and we must join him on the summit. Come !"

She took his hand and raised him to his feet, and together they began the rough ascent towards the Crag. As they passed along the shore of the Tarn of Blood, he saw the fire reflected in the ink-black waters; he made out, too, though dimly, a rough circle of big stones, with a larger flag-stone lying in the centre. Three small fires of bracken and wood, placed in a triangle with its apex towards the Standing Stone on the distant hill, burned briskly, the crackling material sending out sparks that pierced the columns of thick smoke. And in this smoke, peering, shifting, appearing and disappearing, it seemed he saw great faces moving. The flickering light and twirling smoke made clear sight difficult. His bliss, his lethargy were very deep. They left the tarn below them and hand in hand began to climb the final slope.

Whether the physical effort of climbing disturbed the deep pressure of the mood that numbed his senses, or whether the cold draught of wind they met upon the ridge restored some vital detail of To-day, Holt does not know. Something, at any rate, in him wavered suddenly, as though a centre of gravity had shifted slightly. There was a perceptible alteration in the balance of thought and feeling that had held invariable now for many hours. It seemed to him that something heavy lifted, or rather, began to lift—a weight, a shadow, something oppressive that obstructed light. A ray of light, as it were, struggled through the thick darkness that enveloped him. To him, as he paused on the ridge to recover his breath, came this vague suggestion of faint light breaking across the blackness. It was objective.

"See," said the girl in a low voice, "the moon is rising.

It lights the sacred island. The blood-red waters turn to silver."

He saw, indeed, that a huge three-quarter moon now drove with almost visible movement above the distant line of hills; the little tarn gleamed as with silvery armour; the glow of the sacrificial fires showed red across it. He looked down with a shudder into the sheer depth that opened at his feet, then turned to look at his companion. He started and shrank back. Her face, lit by the moon and by the fire, shone pale as death; her black hair framed it with a terrible suggestiveness; the eyes, though brilliant as ever, had a film upon them. She stood in an attitude of both ecstasy and resignation, and one outstretched arm pointed towards the summit where her father stood.

Her lips parted, a marvellous smile broke over her features, her voice was suddenly unfamiliar: "He wears the collar," she uttered. "Come. Our time is here at last, and we are ready. See, he waits for us!"

There rose for the first time struggle and opposition in him; he resisted the pressure of her hand that had seized his own and drew him forcibly along. Whence came the resistance and the opposition he could not tell, but though he followed her, he was aware that the refusal in him strengthened. The weight of darkness that oppressed him shifted a little more, an inner light increased; The same moment they reached the summit and stood beside—the priest. There was a curious sound of fluttering. The figure, he saw, was naked, save for a rough blanket tied loosely about the waist.

"The hour has come at last," cried his deep booming voice that woke echoes from the dark hills about them. "We are alone now with our Gods." And he broke then into a monotonous rhythmic chanting that rose and fell upon the wind, yet in a tongue that sounded strange; his erect figure swayed slightly with its cadences; his black beard swept his naked chest; and his face, turned skywards, shone in the mingled light of moon above and fire below, yet with an added light as well that burned within him rather than without. He was a weird, magnificent figure, a priest of ancient rites invoking his deathless deities upon the unchanging hills.

But upon Holt, too, as he stared in awed amazement, an inner light had broken suddenly. It came as with a dazzling blaze that at first paralysed thought and action. His mind cleared, but too abruptly for movement, either of tongue or hand, to be possible. Then, abruptly, the inner darkness rolled away completely. The light in the wild eyes of the great chanting, swaying figure, he now knew was the light of mania.

The faint fluttering sound increased, and the voice of the girl was oddly mingled with it. The priest had ceased his invocation. Holt, aware that he stood alone, saw the girl go past him carrying a big black bird that struggled with vainly beating wings.

"Behold the sacrifice," she said, as she knelt before her father and held up the victim. "May the Gods accept it as presently They shall accept us too!"

The great figure stooped and took the offering, and with one blow of the knife he held, its head was severed from its body. The blood spattered on the white face of the kneeling girl. Holt was aware for the first time that she, too, was now unclothed; but for a loose blanket, her white body gleamed against the dark heather in the moonlight. At the same moment she rose to her feet, stood upright, turned towards him so that he saw the dark hair streaming across her naked shoulders, and, with a face of ecstasy, yet ever that strange film upon her eyes, her voice came to him on the wind:

"Farewell, yet not farewell! We shall meet, all three, in the underworld. The Gods accept us!"

Turning her face away, she stepped towards the ominous figure behind, and bared her ivory neck and breast to the knife. The eyes of the maniac were upon her own;

she was as helpless and obedient as a lamb before his spell.

Then Holt's horrible paralysis, if only just in time, was lifted. The priest had raised his arm, the bronze knife with its ragged edge gleamed in the air, with the other hand he had already gathered up the thick dark hair, so that the neck lay bare and open to the final blow. But it was two other details, Holt thinks, that set his muscles suddenly free, enabling him to act with the swift judgment which, being wholly unexpected, disconcerted both maniac and victim and frustrated the awful culmination. The dark spots of blood upon the face he loved, and the sudden final fluttering of the dead bird's wings upon the ground—these two things, life actually touching death, released the held-back springs.

He leaped forward. He received the blow upon his left arm and hand. It was his right fist that sent the High Priest to earth with a blow that, luckily, felled him in the direction away from the dreadful brink, and it was his right arm and hand, he became aware some time afterwards only, that were chiefly of use in carrying the fainting girl and her unconscious father back to the shelter of the cottage, and to the best help and comfort he could provide. . . .

It was several years afterwards, in a very different setting, that he found himself spelling out slowly to a little boy the lettering cut into a circlet of bronze the child found on his study table. To the child he told a fairy tale, then dismissed him to play with his mother in the garden. But, when alone, he rubbed away the verdigris with great care, for the circlet was thin and frail with age, as he examined again the little picture of a tripod from which smoke issued, incised neatly in the metal. Below it, almost as sharp as when the Roman craftsman cut it first, was the name Acella. He touched the letters tenderly with his left hand, from which two fingers were missing, then placed it in a drawer of his desk and turned the key.

"That curious name," said a low voice behind his chair. His wife had come in and was looking over his shoulder. "You love it, and I dread it." She sat on the desk beside him, her eyes troubled. "It was the name father used to call me in his illness."

Her husband looked at her with passionate tenderness, but said no word.

"And this," she went on, taking the broken hand in both her own, "is the price you paid to me for his life. I often wonder what strange good deity brought you upon the lonely moor that night, and just in the very nick of time. You remember . . . ?"

"The deity who helps true lovers, of course," he said with a smile, evading the question. The deeper memory, he knew, had closed absolutely in her since the moment of the attempted double crime. He kissed her, murmuring to himself as he did so, but too low for her to hear, "Acella! *My* Acella . . . !"

VI

THE VALLEY OF THE BEASTS

1

A S they emerged suddenly from the dense forest the Indian halted, and Grimwood, his employer, stood beside him, gazing into the beautiful wooded valley that lay spread below them in the blaze of a golden sunset. Both men leaned upon their rifles, caught by the enchantment of the unexpected scene.

"We camp here," said Tooshalli abruptly, after a careful survey. "To-morrow we make a plan."

He spoke excellent English. The note of decision, almost of authority, in his voice was noticeable, but Grimwood set it down to the natural excitement of the moment. Every track they had followed during the last two days, but one track in particular as well, had headed straight for this remote and hidden valley, and the sport promised to be unusual.

"That's so," he replied, in the tone of one giving an order. "You can make camp ready at once." And he sat down on a fallen hemlock to take off his moccasin boots and grease his feet that ached from the arduous day now drawing to a close. Though under ordinary circumstances he would have pushed on for another hour or two, he was not averse to a night here, for exhaustion had come upon him during the last bit of rough going, his eye and muscles were no longer steady, and it was doubtful if he could have shot straight enough to kill. He did not mean to miss a second time.

With his Canadian friend, Iredale, the latter's half-breed, and his own Indian, Tooshalli, the party had set out three weeks ago to find the "wonderful big moose" the Indians reported were travelling in the Snow River country. They soon found that the tale was true; tracks were abundant; they saw fine animals nearly every day, but though carrying good heads, the hunters expected better still and left them alone. Pushing up the river to a chain of small lakes near its source, they then separated into two parties, each with its nine-foot bark canoe, and packed in for three days after the yet bigger animals the Indians agreed would be found in the deeper woods beyond. Excitement was keen, expectation keener still. The day before they separated, Iredale shot the biggest moose of his life, and its head, bigger even than the grand Alaskan heads, hangs in his house to-day. Grimwood's hunting blood was fairly up. His blood was of the fiery, not to say ferocious, quality. It almost seemed he liked killing for its own sake.

Four days after the party broke into two he came upon a gigantic track, whose measurements and length of stride keyed every nerve he possessed to its highest tension.

Tooshalli examined the tracks for some minutes with care. "It is the biggest moose in the world," he said at length, a new expression on his inscrutable red visage.

Following it all that day, they yet got no sight of the big fellow that seemed to be frequenting a little marshy dip of country, too small to be called valley, where willow and undergrowth abounded. He had not yet scented his pursuers. They were after him again at dawn. Towards the evening of the second day Grimwood caught a sudden glimpse of the monster among a thick clump of willows, and the sight of the magnificent head that easily beat all records set his heart beating like a hammer with excitement. He aimed and fired. But the moose, instead of crashing, went thundering away through the further scrub and disappeared, the sound of his plunging

canter presently dying away. Grimwood had missed, even
if he had wounded.

They camped, and all next day, leaving the canoe
behind, they followed the huge track, but though finding
signs of blood, these were not plentiful, and the shot had
evidently only grazed the animal. The travelling was of
the hardest. Towards evening, utterly exhausted, the spoor
led them to the ridge they now stood upon, gazing down
into the enchanting valley that opened at their feet. The
giant moose had gone down into this valley. He would
consider himself safe there. Grimwood agreed with the
Indian's judgment. They would camp for the night and
continue at dawn the wild hunt after "the biggest moose
in the world."

Supper was over, the small fire used for cooking dying
down, with Grimwood became first aware that the Indian
was not behaving quite as usual. What particular detail
drew his attention is hard to say. He was a slow-witted,
heavy man, full-blooded, unobservant; a fact had to hurt
him through his comfort, through his pleasure, before he
noticed it. Yet anyone else must have observed the
changed mood of the Redskin long ago. Tooshalli had
made the fire, fried the bacon, served the tea, and was
arranging the blankets, his own and his employer's, before
the latter remarked upon his—silence. Tooshalli had not
uttered a word for over an hour and a half, since he had
first set eyes upon the new valley, to be exact. And his
employer now noticed the unaccustomed silence, because
after food he liked to listen to wood talk and hunting
lore.

"Tired out, aren't you?" said big Grimwood, looking
into the dark face across the firelight. He resented the
absence of conversation, now that he noticed it. He was
over-weary himself, he felt more irritable than usual,
though his temper was always vile.

"Lost your tongue, eh?" he went on with a growl, as
the Indian returned his stare with solemn, expressionless

face. That dark inscrutable look got on his nerves a bit. "Speak up, man!" he exclaimed sharply. "What's it all about?"

The Englishman had at last realized that there was something to "speak up" about. The discovery, in his present state, annoyed him further. Tooshalli stared gravely, but made no reply. The silence was prolonged almost into minutes. Presently the head turned sideways, as though the man listened. The other watched him very closely, anger growing in him.

But it was the way the Redskin turned his head, keeping his body rigid, that gave the jerk to Grimwood's nerves, providing him with a sensation he had never known in his life before—it gave him what is generally called "the goose-flesh." It seemed to jangle his entire system, yet at the same time made him cautious. He did not like it, this combination of emotions puzzled him.

"Say something, I tell you," he repeated in a harsher tone, raising his voice. He sat up, drawing his great body closer to the fire. "Say something, damn it!"

His voice fell dead against the surrounding trees, making the silence of the forest unpleasantly noticeable. Very still the great woods stood about them; there was no wind, no stir of branches; only the crackle of a snapping twig was audible from time to time, as the night-life moved unwarily sometimes watching the humans round their little fire. The October air had a frosty touch that nipped.

The Redskin did not answer. No muscle of his neck nor of his stiffened body moved. He seemed all ears.

"Well?" repeated the Englishman, lowering his voice this time instinctively. "What d'you hear, God damn it!" The touch of odd nervousness that made his anger grow betrayed itself in his language.

Tooshalli slowly turned his head back again to its normal position, the body rigid as before.

"I hear nothing, Mr. Grimwood," he said, gazing with quiet dignity into his employer's eyes.

This was too much for the other, a man of savage temper at the best of times. He was the type of Englishman who held strong views as to the right way of treating "inferior" races.

"That's a lie, Tooshalli, and I won't have you lie to me. Now what was it? Tell me at once!"

"I hear nothing," repeated the other. "I only think."

"And what is it you're pleased to think?" Impatience made a nasty expression round the mouth.

"I go not," was the abrupt reply, unalterable decision in the voice.

The man's rejoinder was so unexpected that Grimwood found nothing to say at first. For a moment he did not take its meaning; his mind, always slow, was confused by impatience, also by what he considered the foolishness of the little scene. Then in a flash he understood; but he also understood the immovable obstinacy of the race he had to deal with. Tooshalli was informing him that he refused to go into the valley where the big moose had vanished. And his astonishment was so great at first that he merely sat and stared. No words came to him.

"It is——" said the Indian, but used a native term.

"What's that mean?" Grimwood found his tongue, but his quiet tone was ominous.

"Mr. Grimwood, it mean the 'Valley of the Beasts,'" was the reply in a tone quieter still.

The Englishman made a great, a genuine effort at self-control. He was dealing, he forced himself to remember, with a superstitious Redskin. He knew the stubbornness of the type. If the man left him his sport was irretrievably spoilt, for he could not hunt in this wilderness alone, and even if he got the coveted head, he could never, never get it out alone. His native selfishness seconded his effort. Persuasion, if only he could keep back his rising anger, was his rôle to play.

"The Valley of the Beasts," he said, a smile on his lips rather than in his darkening eyes; "but that's just what

we want. It's beasts we're after, isn't it?" His voice
had a false cheery ring that could not have deceived a
child. "But what d'you mean, anyhow—the Valley of the
Beasts?" He asked it with a dull attempt at sympathy.

"It belong to Ishtot, Mr. Grimwood." The man looked
him full in the face, no flinching in the eyes.

"My—our—big moose is there," said the other, who
recognized the name of the Indian Hunting God, and
understanding better, felt confident he would soon persuade his man. Tooshalli, he remembered, too, was
nominally a Christian. "We'll follow him at dawn and
get the biggest head the world has ever seen. You will
be famous," he added, his temper better in hand again.
"Your tribe will honour you. And the white hunters will
pay you much money."

"He go there to save himself. I go not."

The other's anger revived with a leap at this stupid
obstinacy. But, in spite of it, he noticed the odd choice
of words. He began to realize that nothing now would
move the man. At the same time he also realized that
violence on his part must prove worse than useless. Yet
violence was natural to his "dominant" type. "That brute
Grimwood" was the way most men spoke of him.

"Back at the settlement you're a Christian, remember," he tried, in his clumsy way, another line. "And
disobedience means hell-fire. You know that!"

"I a Christian—at the post," was the reply, "but out
here the Red God rule. Ishtot keep that valley for himself. No Indian hunt there." It was as though a granite
boulder spoke.

The savage temper of the Englishman, enforced by the
long difficult suppression, rose wickedly into sudden flame.
He stood up, kicking his blankets aside. He strode across
the dying fire to the Indian's side. Tooshalli also rose.
They faced each other, two humans alone in the wilderness. watched by countless invisible forest eyes.

Tooshalli stood motionless, yet as though he expected

violence from the foolish, ignorant white-face. "You go alone, Mr. Grimwood." There was no fear in him.

Grimwood choked with rage. His words came forth with difficulty, though he roared them into the silence of the forest:

"I pay you, don't I? You'll do what *I* say, not what *you* say!" His voice woke the echoes.

The Indian, arms hanging by his side, gave the old reply.

"I go not," he repeated firmly.

It stung the other into uncontrollable fury.

The beast then came uppermost; it came out. "You've said that once too often, Tooshalli!" and he struck him brutally in the face. The Indian fell, rose to his knees again, collapsed sideways beside the fire, then struggled back into a sitting position. He never once took his eyes from the white man's face.

Beside himself with anger, Grimwood stood over him. "Is that enough? Will you obey me now?" he shouted.

"I go not," came the thick reply, blood streaming from his mouth. The eyes had no flinching in them. "That valley Ishtot keep. Ishtot see us now. *He see you.*" The last words he uttered with strange, almost uncanny emphasis.

Grimwood, arm raised, fist clenched, about to repeat his terrible assault, paused suddenly. His arm sank to his side. What exactly stopped him he could never say. For one thing, he feared his own anger, feared that if he let himself go he would not stop till he had killed— committed murder. He knew his own fearful temper and stood afraid of it. Yet it was not only that. The calm firmness of the Redskin, his courage under pain, and something in the fixed and burning eyes arrested him. Was it also something in the words he had used—"Ishtot see *you*"—that stung him into a queer caution midway in his violence?

He could not say. He only knew that a momentary

sense of awe came over him. He became unpleasantly aware of the enveloping forest, so still, listening in a kind of impenetrable, remorseless silence. This lonely wilderness, looking silently upon what might easily prove murder, laid a faint, inexplicable chill upon his raging blood. The hand dropped slowly to his side again, the fist unclenched itself, his breath came more evenly.

"Look you here," he said, adopting without knowing it the local way of speech. "I ain't a bad man, though your going-on do make a man damned tired. I'll give you another chance." His voice was sullen, but a new note in it surprised even himself. "I'll do that. You can have the night to think it over, Tooshalli—see? Talk it over with your——"

He did not finish the sentence. Somehow the name of the Redskin God refused to pass his lips. He turned away, flung himself into his blankets, and in less than ten minutes, exhausted as much by his anger as by the day's hard going, he was sound asleep.

The Indian, crouching beside the dying fire, had said nothing.   .

Night held the woods, the sky was thick with stars, the life of the forest went about its business quietly, with that wondrous skill which millions of years have perfected. The Redskin, so close to this skill that he instinctively used and borrowed from it, was silent, alert and wise, his outline as inconspicuous as though he merged, like his four-footed teachers, into the mass of the surrounding bush.

He moved perhaps, yet nothing knew he moved. His wisdom, derived from that eternal, ancient mother who from infinite experience makes no mistakes, did not fail him. His soft tread made no sound; his breathing, as his weight, was calculated. The stars observed him, but they did not tell; the light air knew his whereabouts, yet without betrayal. . . .

The chill dawn gleamed at length between the trees,

lighting the pale ashes of an extinguished fire, also of a bulky, obvious form beneath a blanket. The form moved clumsily. The cold was penetrating.

And that bulky form now moved because a dream had come to trouble it. A dark figure stole across its confused field of vision. The form started, but it did not wake. The figure spoke: "Take this," it whispered, handing a little stick, curiously carved. "It is the totem of great Ishtot. In the valley all memory of the White Gods will leave you. Call upon Ishtot. . . . Call on Him if you dare"; and the dark figure glided away out of the dream and out of all remembrance. . . .

2

The first thing Grimwood noticed when he woke was that Tooshalli was not there. No fire burned, no tea was ready. He felt exceedingly annoyed. He glared about him, then got up with a curse to make the fire. His mind seemed confused and troubled. At first he only realized one thing clearly—his guide had left him in the night.

It was very cold. He lit the wood with difficulty and made his tea, and the actual world came gradually back to him. The Red Indian had gone; perhaps the blow, perhaps the superstitious terror, perhaps both, had driven him away. He was alone, that was the outstanding fact. For anything beyond outstanding facts, Grimwood felt little interest. Imaginative speculation was beyond his compass. Close to the brute creation, it seemed, his nature lay.

It was while packing his blankets—he did it automatically, a dull, vicious resentment in him—that his fingers struck a bit of wood that he was about to throw away when its unusual shape caught his attention suddenly. His odd dream came back then. But was it a dream? The bit of wood was undoubtedly a totem stick.

He examined it. He paid it more attention than he meant to, wished to. Yes, it was unquestionably a totem stick. The dream, then, was not a dream. Tooshalli had quit, but, following with Redskin faithfulness some code of his own, had left him the means of safety. He chuckled sourly, but thrust the stick inside his belt. "One never knows," he mumbled to himself.

He faced the situation squarely. He was alone in the wilderness. His capable, experienced woodsman had deserted him. The situation was serious. What should he do? A weakling would certainly retrace his steps, following the track they had made, afraid to be left alone in this vast hinterland of pathless forest. But Grimwood was of another build. Alarmed he might be, but he would not give in. He had the defects of his own qualities. The brutality of his nature argued force. He was determined and a sportsman. He would go on. And ten minutes after breakfast, having first made a *cache* of what provisions were left over, he was on his way—down across the ridge and into the mysterious valley, the Valley of the Beasts.

It looked, in the morning sunlight, entrancing. The trees closed in behind him, but he did not notice. It led him on. . . .

He followed the track of the gigantic moose he meant to kill, and the sweet, delicious sunshine helped him. The air was like wine, the seductive spoor of the great beast, with here and there a faint splash of blood on leaves or ground, lay forever just before his eyes. He found the valley, though the actual word did not occur to him, enticing; more and more he noticed the beauty, the desolate grandeur of the mighty spruce and hemlock, the splendour of the granite bluffs which in places rose above the forest and caught the sun. . . . The valley was deeper, vaster than he had imagined. He felt safe, at home in it, though, again these actual terms did not occur to him. . . . Here he could hide for ever and find peace. . . . He became aware of a new quality in the deep loneliness. The scenery for the first time in his life appealed to him, and the form of the appeal was curious—he felt the comfort of it.

For a man of his habit, this was odd, yet the new sensations stole over him so gently, their approach so gradual, that they were first recognized by his consciousness indirectly. They had already established themselves in him before he noticed them; and the indirectness took this form—that the passion of the chase gave place to an interest in the valley itself. The lust of the hunt, the fierce desire to find and kill, the keen wish, in a word, to see his quarry within range, to aim, to fire, to witness the natural consummation of the long expedition—these had all become measurably less, while the effect of the valley upon him had increased in strength. There was a welcome about it that he did not understand.

The change was singular, yet, oddly enough, it did not occur to him as singular; it was unnatural, yet it did not strike him so. To a dull mind of his unobservant, unanalytical type, a change had to be marked and dramatic before he noticed it; something in the nature of a shock must accompany it for him to recognize it had happened. And there had been no shock. The spoor of the great moose was much cleaner, now that he caught up with the animal that made it; the blood more frequent; he had noticed the spot where it had rested, its huge body leaving a marked imprint on the soft ground; where it had reached up to eat the leaves of saplings here and there was also visible; he had come undoubtedly very near to it, and any minute now might see its great bulk within range of an easy shot. Yet his ardour had somehow lessened.

He first realized this change in himself when it suddenly occurred to him that the animal itself had grown less cautious. It must scent him easily now, since a moose, its sight being indifferent, depends chiefly for its safety upon its unusually keen sense of smell, and the wind came

from behind him. This now struck him as decidedly uncommon: the moose itself was obviously careless of his
close approach. It felt no fear.

It was this inexplicable alteration in the animal's behaviour that made him recognize, at last, the alteration
in his own. He had followed it now for a couple of hours
and had descended some eight hundred to a thousand feet;
the trees were thinner and more sparsely placed; there
were open, park-like places where silver birch, sumach
and maple splashed their blazing colours; and a crystal
stream, broken by many waterfalls, foamed past towards
the bed of the great valley, yet another thousand feet
below. By a quiet pool against some over-arching rocks,
the moose had evidently paused to drink, paused at its
leisure, morever. Grimwood, rising from a close examination of the direction the creature had taken after drink-
ing—the hoof-marks were fresh and very distinct in the
marshy ground about the pool—looked suddenly straight
into the great creature's eyes. It was not twenty yards
from where he stood, yet he had been standing on that
spot for at least ten minutes, caught by the wonder and
loneliness of the scene. The moose, therefore, had been
close beside him all this time. It had been calmly drink-
ing, undisturbed by his presence, unafraid.

The shock came now, the shock that woke his heavy
nature into realization. For some seconds, probably for
minutes, he stood rooted to the ground, motionless, hardly
breathing. He stared as though he saw a vision. The
animal's head was lowered, but turned obliquely somewhat, so that the eyes, placed sideways in its great head,
could see him properly; its immense proboscis hung as
though stuffed upon an English wall; he saw the fore-
feet planted wide apart, the slope of the enormous
shoulders dropping back towards the fine hind-quarters
and lean flanks. It was a magnificent bull. The horns
and head justified his wildest expectations, they were
superb, a record specimen, and a phrase—where had he

heard it?—ran vaguely, as from far distance, through his mind: "the biggest moose in the world."

There was the extraordinary fact, however, that he did not shoot; nor feel the wish to shoot. The familiar instinct, so strong hitherto in his blood, made no sign; the desire to kill apparently had left him. To raise his rifle, aim and fire had become suddenly an absolute impossibility.

He did not move. The animal and the human stared into each other's eyes for a length of time whose interval he could not measure. Then came a soft noise close beside him: the rifle had slipped from his grasp and fallen with a thud into the mossy earth at his feet. And the moose, for the first time now, was moving. With slow, easy stride, its great weight causing a squelching sound as the feet drew out of the moist ground, it came towards him, the bulk of the shoulders giving it an appearance of swaying like a ship at sea. It reached his side, it almost touched him, the magnificent head bent low, the spread of the gigantic horns lay beneath his very eyes. He could have patted, stroked it. He saw, with a touch of pity, that blood trickled from a sore in its left shoulder, matting the thick hair. It sniffed the fallen rifle.

Then, lifting its head and shoulders again, it sniffed the air, this time with an audible sound that shook from Grimwood's mind the last possibility that he witnessed a vision or dreamed a dream. One moment it gazed into his face, its big brown eyes shining and unafraid, then turned abruptly, and swung away at a speed ever rapidly increasing across the park-like spaces till it was lost finally among the dark tangle of undergrowth beyond. And the Englishman's muscles turned to paper, his paralysis passed, his legs refused to support his weight, and he sank heavily to the ground. . . .

3

It seems he slept, slept long and heavily; he sat up,
stretched himself, yawned and rubbed his eyes. The sun
had moved across the sky, for the shadows, he saw, now
ran from west to east, and they were long shadows. He
had slept evidently for hours, and evening was drawing
in. He was aware that he felt hungry. In his pouch-
like pockets, he had dried meat, sugar, matches, tea, and
the little billy that never left him. He would make a fire,
boil some tea and eat.

But he took no steps to carry out his purpose, he felt
disinclined to move, he sat thinking, thinking. . . . What
was he thinking about? He did not know, he could not
say exactly; it was more like fugitive pictures that passed
across his mind. Who, and where, was he? This was
the Valley of the Beasts, that he knew; he felt sure of
nothing else. How long had he been here, and where had
be come from, and why? The questions did not linger for
their answers, almost as though his interest in them was
merely automatic. He felt happy, peaceful, unafraid.

He looked about him, and the spell of this virgin forest
came upon him like a charm; only the sound of falling
water, the murmur of wind sighing among innumerable
branches, broke the enveloping silence. Overhead, beyond
the crests of the towering trees, a cloudless evening sky
was paling into transparent orange, opal, mother of pearl.
He saw buzzards soaring lazily. A scarlet tanager flashed
by. Soon would the owls begin to call and the darkness
fall like a sweet black veil and hide all detail, while the
stars sparkled in their countless thousands. . . .

A glint of something that shone upon the ground caught
his eye—a smooth, polished strip of rounded metal: his
rifle. And he started to his feet impulsively, yet not
knowing exactly what he meant to do. At the sight of
the weapon, something had leaped to life in him, then
faded out, died down, and was gone again.

"I'm—I'm——" he began muttering to himself, but could not finish what he was about to say. His name had disappeared completely. "I'm in the Valley of the Beasts," he repeated in place of what he sought but could not find.

This fact, that he was in the Valley of the Beasts, seemed the only positive item of knowledge that he had. About the name something known and familiar clung, though the sequence that led up to it he could not trace. Presently, nevertheless, he rose to his feet, advanced a few steps, stooped and picked up the shining metal thing, his rifle. He examined it a moment, a feeling of dread and loathing rising in him, a sensation of almost horror that made him tremble, then, with a convulsive movement that betrayed an intense reaction of some sort he could not comprehend, he flung the thing far from him into the foaming torrent. He saw the splash it made, he also saw that same instant a large grizzly bear swing heavily along the bank not a dozen yards from where he stood. It, too, heard the splash, for it started, turned, paused a second, then changed its direction and came towards him. It came up close. Its fur brushed his body. It examined him leisurely, as the moose had done, sniffed, half rose upon its terrible hind legs, opened its mouth so that red tongue and gleaming teeth were plainly visible, then flopped back upon all fours again with a deep growling that yet had no anger in it, and swung off at a quick trot back to the bank of the torrent. He had felt its hot breath upon his face, but he had felt no fear. The monster was puzzled but not hostile. It disappeared.

"They know not——" he sought for the word "man," but could not find it. "They have never been hunted."

The words ran through his mind, if perhaps he was not entirely certain of their meaning; they rose, as it were, automatically; a familiar sound lay in them somewhere. At the same time there rose feelings in him that were equally, though in another way, familiar and quite natural, feelings he had once known intimately but long since laid aside.

What were they? What was their origin? They seemed distant as the stars, yet were actually in his body, in his blood and nerves, part and parcel of his flesh. Long, long ago. . . . Oh, how long, how long?

Thinking was difficult; feeling was what he most easily and naturally managed. He could not think for long; feeling rose up and drowned the effort quickly.

That huge and awful bear—not a nerve, not a muscle quivered in him as its acrid smell rose to his nostrils, its fur brushed down his legs. Yet he was aware that somewhere there was danger, though not here. Somewhere there was attack, hostility, wicked and calculated plans against him—as against that splendid, roaming animal that had sniffed, examined, then gone its own way, satisfied. Yes, active attack, hostility and careful, cruel plans against his safety, but—not here. Here he was safe, secure, at peace; here he was happy; here he could roam at will, no eye cast sideways into forest depths, no ear pricked high to catch sounds not explained, no nostrils quivering to scent alarm. He felt this, but he did not think it. He felt hungry, thirsty too.

Something prompted him now at last to act. His billy lay at his feet, and he picked it up; the matches—he carried them in a metal case whose screw top kept out all moisture—were in his hand. Gathering a few dry twigs, he stooped to light them, then suddenly drew back with the first touch of fear he had yet known.

Fire! What *was* fire? The idea was repugnant to him, it was impossible, he was afraid of fire. He flung the metal case after the rifle and saw it gleam in the last rays of sunset, then sink with a little splash beneath the water. Glancing down at his billy, he realized next that he could not make use of it either, nor of the dark dry dusty stuff he had meant to boil in water. He felt no repugnance, certainly no fear, in connexion with these

things, only he could not handle them, he did not need
them, he had forgotten, yes, "forgotten," what they meant
exactly. This strange forgetfulness was increasing in him
rapidly, becoming more and more complete with every
minute. Yet his thirst must be quenched.

The next moment he found himself at the water's edge;
he stooped to fill his billy; paused, hesitated, examined
the rushing water, then abruptly moved a few feet higher
up the stream, leaving the metal can behind him. His
handling of it had been oddly clumsy, his gestures awkward, even unnatural. He now flung himself down with
an easy, simple motion of his entire body, lowered his
face to a quiet pool he had found, and drank his fill of the
cool, refreshing liquid. But, though unaware of the fact,
he did not drink. He lapped.

Then, crouching where he was, he ate the meat and
sugar from his pockets, lapped more water, moved back a
short distance again into the dry ground beneath the trees,
but moved this time without rising to his feet, curled his
body into a comfortable position and closed his eyes again
to sleep. . . . No single question now raised its head in
him. He felt contentment, satisfaction only. . . .

He stirred, shook himself, opened half an eye and saw,
as he had felt already in slumber, that he was not alone.
In the park-like spaces in front of him, as in the shadowed
fringe of the trees at his back, there was sound and movement, the sound of stealthy feet, the movement of innumerable dark bodies. There was the pad and tread of animals,
the stir of backs, of smooth and shaggy beasts, in countless numbers. Upon this host fell the light of a half
moon sailing high in a cloudless sky; the gleam of stars,
sparkling in the clear night air like diamonds, shone
reflected in hundreds of ever-shifting eyes, most of them
but a few feet above the ground. The whole valley was
alive.

' He sat upon his haunches, staring, staring, but staring
in wonder, not in fear, though the foremost of the great

host were so near that he could have stretched an arm and touched them. It was an ever-moving, ever-shifting throng he gazed at, spell-bound, in the pale light of moon and stars, now fading slowly towards the approaching dawn. And the smell of the forest itself was not sweeter to him in that moment than the mingled perfume, raw, pungent, acrid, of this furry host of beautiful wild animals that moved like a sea, with a strange murmuring, too, like sea, as the myriad feet and bodies passed to and fro together. Nor was the gleam of the starry, phosphorescent eyes less pleasantly friendly than those happy lamps that light home-lost wanderers to cosy rooms and safety. Through the wild army, in a word, poured to him the deep comfort of the entire valley, a comfort which held both the sweetness of invitation and the welcome of some magical home-coming.

No thoughts came to him, but feeling rose in a tide of wonder and acceptance. He was in his rightful place. His nature had come home. There was this dim, vague consciousness in him that after long, futile straying in another place where uncongenial conditions had forced him to be unnatural and therefore terrible, he had returned at last where he belonged. Here, in the Valley of the Beasts, he had found peace, security and happiness. He would be—he was at last—himself.

It was a marvellous, even a magical, scene he watched, his nerves at highest tension yet quite steady, his senses exquisitely alert, yet no uneasiness in the full, accurate reports they furnished. Strong as some deep flood-tide, yet dim, as with untold time and distance, rose over him the spell of long-forgotten memory of a state where he was content and happy, where he was natural. The outlines, as it were, of mighty, primitive pictures, flashed before him, yet were gone again before the detail was filled in.

He watched the great army of the animals, they were all about him now; he crouched upon his haunches in the centre of an ever-moving circle of wild forest life. Great timber wolves he saw pass to and fro, loping past him with long stride and graceful swing; their red tongues lolling out; they swarmed in hundreds. Behind, yet mingling freely with them, rolled the huge grizzlies, not clumsy as their uncouth bodies promised, but swiftly, lightly, easily, their half tumbling gait masking agility and speed. They gambolled, sometimes they rose and stood half upright, they were comely in their mass and power, they rolled past him so close that he could touch them. And the black bear and the brown went with them, bears beyond counting, monsters and little ones, a splendid multitude. Beyond them, yet only a little further back, where the park-like spaces made free movement easier, rose a sea of horns and antlers like a miniature forest in the silvery moonlight. The immense tribe of deer gathered in vast throngs beneath the starlit sky. Moose and caribou, he saw, the mighty wapiti, and the smaller deer in their crowding thousands. He heard the sound of meeting horns, the tread of innumerable hoofs, the occasional pawing of the ground as the bigger creatures manœuvred for more space about them. A wolf, he saw, was licking gently at the shoulder of a great bull-moose that had been injured. And the tide receded, advanced again, once more receded, rising and falling like a living sea whose waves were animal shapes, the inhabitants of the Valley of the Beasts.

Beneath the quiet moonlight they swayed to and fro before him. They watched him, knew him, recognized him. They made him welcome.

He was aware, moreover, of a world of smaller life that formed an under-sea, as it were, numerous under-currents rather, running in and out between the great upright legs of the larger creatures. These, though he could not see them clearly, covered the earth, he was aware, in enormous numbers, darting hither and thither, now hiding, now reappearing, too intent upon their busy purposes to pay him

attention like their huger comrades, yet ever and anon
tumbling against his back, cannoning from his sides,
scampering across his legs even, then gone again with a
scuttering sound of rapid little feet, and rushing back into
the general host beyond. And with this smaller world also
he felt at home.

How long he sat gazing, happy in himself, secure, satisfied, contented, natural, he could not say, but it was long
enough for the desire to mingle with what he saw, to know
closer contact, to become one with them all—long enough
for this deep blind desire to assert itself, so that at length
he began to move from his mossy seat towards them, to
move, moreover, as they moved, and not upright on two
feet.

The moon was lower now, just sinking behind a towering cedar whose ragged crest broke its light into silvery
spray. The stars were a little paler too. A line of faint
red was visible beyond the heights at the valley's eastern
end.

He paused and looked about him, as he advanced
slowly, aware that the host already made an opening in
their ranks and that the bear even nosed the earth in front,
as though to show the way that was easiest for him to
follow. Then, suddenly, a lynx leaped past him into the
low branches of a hemlock, and he lifted his head to admire
its perfect poise. He saw in the same instant the arrival
of the birds, the army of the eagles, hawks and buzzards,
birds of prey—the awakening flight that just precedes the
dawn. He saw the flocks and streaming lines, hiding the
whitening stars a moment as they passed with a prodigious whirr of wings. There came the hooting of an owl
from the tree immediately overhead where the lynx now
crouched, but not maliciously, along its branch.

He started. He half rose to an upright position. He
knew not why he did so, knew not exactly why he started.
But in the attempt to find his new, and, as it now seemed,
his unaccustomed balance, one hand fell against his side

and came in contact with a hard straight thing that projected awkwardly from his clothing. He pulled it out, feeling it all over with his fingers. It was a little stick. He raised it nearer to his eyes, examined it in the light of dawn now growing swiftly, remembered, or half remembered what it was—and stood stock still.

"The totem stick," he mumbled to himself, yet audibly, finding his speech, and finding another thing—a glint of peering memory—for the first time since entering the valley.

A shock like fire ran through his body; he straightened himself, aware that a moment before he had been crawling upon his hands and knees; it seemed that something broke in his brain, lifting a veil, flinging a shutter free. And Memory peered dreadfully through the widening gap.

"I'm—I'm Grimwood," his voice uttered, though below his breath. "Tooshalli's left me. I'm alone. . . !"

He was aware of a sudden change in the animals surrounding him. A big, grey wolf sat three feet away, glaring into his face; at its side an enormous grizzly swayed itself from one foot to the other; behind it, as if looking over its shoulder, loomed a gigantic wapiti, its horns merged in the shadows of the drooping cedar boughs. But the northern dawn was nearer, the sun already close to the horizon. He saw details with sharp distinctness now. The great bear rose, balancing a moment on its massive hind-quarters, then took a step towards him, its front paws spread like arms. Its wicked head lolled horribly, as a huge bull-moose, lowering its horns as if about to charge, came up with a couple of long strides and joined it. A sudden excitement ran quivering over the entire host; the distant ranks moved in a new, unpleasant way; a thousand heads were lifted, ears were pricked, a forest of ugly muzzles pointed up to the wind.

And the Englishman, beside himself suddenly with a sense of ultimate terror that saw no possible escape, stiffened and stood rigid. The horror of his position petrified

him. Motionless and silent he faced the awful army of
his enemies, while the white light of breaking day added
fresh ghastliness to the scene which was the setting for his
cruel death in the Valley of the Beasts.

Above him crouched the hideous lynx, ready to spring
the instant he sought safety in the tree; above it again,
he was aware of a thousand talons of steel, fierce hooked
beaks of iron, and the angry beating of prodigious wings.

He reeled, for the grizzly touched his body with its
outstretched paw; the wolf crouched just before its deadly
spring; in another second he would have been torn to
pieces, crushed, devoured, when terror, operating naturally as ever, released the muscles of his throat and tongue.
He shouted with what he believed was his last breath on
earth. He called aloud in his frenzy. It was a prayer to
whatever gods there be, it was an anguished cry for help
to heaven.

"Ishtot! Great Ishtot, help me!" his voice rang out,
while his hand still clutched the forgotten totem stick.

And the Red Heaven heard him.

Grimwood that same instant was aware of a presence
that, but for his terror of the beasts, must have frightened
him into sheer unconsciousness. A gigantic Red Indian
stood before him. Yet, while the figure rose close in front
of him, causing the birds to settle and the wild animals
to crouch quietly where they stood, it rose also from a
great distance, for it seemed to fill the entire valley with
its influence, its power, its amazing majesty. In some
way, moreover, that he could not understand, its vast
appearance included the actual valley itself with all its
trees, its running streams, its open spaces and its rocky
bluffs. These marked its outline, as it were, the outline
of a superhuman shape. There was a mighty bow, there
was a quiver of enormous arrows, there was this Redskin
figure to whom they belonged.

Yet the appearance, the outline, the face and figure too
—these *were* the valley; and when the voice became audible,

it was the valley itself that uttered the appalling words. It was the voice of trees and wind, and of running, falling water that woke the echoes in the Valley of the Beasts, as, in that same moment, the sun topped the ridge and filled the scene, the outline of the majestic figure too, with a flood of dazzling light:

"You have shed blood in this my valley. . . . *I will not save.* . . !"

The figure melted away into the sunlit forest, merging with the new-born day. But Grimwood saw close against his face the shining teeth, hot fetid breath passed over his cheeks, a power enveloped his whole body as though a mountain crushed him. He closed his eyes. He fell. A sharp, crackling sound passed through his brain, but already unconscious, he did not hear it.

His eyes opened again, and the first thing they took in was—fire. He shrank back instinctively.

"It's all right, old man. We'll bring you round. Nothing to be frightened about." He saw the face of Iredale looking down into his own. Behind Iredale stood Tooshalli. His face was swollen. Grimwood remembered the blow. The big man began to cry.

"Painful still, is it?" Iredale said sympathetically. "Here, swallow a little more of this. It'll set you right in no time."

Grimwood gulped down the spirit. He made a violent effort to control himself, but was unable to keep the tears back. He felt no pain. It was his heart that ached, though why or wherefore, he had no idea.

"I'm all to pieces," he mumbled, ashamed yet somehow not ashamed. "My nerves are rotten. What's happened?" There was as yet no memory in him.

"You've been hugged by a bear, old man. But no bones broken. Tooshalli saved you. He fired in the nick of time—a brave shot, for he might easily have hit you instead of the brute."

"The other brute," whispered Grimwood, as the whisky worked in him and memory came slowly back.

"Where are we?" he asked presently, looking about him.

He saw a lake, canoes drawn up on the shore, two tents, and figures moving. Iredale explained matters briefly, then left him to sleep a bit. Tooshalli, it appeared, travelling without rest, had reached Iredale's camping ground twenty-four hours after leaving his employer. He found it deserted, Iredale and his Indian being on the hunt. When they returned at nightfall, he had explained his presence in his brief native fashion: "He struck me and I quit. He hunt now alone in Ishtot's Valley of the Beasts. He is dead, I think. I come to tell you."

Iredale and his guide, with Tooshalli as leader, started off then and there, but Grimwood had covered a considerable distance, though leaving an easy track to follow. It was the moose tracks and the blood that chiefly guided them. They came up with him suddenly enough—in the grip of an enormous bear.

It was Tooshalli that fired.

The Indian lives now in easy circumstances, all his needs cared for, while Grimwood, his benefactor but no longer his employer, has given up hunting. He is a quiet, easy-tempered, almost gentle sort of fellow, and people wonder rather why he hasn't married. "Just the fellow to make a good father," is what they say; "so kind, good-natured and affectionate." Among his pipes, in a glass case over the mantlepiece, hangs a totem stick. He declares it saved his soul, but what he means by the expression he has never quite explained.

VII

THE CALL

THE incident—story it never was, perhaps—began tamely, almost meanly; it ended upon a note of strange, unearthly wonder that has haunted him ever since. In Headley's memory, at any rate, it stands out as the loveliest, the most amazing thing he ever witnessed. Other emotions, too, contributed to the vividness of the picture. That he had felt jealousy towards his old pal, Arthur Deane, shocked him in the first place; it seemed impossible until it actually happened. But that the jealousy was proved afterwards to have been without a cause shocked him still more. He felt ashamed and miserable.

For him, the actual incident began when he received a note from Mrs. Blondin asking him to the Priory for a week-end, or for longer, if he could manage it.

Captain Arthur Deane, she mentioned, was staying with her at the moment, and a warm welcome awaited him. Iris she did not mention—Iris Manning, the interesting and beautiful girl for whom it was well known he had a considerable weakness. He found a good-sized house party; there was fishing in the little Sussex river, tennis, golf not far away, while two motor cars brought the remoter country across the downs into easy reach. Also there was a bit of duck shooting for those who cared to wake at 3 a. m. and paddle up-stream to the marshes where the birds were feeding.

"Have you brought your gun?" was the first thing Arthur said to him when he arrived. "Like a fool, I left mine in town."

"I hope you haven't," put in Miss Manning; "because

if you have I must get up one fine morning at three
o'clock." She laughed merrily, and there was an under-
note of excitement in the laugh.

Captain Headley showed his surprise. "That you were
a Diana had escaped my notice, I'm ashamed to say," he
replied lightly. "Yet I've known you some years, haven't
I?" He looked straight at her, and the soft yet searching eye, turning from his friend, met his own securely.
She was appraising him, for the hundreth time, and he,
for the hundreth time, was thinking how pretty she was,
and wondering how long the prettiness would last after
marriage.

"I'm not," he heard her answer. "That's just it. But
I've promised."

"Rather!" said Arthur gallantly. "And I shall hold
you to it," he added still more gallantly—too gallantly,
Headley thought. "I couldn't possibly get up at cock-
crow without a very special inducement, could I, now?
You know me, Dick!"

"Well, anyhow, I've brought my gun," Headley replied evasively, "so you've no excuse, either of you. You'll
have to go." And while they were laughing and chattering about it, Mrs. Blondin clinched the matter for them.
Provisions were hard to come by; the larder really needed
a brace or two of birds; it was the least they could do in
return for what she called amusingly her "Armistice hospitality."

"So I expect you to get up at three," she chaffed
them, "and return with your Victory birds."

It was from this preliminary skirmish over the tea-
table on the law five minutes after his arrival that Dick
Headley realized easily enough the little game in progress.
As a man of experience, just on the wrong side of forty,
it was not difficult to see the cards each held. He sighed.
Had he guessed an intrigue was on foot he would not
have come, yet he might have known that wherever his
hostess was, there were the vultures gathered together.

Matchmaker by choice and instinct, Mrs. Blondin could not help herself. True to her name, she was always balancing on matrimonial tightropes—for others.

Her cards, at any rate, were obvious enough; she had laid them on the table for him. He easily read her hand. The next twenty-four hours confirmed this reading. Having made up her mind that Iris and Arthur were destined for each other, she had grown impatient; they had been ten days together, yet Iris was still free. They were good friends only. With calculation, she, therefore, took a step that must bring things further. She invited Dick Headley, whose weakness for the girl was common knowledge. The card was indicated; she played it. Arthur must come to the point or see another man carry her off. This, at least, she planned, little dreaming that the dark King of Spades would interfere.

Miss Manning's hand also was fairly obvious, for both men were extremely eligible *partis*. She was getting on; one or other was to become her husband before the party broke up. This, in crude language, was certainly in her cards, though, being a nice and charming girl, she might camouflage it cleverly to herself and others. Her eyes, on each man in turn when the shooting expedition was being discussed, revealed her part in the little intrigue clearly enough. It was all, thus far, as commonplace as could be.

But there were two more hands Headley had to read —his own and his friend's; and these, he admitted honestly, were not so easy. To take his own first. It was true he was fond of the girl and had often tried to make up his mind to ask her. Without being conceited, he had good reason to believe his affection was returned and that she would accept him. There was no ecstatic love on either side, for he was no longer a boy of twenty, nor was she unscathed by tempestuous love affairs that had scorched the first bloom from her face and heart. But they understood one another; they were an honest couple;

she was tired of flirting; both wanted to marry and settle down. Unless a better man turned up she probably would say "Yes" without humbug or delay. It was this last reflection that brought him to the final hand he had to read.

Here he was puzzled. Arthur Deane's rôle in the tea-cup strategy, for the first time since they had known one another, seemed strange, uncertain. Why? Because, though paying no attention to the girl openly, he met her clandestinely, unknown to the rest of the house-party, and above all without telling his intimate pal—at three o'clock in the morning.

The house-party was in full swing, with a touch of that wild, reckless gaiety which followed the end of the war: "Let us be happy before a worse thing comes upon us," was in many hearts. After a crowded day they danced till early in the morning, while doubtful weather prevented the early shooting expedition after duck. The third night Headley contrived to disappear early to bed. He lay there thinking. He was puzzled over his friend's rôle, over the clandestine meeting in particular. It was the morning before, waking very early, he had been drawn to the window by an unusual sound—the cry of a bird. Was it a bird? In all his experience he had never heard such a curious, half-singing call before. He listened a moment, thinking it must have been a dream, yet with the odd cry still ringing in his ears. It was repeated close beneath his open window, a long, low-pitched cry with three distinct following notes in it.

He sat up in bed and listened hard. No bird that he knew could make such sounds. But it was not repeated a third time, and out of sheer curiosity he went to the window and looked out. Dawn was creeping over the distant downs; he saw their outline in the grey pearly light; he saw the lawn below, stretching down to the little river at the bottom, where a curtain of faint mist hung in the air. And on this lawn he also saw Arthur Deane—with Iris Manning.

Of course, he reflected, they were going after the duck.
He turned to look at his watch; it was three o'clock. The
same glance, however, showed him his gun standing in
the corner. So they were going without a gun. A sharp
pang of unexpected jealousy shot through him. He was
just going to shout out something or other, wishing them
good luck, or asking if they had found another gun, perhaps, when a cold touch crept down his spine. The same
instant his heart contracted. Deane had followed the girl
into the summer-house, which stood on the right. It was
not the shooting expedition at all. Arthur was meeting
her for another purpose. The blood flowed back, filling his
head. He felt an eavesdropper, a sneak, a detective; but,
for all that, he felt also jealous. And his jeaolusy seemed
chiefly because Arthur had not told him.

' Of this, then, he lay thinking in bed on the third
night. The following day he had said nothing, but had
crossed the corridor and put the gun in his friend's room.
Arthur, for his part, had said nothing either. For the
first time in their long, long friendship, there lay a secret
between them. To Headley the unexpected revelation came
with pain.

For something like a quarter of a century these two
had been bosom friends; they had camped together, been
in the army together, taken their pleasure together, each
the full confidant of the other in all the things that go
to make up men's lives. Above all, Headley had been the
one and only recipient of Arthur's unhappy love story.
He knew the girl, knew his friend's deep passion, and
also knew his terrible pain when she was lost at sea.
Arthur was burnt out, finished, out of the running, so far
as marriage was concerned. He was not a man to love a
second time. It was a great and poignant tragedy. Headley, as confidant, knew all. But more than that—Arthur,
on his side, knew his friend's weakness for Iris Manning,
knew that a marriage was still possible and likely between
them. They were true as steel to one another, and each

man, oddly enough, had once saved the other's life, thus adding to the strength of a great natural tie.

Yet now one of them, feigning innocence by day, even indifference, secretly met his friend's girl by night, and kept the matter to himself. It seemed incredible. With his own eyes Headley had seen him on the lawn, passing in the faint grey light through the mist into the summer-house, where the girl had just preceded him. He had not seen her face, but he had seen the skirt sweep round the corner of the wooden pillar. He had not waited to see them come out again.

So he now lay wondering what rôle his old friend was playing in this little intrigue that their hostess, Mrs. Blondin, helped to stage. And, oddly enough, one minor detail stayed in his mind with a curious vividness. As naturalist, hunter, nature-lover, the cry of that strange bird, with its three mournful notes, perplexed him exceedingly.

A knock came at his door, and the door pushed open before he had time to answer. Deane himself came in.

"Wise man," he exclaimed in an easy tone, "got off to bed. Iris was asking where you were." He sat down on the edge of the mattress, where Headley was lying with a cigarette and an open book he had not read. The old sense of intimacy and comradeship rose in the latter's heart. Doubt and suspicion faded. He prized his great friendship. He met the familiar eyes. "Impossible," he said to himself, "absolutely impossible! He's not playing a game; he's not a rotter!" He pushed over his cigarette case, and Arthur lighted one.

"Done in," he remarked shortly, with the first puff. "Can't stand it any more. I'm off to town to-morrow."

Headley stared in amazement. "Fed up already?" he asked. "Why, I rather like it. It's quite amusing. What's wrong, old man?"

"This match-making," said Deane bluntly. "Always throwing that girl at my head. If it's not the duck-shooting stunt at 3 a. m., it's something else. She doesn't care for me and I don't care for her. Besides——"

He stopped, and the expression of his face changed suddenly. A sad, quiet look of tender yearning came into his clear brown eyes.

"*You* know, Dick," he went on in a low, half-reverent tone. "I don't want to marry. I never can."

Dick's heart stirred within him. "Mary," he said, understandingly.

The other nodded, as though the memories were still too much for him. "I'm still miserably lonely for her," he said. "Can't help it simply. I feel utterly lost without her. Her memory to me is everything." He looked deep into his pal's eyes. "I'm married to that," he added very firmly.

They pulled their cigarettes a moment in silence. They belonged to the male type that conceals emotion behind schoolboy language.

"It's hard luck," said Headley gently, "rotten luck, old man, I understand." Arthur's head nodded several times in succession as he smoked. He made no remark for some minutes. Then presently he said, as though it had no particular importance—for thus old friends show frankness to each other—"Besides, anyhow, it's you the girl's dying for, not me. She's blind as a bat, old Blondin. Even when I'm with her—thrust with her by that old matchmaker for my sins—it's you she talks about. All the talk leads up to you and yours. She's devilish fond of you." He paused a moment and looked searchingly into his friend's face. "I say, old man—are you—I mean, do you mean business there? Because—excuse me interfering—but you'd better be careful. She's a good sort, you know, after all."

"Yes, Arthur, I do like her a bit," Dick told him frankly. "But I can't make up my mind quite. You see, it's like this——"

And they talked the matter over as old friends will, until finally Arthur chucked his cigarette into the grate and got up to go. "Dead to the world," he said, with a yawn. "I'm off to bed. Give you a chance, too," he added with a laugh. It was after midnight.

The other turned, as though something had suddenly occurred to him.

"By the bye, Arthur," he said abruptly, "what bird makes this sound? I heard it the other morning. Most extraordinary cry. You know everything that flies. What is it?" And, to the best of his ability, he imitated the strange three-note cry he had heard in the dawn two mornings before.

To his amazement and keen distress, his friend, with a sound like a stifled groan, sat down upon the bed without a word. He seemed startled. His face was white. He stared. He passed a hand, as in pain, across his forehead.

"Do it again," he whispered, in a hushed, nervous voice. "Once again—for me."

And Headley, looking at him, repeated the queer notes, a sudden revulsion of feeling rising through him. "He's fooling me after all," ran in his heart, "my old, old pal——"

There was silence for a full minute. Then Arthur, stammering a bit, said lamely, a certain hush in his voice still: "Where in the world did you hear that—and *when?*"

Dick Headley sat up in bed. He was not going to lose this friendship, which, to him, was more than the love of woman. He must help. His pal was in distress and difficulty. There were circumstances, he realized, that might be too strong for the best man in the world—sometimes. No, by God, he would play the game and help him out!

"Arthur, old chap," he said affectionately, almost tenderly. "I heard it two mornings ago—on the lawn below my window here. It woke me up. I—I went to look. Three in the morning, about."

Arthur amazed him then. He first took another cigarette and lit it steadily. He looked round the room vaguely, avoiding, it seemed, the other's eyes. Then he turned, pain in his face, and gazed straight at him.

"You saw—nothing?" he asked in a louder voice, but a voice that had something very real and true in it. It reminded Headley of the voice he heard when he was fainting from exhaustion, and Arthur had said, "Take it, I tell you. I'm all right," and had passed over the flask, though his own throat and sight and heart were black with thirst. It was a voice that had command in it, a voice that did not lie because it could not—yet did lie and could lie—when occasion warranted.

Headley knew a second's awful struggle.

"Nothing," he answered quietly, after his little pause. "Why?"

For perhaps two minutes his friend hid his face. Then he looked up.

"Only," he whispered, "because that was our secret lover's cry. It seems so strange you heard it and not I. I've felt her so close of late—Mary!"

The white face held very steady, the firm lips did not tremble, but it was evident that the heart knew anguish that was deep and poignant. "We used it to call each other—in the old days. It was our private call. No one else in the world knew it but Mary and myself."

Dick Headley was flabbergasted. He had no time to think, however.

"It's odd you should hear it and not I," his friend repeated. He looked hurt, bewildered, wounded. Then suddenly his face brightened. "I know," he cried suddenly. "You and I are pretty good pals. There's a tie between us and all that. Why, it's tel—telepathy, or whatever they call it. That's what it is."

He got up abruptly. Dick could think of nothing to

say but to repeat the other's words. "Of course, of course.
That's it," he said, "telepathy." He stared—anywhere
but at his pal.

"Night, night!" he heard from the door, and before
he could do more than reply in similar vein Arthur was
gone.

He lay for a long time, thinking, thinking. He found
it all very strange. Arthur in this emotional state was
new to him. He turned it over and over. Well, he had
known good men behave queerly when wrought up. That
recognition of the bird's cry was strange, of course, but—
he knew the cry of a bird when he heard it, though he
might not know the actual bird. That was no human
whistle. Arthur was—inventing. No, that was not possible. He was worked up, then, over something, a bit
hysterical perhaps. It had happened before, though in a
milder way, when his heart attacks came on. They affected
his nerves and head a little, it seemed. He was a deep
sort, Dick remembered. Thought turned and twisted in
him, offering various solutions, some absurd, some likely.
He was a nervous, high-strung fellow underneath, Arthur
was. He remembered that. Also he remembered, anxiously again, that his heart was not quite sound, though
what that had to do with the present tangle he did not
see.

Yet it was hardly likely that he would bring in Mary
as an invention, an excuse—Mary, the most sacred memory
in his life, the deepest, truest, best. He had sworn, anyhow, that Iris Manning meant nothing to him.

Through all his speculations, behind every thought,
ran this horrid working jealousy. It poisoned him. It
twisted truth. It moved like a wicked snake through mind
and heart. Arthur, gripped by his new, absorbing love
for Iris Manning, lied. He couldn't believe it, he didn't
believe it, he wouldn't believe it—yet jealousy persisted
in keeping the idea alive in him. It was a dreadful
thought. He fell asleep on it.

But his sleep was uneasy with feverish, unpleasant
dreams that rambled on in fragments without coming to
conclusion. Then, suddenly, the cry of the strange bird
came into his dream. He started, turned over, woke up.
The cry still continued. It was not a dream. He jumped
out of bed.

The room was grey with early morning, the air fresh
and a little chill. The cry came floating over the lawn
as before. He looked out, pain clutching at his heart.
Two figures stood below, a man and a girl, and the man
was Arthur Deane. Yet the light was so dim, the morning being overcast, that had he not expected to see his
friend, he would scarcely have recognized the familiar form
in that shadowy outline that stood close beside the girl.
Nor could he, perhaps, have recognized Iris Manning.
Their backs were to him. They moved away, disappearing again into the little summer-house, and this time—he
saw it beyond question—the two were hand in hand.
Vague and uncertain as the figures were in the early twilight, he was sure of that.

The first disagreeable sensation of surprise, disgust,
anger that sickened him turned quickly, however, into one
of another kind altogether. A curious feeling of superstitious dread crept over him, and a shiver ran again along
his nerves.

"Hallo, Arthur!" he called from the window. There
was no answer. His voice was certainly audible in the
summer-house. But no one came. He repeated the call
a little louder, waited in vain for thirty seconds, then came,
the same moment, to a decision that even surprised himself,
for the truth we he could no longer bear the suspense of
waiting. He must see his friend at once and have it out
with him. He turned and went deliberately down the corridor to Deane's bedroom. He would wait there for his
return and know the truth from his own lips. But also
another thought had come—the gun. He had quite for-

gotten it—the safety-catch was out of order. He had not warned him.

He found the door closed but not locked; opening it cautiously, he went in.

But the unexpectedness of what he saw gave him a genuine shock. He could hardly suppress a cry. Everything in the room was neat and orderly, no sign of disturbance anywhere, and it was not empty. There, in bed, before his very eyes, was Arthur. The clothes were turned back a little; he saw the pyjamas open at the throat; he lay sound asleep, deeply, peacefully asleep.

So surprised, indeed, was Headley that, after staring a moment, almost unable to believe his sight, he then put out a hand and touched him gently, cautiously on the forehead. But Arthur did not stir or wake; his breathing remained deep and regular. He lay sleeping like a baby.

Headley glanced round the room, noticed the gun in the corner where he himself had put it the day before, and then went out, closing the door behind him softly.

Arthur Deane, however, did not leave for London as he had intended, because he felt unwell and kept to his room upstairs. It was only a slight attack, apparently, but he must lie quiet. There was no need to send for a doctor; he knew just what to do; these passing attacks were common enough. He would be up and about again very shortly. Headley kept him company, saying no single word of what had happened. He read aloud to him, chatted and cheered him up. He had no other visitors. Within twenty-four hours he was himself once more. He and his friend had planned to leave the following day.

But Headley, that last night in the house, felt an odd uneasiness and could not sleep. All night long he sat up reading, looking out of the window, smoking in a chair where he could see the stars and hear the wind and watch the huge shadow of the downs. The house lay very still as the hours passed. He dozed once or twice. Why did he sit up in this unnecessary way? Why did he leave his door ajar so that the slightest sound of another door opening, or of steps passing along the corridor, must reach him? Was he anxious for his friend? Was he suspicious? What was his motive, what his secret purpose?

Headley did not know, and could not even explain it to himself. He felt uneasy, that was all he knew. Not for worlds would he have let himself go to sleep or lose full consciousness that night. It was very odd; he could not understand himself. He merely obeyed a strange, deep instinct that bade him wait and watch. His nerves were jumpy; in his heart lay some unexplicable anxiety that was pain.

The dawn came slowly; the stars faded one by one; the line of the downs showed their grand bare curves against the sky; cool and cloudless the September morning broke above the little Sussex pleasure house. He sat and watched the east grow bright. The early wind brought a scent of marshes and the sea into his room. Then suddenly it brought a sound as well—the haunting cry of the bird with its three following notes. And this time there came an answer.

Headley knew then why he had sat up. A wave of emotion swept him as he heard—an emotion he could not attempt to explain. Dread, wonder, longing seized him. For some seconds he could not leave his chair because he did not dare to. The low-pitched cries of call and answer rang in his ears like some unearthly music. With an effort he started up, went to the window and looked out.

This time the light was sharp and clear. No mist hung in the air. He saw the crimsoning sky reflected like a band of shining metal in the reach of river beyond the lawn. He saw dew on the grass, a sheet of pallid silver. He saw the summer-house, empty of any passing figures. For this time the two figures stood plainly in view before his eyes upon the lawn. They stood there, hand in hand, sharply defined, unmistakable in form and outline, their faces, moreover, turned upwards to the window where he stood, staring down in pain and amazement at them—at Arthur Deane and *Mary*.

They looked into his eyes. He tried to call, but no sound left his throat. They began to move across the dew-soaked lawn. They went, he saw, with a floating, undulating motion towards the river shining in the dawn. Their feet left no marks upon the grass. They reached the bank, but did not pause in their going. They rose a little, floating like silent birds across the river. Turning in mid-stream, they smiled towards him, waved their hands with a gesture of farewell, then, rising still higher into the opal dawn, their figures passed into the distance slowly, melting away against the sunlit marshes and the shadowing downs beyond. They disappeared.

Headley never quite remembers actually leaving the window, crossing the room, or going down the passage. Perhaps he went at once, perhaps he stood gazing into the air above the downs for a considerable time, unable to tear himself away. He was in some marvellous dream, it seemed. The next thing he remembers, at any rate, was that he was standing beside his friend's bed, trying, in his distraught anguish of heart, to call him from that sleep which, on earth, knows no awakening.

VIII

EGYPTIAN SORCERY

1

SANFIELD paused as he was about to leave the Underground station at Victoria, and cursed the weather. When he left the City it was fine; now it was pouring with rain, and he had neither overcoat nor umbrella. Not a taxi was discoverable in the dripping gloom. He would get soaked before he reached his rooms in Sloane Street.

He stood for some minutes, thinking how vile London was in February, and how depressing life was in general. He stood also, in that moment, though he knew it not, upon the edge of a singular adventure. Looking back upon it in later years, he often remembered this particularly wretched moment of a pouring wet February evening, when everything seemed wrong, and Fate had loaded the dice against him, even in the matter of weather and umbrellas.

Fate, however, without betraying her presence, was watching him through the rain and murk; and Fate, that night, had strange, mysterious eyes. Fantastic cards lay up her sleeve. The rain, his weariness and depression, his physical fatigue especially, seemed the conditions she required before she played these curious cards. Something new and wonderful fluttered close. Romance flashed by him across the driving rain and touched his cheek. He was too exasperated to be aware of it.

Things had gone badly that day at the office, where he was junior partner in a small firm of engineers. Threatened trouble at the works had come to a head. A strike seemed imminent. To add to his annoyance, a new client, whose custom was of supreme importance, had just complained bitterly of the delay in the delivery of his machinery. The senior partners had left the matter in Sanfield's hands; he had not succeeded. The angry customer swore he would hold the firm to its contract. They could deliver or pay up—whichever suited them. The junior partner had made a mess of things.

The final words on the telephone still rang in his ears as he stood sheltering under the arcade, watching the downpour, and wondering whether he should make a dash for it or wait on the chance of its clearing up—when a further blow was dealt him as the rain-soaked poster of an evening paper caught his eye: "Riots in Egypt. Heavy Fall in Egyptian Securities," he read with blank dismay. Buying a paper he turned feverishly to the City article— to find his worst fears confirmed. Delta Lands, in which nearly all his small capital was invested, had declined a quarter on the news, and would evidently decline further still. The riots were going on in the towns nearest to their property. Banks had been looted, crops destroyed; the trouble was deep-seated.

So grave was the situation that mere weather seemed suddenly of no account at all. He walked home doggedly in the drenching rain, paying less attention to it than if it had been Scotch mist. The water streamed from his hat, dripped down his back and neck, splashed him with mud and grime from head to foot. He was soaked to the skin. He hardly noticed it. His capital had depreciated by half, at least, and possibly was altogether lost; his position at the office was insecure. How could mere weather matter?

Sitting, eventually, before his fire in dry clothes, after an apology for a dinner he had no heart to eat, he reviewed the situation. He faced a possible total loss of his private capital. Next, the position of his firm caused him grave uneasiness, since, apart from his own mishandling of the new customer, the threatened strike might ruin it completely; a long strain on its limited finances was out of the question. George Sanfield certainly saw things at their worst. He was now thirty-five. A fresh start—the mere idea of it made him shudder—occurred as a possibility in the near future. Vitality, indeed, was at a low ebb, it seemed. Mental depression, great physical fatigue, weariness of life in general made his spirits droop alarmingly, so that almost he felt tired of living. His tie with existence, at any rate, just then was dangerously weak.

Thought turned next to the man on whose advice he had staked his all in Delta Lands. Morris had important Egyptian interests in various big companies and enterprises along the Nile. He had first come to the firm with a letter of introduction upon some business matter, which the junior partner had handled so successfully that acquaintance thus formed had ripened into a more personal tie. The two men had much in common; their temperaments were suited; understanding grew between them; they felt at home and comfortable with one another. They became friends; they felt a mutual confidence. When Morris paid his rare visits to England, they spent much time together; and it was on one of these occasions that the matter of the Egyptian shares was mentioned, Morris urgently advising their purchase.

Sanfield explained his own position clearly enough, but his friend was so confident and optimistic that the purchase eventually had been made. There had been, moreover, Sanfield now remembered, the flavour of a peculiarly intimate and personal kind about the deal. He had remarked it, with a touch of surprise, at the moment, though really it seemed natural enough. Morris was very earnest, holding his friend's interest at heart; he was affectionate almost.

"I'd like to do you this good turn, old man," he said. "I have the strong feeling, somehow, that I owe you this, though heaven alone knows why!" After a pause he added, half shyly: "It may be one of those old memories we hear about nowadays cropping up out of some previous life together." Before the other could reply, he went on to explain that only three men were in the parent syndicate, the shares being unobtainable. "I'll set some of my own aside for you—four thousand or so, if you like."

They laughed together; Sanfield thanked him warmly; the deal was carried out. But the recipient of the favour had wondered a little at the sudden increase of intimacy even while he liked it and responded.

Had he been a fool, he now asked himself, to swallow the advice, putting all his eggs into a single basket? He knew very little about Morris after all. . . . Yet, while reflection showed him that the advice was honest, and the present riots no fault of the adviser's, he found his thoughts turning in a steady stream towards the man. The affairs of the firm took second place. It was Morris, with his deep-set eyes, his curious ways, his dark skin burnt brick-red by a fierce Eastern sun; it was Morris, looking almost like an Egyptian, who stood before him as he sat thinking gloomily over his dying fire.

He longed to talk with him, to ask him questions, to seek advice. He saw him very vividly against the screen of thought; Morris stood beside him now, gazing out across the limitless expanse of tawny sand. He had in his eyes the "distance" that sailors share with men whose life has been spent amid great trackless wastes. Morris, more-over, now he came to think of it, seemed always a little out of place in England. He had few relatives and, ap-parently, no friends; he was always intensely pleased when the time came to return to his beloved Nile. He had once mentioned casually a sister who kept house for him when duty detained him in Cairo, but, even here, he was something of an Oriental, rarely speaking of his women folk. Egypt, however, plainly drew him like a magnet. Resistance involved disturbance in his being, even ill-health. Egypt was "home" to him, and his friend, though he had never been there, felt himself its potent spell.

Another curious trait Sanfield remembered, too—his friend's childish superstition; his belief, or half-belief, in magic and the supernatural. Sanfield, amused, had ascribed it to the long sojourn in a land where anything unusual is at once ascribed to spiritual agencies. Morris owed his entire fortune, if his tale could be believed, to the magical apparition of an unearthly kind in some lonely *wadi* among the Bedouins. A sand-diviner had influenced another successful speculation. . . . He was a picturesque figure, whichever way one took him: yet a successful business man into the bargain.

These reflections and memories, on the other hand, brought small comfort to the man who had tempted Fate by following his advice. It was only a little strange how Morris now dominated his thoughts, directing them towards himself. Morris was in Egypt at the moment.

He went to bed at length, filled with uneasy misgivings, but for a long time he could not sleep. He tossed restlessly, his mind still running on the subject of his long reflections. He ached with tiredness. He dropped off at last. Then came a nightmare dream, in which the firm's works were sold for nearly nothing to an old Arab sheikh who wished to pay for them—in goats. He woke up in a cold perspiration. He had uneasy thoughts. His fancy was travelling. He could not rest.

To distract his mind, he turned on the light and tried to read, and, eventually, towards morning, fell into a sleep of sheer exhaustion. And his final thought—he knew not exactly why—was a sentence Morris had made use of long ago: "I feel I owe you a good turn; I'd like to do something for you. . . ."

This was the memory in his mind as he slipped off into unconsciousness.

But what happens when the mind is unconscious and

the tired body lies submerged in deep sleep, no man, they
say, can really tell.

2

The next thing he knew he was walking along a sun-
baked street in some foreign town that was familiar, although, at first, its name escaped him. Colour, softness,
and warmth pervaded it; there was sparkle and lightness
in the exhilarating air; it was an Eastern town.

Though early morning, a number of people were
already stirring; strings of camels passed him, loaded with
clover, bales of merchandise, and firewood. Gracefully-
draped women went by silently, carrying water jars of
burnt clay upon their heads. Rude wooden shutters were
being taken down in the bazaars; the smoke of cooking-
fires rose in the blue spirals through the quiet air. He
felt strangely at home and happy. The light, the radiance stirred him. He passed a mosque from which the
worshippers came pouring in a stream of colour.

Yet, though an Eastern town, it was not wholly Oriental, for he saw that many of the buildings were of semi-
European design, and that the natives sometimes wore
European dress, except for the fez upon the head. Among
them were Europeans, too. Staring into the faces of the
passers-by he found, to his vexation, that he could not
focus sight as usual, and that the nearer he approached,
the less clearly he discerned the features. The faces, upon
close attention, at once grew shadowy, merged into each
other, or, in some odd fashion, melted into the dazzling
sunshine that was their background. All his attempts in
this direction failed; impatience seized him; of surprise,
however, he was not conscious. Yet this mingled vagueness and intensity seemed perfectly natural.

Filled with a stirring curiosity, he made a strong effort
to concentrate his attention, only to discover that this
vagueness, this difficulty of focus, lay in his own being,
too. He wandered on, unaware exactly where he was go-

ing, yet not much perturbed, since there was an objective in view, he knew, and this objective *must* eventually be reached. Its nature, however, for the moment entirely eluded him.

The sense of familiarity, meanwhile, increased; he had been in this town before, although not quite within recoverable memory. It seemed, perhaps, the general atmosphere, rather than the actual streets, he knew; a certain perfume in the air, a tang of indefinable sweetness, a vitality in the radiant sunshine. The dark faces that he could not focus, he yet knew; the flowing garments of blue and red and yellow, the softly-slippered feet, the slouching camels, the burning human eyes that faded ere he fully caught them—the entire picture in this blazing sunlight lay half-hidden, half-revealed. And an extraordinary sense of happiness and well-being flooded him as he walked; he felt at home; comfort and bliss stole over him. Almost he knew his way about. This was a place he loved and knew.

The complete silence, moreover, did not strike him as peculiar until, suddenly, it was broken in a startling fashion. He heard his own name spoken. It sounded close beside his ear.

"George Sanfield!" The voice was familiar. Morris called him. He realized then the truth. He was, of course, in Cairo.

Yet, instead of turning to discover the speaker at his side, he hurried forward, as though he knew that the voice had come through distance. His consciousness cleared and lightened; he felt more alive; his eyes now focused the passers-by without difficulty. He was there to find Morris, and Morris was directing him. All was explained and natural again. He hastened. But, even while he hastened, he knew that his personal desire to speak with his friend about Egyptian shares and Delta Lands was not his single object. Behind it, further in among as yet unstirring shadows, lay another deeper purpose. Yet he did not trouble about it, nor make a conscious effort at discovery. Morris was doing him that "good turn I feel I owe you." This conviction filled him overwhelmingly. The question of how and why did not once occur to him. A strange, great happiness rose in him.

Upon the outskirts of the town now, he found himself approaching a large building in the European style, with wide verandas and a cultivated garden filled with palm trees. A well-kept drive of yellow sand led to its chief entrance, and the man in khaki drill and riding-breeches walking along this drive, not ten yards in front of him, was—Morris. He overtook him, but his cry of welcome recognition was not answered. Morris, walking with bowed head and stooping shoulders, seemed intensely preoccupied; he had not heard the call.

"Here I am, old fellow!" exclaimed his friend, holding out a hand. "I've come, you see . . . !" then paused aghast before the altered face. Morris paid no attention. He walked straight on as though he had not heard. It was the distraught and anguished expression on the drawn and haggard features that impressed the other most. The silence he took without surprise.

It was the pain and suffering in his friend that occupied him. The dark rims beneath heavy eyes, the evidence of sleepless nights, of long anxiety and ceaseless dread, afflicted him with their too-plain story. The man was overwhelmed with some great sorrow. Sanfield forgot his personal trouble; this larger, deeper grief usurped its place entirely.

"Morris! Morris!" he cried yet more eagerly than before. "I've come, you see. Tell me what's the matter. I believe—that I can—help you . . . !"

The other turned, looking past him through the air. He made no answer. The eyes went through him. He walked straight on, and Sanfield walked at his side in silence. Through the large door they passed together, Morris paying as little attention to him as though he were not there, and in the small chamber they now entered, evidently a waiting-room, an Egyptian servant approached, uttered some inaudible words, and then withdrew, leaving them alone together.

It seemed that time leaped forward, yet stood still; the passage of minutes, that is to say, was irregular, almost fanciful. Whether the interval was long or short, however, Morris spent it pacing up and down the little room, his hands thrust deep into his pockets, his mind oblivious of all else but his absorbing anxiety and grief. To his friend, who watched him by the wall with intense desire to help, he paid no attention. The latter's spoken words went by him, entirely unnoticed; he gave no sign of seeing him; his eyes, as he paced up and down, muttering inaudibly to himself, were fixed every few seconds on an inner door. Beyond that door, Sanfield now divined, lay someone who hesitated on the narrow frontier between life and death.

It opened suddenly and a man, in overall and rubber gloves, came out, his face grave yet with faint signs of hope about it—a doctor, clearly, straight from the operating table. Morris, standing rigid in his tracks, listened to something spoken, for the lips were in movement, though no words were audible. The operation, Sanfield divined, had been successful, though danger was still present. The two men passed out, then, into the hall and climbed a wide staircase to the floor above, Sanfield following noiselessly, though so close that he could touch them. Entering a large, airy room where French windows, carefully shaded with green blinds opened on to a veranda, they approached a bed. Two nurses bent over it. The occupant was at first invisible.

Events had moved with curious rapidity. All this had happened, it seemed, in a single moment, yet with the irregular effect already mentioned which made Sanfield feel it might, equally, have lasted hours. But, as he stood behind Morris and the surgeon at the bed, the deeps

in him opened suddenly, and he trembled under a shock
of intense emotion that he could not understand. As with
a stroke of lightning some heavenly fire set his heart aflame
with yearning. The very soul in him broke loose with
passionate longing that *must* find satisfaction. It came
to him in a single instant with the certain knowledge of
an unconquerable conviction. Hidden, yet ever waiting,
among the broken centuries, there now leaped upon him
this flash of memory—the memory of some sweet and
ancient love Time might veil yet could not kill.

He ran forward, past the surgeon and the nurses, past
Morris who bent above the bed with a face ghastly from
anxiety. He gazed down upon the fair girl lying there,
her unbound hair streaming over the pillow. He saw, and
he remembered. And an uncontrollable cry of recognition
left his lips. . . .

The irregularity of the passing minutes became so
marked then, that he might well have passed outside their
measure altogether, beyond what men call Time; duration, interval, both escaped. Alone and free with his eternal love, he was safe from all confinement, free, it seemed,
either of time or space. His friend, however, was vaguely
with him during the amazing instant. He felt acutely
aware of the need each had, respectively, for the other,
born of a heritage the Past had hidden over-long. Each,
it was clear, could do the other a good turn. . . . Sanfield, though unable to describe or disentangle later, knew,
while it lasted, this joy of full, delicious understanding. . . .

The strange, swift instant of recognition passed and
disappeared. The cry, Sanfield realized, on coming back
to the Present, had been soundless and inaudible as before.
No one observed him; no one stirred. The girl, on that
bed beside the opened windows, lay evidently dying. Her
breath came in gasps, her chest heaved convulsively, each
attempt at recovery was slower and more painful than
the one before. She was unconscious. Sometimes her
breathing seemed to stop. It grew weaker, as the pulse

grew fainter. And Sanfield, transfixed as with paralysis, stood watching, waiting, an intolerable yearning in his heart to help. It seemed to him that he waited with a purpose.

This purpose suddenly became clear. He knew why he waited. There was help to be given. He was the one to give it.

The girl's vitality and ebbing nerves, her entire physical organism now fading so quickly towards that final extinction which meant death—could these but be stimulated by a new tide of life, the danger-point now fast approaching might be passed, and recovery must follow. This impetus, he knew suddenly, he could supply. How, he could not tell. It flashed upon him from beyond the stars, as from ancient store of long-forgotten, long-neglected knowledge. It was enough that he felt confident and sure. His soul burned within him; the strength of an ancient and unconquerable love rose through his being. He would try.

The doctor, he saw, was in the act of giving his last aid in the form of a hypodermic injection, Morris and the nurses looking on. Sanfield observed the sharp quick rally, only too faint, too slight; he saw the collapse that followed. The doctor, shrugging his shoulders, turned with a look that could not express itself in words, and Morris, burying his face in his hands, knelt by the bed, shaken with convulsive sobbing. It was the end.

In which moment, precisely, the strange paralysis that had bound Sanfield momentarily, was lifted from his being, and an impelling force, obeying his immense desire, invaded him. He knew how to act. His will, taught long ago, yet long-forgotten, was set free.

"You have come back to me at last," he cried in his anguish and his power, though the voice was, as ever, inaudible and soundless, *"I shall not let you go! . . ."*

Drawn forward nearer and nearer to the bed, he leaned down, as if to kiss the pale lips and streaming hair. But his knowledge operated better than he knew. In the tremendous grip of that power which spins the stars and suns, while drawing souls into manifestation upon a dozen planets, he raced, he dived, he plunged, helpless, yet driven by the creative stress of love and sacrifice towards some eternal purpose. Caught in what seemed a vortex of amazing force, he sank away, as a straw is caught and sunk within the suction of a mighty whirlpool. His memory of Morris, of the doctor, of the girl herself, passed utterly. His entire personality became merged, lost, obliterated. He was aware of nothing; not even aware of nothingness. He lost consciousness. . . .

3

The reappearance was as sudden as the obliteration. He emerged. There had been interval, duration, time. He was not aware of them. A spasm of blinding pain shot through him. He opened his eyes. His whole body was a single devouring pain. He felt cramped, confined, uncomfortable. He must escape. He thrashed about. Someone seized his arm and held it. With a snarl he easily wrenched it free.

He was in bed. How had he come to this? An accident? He saw the faces of nurse and doctor bending over him, eager, amazed, surprised, a trifle frightened. Vague memories floated to him. Who was he? Where had he come from? And where was . . . where was . . . someone . . . who was dearer to him than life itself? He looked about him: the room, the faces, the French windows, the veranda, all seemed only half familiar. He looked, he searched for . . . someone . . . but in vain. . . .

A spasm of violent pain burned through his body like a fire, and he shut his eyes. He groaned. A voice sounded just above him: "Take this, dear. Try and swallow a little. It will relieve you. Your brother will be back in a moment. You are much better already."

He looked up at the nurse; he drank what she gave him.

"My brother!" he murmured. "I don't understand. I have no brother." Thirst came over him; he drained the glass. The nurse, wearing a startled look, moved away. He watched her go. He pointed at her with his hand, meaning to say something that he instantly forgot—as he saw his own bare arm. Its dreadful thinness shocked him. He must have been ill for months. The arm, wasted almost to nothing, showed the bone. He sank back exhausted, the sleeping draught began to take effect. The nurse returned quietly to a chair beside the bed, from which she watched him without ceasing as the long minutes passed. . . .

He found it difficult to collect his thoughts, to keep them in his mind when caught. There floated before him a series of odd scenes like coloured pictures in an endless flow. He was unable to catch them. Morris was with him always. They were doing quite absurd, impossible things. They rode together across the desert in the dawn, they wandered through old massive temples, they saw the sun set behind mud villages mid wavering palms, they drifted down a river in a sailing boat of quaint design. It had an enormous single sail. Together they visited tombs cut in the solid rock, hot airless corridors, and huge, dim, vaulted chambers underground. There was an icy wind by night, fierce burning sun by day. They watched vast troops of stars pass down a stupendous sky. . . . They knew delight and tasted wonder. Strange memories touched them. . . .

"Nurse!" he called aloud, returning to himself again, and remembering that he must speak with his friend about something—he failed to recall exactly what. "Please ask Mr. Morris to come to me."

"At once, dear. He's only in the next room waiting for you to wake." She went out quickly, and he heard her voice in the passage. It sank to a whisper as she came back with Morris, yet every syllable reached him distinctly:

". . . and pay no attention if she wanders a little; just ignore it. She's turned the corner, thank God, and that's the chief thing." Each word he heard with wonder and perplexity, with increasing irritability too.

"I'm a hell of a wreck," he said, as Morris came, beaming, to the bedside. "Have I been ill long? It's frightfully decent of you to come, old man."

But Morris, staggered at this greeting, stopped abruptly, half turning to the nurse for guidance. He seemed unable to find words. Sanfield was extremely annoyed; he showed his feeling. "I'm *not* balmy, you old ass!" he shouted. "I'm all right again, though very weak. But I wanted to ask you—oh, I remember now—I wanted to ask you about my—er—*Deltas.*"

"My poor dear Maggie," stammered Morris, fumbling with his voice. "Don't worry about your few shares, darling. Deltas are all right—it's *you* we——"

"Why, the devil, do you call me Maggie?" snapped the other viciously. "And 'darling'!" He felt furious, exasperated. "Have *you* gone balmy, or have I? What in the world are you two up to?" His fury tired him. He lay back upon his pillows, fuming. Morris took a chair beside the bed; he put a hand gently on his wasted arm.

"My darling girl," he said, in what was intended to be a soothing voice, though it stirred the sick man again to fury beyond expression, "you must really keep quiet for a bit. You've had a very severe operation"—his voice shook a little—"but, thank God, you've pulled through and are now on the way to recovery. You are my sister Maggie. It will all come back to you when you're rested——"

"Maggie, indeed!" interrupted the other, trying to sit up again, but too weak to compass it. "Your sister! You bally idiot! Don't you know me? I wish to God the nurse wouldn't 'dear' me in that senseless way. And you,

with your atrocious 'darling.' I'm not your precious sister
Maggie. I'm—I'm George San——"

But even as he said it, there passed over him some
dim lost fragment of a wild, delicious memory he could
not seize. Intense pleasure lay in it, could he but recover
it. He knew a sweet, forgotten joy. His broken, troubled
mind lay searching frantically but without success. It
dazzled him. It shook him with an indescribable emotion
—of joy, of wonder, of deep sweet confusion. A rapt
happiness rose in him, yet pain, like a black awful shutter, closed in upon the happiness at once. He remembered
a girl. But he remembered, too, that he had seen her
die. Who was she? Had he lost her . . . again . . . !

"My dear fellow," he faltered in a weaker voice to
Morris, "my brain's in a whirl. I'm sorry. I suppose I've
had some blasted concussion—haven't I?"

But the man beside his bed, he saw, was startled. An
extraordinary look came into his face, though he tried to
hide it with a smile.

"My shares!" cried Sanfield, with a half scream.
"Four thousand of them!"

Whereupon Morris blanched. "George Sanfield!" he
muttered, half to himself, half to the nurse who hurried
up. "That voice! The very number too!" He looked
white and terrified, as if he had seen a ghost. A whispered colloquy ensued between him and the nurse. It was
inaudible.

"Now, dearest Maggie," he said at length, making evi-
dently a tremendous effort, "do try and lie quiet for a bit.
Don't bother about George Sanfield, my London friend.
His shares are quite safe. You've heard me speak of him.
It's all right, my darling, quite all right. Oh, believe me!
I'm your brother."

"Maggie . . . !" whispered the man to himself upon
the bed, whereupon Morris stooped, and, to his intense
horror, kissed him on the cheek. But his horror seemed

merged at once in another personality that surged through and over his entire being, drowning memory and recognition hopelessly. "Darling," he murmured. He realized that he was mad, of course. It seemed he fainted. . . .

The momentary unconsciousness soon passed, at any rate. He opened his eyes again. He saw a palm tree out of the window. He knew positively he was *not* mad, whatever else he might be. Dead perhaps? He felt the sheets, the mattress, the skin upon his face. No, he was alive all right. The dull pains where the tight bandages oppressed him were also real. He was among substantial, earthly things. The nurse, he noticed, regarded him anxiously. She was a pleasant-looking young woman. He smiled; and, with an expression of affectionate, even tender pleasure, she smiled back at him.

"You feel better now, a little stronger," she said softly. "You've had a sleep, Miss Margaret." She said "Miss Margaret" with a conscious effort. It was better, perhaps, than "dear"; but his anger rose at once. He was too tired, however, to express his feelings. There stole over him, besides, the afflicting consciousness of an alien personality that was familiar, and yet not his. It strove to dominate him. Only by a great effort could he continue to think his own thoughts. This other being kept trying to intrude, to oust him, to take full possession. It resented his presence with a kind of violence.

He sighed. So strong was the feeling of another personality trying to foist itself upon his own, upon his mind, his body, even upon his very face, that he turned instinctively to the nurse, though unaware exactly what he meant to ask her for.

"My hand-glass, please," he heard himself saying— with horror. The phrase was not his own. Glass or mirror were the words *he* would have used.

A moment later he was staring with acute and ghastly terror at a reflection that was not his own. It was the face of the dead girl he saw within the silver-handled, woman's hand-glass he held up.

* * * * *

The dream with its amazing, vivid detail haunted him for days, even coming between him and his work. It seemed far more real, more vivid than the commonplace events of life that followed. The occurrences of the day were pale compared to its overpowering intensity. And a cable, received the very next afternoon, increased this sense of actual truth—of something that had really happened.

"Hold shares writing Morris."

Its brevity added a convincing touch. He was aware of Egypt even in Throgmorton Street. Yet it was the face of the dead, or dying, girl that chiefly haunted him. She remained in his thoughts, alive and sweet and exquisite. Without her he felt incomplete, his life a failure. He thought of nothing else.

The affairs at the office, meanwhile, went well; unexpected success attended them; there was no strike; the angry customer was pacified. And when the promised letter came from Morris, Sanfield's hands trembled so violently that he could hardly tear it open. Nor could he read it calmly. The assurance about his precious shares scarcely interested him. It was the final paragraph that set his heart beating against his ribs as though a hammer lay inside him:

" . . . I've had great trouble and anxiety, though, thank God, the danger is over now. I forget if I ever mentioned my sister, Margaret, to you. She keeps house for me in Cairo, when I'm there. She is my only tie in life. Well, a severe operation she had to undergo, all but finished her. To tell you the truth, she very nearly died, for the doctor gave her up. You'll smile when I tell you that odd things happened—at the very last moment. I can't explain it, nor can the doctor. It rather terrified me. But at the very moment when we thought her gone, something revived in her. She became full of unexpected life and vigor. She was even violent—whereas, a moment before, she had not the strength to speak, much less to move. It was rather wonderful, but it was terrible too.

"You don't believe in these things, I know, but I must tell you, because, when she recovered consciousness, she began to babble about yourself, using your name, though she has rarely, if ever, heard it, and even speaking—you won't believe this, of course!— of your shares in Deltas, giving the *exact* number that you hold. When you write, please tell me if you were very anxious about these? Also, whether your thoughts were directed particularly to me? I thought a good deal about you, knowing you might be uneasy, but my mind was pretty full, as you will understand, of her operation at the time. The climax, when all this happened, was about 11 a. m. on February 13th.

"Don't fail to tell me this, as I'm particularly interested in what you may have to say.

"And, now, I want to ask a great favor of you. The doctor forbids Margaret to stay here during the hot weather, so I'm sending her home to some cousins in Yorkshire, as soon as she is fit to travel. It would be most awfully kind—I know how women bore you—if you could manage to meet the boat and help her on her way through London. I'll let you know dates and particulars later, when I hear that you will do this for me. . . ."

Sanfield hardly read the remainder of the letter, which dealt with shares and business matters. But a month later he stood on the dock-pier at Tilbury, watching the approach of the tender from the *Egyptian Mail*.

He saw it make fast; he saw the stream of passengers pour down the gangway; and he saw among them the tall, fair woman of his dream. With a beating heart he went to meet her. . . .

IX

THE DECOY

IT belonged to the category of unlovely houses about which an ugly superstition clings, one reason being, perhaps, its inability to inspire interest in itself without assistance. It seemed too ordinary to possess individuality, much less to exert an influence. Solid and ungainly, its huge bulk dwarfing the park timber, its best claim to notice was a negative one—it was unpretentious.

From the little hill its expressionless windows stared across the Kentish Weald, indifferent to weather, dreary in winter, bleak in spring, unblessed in summer. Some colossal hand had tossed it down, then let it starve to death, a country mansion that might well strain the adjectives of advertisers and find inheritors with difficulty. Its soul had fled, said some; it had committed suicide, thought others; and it was an inheritor, before he killed himself in the library, who thought this latter, yielding, apparently, to an hereditary taint in the family. For two other inheritors followed suit, with an interval of twenty years between them, and there was no clear reason to explain the three disasters. Only the first owner, indeed, lived permanently in the house, the others using it in the summer months and then deserting it with relief. Hence, when John Burley, present inheritor, assumed possession, he entered a house about which clung an ugly superstition, based, nevertheless, upon a series of undeniably ugly facts.

This century deals harshly with superstitious folk, deeming them fools or charlatans; but John Burley, robust, contemptuous of half lights, did not deal harshly with them, because he did not deal with them at all. He was hardly aware of their existence. He ignored them as he ignored, say, the Esquimaux, poets, and other human aspects that did not touch his scheme of life. A successful business man, he concentrated on what was real; he dealt with business people. His philanthropy, on a big scale, was also real; yet, though he would have denied it vehemently, he had his superstition as well. No man exists without some taint of superstition in his blood; the racial heritage is too rich to be escaped entirely. Burley's took this form—that unless he gave his tithe to the poor he would not prosper. This ugly mansion, he decided, would make an ideal Convalescent Home.

"Only cowards or lunatics kill themselves," he declared flatly, when his use of the house was criticized. "I'm neither one nor t'other." He let out his gusty, boisterous laugh. In his invigorating atmosphere such weakness seemed contemptible, just as superstition in his presence seemed feeblest ignorance. Even its picturesqueness faded. "I can't conceive," he boomed, "can't even imagine to myself," he added emphatically, "the state of mind in which a man can think of suicide, much less do it." He threw his chest out with a challenging air. "I tell you, Nancy, it's either cowardice or mania. And I've no use for either."

Yet he was easy-going and good-humoured in his denunciation. He admitted his limitations with a hearty laugh his wife called noisy. Thus he made allowances for the fairy fears of sailorfolk, and had even been known to mention haunted ships his companies owned. But he did so in the terms of tonnage and £ s. d. His scope was big; details were made for clerks.

His consent to pass a night in the mansion was the consent of a practical business man and philanthropist who dealt condescendingly with foolish human nature. It was based on the common-sense of tonnage and £ s. d. The local newspapers had revived the silly story of the suicides, calling attention to the effect of the superstition upon the fortunes of the house, and so, possibly, upon the fortunes of its present owner. But the mansion, otherwise a white elephant, was precisely ideal for his purpose, and so trivial a matter as spending a night in it should not stand in the way. "We must take people as we find them, Nancy."

His young wife had her motive, of course, in making the proposal, and, if she was amused by what she called "spook-hunting," he saw no reason to refuse her the indulgence. He loved her, and took her as he found her—late in life. To allay the superstitions of prospective staff and patients and supporters, all, in fact, whose goodwill was necessary to success, he faced this boredom of a night in the building before its opening was announced. "You see, John, if you, the owner, do this, it will nip damaging talk in the bud. If anything went wrong later it would only be put down to this suicide idea, this haunting influence. The Home will have a bad name from the start. There'll be endless trouble. It will be a failure."

"You think my spending a night there will stop the nonsense?" he inquired.

"According to the old legend it breaks the spell," she replied. "That's the condition, anyhow."

"But somebody's sure to die there sooner or later," he objected. "We can't prevent that."

"We can prevent people whispering that they died unnaturally." She explained the working of the public mind.

"I see," he replied, his lip curling, yet quick to gauge the truth of what she told him about collective instinct.

"Unless *you* take poison in the hall," she added laughingly, "or elect to hang yourself with your braces from the hat peg."

"I'll do it," he agreed, after a moment's thought. "I'll sit up with you. It will be like a honeymoon over again, you and I on the spree—eh?" He was even interested now; the boyish side of him was touched perhaps; but his enthusiasm was less when she explained that three was a better number than two on such an expedition.

"I've often done it before, John. We were always three."

"Who?" he asked bluntly. He looked wonderingly at her, but she answered that if anything went wrong a party of three provided a better margin for help. It was sufficiently obvious. He listened and agreed. "I'll get young Mortimer," he suggested. "Will he do?"

She hesitated. "Well—he's cheery; he'll be interested, too. Yes, he's as good as another." She seemed indifferent.

"And he'll make the time pass with his stories," added her husband.

So Captain Mortimer, late officer on a T.B.D., a "cheery lad," afraid of nothing, cousin of Mrs. Burley, and now filling a good post in the company's London offices, was engaged as third hand in the expedition. But Captain Mortimer was young and ardent, and Mrs. Burley was young and pretty and ill-mated, and John Burley was a neglectful, and self-satisfied husband.

Fate laid the trap with cunning, and John Burley, blind-eyed, careless of detail, floundered into it. He also floundered out again, though in a fashion none could have expected of him.

The night agreed upon eventually was as near to the shortest in the year as John Burley could contrive—June 18th—when the sun set at 8:18 and rose about a quarter to four. There would be barely three hours of true darkness. "You're the expert," he admitted, as she explained that sitting through the actual darkness only was required, not necessarily from sunset to sunrise. "We'll do the thing properly. Mortimer's not very keen, he had a dance or something," he added, noticing the look of annoyance that flashed swiftly in her eyes; "but he got out of it. He's coming." The pouting expression of the spoilt woman amused him. "Oh, no, he didn't need much persuading really," he assured her. "Some girl or other, of course.

He's young, remember." To which no comment was forthcoming, though the implied comparison made her flush.

They motored from South Audley Street after an early
tea, in due course passing Sevenoaks and entering the
Kentish Weald; and, in order that the necessary adver-
tisement should be given, the chauffeur, warned strictly
to keep their purpose quiet, was to put up at the country
inn and fetch them an hour after sunrise; they would
breakfast in London. "He'll tell everybody," said his
practical and cynical master; "the local newspaper will
have it all next day. A few hours' discomfort is worth
while if it ends the nonsense. We'll read and smoke, and
Mortimer shall tell us yarns about the sea." He went
with the driver into the house to superintend the arrangement of the room, the lights, the hampers of food, and
so forth, leaving the pair upon the lawn.

"Four hours isn't much, but it's something," whispered
Mortimer, alone with her for the first time since they
started. "It's simply ripping of you to have got me in.
You look divine to-night. You're the most wonderful
woman in the world." His blue eyes shone with the hungry
desire he mistook for love. He looked as if he had blown
in from the sea, for his skin was tanned and his light hair
bleached a little by the sun. He took her hand, drawing
her out of the slanting sunlight towards the rhododendrons.

"I didn't, you silly boy. It was John suggested your
coming." She released her hand with an affected effort.
"Besides, you overdid it—pretending you had a dance."

"You could have objected," he said eagerly, "and didn't.
Oh, you're too lovely, you're delicious!" He kissed her
suddenly with passion. There was a tiny struggle, in
which she yielded too easily, he thought.

"Harry, you're an idiot!" she cried breathlessly, when
he let her go. "I really don't know how you dare! And
John's your friend. Besides, you know"—she glanced
round quickly—"it isn't safe here." Her eyes shone happily, her cheeks were flaming. She looked what she was, a

pretty, young, lustful animal, false to ideals, true to selfish passion only. "Luckily," she added, "he trusts me too fully to think anything."

The young man, worship in his eyes, laughed gaily. "There's no harm in a kiss," he said. "You're a child to him, he never thinks of you as a woman. Anyhow, his head's full of ships and kings and scaling-wax," he comforted her, while respecting her sudden instinct which warned him not to touch her again, "and he never sees anything. Why, even at ten yards——"

From twenty yards away a big voice interrupted him, as John Burley came round a corner of the house and across the lawn towards them. The chauffeur, he announced, had left the hampers in the room on the first floor and gone back to the inn. "Let's take a walk round," he added, joining them, "and see the garden. Five minutes before sunset we'll go in and feed." He laughed. "We must do the thing faithfully, you know, mustn't we, Nancy? Dark to dark, remember. Come on, Mortimer" —he took the young man's arm—"a last look round before we go in and hang ourselves from adjoining hooks in the matron's room!" He reached out his free hand towards his wife.

"Oh, hush, John!" she said quickly. "I don't like— especially now the dusk is coming." She shivered, as though it were a genuine little shiver, pursing her lips deliciously as she did so; whereupon he drew her forcibly to him, saying he was sorry, and kissed her exactly where she had been kissed two minutes before, while young Mortimer looked on. "We'll take care of you between us," he said. Behind a broad back the pair exchanged a swift but meaning glance, for there was that in his tone which enjoined wariness, and perhaps after all he was not so blind as he appeared. They had their code, these two. "All's well," was signalled; "but another time be more careful!"

There still remained some minutes' sunlight before the huge red ball of fire would sink behind the wooded hills, and the trio, talking idly, a flutter of excitement in two hearts certainly, walked among the roses. It was a perfect evening, windless, perfumed, warm. Headless shadows preceded them gigantically across the lawn as they moved, and one side of the great building lay already dark; bats were flitting, moths darted to and fro above the azalea and rhododendron clumps. The talk turned chiefly on the uses of the mansion as a Convalescent Home, its probable running cost, suitable staff, and so forth.

"Come along," John Burley said presently, breaking off and turning abruptly, "we must be inside, actually inside, before the sun's gone. We must fulfil the conditions faithfully," he repeated, as though fond of the phrase. He was in earnest over everything in life, big or little, once he set his hand to it.

They entered, this incongruous trio of ghost-hunters, no one of them really intent upon the business in hand, and went slowly upstairs to the great room where the hampers lay. Already in the hall it was dark enough for three electric torches to flash usefully and help their steps as they moved with caution, lighting one corner after another. The air inside was chill and damp. "Like an unused museum," said Mortimer. "I can smell the specimens." They looked about them, sniffing. "That's humanity," declared his host, employer, friend, "with cement and whitewash to flavour it"; and all three laughed as Mrs. Burley said she wished they had picked some roses and brought them in. Her husband was again in front on the broad staircase, Mortimer just behind him, when she called out. "I don't like being last," she exclaimed. It's so black behind me in the hall. I'll come between you two," and the sailor took her outstretched hand, squeezing it, as he passed her up. "There's a figure, remember," she said hurriedly, turning to gain her husband's attention, as when she touched wood at home. "A figure is seen; that's part of the story. The figure of a man." She gave a tiny shiver of pleasurable, half-imagined alarm as she took his arm.

"I hope we shall see it," he mentioned prosaically.

"I hope we shan't," she replied with emphasis. "It's only seen before—something happens." Her husband said nothing, while Mortimer remarked facetiously that it would be a pity if they had their trouble for nothing. "Something can hardly happen to all three of us," he said lightly, as they entered a large room where the paperhangers had conveniently left a rough table of bare planks. Mrs. Burley, busy with her own thoughts, began to unpack the sandwiches and wine. Her husband strolled over to the window. He seemed restless.

"So this," his deep voice startled her, "is where one of us"—he looked round him—"is to——"

"John!" She stopped him sharply, with impatience. "Several times already I've begged you." Her voice rang rather shrill and querulous in the empty room, a new note in it. She was beginning to feel the atmosphere of the place, perhaps. On the sunny lawn it had not touched her, but now, with the fall of night, she was aware of it, as shadow called to shadow and the kingdom of darkness gathered power. Like a great whispering gallery, the whole house listened.

"Upon my word, Nancy," he said with contrition, as he came and sat down beside her, "I quite forgot again. Only I cannot take it seriously. It's so utterly unthinkable to me that a man——"

"But why evoke the idea at all?" she insisted in a lowered voice, that snapped despite its faintness. "Men, after all, don't do such things for nothing."

"We don't know everything in the universe, do we?" Mortimer put in, trying clumsily to support her. "All I know just now is that I'm famished and this veal and ham pie is delicious." He was very busy with his knife and fork. His foot rested lightly on her own beneath the table; he could not keep his eyes off her face; he was continually passing new edibles to her.

"No," agreed John Burley, "not everything. You're right there."

She kicked the younger man gently, flashing a warning with her eyes as well, while her husband, emptying his glass, his head thrown back, looked straight at them over the rim, apparently seeing nothing. They smoked their cigarettes round the table, Burley lighting a big cigar. "Tell us about the figure, Nancy?" he inquired. "At least there's no harm in that. It's new to me. I hadn't heard about a figure." And she did so willingly, turning her chair sideways from the dangerous, reckless feet. Mortimer could now no longer touch her. "I know very little," she confessed; "only what the paper said. It's a man. . . . And he changes."

"How changes?" asked her husband. "Clothes, you mean, or what?"

Mrs. Burley laughed, as though she was glad to laugh, Then she answered: "According to the story, he shows himself each time to the man——"

"The man who——?"

"Yes, yes, of course. He appears to the man who dies —as himself."

"H'm," grunted her husband, naturally puzzled. He stared at her.

"Each time the chap saw his own double"—Mortimer came this time usefully to the rescue—"before he did it."

Considerable explanation followed, involving much psychic jargon from Mrs. Burley, which fascinated and impressed the sailor, who thought her as wonderful as she was lovely, showing it in his eyes for all to see. John Burley's attention wandered. He moved over to the window, leaving them to finish the discussion between them; he took no part in it, made no comment even, merely listening idly and watching them with an air of absent-mindedness through the cloud of cigar smoke round his head. He moved from window to window, ensconcing himself in turn in each deep embrasure, examining the fastenings, measuring the thickness of the stonework with his handkerchief. He seemed restless, bored, obviously out of place in this ridiculous expedition. On his big massive face lay a quiet, resigned expression his wife had never seen before. She noticed it now as, the discussion ended, the pair tidied away the *débris* of dinner, lit the spirit lamp for coffee and laid out a supper which would be very welcome with the dawn. A draught passed through the room, making the papers flutter on the table. Mortimer turned down the smoking lamps with care.

"Wind's getting up a bit—from the south," observed Burley from his niche, closing one-half of the casement window as he said it. To do this, he turned his back a moment, fumbling for several seconds with the latch, while Mortimer, noting it, seized his sudden opportunity with the foolish abandon of his age and temperament. Neither he nor his victim perceived that, against the outside darkness, the interior of the room was plainly reflected in the window-pane. One reckless, the other terrified, they snatched the fearful joy, which might, after all, have been lengthened by another full half-minute, for the head they feared, followed by the shoulders, pushed through the side of the casement still open, and remained outside, taking in the night.

"A grand air," said his deep voice, as the head drew in again. "I'd like to be at sea a night like this." He left the casement open and came across the room towards them. "Now," he said cheerfully, arranging a seat for himself, "let's get comfortable for the night. Mortimer, we expect stories from you without ceasing, until dawn or the ghost arrives. Horrible stories of chains and headless men, remember. Make it a night we shan't forget in a hurry." He produced his gust of laughter.

They arranged their chairs, with other chairs to put their feet on, and Mortimer contrived a footstool by means

of a hamper for the smallest feet; the air grew thick with
tobacco smoke; eyes flashed and answered, watched perhaps as well; ears listened and perhaps grew wise; occasionally, as a window shook, they started and looked round;
there were sounds about the house from time to time, when
the entering wind, using broken or open windows, set loose
objects rattling.

But Mrs. Burley vetoed horrible stories with decision.
A big, empty mansion, lonely in the country, and even
with the comfort of John Burley and a lover in it, has
its atmosphere. Furnished rooms are far less ghostly.
This atmosphere now came creeping everywhere, through
spacious halls and sighing corridors, silent, invisible, but
all-pervading, John Burley alone impervious to it, unaware of its soft attack upon the nerves. It entered possibly with the summer night wind, but possibly it was
always there. . . . And Mrs. Burley looked often at her
husband, sitting near her at an angle; the light fell on
his fine strong face; she felt that, though apparently so
calm and quiet, he was really very restless; something
about him was a little different; she could not define it;
his mouth seemed set as with an effort; he looked, she
thought curiously to herself, patient and very dignified;
he was rather a dear after all. Why did she think the face
inscrutable? Her thoughts wandered vaguely, unease, discomfort among them somewhere, while the heated blood
—she had taken her share of wine—seethed in her.

Burley turned to the sailor for more stories. "Sea
and wind in them," he asked. "No horrors, remember!"
and Mortimer told a tale about the shortage of rooms at
a Welsh seaside place where spare rooms fetched fabulous
prices, and one man alone refused to let—a retired captain
of a South Seas trader, very poor, a bit crazy apparently.
He had two furnished rooms in his house worth twenty
guineas a week. The rooms faced south; he kept them full
of flowers; but he would not let. An explanation of his
unworldly obstinacy was not forthcoming until Mortimer—

they fished together—gained his confidence. "The South Wind lives in them," the old fellow told him. "I keep them free for her."

"For *her?*"

"It was on the South Wind my love came to me," said the other softly; "and it was on the South Wind that she left——"

It was an odd tale to tell in such company, but he told it well.

"Beautiful," thought Mrs. Burley. Aloud she said a quiet, "Thank you. By 'left,' I suppose he meant she died or ran away?"

John Burley looked up with a certain surprise. "We ask for a story," he said, "and you give us a poem." He laughed. "You're in love, Mortimer," he informed him, "and with my wife probably."

"Of course I am, sir," replied the young man gallantly. "A sailor's heart, you know," while the face of the woman turned pink, then white. She knew her husband more intimately than Mortimer did, and there was something in his tone, his eyes, his words, she did not like. Harry was an idiot to choose such a tale. An irritated annoyance stirred in her, close upon dislike. "Anyhow, it's better than horrors," she said hurriedly.

"Well," put in her husband, letting forth a minor gust of laughter, "it's possible, at any rate. Though one's as crazy as the other." His meaning was not wholly clear. "If a man really loved," he added in his blunt fashion, "and was tricked by her, I could almost conceive his——"

"Oh, don't preach, John, for Heaven's sake. You're so dull in the pulpit." But the interruption only served to emphasize the sentence which, otherwise, might have been passed over.

"Could conceive his finding life so worthless," persisted the other, "that——" He hesitated. "But there, now, I promised I wouldn't," he went on, laughing good-humouredly. Then, suddenly, as though in spite of himself, driven it seemed: "Still, under such conditions, he might show his contempt for human nature and for life by——"

It was a tiny stifled scream that stopped him this time.

"John, I hate, I loathe you, when you talk like that. And you've broken your word again." She was more than petulant; a nervous anger sounded in her voice. It was the way he had said it, looking from them towards the window, that made her quiver. She felt him suddenly as a man; she felt afraid of him.

Her husband made no reply; he rose and looked at his watch, leaning sideways towards the lamp, so that the expression of his face was shaded. "Two o'clock," he remarked. "I think I'll take a turn through the house. I may find a workman asleep or something. Anyhow, the light will soon come now." He laughed; the expression of his face, his tone of voice, relieved her momentarily. He went out. They heard his heavy tread echoing down the carpetless long corridor.

Mortimer began at once. "Did he mean anything?" he asked breathlessly. "He doesn't love you the least little bit, anyhow. He never did. I do. You're wasted on him. You belong to me." The words poured out. He covered her face with kisses. "Oh, I didn't mean *that*," he caught between the kisses.

The sailor released her, staring. "What then?" he whispered. "Do you think he saw us on the lawn?" He paused a moment, as she made no reply. The steps were audible in the distance still. "I know!" he exclaimed suddenly. "It's the blessed house he feels. That's what it is. He doesn't like it."

A wind sighed through the room, making the papers flutter; something rattled; and Mrs. Burley started. A loose end of rope swinging from the paperhanger's ladder caught her eye. She shivered slightly.

"He's different," she replied in a low voice, nestling very close again, "and so restless. Didn't you notice what he said just now—that under certain conditions he could

understand a man"—she hesitated—"doing it," she concluded, a sudden drop in her voice. "Harry," she looked
full into his eyes, "that's not like him. He didn't say
that for nothing."

"Nonsense! He's bored to tears, that's all. And the
house it getting on your nerves, too." He kissed her tenderly. Then, as she responded, he drew her nearer still
and held her passionately, mumbling incoherent words,
among which "nothing to be afraid of" was distinguishable. Meanwhile, the steps were coming nearer. She
pushed him away. "You must behave yourself. I insist.
You shall, Harry," then buried herself in his arms, her face
hidden against his neck—only to disentangle herself the
next instant and stand clear of him. "I hate you, Harry,"
she exclaimed sharply, a look of angry annoyance flashing across her face. "And I *hate* myself. Why do you
treat me——?" She broke off as the steps came closer,
patted her hair straight, and stalked over to the open
window.

"I believe after all you're only playing with me," he
said viciously. He stared in surprised disappointment,
watching her. "It's him you really love," he added jeal-
ously. He looked and spoke like a petulant spoilt boy.

She did not turn her head. "He's always been fair to
me, kind and generous. He never blames me for anything. Give me a cigarette and don't play the stage hero.
My nerves are on edge, to tell you the truth." Her voice
jarred harshly, and as he lit her cigarette he noticed that
her lips were trembling; his own hand trembled too. He
was still holding the match, standing beside her at the
window-sill, when the steps crossed the threshold and John
Burley came into the room. He went straight up to the
table and turned the lamp down. "It was smoking," he
remarked. "Didn't you see?"

"I'm sorry, sir," and Mortimer sprang forward, too
late to help him. "It was the draught as you pushed
the door open." The big man said, "Ah!" and drew a

chair over, facing them. "It's just *the* very house," he
told them. "I've been through every room on this floor.
It will make a splendid Home, with very little alteration,
too." He turned round in his creaking wicker chair and
looked up at his wife, who sat swinging her legs and
smoking in the window embrasure. "Lives will be saved
inside these old walls. It's a good investment," he went
on, talking rather to himself it seemed. "People will die
here, too——"

"Hark!" Mrs. Burley interrupted him. "That noise
—what is it?" A faint thudding sound in the corridor
or in the adjoining room was audible, making all three
look round quickly, listening for a repetition, which did
not come. The papers fluttered on the table, the lamps
smoked an instant.

"Wind," observed Burley calmly, "our little friend, the
South Wind. Something blown over again, that's all."
But, curiously, the three of them stood up. "I'll go and
see," he continued. "Doors and windows are all open
to let the paint dry." Yet he did not move; he stood
there watching a white moth that dashed round and round
the lamp, flopping heavily now and again upon the bare
deal table.

"Let me go, sir," put in Mortimer eagerly. He was
glad of the chance; for the first time he, too, felt uncomfortable. But there was another who, apparently,
suffered a discomfort greater than his own and was accordingly even more glad to get away. "I'll go," Mrs. Burley
announced, with decision. "I'd like to. I haven't been
out of this room since we came. I'm not an atom afraid."

It was strange that for a moment she did not make a
move either; it seemed as if she waited for something.
For perhaps fifteen seconds no one stirred or spoke. She
knew by the look in her lover's eyes that he had now
become aware of the slight, indefinite change in her husband's manner, and was alarmed by it. The fear in him
woke her contempt; she suddenly despised the youth, and

was conscious of a new, strange yearning towards her husband; against her worked nameless pressures, troubling her being. There was an alteration in the room, she thought; something had come in. The trio stood listening to the gentle wind outside, waiting for the sound to be repeated; two careless, passionate young lovers and a man stood waiting, listening, watching in that room; yet it seemed there were five persons altogether and not three, for two guilty consciences stood apart and separate from their owners. John Burley broke the silence.

"Yes, you go, Nancy. Nothing to be afraid of—there. It's only wind." He spoke as though he meant it.

Mortimer bit his lips. "I'll come with you," he said instantly. He was confused. "Let's all three go. I don't think we ought to be separated." But Mrs. Burley was already at the door. "I insist," she said, with a forced laugh. "I'll call if I'm frightened," while her husband, saying nothing, watched her from the table.

"Take this," said the sailor, flashing his electric torch as he went over to her. "Two are better than one." He saw her figure exquisitely silhouetted against the black corridor beyond; it was clear she wanted to go; any nervousness in her was mastered by a stronger emotion still; she was glad to be out of their presence for a bit. He had hoped to snatch a word of explanation in the corridor, but her manner stopped him. Something else stopped him, too.

"First door on the left," he called out, his voice echoing down the empty length. "That's the room where the noise came from. Shout if you want us."

He watched her moving away, the light held steadily in front of her, but she made no answer, and he turned back to see John Burley lighting his cigar at the lamp chimney, his face thrust forward as he did so. He stood a second, watching him, as the lips sucked hard at the cigar to make it draw; the strength of the features was emphasized to sternness. He had meant to stand by the door and listen for the least sound from the adjoining room, but now found his whole attention focused on the face above the lamp. In that minute he realized that Burley had wished—had meant—his wife to go. In that minute also he forgot his love, his shameless, selfish little mistress, his worthless, caddish little self. For John Burley looked up. He straightened slowly, puffing hard and quickly to make sure his cigar was lit, and faced him. Mortimer moved forward into the room, self-conscious, embarrassed, cold.

"Of course it was only wind," he said lightly, his one desire being to fill the interval while they were alone with commonplaces. He did not wish the other to speak. "Dawn wind, probably." He glanced at his wrist-watch. "It's half-past two already, and the sun gets up at a quarter to four. It's light by now, I expect. The shortest night is never quite dark." He rambled on confusedly, for the other's steady, silent stare embarrassed him. A faint sound of Mrs. Burley moving in the next room made him stop a moment. He turned instinctively to the door, eager for an excuse to go.

"That's nothing," said Burley, speaking at last and in a firm quiet voice. "Only my wife, glad to be alone— my young and pretty wife. She's all right. I know her better than you do. Come in and shut the door."

Mortimer obeyed. He closed the door and came close to the table, facing the other, who at once continued.

"If I thought," he said, in that quiet deep voice, "that you two were serious"—he uttered his words very slowly, with emphasis, with intense severity—"do you know what I should do? I will tell you, Mortimer. I should like one of us two—you or myself—to remain in this house, dead."

His teeth gripped his cigar tightly; his hands were clenched; he went on through a half-closed mouth. His eyes blazed steadily.

"I trust her so absolutely—understand me?—that my

belief in women, in human beings, would go.   And with
it the desire to live.   Understand me?"

Each word to the young careless fool was a blow in
the face, yet it was the softest blow, the flash of a big
deep heart, that hurt the most.   A dozen answers—denial,
explanation, confession, taking all guilt upon himself—
crowded his mind, only to be dismissed.   He stood motionless and silent, staring hard into the other's eyes.   No
word passed his lips; there was no time in any case.   It
was in this position that Mrs. Burley, entering at that
moment, found them.   She saw her husband's face; the
other man stood with his back to her.   She came in with
a little nervous laugh.   "A bell-rope swinging in the wind
and hitting a sheet of metal before the fireplace," she
informed them.   And all three laughed together then,
though each laugh had a different sound.   "But I hate
this house," she added.   "I wish we had never come."

"The moment there's light in the sky," remarked her
husband quietly, "we can leave.   That's the contract; let's
see it through.   Another half-hour will do it.   Sit down,
Nancy, and have a bite of something."   He got up and
placed a chair for her.   "I think I'll take another look
round."   He moved slowly to the door.   "I may go out
on to the lawn a bit and see what the sky is doing."

It did not take half a minute to say the words, yet
to Mortimer it seemed as though the voice would never end.
His mind was confused and troubled.   He loathed himself, he loathed the woman through whom he had got into
this awkward mess.

The situation had suddenly become extremely painful;
he had never imagined such a thing; the man he had
thought blind had after all seen everything—known it all
along, watched them, waited.   And the woman, he was
now certain, loved her husband; she had fooled him, Mortimer, all along, amusing herself.

"I'll come with you, sir.   Do let me," he said suddenly.
Mrs. Burley stood pale and uncertain between them.   She

looked scared. What has happened, she was clearly wondering.

"No, no, Harry"—he called him "Harry" for the first time—"I'll be back in five minutes at most. My wife mustn't be alone either." And he went out.

The young man waited till the footsteps sounded some distance down the corridor, then turned, but he did not move forward; for the first time he let pass unused what he called "an opportunity." His passion had left him; his love, as he once thought it, was gone. He looked at the pretty woman near him, wondering blankly what he had ever seen there to attract him so wildly. He wished to Heaven he was out of it all. He wished he were dead. John Burley's words suddenly appalled him.

One thing he saw plainly—she was frightened. This opened his lips.

"What's the matter?" he asked, and his hushed voice shirked the familiar Christian name. "Did you see anything?" He nodded his head in the direction of the adjoining room. It was the sound of his own voice addressing her coldly that made him abruptly see himself as he really was, but it was her reply, honestly given, in a faint even voice, that told him she saw her own self too with similar clarity. God, he thought, how revealing a tone, a single word can be!

"I saw—nothing. Only I feel uneasy—dear." That "dear" was a call for help.

"Look here," he cried, so loud that she held up a warning finger, "I'm—I've been a damned fool, a cad! I'm most frightfully ashamed. I'll do anything—*anything* to get it right." He felt cold, naked, his worthlessness laid bare; she felt, he knew, the same. Each revolted suddenly from the other. Yet he knew not quite how or wherefore this great change had thus abruptly come about, especially on her side. He felt that a bigger, deeper emotion than he could understand was working on them, making mere physical relationships seem empty, trivial, cheap and vulgar. His cold increased in face of this utter ignorance.

"Uneasy?" he repeated, perhaps hardly knowing exactly why he said it. "Good Lord, but he can take care of himself——"

"Oh, *he* is a man," she interrupted; "yes."

Steps were heard, firm, heavy steps, coming back along the corridor. It seemed to Mortimer that he had listened to this sound of steps all night, and would listen to them till he died. He crossed to the lamp and lit a cigarette, carefully this time, turning the wick down afterwards. Mrs. Burley also rose, moving over towards the door, away from him. They listened a moment to these firm and heavy steps, the tread of a man, John Burley. A man . . . and a philanderer, flashed across Mortimer's brain like fire, contrasting the two with fierce contempt for himself. The tread became less audible. There was distance in it. It had turned in somewhere.

"There!" she exclaimed in a hushed tone. "He's gone in."

"Nonsense! It passed us. He's going out on to the lawn."

The pair listened breathlessly for a moment, when the sound of steps came distinctly from the adjoining room, walking across the boards, apparently towards the window.

"There!" she repeated. "He did go in." Silence of perhaps a minute followed, in which they heard each other's breathing. "I don't like his being alone—in there," Mrs. Burley said in a thin faltering voice, and moved as though to go out. Her hand was already on the knob of the door, when Mortimer stopped her with a violent gesture.

"Don't! For God's sake, don't!" he cried, before she could turn it. He darted forward. As he laid a hand upon her arm a thud was audible through the wall. It was a heavy sound, and this time there was no wind to cause it.

"It's only that loose swinging thing," he whispered thickly, a dreadful confusion blotting out clear thought and speech.

"There was no loose swaying thing at all," she said in a failing voice, then reeled and swayed against him. "I invented that. There was nothing." As he caught her, staring helplessly, it seemed to him that a face with lifted lids rushed up at him. He saw two terrified eyes in a patch of ghastly white. Her whisper followed, as she sank into his arms. "It's John. He's——"

At which instant, with terror at its climax, the sound of steps suddenly became audible once more—the firm and heavy tread of John Burley coming out again into the corridor. Such was their amazement and relief that they neither moved nor spoke. The steps drew nearer. The pair seemed petrified; Mortimer did not remove his arms, nor did Mrs. Burley attempt to release herself. They stared at the door and waited. It was pushed wider the next second, and John Burley stood beside them. He was so close he almost touched them—there in each other's arms.

"Jack, dear!" cried his wife, with a searching tenderness that made her voice seem strange.

He gazed a second at each in turn. "I'm going out on to the lawn for a moment," he said quietly. There was no expression on his face; he did not smile, he did not frown; he showed no feeling, no emotion—just looked into their eyes, and then withdrew round the edge of the door before either could utter a word in answer. The door swung to behind him. He was gone.

"He's going to the lawn. He said so." It was Mortimer speaking, but his voice shook and stammered. Mrs. Burley had released herself. She stood now by the table, silent, gazing with fixed eyes at nothing, her lips parted, her expression vacant. Again she was aware of an alteration in the room; something had gone out. . . . He watched her a second, uncertain what to say or do. It was the face of a drowned person, occurred to him. Something intangible, yet almost visible stood between them in that narrow space. Something had ended, there before his eyes, definitely ended. The barrier between them rose higher, denser. Through this barrier her words came to him with an odd whispering remoteness.

"Harry. . . . You saw? You noticed?"

"What d'you mean?" he said gruffly. He tried to feel angry, contemptuous, but his breath caught absurdly.

"Harry—he was different. The eyes, the hair, the"—her face grew like death—"the twist in his face——"

"What on earth are you saying? Pull yourself together." He saw that she was trembling down the whole length of her body, as she leaned against the table for support. His own legs shook. He stared hard at her.

"Altered, Harry . . . altered." Her horrified whisper came at him like a knife. For it was true. He, too, had noticed something about the husband's appearance that was not quite normal. Yet, even while they talked, they heard him going down the carpetless stairs; the sounds ceased as he crossed the hall; then came the noise of the front door hanging, the reverberation even shaking the room a little where they stood.

Mortimer went over to her side. He walked unevenly.

"My dear! For God's sake—this is sheer nonsense. Don't let yourself go like this. I'll put it straight with him—it's all my fault." He saw by her face that she did not understand his words; he was saying the wrong thing altogether; her mind was utterly elsewhere. "He's all right," he went on hurriedly. "He's out on the lawn now——"

He broke off at the sight of her. The horror that fastened on her brain plastered her face with deathly whiteness.

"That was not John at all!" she cried, a wail of misery and terror in her voice. She rushed to the window and he followed. To his immense relief a figure moving below was plainly visible. It was John Burley. They saw him in the faint grey of the dawn, as he crossed the lawn, going away from the house. He disappeared.

"There you are! See?" whispered Mortimer reassuringly. "He'll be back in——" when a sound in the adjoining room, heavier, louder than before, cut appallingly across his words, and Mrs. Burley, with that wailing scream, fell back into his arms. He caught her only just in time, for she stiffened into ice, daft with the uncomprehended terror of it all, and helpless as a child.

"Darling, my darling—oh, God!" He bent, kissing her face wildly. He was utterly distraught.

"Harry! Jack—oh, oh!" she wailed in her anguish. "It took on his likeness. It deceived us . . . to give him time. He's done it."

She sat up suddenly. "Go," she said, pointing to the room beyond, then sank fainting, a dead weight in his arms.

He carried her unconscious body to a chair, then entering the adjoining room he flashed his torch upon the body of her husband hanging from a bracket in the wall. He cut it down five minutes too late.

X

THE MAN WHO FOUND OUT
(A NIGHTMARE)

1

PROFESSOR MARK EBOR, the scientist, led a double life, and the only persons who knew it were his assistant, Dr. Laidlaw, and his publishers. But a double life need not always be a bad one, and, as Dr. Laidlaw and the gratified publishers well knew, the parallel lives of this particular man were equally good, and indefinitely produced would certainly have ended in a heaven somewhere that can suitably contain such strangely opposite characteristics as his remarkable personality combined.

For Mark Ebor, F.R.S., etc., etc., was that unique combination hardly ever met with in actual life, a man of science and a mystic.

As the first, his name stood in the gallery of the great, and as the second—but there came the mystery! For under the pseudonym of "Pilgrim" (the author of that brilliant series of books that appealed to so many), his identity was as well concealed as that of the anonymous writer of the weather reports in a daily newspaper. Thousands read the sanguine, optimistic, stimulating little books that issued annually from the pen of "Pilgrim," and thousands bore their daily burdens better for having read; while the Press generally agreed that the author, besides being an incorrigible enthusiast and optimist, was also—a woman; but no one ever succeeded in penetrating the veil of anonymity and discovering that "Pilgrim" and the biologist were one and the same person.

Mark Ebor, as Dr. Laidlaw knew him in his laboratory, was one man; but Mark Ebor, as he sometimes saw him after work was over, with rapt eyes and ecstatic face, discussing the possibilities of "union with God" and the future of the human race, was quite another.

"I have always held, as you know," he was saying one evening as he sat in the little study beyond the laboratory with his assistant and intimate, "that Vision should play a large part in the life of the awakened man—not to be regarded as infallible, of course, but to be observed and made use of as a guide-post to possibilities——"

"I am aware of your peculiar views, sir," the young doctor put in deferentially, yet with a certain impatience.

"For Visions come from a region of the consciousness where observation and experiment are out of the question," pursued the other with enthusiasm, not noticing the interruption, "and, while they should be checked by reason afterwards, they should not be laughed at or ignored. All inspiration, I hold, is of the nature of interior Vision, and all our best knowledge has come—such is my confirmed belief—as a sudden revelation to the brain prepared to receive it——"

"Prepared by hard work first, by concentration, by the closest possible study of ordinary phenomena," Dr. Laidlaw allowed himself to observe.

"Perhaps," sighed the other; "but by a process, none the less, of spiritual illumination. The best match in the world will not light a candle unless the wick be first suitably prepared."

It was Laidlaw's turn to sigh. He knew so well the impossibility of arguing with his chief when he was in the regions of the mystic, but at the same time the respect he felt for his tremendous attainments was so sincere that he always listened with attention and deference, wondering how far the great man would go and to what end this curious combination of logic and "illumination" would eventually lead him.

"Only last night," continued the elder man, a sort of light coming into his rugged features, "the vision came to me again—the one that has haunted me at intervals ever since my youth, and that will not be denied."

Dr. Laidlaw fidgeted in his chair.

"About the Tablets of the Gods, you mean—and that they lie somewhere hidden in the sands," he said patiently. A sudden gleam of interest came into his face as he turned to catch the professor's reply.

"And that I am to be the one to find them, to decipher them, and to give the great knowledge to the world——"

"Who will not believe," laughed Laidlaw shortly, yet interested in spite of his thinly-veiled contempt.

"Because even the keenest minds, in the right sense of the word, are hopelessly—unscientific," replied the other gently, his face positively aglow with the memory of his vision. "Yet what is more likely," he continued after a moment's pause, peering into space with rapt eyes that saw things too wonderful for exact language to describe, "than that there should have been given to man in the first ages of the world some record of the purpose and problem that had been set him to solve? In a word," he cried, fixing his shining eyes upon the face of his perplexed assistant, "that God's messengers in the far-off ages should have given to His creatures some full statement of the secret of the world, of the secret of the soul, of the meaning of life and death—the explanation of our being here, and to what great end we are destined in the ultimate fullness of things?"

Dr. Laidlaw sat speechless. These outbursts of mystical enthusiasm he had witnessed before. With any other man he would not have listened to a single sentence, but to Professor Ebor, man of knowledge and profound investigator, he listened with respect, because he regarded this condition as temporary and pathological, and in some sense a reaction from the intense strain of the prolonged mental concentration of many days.

He smiled, with something between sympathy and resignation as he met the other's rapt gaze.

"But you have said, sir, at other times, that you consider the ultimate secrets to be screened from all possible——"

"The *ultimate* secrets, yes," came the unperturbed reply; "but that there lies buried somewhere an indestructible record of the secret meaning of life, originally known to men in the days of their pristine innocence, I am convinced. And, by this strange vision so often vouchsafed to me, I am equally sure that one day it shall be given to me to announce to a weary world this glorious and terrific message."

And he continued at great length and in glowing language to describe the species of vivid dream that had come to him at intervals since earliest childhood, showing in detail how he discovered these very Tablets of the Gods, and proclaimed their splendid contents—whose precise nature was always, however, withheld from him in the vision—to a patient and suffering humanity.

"The *Scrutator,* sir, well described 'Pilgrim' as the Apostle of Hope," said the young doctor gently, when he had finished; "and now, if that reviewer could hear you speak and realize from what strange depths comes your simple faith——"

The professor held up his hand, and the smile of a little child broke over his face like sunshine in the morning.

"Half the good my books do would be instantly destroyed," he said saidly; "they would say that I wrote with my tongue in my cheek. But wait," he added significantly; "wait till I find these Tablets of the Gods! Wait till I hold the solutions of the old world-problems in my hands! Wait till the light of this new revelation breaks upon confused humanity, and it wakes to find its bravest hopes justified! Ah, then, my dear Laidlaw——"

He broke off suddenly; but the doctor, cleverly guessing the thought in his mind, caught him up immediately.

"Perhaps this very summer," he said, trying hard to make the suggestion keep pace with honesty; "in your explorations in Assyria—your digging in the remote civilization of what was once Chaldea, you may find—what you dream of——"

The professor held up his hand, and the smile of a fine old face.

"Perhaps," he murmured softly, "perhaps!"

And the young doctor, thanking the gods of science that his leader's aberrations were of so harmless a character, went home strong in the certitude of his knowledge of externals, proud that he was able to refer his visions to self-suggestion, and wondering complaisantly whether in his old age he might not after all suffer himself from visitations of the very kind that afflicted his respected chief.

And as he got into bed and thought again of his master's rugged face, and finely shaped head, and the deep lines traced by years of work and self-discipline, he turned over on his pillow and fell asleep with a sigh that was half of wonder, half of regret.

2

It was in February, nine months later, when Dr. Laidlaw made his way to Charing Cross to meet his chief after his long absence of travel and exploration. The vision about the so-called Tablets of the Gods had meanwhile passed almost entirely from his memory.

There were few people in the train, for the stream of traffic was now running the other way, and he had no difficulty in finding the man he had come to meet. The shock of white hair beneath the low-crowned felt hat was alone enough to distinguish him by easily.

"Here I am at last!" exclaimed the professor, somewhat wearily, clasping his friend's hand as he listened to the young doctor's warm greetings and questions. "Here I am—a little older, and *much* dirtier than when you last saw me!" He glanced down laughingly at his travel-stained garments.

"And *much* wiser," said Laidlaw, with a smile, as he bustled about the platform for porters and gave his chief the latest scientific news.

At last they came down to practical considerations.

"And your luggage—where is that? You must have tons of it, I suppose?" said Laidlaw.

"Hardly anything," Professor Ebor answered. "Nothing, in fact, but what you see."

"Nothing but this hand-bag?" laughed the other, thinking he was joking.

"And a small portmanteau in the van," was the quiet reply. "I have no other luggage."

"You have no other luggage?" repeated Laidlaw, turning sharply to see if he were in earnest.

"Why should I need more?" the professor added simply.

Something in the man's face, or voice, or manner—the doctor hardly knew which—suddenly struck him as strange. There was a change in him, a change so profound—so little on the surface, that is—that at first he had not become aware of it. For a moment it was as though an utterly alien personality stood before him in that noisy, bustling throng. Here, in all the homely, friendly turmoil of a Charing Cross crowd, a curious feeling of cold passed over his heart, touching his life with icy finger, so that he actually trembled and felt afraid.

He looked up quickly at his friend, his mind working with startled and unwelcome thoughts.

"Only this?" he repeated, indicating the bag. "But where's all the stuff you went away with, And—have you brought nothing home—no treasures?"

"This is all I have," the other said briefly. The pale smile that went with the words caused the doctor a second indescribable sensation of uneasiness. Something was very wrong, something was very queer; he wondered now that he had not noticed it sooner.

"The rest follows, of course, by slow freight," he added tactfully, and as naturally as possible. "But come, sir, you must be tired and in want of food after your long journey. I'll get a taxi at once, and we can see about the other luggage afterwards."

It seemed to him he hardly knew quite what he was saying; the change in his friend had come upon him so suddenly and now grew upon him more and more distressingly. Yet he could not make out exactly in what it consisted. A terrible suspicion began to take shape in his mind, troubling him dreadfully.

"I am neither very tired, nor in need of food, thank you," the professor said quietly. "And this is all I have. There is no luggage to follow. I have brought home nothing—nothing but what you see."

His words conveyed finality. They got into a taxi, tipped the porter, who had been staring in amazement at the venerable figure of the scientist, and were conveyed slowly and noisily to the house in the north of London where the laboratory was, the scene of their labours of years.

And the whole way Professor Ebor uttered no word, nor did Dr. Laidlaw find the courage to ask a single question.

It was only late that night, before he took his departure, as the two men were standing before the fire in the study—that study where they had discussed so many problems of vital and absorbing interest—that Dr. Laidlaw at last found strength to come to the point with direct questions. The professor had been giving him a superficial and desultory account of his travels, of his journeys by camel, of his encampments among the mountains and in the desert, and of his explorations among the buried temples, and, deeper, into the waste of the pre-historic sands, when suddenly the doctor came to the desired point with a kind of nervous rush, almost like a frightened boy.

"And you found——" he began stammering, looking hard at the other's dreadfully altered face, from which every line of hope and cheerfulness seemed to have been obliterated as a sponge wipes markings from a slate—"you found——"

"I found," replied the other, in a solemn voice, and it was the voice of the mystic rather than the man of science—"I found what I went to seek. The vision never once failed me. It led me straight to the place like a star in the heavens. I found—the Tablets of the Gods."

Dr. Laidlaw caught his breath, and steadied himself on the back of a chair. The words fell like particles of ice upon his heart. For the first time the professor had uttered the well-known phrase without the glow of light and wonder in his face that always accompanied it.

"You have—brought them?" he faltered.

"I have brought them home," said the other, in a voice with a ring like iron; "and I have—deciphered them."

Profound despair, the bloom of outer darkness, the dead sound of a hopeless soul freezing in the utter cold of space seemed to fill in the pauses between the brief sentences. A silence followed, during which Dr. Laidlaw saw nothing but the white face before him alternately fade and return. And it was like the face of a dead man.

"They are, alas, indestructible," he heard the voice continue, with its even, metallic ring.

"Indestructible," Laidlaw repeated mechanically, hardly knowing what he was saying.

Again a silence of several minutes passed, during which, with a creeping cold about his heart, he stood and stared into the eyes of the man he had known and loved so long—aye, and worshipped, too; the man who had first opened his own eyes when they were blind, and had led him to the gates of knowledge, and no little distance along the difficult path beyond; the man who, in another direction, had passed on the strength of his faith into the hearts of thousands by his books.

"I may see them?" he asked at last, in a low voice he hardly recognized as his own. "You will let me know—their message?"

Professor Ebor kept his eyes fixedly upon his assistant's face as he answered, with a smile that was more like the grin of death than a living human smile.

"When I am gone," he whispered; "when I have passed away. Then you shall find them and read the translation I have made. And then, too, in your turn, you must try, with the latest resources of science at your disposal to aid you, to compass their utter destruction." He paused a moment, and his face grew pale as the face of a corpse. "Until that time," he added presently, without looking up, "I must ask you not to refer to the subject again—and to keep my confidence meanwhile—*ab—so—lute—ly.*"

3

A year passed slowly by, and at the end of it Dr. Laidlaw had found it necessary to sever his working connexion with his friend and one-time leader. Professor Ebor was no longer the same man. The light had gone out of his life; the laboratory was closed; he no longer put pen to paper or applied his mind to a single problem. In the short space of a few months he had passed from a hale and hearty man of late middle life to the condition of old age—a man collapsed and on the edge of dissolution. Death, it was plain, lay waiting for him in the shadows of any day—and he knew it.

To describe faithfully the nature of this profound alteration in his character and temperament is not easy, but Dr. Laidlaw summed it up to himself in three words: *Loss of Hope.* The splendid mental powers remained indeed undimmed, but the incentive to use them—to use them for the help of others—had gone. The character still held

to its fine and unselfish habits of years, but the far goal
to which they had been the leading strings had faded away.
The desire for knowledge—knowledge for its own sake—
had died, and the passionate hope which hitherto had animated with tireless energy the heart and brain of this
splendidly equipped intellect had suffered total eclipse.
The central fires had gone out. Nothing was worth doing,
thinking, working for. There *was* nothing to work for
any longer!

The professor's first step was to recall as many of his
books as possible; his second to close his laboratory and
stop all research. He gave no explanation, he invited no
questions. His whole personality crumbled away, so to
speak, till his daily life became a mere mechanical process
of clothing the body, feeding the body, keeping it in good
health so as to avoid physical discomfort, and, above all,
doing nothing that could interfere with sleep. The professor did everything he could to lengthen the hours of
sleep, and therefore of forgetfulness.

It was all clear enough to Dr. Laidlaw. A weaker man,
he knew, would have sought to lose himself in one form
or another of sensual indulgence—sleeping-draughts, drink,
the first pleasures that came to hand. Self-destruction
would have been the method of a little bolder type; and
deliberate evil-doing, poisoning with his awful knowledge
all he could, the means of still another kind of man. Mark
Ebor was none of these. He held himself under fine control, facing silently and without complaint the terrible
facts he honestly believed himself to have been unfortunate
enough to discover. Even to his intimate friend and assistant, Dr. Laidlaw, he vouchsafed no word of true explanation or lament. He went straight forward to the end,
knowing well that the end was not very far away.

And death came very quietly one day to him, as he
was sitting in the arm-chair of the study, directly facing
the doors of the laboratory—the doors that no longer
opened. Dr. Laidlaw, by happy chance, was with him at

the time, and just able to reach his side in response to the sudden painful efforts for breath; just in time, too, to catch the murmured words that fell from the pallid lips like a message from the other side of the grave.

"Read them, if you must; and, if you can—destroy. But"—his voice sank so low that Dr. Laidlaw only just caught the dying syllables—"but—never, never—give them to the world."

And like a grey bundle of dust loosely gathered up in an old garment the professor sank back into his chair and expired.

But this was only the death of the body. His spirit had died two years before.

4

The estate of the dead man was small and uncomplicated, and Dr. Laidlaw, as sole executor and residuary legatee, had no difficulty in settling it up. A month after the funeral he was sitting alone in his upstairs library, the last sad duties completed, and his mind full of poignant memories and regrets for the loss of a friend he had revered and loved, and to whom his debt was so incalculably great. The last two years, indeed, had been for him terrible. To watch the swift decay of the greatest combination of heart and brain he had ever known, and to realize he was powerless to help, was a source of profound grief to him that would remain to the end of his days.

At the same time an insatiable curiosity possessed him. The study of dementia was, of course, outside his special province as a specialist, but he knew enough of it to understand how small a matter might be the actual cause of how great an illusion, and he had been devoured from the very beginning by a ceaseless and increasing anxiety to know what the professor had found in the sands of "Chaldea," what these precious Tablets of the Gods might be, and particularly—for this was the real cause that had sapped the man's sanity and hope—what the inscription was that he had believed to have deciphered thereon.

The curious feature of it all to his own mind was, that whereas his friend had dreamed of finding a message of glorious hope and comfort, he had apparently found (so far as he had found anything intelligible at all, and not invented the whole thing in his dementia) that the secret of the world, and the meaning of life and death, was of so terrible a nature that it robbed the heart of courage and the soul of hope. What, then, could be the contents of the little brown parcel the professor had bequeathed to him with his pregnant dying sentences?

Actually his hand was trembling as he turned to the writing-table and began slowly to unfasten a small old-fashioned desk on which the small gilt initials "M.E." stood forth as a melancholy memento. He put the key into the lock and half turned it. Then, suddenly, he stopped and looked about him. Was that a sound at the back of the room? It was just as though someone had laughed and then tried to smother the laugh with a cough. A slight shiver ran over him as he stood listening.

"This is absurd," he said aloud; "too absurd for belief—that I should be so nervous! It's the effect of curiosity unduly prolonged." He smiled a little sadly and his eyes wandered to the blue summer sky and the plane trees swaying in the wind below his window. "It's the reaction," he continued. "The curiosity of two years to be quenched in a single moment! The nervous tension, of course, must be considerable."

He turned back to the brown desk and opened it without further delay. His hand was firm now, and he took out the paper parcel that lay inside without a tremor. It was heavy. A moment later there lay on the table before him a couple of weather-worn plaques of grey stone—they looked like stone, although they felt like metal—on which he saw markings of a curious character that might have been the mere tracings of natural forces through the ages,

or, equally well, the half-obliterated hieroglyphics cut upon
their surface in past centuries by the more or less untutored
hand of a common scribe.

He lifted each stone in turn and examined it carefully. It seemed to him that a faint glow of heat passed
from the substance into his skin, and he put them down
again suddenly, as with a gesture of uneasiness.

"A very clever, or a very imaginative man," he said to
himself, "who could squeeze the secrets of life and death
from such broken lines as those!"

Then he turned to a yellow envelope lying beside them
in the desk, with the single word on the outside in the
writing of the professor—the word *Translation*.

"Now," he thought, taking it up with a sudden violence to conceal his nervousness, "now for the great solution. Now to learn the meaning of the worlds, and why
mankind was made, and why discipline is worth while, and
sacrifice and pain the true law of advancement."

There was the shadow of a sneer in his voice, and yet
something in him shivered at the same time. He held the
envelope as though weighing it in his hand, his mind pon-
dering many things. Then curiosity won the day, and he
suddenly tore it open with the gesture of an actor who
tears open a letter on the stage, knowing there is no real
writing inside at all.

A page of finely written script in the late scientist's
handwriting lay before him. He read it through from
beginning to end, missing no word, uttering each syllable
distinctly under his breath as he read.

The pallor of his face grew ghastly as he neared the
end. He began to shake all over as with ague. His breath
came heavily in gasps. He still gripped the sheet of
paper, however, and deliberately, as by an intense effort
of will, read it through a second time from beginning to
end. And this time, as the last syllable dropped from
his lips, the whole face of the man flamed with a sudden
and terrible anger. His skin became deep, deep red, and

he clenched his teeth. With all the strength of his vigorous soul he was struggling to keep control of himself.

For perhaps five minutes he stood there beside the table without stirring a muscle. He might have been carved out of stone. His eyes were shut, and only the heaving of the chest betrayed the fact that he was a living being. Then, with a strange quietness, he lit a match and applied it to the sheet of paper he held in his hand. The ashes fell slowly about him, piece by piece, and he blew them from the window-sill into the air, his eyes following them as they floated away on the summer wind that breathed so warmly over the world.

He turned back slowly into the room. Although his actions and movements were absolutely steady and controlled, it was clear that he was on the edge of violent action. A hurricane might burst upon the still room any moment. His muscles were tense and rigid. Then, suddenly, he whitened, collapsed, and sank backwards into a chair, like a tumbled bundle of inert matter. He had fainted.

In less than half an hour he recovered consciousness and sat up. As before, he made no sound. Not a syllable passed his lips. He rose quietly and looked about the room.

Then he did a curious thing.

Taking a heavy stick from the rack in the corner he approached the mantlepiece, and with a heavy shattering blow he smashed the clock to pieces. The glass fell in shivering atoms.

"Cease your lying voice for ever," he said, in a curiously still, even tone. "There is no such thing as *time!*"

He took the watch from his pocket, swung it round several times by the long gold chain, smashed it into smithereens against the wall with a single blow, and then walked into his laboratory next door, and hung its broken body on the bones of the skeleton in the corner of the room.

"Let one damned mockery hang upon another," he

said smiling oddly. "Delusions, both of you, and cruel as false !"

He slowly moved back to the front room. He stopped opposite the bookcase where stood in a row the "Scriptures of the World," choicely bound and exquisitely printed, the late professor's most treasured possession, and next to them several books signed "Pilgrim."

One by one he took them from the shelf and hurled them through the open window.

"A devil's dreams ! A devil's foolish dreams !" he cried, with a vicious laugh.

Presently he stopped from sheer exhaustion. He turned his eyes slowly to the wall opposite, where hung a weird array of Eastern swords and daggers, scimitars and spears, the collections of many journeys. He crossed the room and ran his finger along the edge. His mind seemed to waver.

"No," he muttered presently; "not that way. There are easier and better ways than that."

He took his hat and passed downstairs into the street.

5

It was five o'clock, and the June sun lay hot upon the pavement. He felt the metal door-knob burn the palm of his hand.

"Ah, Laidlaw, this is well met," cried a voice at his elbow; "I was in the act of coming to see you. I've a case that will interest you, and besides, I remembered that you flavoured your tea with orange leaves !—and I admit——"

It was Alexis Stephen, the great hypnotic doctor.

"I've had no tea to-day," Laidlaw said, in a dazed manner, after staring for a moment as though the other had struck him in the face. A new idea had entered his mind.

"What's the matter ?" asked Dr. Stephen quickly. "Something's wrong with you. It's this sudden heat, or overwork. Come, man, let's go inside."

A sudden light broke upon the face of the younger man, the light of a heaven-sent inspiration. He looked into his friend's face, and told a direct lie.

"Odd," he said, "I myself was just coming to see you. I have something of great importance to test your confidence with. But in *your* house, please," as Stephen urged him towards his own door—"in your house. It's only round the corner, and I—I cannot go back there—to my rooms—till I have told you."

"I'm your patient—for the moment," he added stammeringly as soon as they were seated in the privacy of the hypnotist's sanctum, "and I want—er——"

"My dear Laidlaw," interrupted the other, in that soothing voice of command which had suggested to many a suffering soul that the cure for its pain lay in the powers of its own reawakened will, "I am always at your service, as you know. You have only to tell me what I can do for you, and I will do it." He showed every desire to help him out. His manner was indescribably tactful and direct.

Dr. Laidlaw looked up into his face.

"I surrender my will to you," he said, already calmed by the other's healing presence, "and I want you to treat me hypnotically—and at once. I want you to suggest to me"—his voice became very tense—"that I shall forget—forget till I die—everything that has occurred to me during the last two hours; till I die, mind," he added, with solemn emphasis, "till I die."

He floundered and stammered like a frightened boy. Alexis Stephen looked at him fixedly without speaking.

"And further," Laidlaw continued, "I want you to ask me no questions. I wish to forget for ever something I have recently discovered—something so terrible and yet so obvious that I can hardly understand why it is not patent to every mind in the world—for I have had a moment of absolute *clear vision*—of merciless clairvoyance. But I

want no one else in the whole world to know what it is—
least of all, old friend, yourself."

He talked in utter confusion, and hardly knew what
he was saying. But the pain on his face and the anguish
in his voice were an instant passport to the other's heart.

"Nothing is easier," replied Dr. Stephen, after a hesitation so slight that the other probably did not even notice
it. "Come into my other room where we shall not be disturbed. I can heal you. Your memory of the last two
hours shall be wiped out as though it had never been.
You can trust me absolutely."

"I know I can," Laidlaw said simply, as he followed
him in.

6

An hour later they passed back into the front room
again. The sun was already behind the houses opposite,
and the shadows began to gather.

"I went off easily?" Laidlaw asked.

"You were a little obstinate at first. But though you
came in like a lion, you went out like a lamb. I let you
sleep a bit afterwards.

Dr. Stephen kept his eyes rather steadily upon his
friend's face.

"What were you doing by the fire before you came
here?" he asked, pausing, in a casual tone, as he lit a
cigarette and handed the case to his patient.

"I? Let me see. Oh, I know; I was worrying my
way through poor old Ebor's papers and things. I'm his
executor, you know. Then I got weary and came out for
a whiff of air." He spoke lightly and with perfect natural-
ness. Obviously he was telling the truth. "I prefer specimens to papers," he laughed cheerily.

"I know, I know," said Dr. Stephen, holding a lighted
match for the cigarette. His face wore an expression of
content. The experiment had been a complete success.

The memory of the last two hours was wiped out utterly.
Laidlaw was already chatting gaily and easily about a
dozen other things that interested him. Together they
went out into the street, and at his door Dr. Stephen left
him with a joke and a wry face that made his friend laugh
heartily.

"Don't dine on the professor's old papers by mistake,"
he cried, as he vanished down the street.

Dr. Laidlaw went up to his study at the top of the
house. Half way down he met his housekeeper, Mrs.
Fewings. She was flustered and excited, and her face was
very red and perspiring.

"There've been burglars here," she cried excitedly, "or
something funny! All your things is just any'ow, sir. I
found everything all about everywhere!" She was very
confused. In this orderly and very precise establishment
it was unusual to find a thing out of place.

"Oh, my specimens!" cried the doctor, dashing up the
rest of the stairs at top speed. "Have they been touched
or——"

He flew to the door of the laboratory. Mrs. Fewings
panted up heavily behind him.

"The labatry ain't been touched," she explained, breathlessly, "but they smashed the libry clock and they've 'ung
your gold watch, sir, on the skelinton's hands. And the
books that weren't no value they flung out er the window
just like so much rubbish. They must have been wild
drunk, Dr. Laidlaw, sir!"

The young scientist made a hurried examination of
the rooms. Nothing of value was missing. He began to
wonder what kind of burglars they were. He looked up
sharply at Mrs. Fewings standing in the doorway. For a
moment he seemed to cast about in his mind for something.

"Odd," he said at length. "I only left here an hour
ago and everything was all right then."

"Was it, sir? Yes, sir." She glanced sharply at him.

Her room looked out upon the courtyard, and she must have seen the books come crashing down, and also have heard her master leave the house a few minutes later.

"And what's this rubbish the brutes have left?" he cried, taking up two slabs of worn gray stone, on the writing-table. "Bath brick, or something, I do declare."

He looked very sharply again at the confused and troubled housekeeper.

"Throw them on the dust heap, Mrs. Fewings, and— and let me know if anything is missing in the house, and I will notify the police this evening."

When she left the room he went into the laboratory and took his watch off the skeleton's fingers. His face wore a troubled expression, but after a moment's thought it cleared again. His memory was a complete blank.

"I suppose I left it on the writing-table when I went out to take the air," he said. And there was no one present to contradict him.

He crossed to the window and blew carelessly some ashes of burned paper from the sill, and stood watching them as they floated away lazily over the tops of the trees.

XI

THE EMPTY SLEEVE

1

THE Gilmer brothers were a couple of fussy and pernickety old bachelors of a rather retiring, not to say timid, disposition. There was grey in the pointed beard of John, the elder, and if any hair had remained to William it would also certainly have been of the same shade. They had private means. Their main interest in life was the collection of violins, for which they had the instinctive *flair* of true connoisseurs. Neither John nor William, however, could play a single note. They could only pluck the open strings. The production of tone, so necessary before purchase, was done vicariously for them by another.

The only objection they had to the big building in which they occupied the roomy top floor was that Morgan, liftman and caretaker, insisted on wearing a billycock with his uniform after six o'clock in the evening, with a result disastrous to the beauty of the universe. For "Mr. Morgan," as they called him between themselves, had a round and pasty face on the top of a round and conical body. In view, however, of the man's other rare qualities—including his devotion to themselves—this objection was not serious.

He had another peculiarity that amused them. On being found fault with, he explained nothing, but merely repeated the words of the complaint.

"Water in the bath wasn't really hot this morning, Morgan!"

"Water in the bath not reely 'ot, wasn't it, sir?"

Or, from William, who was something of a faddist:

"My jar of sour milk came up late yesterday, Morgan."

"Your jar sour milk come up late, sir, yesterday?"

Since, however, the statement of a complaint invariably resulted in its remedy, the brothers had learned to look for no further explanation. Next morning the bath *was* hot, the sour milk *was* "brortup" punctually. The uniform and billycock hat, though, remained an eyesore and source of oppression.

On this particular night John Gilmer, the elder, returning from a Masonic rehearsal, stepped into the lift and found Mr. Morgan with his hand ready on the iron rope.

"Fog's very thick outside," said Mr. John pleasantly; and the lift was a third of the way up before Morgan had completed his customary repetition: "Fog very thick outside, yes, sir." And Gilmer then asked casually if his brother were alone, and received the reply that Mr. Hyman had called and had not yet gone away.

Now this Mr. Hyman was a Hebrew, and, like themselves, a connoisseur in violins, but, unlike themselves, who only kept their specimens to look at, he was a skilful and exquisite player. He was the only person they ever permitted to handle their pedigree instruments, to take them from the glass cases where they reposed in silent splendour, and to draw the sound out of their wondrous painted hearts of golden varnish. The brothers loathed to see his fingers touch them, yet loved to hear their singing voices in the room, for the latter confirmed their sound judgment as collectors, and made them certain their money had been well spent. Hyman, however, made no attempt to conceal his contempt and hatred for the mere collector. The atmosphere of the room fairly pulsed with these opposing forces of silent emotion when Hyman played and the Gilmers, alternately writhing and admiring, listened. The occasions, however, were not frequent. The Hebrew only came by invitation, and both brothers made

a point of being in. It was a very formal proceeding—
something of a sacred rite almost.

John Gilmer, therefore, was considerably surprised by
the information Morgan had supplied. For one thing,
Hyman, he had understood, was away on the Continent.

"Still in there, you say?" he repeated, after a moment's
reflection.

"Still in there, Mr. John, sir." Then, concealing his
surprise from the liftman, he fell back upon his usual mild
habit of complaining about the billycock hat and the uniform.

"You really should try and remember, Morgan," he
said, though kindly. "That hat does *not* go well with that
uniform!"

Morgan's pasty countenance betrayed no vestige of expression. "'At don't go well with the yewniform, sir,"
he repeated, hanging up the disreputable bowler and replac-
ing it with a gold-braided cap from the peg. "No, sir, it
don't, do it?" he added cryptically, smiling at the trans-
formation thus effected.

And the lift then halted with an abrupt jerk at the
top floor. By somebody's carelessness the landing was in
darkness, and, to make things worse, Morgan, clumsily
pulling the iron rope, happened to knock the billycock from
its peg so that his sleeve, as he stooped to catch it, struck
the switch and plunged the scene in a moment's complete
obscurity.

And it was then, in the act of stepping out before the
light was turned on again, that John Gilmer stumbled
against something that shot along the landing past the
open door. First he thought it must be a child, then a
man, then—an animal. Its movement was rapid yet
stealthy. Starting backwards instinctively to allow it room
to pass, Gilmer collided in the darkness with Morgan, and
Morgan incontinently screamed. There was a moment of
stupid confusion. The heavy framework of the lift shook
a little, as though something had stepped into it and then

as quickly jumped out again. A rushing sound followed that resembled footsteps, yet at the same time was more like gliding—someone in soft slippers or stockinged feet, greatly hurrying. Then came silence again. Morgan sprang to the landing and turned up the electric light. Mr. Gilmer, at the same moment, did likewise to the switch in the lift. Light flooded the scene. Nothing was visible.

"Dog or cat, or something, I suppose, wasn't it?" exclaimed Gilmer, following the man out and looking round with bewildered amazement upon a deserted landing. He knew quite well, even while he spoke, that the words were foolish.

"Dog or cat, yes, sir, or—something," echoed Morgan, his eyes narrowed to pin-points, then growing large, but his face stolid.

"The light should have been on." Mr. Gilmer spoke with a touch of severity. The little occurrence had curiously disturbed his equanimity. He felt annoyed, upset, uneasy.

For a perceptible pause the liftman made no reply, and his employer, looking up, saw that, besides being flustered, he was white about the jaws. His voice, when he spoke, was without its normal assurance. This time he did not merely repeat. He explained.

"The light *was* on, sir, when last *I* come up!" he said, with emphasis, obviously speaking the truth. "Only a moment ago," he added.

Mr. Gilmer, for some reason, felt disinclined to press for explanations. He decided to ignore the matter.

Then the lift plunged down again into the depths like a diving-bell into water; and John Gilmer, pausing a moment first to reflect, let himself in softly with his latch-key, and, after hanging up hat and coat in the hall, entered the big sitting-room he and his brother shared in common.

The December fog that covered London like a dirty blanket had penetrated, he saw, into the room. The objects in it were half shrouded in the familiar yellowish haze.

2

In dressing-gown and slippers, William Gilmer, almost invisible in his armchair by the gas-stove across the room, spoke at once. Through the thick atmosphere his face gleamed, showing an extinguished pipe hanging from his lips. His tone of voice conveyed emotion, an emotion he sought to suppress, of a quality, however, not easy to define.

"Hyman's been here," he announced abruptly. "You must have met him. He's this very instant gone out."

It was quite easy to see that something had happened, for "scenes" leave disturbance behind them in the atmosphere. But John made no immediate reference to this. He replied that he had seen no one—which was strictly true —and his brother thereupon, sitting bolt upright in the chair, turned quickly and faced him. His skin, in the foggy air, seemed paler than before.

"That's odd," he said nervously.

"What's odd?" asked John.

"That you didn't see—anything. You ought to have run into one another on the doorstep." His eyes went peering about the room. He was distinctly ill at ease. "You're positive you saw no one? Did Morgan take him down before you came? Did Morgan see him?" He asked several questions at once.

"On the contrary, Morgan told me he was still here with you. Hyman probably walked down, and didn't take the lift at all," he replied. "That accounts for neither of us seeing him." He decided to say nothing about the occurrence in the lift, for his brother's nerves, he saw plainly, were on edge.

William then stood up out of his chair, and the skin of his face changed its hue, for whereas a moment ago it

was merely pale, it had now altered to a tint that lay somewhere between white and a livid grey.   The man was
fighting internal terror.   For a moment these two brothers
of middle age looked each other straight in the eye.   Then
John spoke:

"What's wrong, Billy?" he asked quietly.   "Something's upset you.   What brought Hyman in this way—
unexpectedly?   I thought he was still in Germany."

The brothers, affectionate and sympathetic, understood
one another perfectly.   They had no secrets.   Yet for
several minutes the younger one made no reply.   It seemed
difficult to choose his words apparently.

"Hyman played, I suppose—on the fiddles?"   John
helped him, wondering uneasily what was coming.   He
did not care much for the individual in question, though
his talent was of such great use to them.

The other nodded in the affirmative, then plunged into
rapid speech, talking under his breath as though he feared
someone might overhear.   Glancing over his shoulder down
the foggy room, he drew his brother close.

"Hyman came," he began, "unexpectedly.   He hadn't
written, and I hadn't asked him.   You hadn't either, I
suppose?"

John shook his head.

"When I came in from the dining-room I found him
in the passage.   The servant was taking away the dishes,
and he had let himself in while the front door was ajar.
Pretty cool, wasn't it?"

"He's an original," said John, shrugging his
shoulders.   "And you welcomed him?" he asked.

"I asked him in, of course.   He explained he had
something glorious for me to hear.   Silenski had played
it in the afternoon, and he had bought the music since.
But Silenski's 'Strad' hadn't the power—it's thin on the
upper strings, you remember, unequal, patchy—and he
said no instrument in the world could do it justice but our

'Joseph'—the small Guarnerius, you know, which he swears is the most perfect in the world."

"And what was it? Did he play it?" asked John, growing more uneasy as he grew more interested. With relief he glanced round and saw the matchless little instrument lying there safe and sound in its glass case near the door.

"He played it—divinely: a Zigeuner Lullaby, a fine, passionate, rushing bit of inspiration, oddly misnamed 'lullaby.' And, fancy, the fellow had memorized it already! He walked about the room on tiptoe while he played it, complaining of the light——"

"Complaining of the light?"

"Said the thing was crepuscular, and needed dusk for its full effect. I turned the lights out one by one, till finally there was only the glow of the gas logs. He insisted. You know that way he has with him? And then he got over me in another matter: insisted on using some special strings he had brought with him, and put them on, too, himself—thicker than the A and E *we* use."

For though neither Gilmer could produce a note, it was their pride that they kept their precious instruments in perfect condition for playing, choosing the exact thickness and quality of strings that suited the temperament of each violin; and the little Guarnerius in question always "sang" best, they held, with thin strings.

"Infernal insolence," exclaimed the listening brother, wondering what was coming next. "Played it well, though, didn't he, this Lullaby thing?" he added, seeing that William hesitated. As he spoke he went nearer, sitting down close beside him in a leather chair.

"Magnificent! Pure fire of genius!" was the reply with enthusiasm, the voice at the same time dropping lower. "Staccato like a silver hammer; harmonics like flutes, clear, soft, ringing; and the tone—well, the G string was a baritone, and the upper registers creamy and mel-

low as a boy's voice. John," he added, "that Guarnerius
is the very pick of the period and"—again he hesitated—
"Hyman loves it. He'd give his soul to have it."

The more John heard, the more uncomfortable it made
him. He had always disliked this gifted Hebrew, for in
his secret heart he knew that he had always feared and
distrusted him. Sometimes he had felt half afraid of him;
the man's very forcible personality was too insistent to be
pleasant. His type was of the dark and sinister kind, and
he possessed a violent will that rarely failed of accom-
plishing its desire.

"Wish I'd heard the fellow play," he said at length,
ignoring his brother's last remark, and going on to speak
of the most matter-of-fact details he could think of. "Did
he use the Dodd bow, or the Tourte? That Dodd I picked
up last month, you know, is the most perfectly balanced I
have ever——"

He stopped abruptly, for William had suddenly got
upon his feet and was standing there, searching the room
with his eyes. A chill ran down John's spine as he watched
him.

"What is it, Billy?" he asked sharply. "Hear anything?"

William continued to peer about him through the thick
air.

"Oh, nothing, probably," he said, an odd catch in his
voice; "only—— I keep feeling as if there was somebody listening. Do you think, perhaps"—he glanced over
his shoulder—"there is someone at the door? I wish—I
wish you'd have a look, John."

John obeyed, though without great eagerness. Crossing the room slowly, he opened the door, then switched on
the light. The passage leading past the bathroom towards the bedrooms beyond was empty. The coats hung
motionless from their pegs.

"No one, of course," he said, as he closed the door
and came back to the stove. He left the light burning in

the passage. It was curious the way both brothers had this impression that they were not alone, though only one of them spoke of it.

"Used the Dodd or the Tourte, Billy—which?" continued John in the most natural voice he could assume.

But at that very same instant the water started to his eyes. His brother, he saw, was close upon the thing he really had to tell. But he had stuck fast.

3

By a great effort John Gilmer composed himself and remained in his chair. With detailed elaboration he lit a cigarette, staring hard at his brother over the flaring match while he did so. There he sat in his dressing-gown and slippers by the fireplace, eyes downcast, fingers playing idly with the red tassel. The electric light cast heavy shadows across the face. In a flash then, since emotion may sometimes express itself in attitude even better than in speech, the elder brother understood that Billy was about to tell him an unutterable thing.

By instinct he moved over to his side so that the same view of the room confronted him.

"Out with it, old man," he said, with an effort to be natural. "Tell me what you saw."

Billy shuffled slowly round and the two sat side by side, facing the fog-draped chamber.

"It was like this," he began softly, "only I was standing instead of sitting, looking over to that door as you and I do now. Hyman moved to and fro in the faint glow of the gas logs against the far wall, playing that "crepuscular' thing in his most inspired sort of way, so that the music seemed to issue from himself rather than from the shining bit of wood under his chin, when—I noticed something coming over me that was"—he hesitated, searching for words—"that wasn't *all* due to the music," he finished abruptly.

"His personality put a bit of hypnotism on you, eh?"
William shrugged his shoulders.

"The air was thickish with fog and the light was dim,
cast upwards upon him from the stove," he continued.
"I admit all that. But there wasn't light enough to throw
shadows, you see, and——"

"Hyman looked queer?" the other helped him quickly.
Billy nodded his head without turning.

"Changed there before my very eyes"—he whispered
it—"turned animal——"

"Animal?" John felt his hair rising.

"That's the only way I can put it. His face and hands
and body turned otherwise than usual. I lost the sound
of his feet. When the bow-hand or the fingers on the
strings passed into the light, they were"—he uttered a
soft, shuddering little laugh—"furry, oddly divided, the
fingers massed together. And he paced stealthily. I
thought every instant the fiddle would drop with a crash
and he would spring at me across the room."

"My dear chap——"

"He moved with those big, lithe, striding steps one
sees"—John held his breath in the little pause, listening
keenly—"one sees those big brutes make in the cages when
their desire is aflame for food or escape, or—or fierce, passionate desire for anything they want with their whole
nature——"

"The big felines!" John whistled softly.

"And every minute getting nearer and nearer to the
door, as though he meant to make a sudden rush for it
and get out."

"With the violin! Of course you stopped him?"

"In the end. But for a long time, I swear to you, I
found it difficult to know what to do, even to move. I
couldn't get my voice for words of any kind; it was like
a spell."

"It *was* a spell," suggested John firmly.

"Then, as he moved, still playing," continued the

other, "he seemed to grow smaller; to shrink down below
the line of the gas. I thought I should lose sight of him
altogether. I turned the light up suddenly. There he
was over by the door—crouching."

"Playing on his knees, you mean?"

William closed his eyes in an effort to visualize it
again.

"Crouching," he repeated, at length, "close to the floor.
At least, I think so. It all happened so quickly, and I
felt so bewildered, it was hard to see straight. But at
first I could have sworn he was half his natural size. I
called to him, I think I swore at him—I forget exactly,
but I know he straightened up at once and stood before me
down there in the light"—he pointed across the room to
the door—"eyes gleaming, face white as chalk, perspiring
like midsummer, and gradually filling out, straightening
up, whatever you like to call it, to his natural size and appearance again. It was the most horrid thing I've ever
seen."

"As an—animal, you saw him still?"

"No; human again. Only much smaller."

"What did he say?"

Billy reflected a moment.

"Nothing that I can remember," he replied. "You
see, it was all over in a few seconds. In the full light, I
felt so foolish, and nonplussed at first. To see him normal
again baffled me. And, before I could collect myself, he
had let himself out into the passage, and I heard the front
door slam. A minute later—the same second almost, it
seemed—you came in. I only remember grabbing the violin and getting it back safely under the glass case. The
strings were still vibrating."

The account was over. John asked no further questions. Nor did he say a single word about the lift, Morgan, or the extinguished light on the landing. There fell
a longish silence between the two men; and then, while
they helped themselves to a generous supply of whisky-

and-soda before going to bed, John looked up and spoke:

"If you agree, Billy," he said quietly, "I think I might write and suggest to Hyman that we shall no longer have need for his services."

And Billy, acquiescing, added a sentence that expressed something of the singular dread lying but half concealed in the atmosphere of the room, if not in their minds as well:

"Putting it, however, in a way that need not offend him."

"Of course. There's no need to be rude, is there?"

Accordingly, next morning the letter was written; and John, saying nothing to his brother, took it round himself by hand to the Hebrew's rooms near Euston. The answer he dreaded was forthcoming:

"Mr. Hyman's still away abroad," he was told. "But we're forwarding letters; yes. Or I can give you 'is address if you'll prefer it." The letter went, therefore, to the number in Königstrasse, Munich, thus obtained.

Then, on his way back from the insurance company where he went to increase the sum that protected the small Guarnerius from loss by fire, accident, or theft, John Gilmer called at the offices of certain musical agents and ascertained that Silenski, the violinist, was performing at the time in Munich. It was only some days later, though, by diligent inquiry, he made certain that at a concert on a certain date the famous virtuoso had played a Zigeuner Lullaby of his own composition—the very date, it turned out, on which he himself had been to the Masonic rehearsal at Mark Masons' Hall.

John, however, said nothing of these discoveries to his brother William.

4

It was about a week later when a reply to the letter came from Munich—a letter couched in somewhat offensive terms, though it contained neither words nor phrases that could actually be found fault with. Isidore Hyman was hurt and angry. On his return to London a month or so later, he proposed to call and talk the matter over. The offensive part of the letter lay, perhaps, in his definite assumption that he could persuade the brothers to resume the old relations. John, however, wrote a brief reply to the effect that they had decided to buy no new fiddles; their collection being complete, there would be no occasion for them to invite his services as a performer. This was final. No answer came, and the matter seemed to drop. Never for one moment, though, did it leave the consciousness of John Gilmer. Hyman had said that he would come, and come assuredly he would. He secretly gave Morgan instructions that he and his brother for the future were always "out" when the Hebrew presented himself.

"He must have gone back to Germany, you see, almost at once after his visit here that night," observed William —John, however, making no reply.

One night towards the middle of January the two brothers came home together from a concert in Queen's Hall, and sat up later than usual in their sitting-room discussing over their whisky and tobacco the merits of the pieces and performers. It must have been past one o'clock when they turned out the lights in the passage and retired to bed. The air was still and frosty; moonlight over the roofs—one of those sharp and dry winter nights that now seem to visit London rarely.

"Like the old-fashioned days when we were boys," remarked William, pausing a moment by the passage window and looking out across the miles of silvery, sparkling roofs.

"Yes," added John; "the ponds freezing hard in the fields, rime on the nursery windows, and the sound of a horse's hoofs coming down the road in the distance, eh?" They smiled at the memory, then said good night, and separated. Their rooms were at opposite ends of the corridor; in between were the bathroom, dining-room, and sitting-room. It was a long, straggling flat. Half an hour later both brothers were sound asleep, the flat silent, only a dull murmur rising from the great city outside, and the moon sinking slowly to the level of the chimneys.

Perhaps two hours passed, perhaps three, when John Gilmer, sitting up in bed with a start, wide-awake and frightened, knew that someone was moving about in one of the three rooms that lay between him and his brother. He had absolutely no idea why he should have been frightened, for there was no dream or nightmare-memory that he brought over from unconsciousness, and yet he realized plainly that the fear he felt was by no means a foolish and unreasoning fear. It had a cause and a reason. Also—which made it worse—it was fully warranted. Something in his sleep, forgotten in the instant of waking, had happened that set every nerve in his body on the watch. He was positive only of two things—first, that it was the entrance of this person, moving so quietly there in the flat, that sent the chills down his spine; and, secondly, that this person was *not* his brother William.

John Gilmer was a timid man. The sight of a burglar, his eyes black-masked, suddenly confronting him in the passage, would most likely have deprived him of all power of decision—until the burglar had either shot him or escaped. But on this occasion some instinct told him that it was no burglar, and that the acute distress he experienced was not due to any message of ordinary physical fear. The thing that had gained access to his flat while he slept had first come—he felt sure of it—into his room, and had passed very close to his own bed, before going on. It had then doubtless gone to his brother's room, visiting them both stealthily to make sure they slept. And its mere passage through his room had been enough to wake him and set these drops of cold perspiration upon his skin.

For it was—he felt it in every fibre of his body—something hostile.

The thought that it might at that very moment be in the room of his brother, however, brought him to his feet on the cold floor, and set him moving with all the determination he could summon towards the door. He looked cautiously down an utterly dark passage; then crept on tiptoe along it. On the wall were old-fashioned weapons that had belonged to his father; and feeling a curved, sheathless sword that had come from some Turkish campaign of years gone by, his fingers closed tightly round it, and lifted it silently from the three hooks whereon it lay. He passed the doors of the bathroom and dining-room, making instinctively for the big sitting-room where the violins were kept in their glass cases. The cold nipped him. His eyes smarted with the effort to see in the darkness. Outside the closed door he hesitated.

Putting his ear to the crack, he listened. From within came a faint sound of someone moving. The same instant there rose the sharp, delicate "ping" of a violin-string being plucked; and John Gilmer, with nerves that shook like the vibrations of that very string, opened the door wide with a fling and turned on the light at the same moment. The plucked string still echoed faintly in the air.

The sensation that met him on the threshold was the well-known one that things had been going on in the room which his unexpected arrival had that instant put a stop to. A second earlier and he would have discovered it all in the act. The atmosphere still held the feeling of rushing, silent movement with which the things had raced back to their normal, motionless positions. The immobility of the furniture was a mere attitude hurriedly assumed, and the moment his back was turned the whole business, whatever it might be, would begin again. With this presentment of the room, however—a purely imaginative one—came another, swiftly on its heels.

For one of the objects, less swift than the rest, had not quite regained its "attitude" of repose. It still moved. Below the window curtains on the right, not far from the shelf that bore the violins in their glass cases, he made it out, slowly gliding along the floor. Then, even as his eye caught it, it came to rest.

And, while the cold perspiration broke out all over him afresh, he knew that this still moving item was the cause both of his waking and of his terror. This was the disturbance whose presence he had divined in the flat without actual hearing, and whose passage through his room, while he yet slept, had touched every nerve in his body as with ice. Clutching his Turkish sword tightly, he drew back with the utmost caution against the wall and watched, for the singular impression came to him that the movement was not that of a human being crouching, but rather of something that pertained to the animal world. He remembered, flash-like, the movements of reptiles, the stealth of the larger felines, the undulating glide of great snakes. For the moment, however, it did not move, and they faced one another.

The other side of the room was but dimly lighted, and the noise he made clicking up another electric lamp brought the thing flying forward again—towards himself. At such a moment it seemed absurd to think of so small a detail, but he remembered his bare feet, and, genuinely frightened, he leaped upon a chair and swished with his sword through the air about him. From this better point of view, with the increased light to aid him, he then saw two things—first, that the glass case usually covering the Guarnerius violin had been shifted; and, secondly, that the moving object was slowly elongating itself into an upright position. Semi-erect, yet most oddly, too, like a creature on its hind legs, it was coming swiftly towards him. It was making for the door—and escape.

The confusion of ghostly fear was somehow upon him so that he was too bewildered to see clearly, but he had sufficient self-control, it seemed, to recover a certain power of action; for the moment the advancing figure was near enough for him to strike, that curved scimitar flashed and whirred about him, with such misdirected violence, however, that he not only failed to strike it even once, but at the same time lost his balance and fell forward from the chair whereon he perched—straight into it.

And then came the most curious thing of all, for as he dropped, the figure also dropped, stooped low down, crouched, dwindled amazingly in size, and rushed past him close to the ground like an animal on all fours. John Gilmer screamed, for he could no longer contain himself. Stumbling over the chair as he turned to follow, cutting and slashing wildly with his sword, he saw halfway down the darkened corridor beyond the scuttling outline of, apparently, an enormous—cat!

The door into the outer landing was somehow ajar, and the next second the beast was out, but not before the steel had fallen with a crashing blow upon the front disappearing leg, almost severing it from the body.

It was dreadful. Turning up the lights as he went, he ran after it to the outer landing. But the thing he followed was already well away, and he heard, on the floor below him, the same oddly gliding, slithering, stealthy sound, yet hurrying, that he had heard weeks before when something had passed him in the lift and Morgan, in his terror, had likewise cried aloud.

For a time he stood there on that dark landing, listening, thinking, trembling; then turned into the flat and shut the door. In the sitting-room he carefully replaced the glass case over the treasured violin, puzzled to the point of foolishness, and strangely routed in his mind. For the violin itself, he saw, had been dragged several inches from its cushioned bed of plush.

Next morning, however, he made no allusion to the occurrence of the night. His brother apparently had not been disturbed.

5

The only thing that called for explanation—an explanation not fully forthcoming—was the curious aspect of Mr. Morgan's countenance. The fact that this individual gave notice to the owners of the building, and at the end of the month left for a new post, was, of course, known to both brothers; whereas the story he told in explanation of his face was known only to the one who questioned him about it—John. And John, for reasons best known to himself, did not pass it on to the other. Also, for reasons best known to himself, he did not cross-question the liftman about those singular marks, or report the matter to the police.

Mr. Morgan's pasty visage was badly scratched, and there were red lines running from the cheek into the neck that had the appearance of having been produced by sharp points viciously applied—claws. He had been disturbed by a noise in the hall, he said, about three in the morning, a scuffle had ensued in the darkness, but the intruder had got clear away. . . .

"A cat or something of the kind, no doubt," suggested John Gilmer at the end of the brief recital. And Morgan replied in his usual way: "A cat, or something of the kind, Mr. John, no doubt."

All the same, he had not cared to risk a second encounter, but had departed to wear his billycock and uniform in a building less haunted.

Hyman, meanwhile, made no attempt to call and talk over his dismissal. The reason for this was only apparent, however, several months later when, quite by chance, coming along Piccadilly in an omnibus, the brothers found themselves seated opposite to a man with a thick black beard and blue glasses. William Gilmer hastily rang the bell and got out, saying something half intelligible about feeling faint. John followed him.

"Did you see who it was?" he whispered to his brother the moment they were safely on the pavement.

John nodded.

"Hyman, in spectacles. He's grown a beard, too."

"Yes, but did you also notice——"

"What?"

"He had an empty sleeve."

"An empty sleeve?"

"Yes," said William; "he's lost an arm."

There was a long pause before John spoke. At the door of their club the elder brother added:

"Poor devil! He'll never again play on"—then, suddenly changing the preposition—"*with* a pedigree violin!"

And that night in the flat, after William had gone to bed, he looked up a curious old volume he had once picked up on a second-hand bookstall, and read therein quaint descriptions of how the "desire-body of a violent man" may assume animal shape, operate on concrete matter even at a distance; and, further, how a wound inflicted thereon can reproduce itself upon its physical counterpart by means of the mysterious so-called phenomenon of "re-percussion."

XII

WIRELESS CONFUSION

"GOOD night, Uncle," whispered the child, as she climbed on to his knee and gave him a resounding kiss. "It's time for me to disappop into bed—at least, so mother says."

"Disappop, then," he replied, returning her kiss, "although I doubt. . . ."

He hesitated. He remembered the word was her father's invention, descriptive of the way rabbits pop into their holes and disappear, and the way *good* children should leave the room the instant bed-time was announced. The father—his twin brother—seemed to enter the room and stand beside them. "Then give me another kiss, and disappop!" he said quickly. The child obeyed the first part of his injunction, but had not obeyed the second when the queer thing happened. She had not left his knee; he was still holding her at the full stretch of both arms; he was staring into her laughing eyes, when she suddenly went far away into an extraordinary distance. She retired. Minute, tiny, but still in perfect proportion and clear as before, she was withdrawn in space till she was small as a doll. He saw his own hands holding her, and they too were minute. Down this long corridor of space, as it were, he saw her diminutive figure.

"Uncle!" she cried, yet her voice was loud as before, "but what a funny face! You're pretending you've seen a ghost"—and she was gone from his knee and from the room, the door closing quietly behind her. He saw her cross the floor, a tiny figure. Then, just as she reached the door, she became of normal size again, as if she crossed a line.

He felt dizzy. The loud voice close to his ear issuing from a diminutive figure half a mile away had a distress-ing effect upon him. He knew a curious qualm as he sat there in the dark. He heard the wind walking round the house, trying the doors and windows. He was troubled by a memory he could not seize.

Yet the emotion instantly resolved itself into one of per-sonal anxiety: something had gone wrong with his eyes. Sight, his most precious possession as an artist, was of course affected. He was conscious of a little trembling in him, as he at once began trying his sight at various objects —his hands, the high ceiling, the trees dim in the twilight on the lawn outside. He opened a book and read half a dozen lines, at changing distances; finally he stared care-fully at the second hand of his watch. "Right as a trivet!" he exclaimed aloud. He emitted a long sigh; he was im-mensely relieved. "Nothing wrong with my eyes."

He thought about the actual occurrence a great deal— he felt as puzzled as any other normal person must have felt. While he held the child actually in his arms, grip-ping her with both hands, he had seen her suddenly half a mile away. "Half a mile!" he repeated under his breath, "why it was even more, it was easily a mile." It had been exactly as though he suddenly looked at her down the wrong end of a powerful telescope. It had really hap-pened; he could not explain it; there was no more to be said.

This was the first time it happened to him.

At the theatre, a week later, when the phenomenon was repeated, the stage he was watching fixedly at the moment went far away, as though he saw it from a long way off. The distance, so far as he could judge, was the same as before, about a mile. It was an Eastern scene, realistically costumed and produced, that without an instant's warning withdrew. The entire stage went with it, although he did

not actually see it go.   He did not see movement, that is.
It was suddenly remote, while yet the actors' voices, the
orchestra, the general hubbub retained their normal
volume.   He experienced again the distressing dizziness;
he closed his eyes, covering them with his hand, then rub-
bing the eyeballs slightly; and when he looked up the next
minute, the world was as it should be, as it had been, at
any rate.   Unwilling to experience a repetition of the
thing in a public place, however, and fortunately being
alone, he left the theatre at the end of the act.

Twice this happened to him, once with an individual,
his brother's child, and once with a landscape, an Eastern
stage scene.   Both occurrences were within the week, during which time he had been considering a visit to the
oculist, though without putting his decision into execution.
He was the kind of man that dreaded doctors, dentists,
oculists, always postponing, always finding reasons for
delay.   He found reasons now, the chief among them being
an unwelcome one—that it was perhaps a brain specialist,
rather than an oculist, he ought to consult.   This particular notion hung unpleasantly about his mind, when, the
day after the theatre visit, the thing recurred, but with a
startling difference.

While idly watching a blue-bottle fly that climbed the
window-pane with remorseless industry, only to slip down
again at the very instant when escape into the open air
was within its reach, the fly grew abruptly into gigantic
proportions, became blurred and indistinct as it did so,
covered the entire pane with its furry, dark, ugly mass,
and frightened him so that he stepped back with a cry
and nearly lost his balance altogether.   He collapsed into
a chair.   He listened with closed eyes.   The metallic buzz-
ing was audible, a small, exasperating sound, ordinarily
unable to stir any emotion beyond a mild annoyance.   Yet
it was terrible; that so huge an insect should make so faint
a sound seemed to him terrible.

At length he cautiously opened his eyes.   The fly was

of normal size once more. He hastily flicked it out of the window.

An hour later he was talking with the famous oculist in Harley Street . . . about the advisability of starting reading-glasses. He found it difficult to relate the rest. A curious shyness restrained him.

"Your optic nerves might belong to a man of twenty," was the verdict. "Both are perfect. But at your age it is wise to save the sight as much as possible. There is a slight astigmatism. . . ." And a prescription for the glasses was written out. It was only when paying the fee, and as a means of drawing attention from the awkward moment, that his story found expression. It seemed to come out in spite of himself. He made light of it even then, telling it without conviction. It seemed foolish suddenly as he told it. "How very odd," observed the oculist vaguely, "dear me, yes, curious indeed. But that's nothing. H'm, h'm!" Either it was no concern of his, or he deemed it negligible. . . . His only other confidant was a friend of psychological tendencies who was interested and eager to explain. It is on the instant plausible explanation of anything and everything that the reputation of such folk depends; this one was true to type: "A spontaneous invention, my dear fellow—a pictorial rendering of your thought. You are a painter, aren't you? Well, this is merely a rendering in picture-form of"—he paused for effect, the other hung upon his words—"of the odd expression 'disappop.' "

"Ah!" exclaimed the painter.

"You see everything pictorially, of course, don't you?"

"Yes—as a rule."

"There you have it. Your painter's psychology saw the child 'disappopping.' That's all."

"And the fly?" but the fly was easily explained, since it was merely the process reversed. "Once a process has established itself in your mind, you see, it may act in either direction. When a madman says 'I'm afraid Smith will

do me an injury,' it means, 'I will do an injury to Smith.'"
And he repeated with finality, "That's it."

The explanations were not very satisfactory, the illus-
tration even tactless, but then the problem had not been
stated quite fully. Neither to the oculist nor to the other
had all the facts been given. The same shyness had been a
restraining influence in both cases; a detail had been
omitted, and this detail was that he connected the occurrences somehow with his brother whom the war had taken.

The phenomenon made one more appearance—the last
—before its character, its field of action rather, altered.
He was reading a book when the print became now large,
now small; it blurred, grew remote and tiny, then so huge
that a single word, a letter even, filled the whole page. He
felt as if someone were playing optical tricks with the
mechanism of his eyes, trying first one, then another focus.

More curious still, the meaning of the words themselves
became uncertain; he did not understand them any more;
the sentences lost their meaning, as though he read a
strange language, or a language little known. The flash
came then—someone was using his eyes—someone else was
looking through them.

No, it was not his brother. The idea was preposterous
in any case. Yet he shivered again, as when he heard the
walking wind, for an uncanny conviction came over him
that it was someone who did not understand eyes but was
manipulating their mechanism experimentally. With the
conviction came also this: that, while not his brother, it
was someone connected with his brother.

Here, moreover, was an explanation of sorts, for if the
supernatural existed—he had never troubled his head about
it—he could accept this odd business as a manifestation,
and leave it at that. He did so, and his mind was eased.
This was his attitude: "The supernatural may exist. Why
not? We cannot know. But we can watch." His eyes and
brain, at any rate, were proved in good condition.

He watched. No change of focus, no magnifying or

diminishing, came again. For some weeks he noticed nothing unusual of any kind, except that his mind often filled now with Eastern pictures. Their sudden irruption caught his attention, but no more than that; they were sometimes blurred and sometimes vivid; he had never been in the East; he attributed them to his constant thinking of his brother, missing in Mesopotamia these six months. Photographs in magazines and newspapers explained the rest. Yet the persistence of the pictures puzzled him: tents beneath hot cloudless skies, palms, a stretch of desert, dry watercourses, camels, a mosque, a minaret—typical snatches of this kind flashed into his mind with a sense of faint familiarity often. He knew, again, the return of a fugitive memory he could not seize. . . . He kept a note of the dates, all of them subsequent to the day he read his brother's fate in the official Roll of Honour: "Believed missing; now killed." Only when the original phenomenon returned, but in its altered form, did he stop the practice. The change then affected his life too fundamentally to trouble about mere dates and pictures.

For the phenomenon, shifting its field of action, abruptly became mental, and the singular change of focus took place now in his mind. Events magnified or contracted themselves out of all relation with their intrinsic values, sense of proportion went hopelessly astray. Love, hate and fear experienced sudden intensification, or abrupt dwindling into nothing; the familiar everyday emotions, commonplace daily acts, suffered exaggerated enlargement, or reduction into insignificance, that threatened the stability of his personality. Fortunately, as stated, they were of brief duration; to examine them in detail were to touch the painful absurdities of incipient mania almost; that a lost collar stud could block his exasperated mind for hours, filling an entire day with emotion, while a deep affection of long standing could ebb towards complete collapse suddenly without apparent cause . . . !

It was the unexpected suddenness of Turkey's spec-

tacular defeat that closed the painful symptoms. The
Armistice saw them go. He knew a quick relief he was
unable to explain. The telegram that his brother was alive
and safe came *after* his recovery of mental balance. It was
a shock. But the phenomena had ceased before the shock.

It was in the light of his brother's story that he reviewed the puzzling phenomena described. The story was
not more curious than many another, perhaps, yet the details were queer enough. That a wounded Turk to whom
he gave water should have remembered gratitude was likely
enough, for all travellers know that these men are kindly
gentlemen at times; but that this Mohammedan peasant
should have been later a member of a prisoner's escort and
have provided the means of escape and concealment—
weeks in a dry watercourse and months in a hut outside
the town—seemed an incredible stroke of good fortune.
"He brought me food and water three times a week. I
had no money to give him, so I gave him my Zeiss glasses.
I taught him a bit of English too. But he liked the glasses
best. He was never tired of playing with 'em—making big
and little, as he called it. He learned precious little English. . . ."

"My pair, weren't they?" interrupted his brother. "My
old climbing glasses."

"Your present to me when I went out, yes. So really
you helped me to save my life. I told the old Turk that.
I was always thinking about you."

"And the Turk?"

"No doubt. . . . Through *my* mind, that is. At any
rate, he asked a lot of questions about you. I showed him
your photo. He died, poor chap—at least they told me
so. Probably they shot him."

XIII

CONFESSION

THE fog swirled slowly round him, driven by a heavy movement of its own, for of course there was no wind. It hung in poisonous thick coils and loops; it rose and sank; no light penetrated it directly from street lamp or motor-car, though here and there some big shop-window shed a glimmering patch upon its ever-shifting curtain.

O'Reilly's eyes ached and smarted with the incessant effort to see a foot beyond his face. The optic nerve grew tired, and sight, accordingly, less accurate. He coughed as he shuffled forward cautiously through the choking gloom. Only the stifled rumble of crawling traffic persuaded him he was in a crowded city at all—this, and the vague outlines of groping figures, hugely magnified, emerging suddenly and disappearing again, as they fumbled along inch by inch towards uncertain destinations.

The figures, however were human beings; they were real. That much he knew. He heard their muffled voices, now close, now distant, strangely smothered always. He also heard the tapping of innumerable sticks, feeling for iron railings or the kerb. These phantom outlines represented living people. He was not alone.

It was the dread of finding himself *quite* alone that haunted him, for he was still unable to cross an open space without assistance. He had the physical strength, it was the mind that failed him. Midway the panic terror might descend upon him, he would shake all over, his will dissolve, he would shriek for help, run wildly—into the traffic probably—or, as they called it in his North

Ontario home, "throw a fit" in the street before advancing wheels. He was not yet entirely cured, although under
ordinary conditions he was safe enough, as Dr. Henry had
assured him.

When he left Regent's Park by Tube an hour ago the
air was clear, the November sun shone brightly, the pale
blue sky was cloudless, and the assumption that he could
manage the journey across London Town alone was justified. The following day he was to leave for Brighton for
the week of final convalescence: this little preliminary test
of his powers on a bright November afternoon was all to
the good. Doctor Henry furnished minute instructions:
"You change at Piccadilly Circus—without leaving the
underground station, mind—and get out at South Kensington. You know the address of your V.A.D. friend. Have
your cup of tea with her, then come back the same way to
Regent's Park. Come back before dark—say six o'clock
at latest. It's better." He had described exactly what
turns to take after leaving the station, so many to the
right, so many to the left; it was a little confusing, but the
distance was short. "You can always ask. You can't possibly go wrong."

The unexpected fog, however, now blurred these instructions in a confused jumble in his mind. The failure
of outer sight reacted upon memory. The V.A.D. besides
had warned him her address was "not easy to find the
first time. The house lies in a backwater. But with your
'backwoods' instincts you'll probably manage it better than
any Londoner!" She, too, had not calculated upon the fog.

When O'Reilly came up the stairs at South Kensington
Station, he emerged into such murky darkness that he
thought he was still underground. An impenetrable
world lay round him. Only a raw bite in the damp atmosphere told him he stood beneath an open sky. For some
little time he stood and stared—a Canadian soldier, his
home among clear brilliant spaces, now face to face for the
first time in his life with that thing he had so often read

about—a bad London fog. With keenest interest and surprise he "enjoyed" the novel spectacle for perhaps ten minutes, watching the people arrive and vanish, and wondering why the station lights stopped dead the instant they touched the street—then, with a sense of adventure—it cost an effort—he left the covered building and plunged into the opaque sea beyond.

Repeating to himself the directions he had received—first to the right, second to the left, once more to the left, and so forth—he checked each turn, assuring himself it was impossible to go wrong. He made correct if slow progress, until someone blundered into him with an abrupt and startling question: "Is this right, do you know, for South Kensington Station?"

It was the suddenness that startled him; one moment there was no one, the next they were face to face, another, and the stranger had vanished into the gloom with a courteous word of grateful thanks. But the little shock of interruption had put memory out of gear. Had he already turned twice to the right, or had he not? O'Reilly realized sharply he had forgotten his memorized instructions. He stood still, making strenuous efforts at recovery, but each effort left him more uncertain than before. Five minutes later he was lost as hopelessly as any townsman who leaves his tent in the backwoods without blazing the trees to ensure finding his way back again. Even the sense of direction, so strong in him among his native forests, was completely gone. There were no stars, there was no wind, no smell, no sound of running water. There was nothing anywhere to guide him, nothing but occasional dim outlines, groping, shuffling, emerging and disappearing in the eddying fog, but rarely coming within actual speaking, much less touching, distance. He was lost utterly; more, he was alone.

Yet not *quite* alone—the thing he dreaded most. There were figures still in his immediate neighborhood. They emerged, vanished, reappeared, dissolved. No, he was not

quite alone. He saw these thickenings of the fog, he
heard their voices, the tapping of their cautious sticks,
their shuffling feet as well. They were real. They moved,
it seemed, about him in a circle, never coming very close.

"But they're real," he said to himself aloud, betraying
the weak point in his armour. "They're human beings
right enough. I'm positive of that."

He had never argued with Dr. Henry—he wanted to
get well; he had obeyed implicitly, believing everything
the doctor told him—up to a point. But he had always
had his own idea about these "figures," because, among
them, were often enough his own pals from the Somme,
Gallipoli, the Mespot horror, too. And he ought to know
his own pals when he saw them! At the same time he
knew quite well he had been "shocked," his being dis-
located; half dissolved as it were, his system pushed into
some lopsided condition that meant inaccurate registra-
tion. True. He grasped that perfectly. But, in that
shock and dislocation, had he not possibly picked up
another gear? Were there not gaps and broken edges,
pieces that no longer dovetailed, fitted as usual, interstices,
in a word? Yes, that was the word—interstices. Cracks,
so to speak, between his perception of the outside world
and his inner interpretation of these? Between memory
and recognition? Between the various states of consciousness that usually dovetailed so neatly that the joints were
normally imperceptible?

His state, he well knew, was abnormal, but were his
symptoms on that account unreal? Could not these "interstices" be used by—others? When he saw his "figures,"
he used to ask himself: "Are not these the real ones, and
the others—the human beings—unreal?"

This question now revived in him with a new intensity.
Were these figures in the fog real or unreal? The man
who had asked the way to the station, was he not, after
all, a shadow merely?

By the use of his cane and foot and what of sight was

left to him he knew that he was on an island. A lamp-post stood up solid and straight beside him, shedding its faint patch of glimmering light. Yet there were railings, however, that puzzled him, for his stick hit the metal rods distinctly in a series. And there should be no railings round an island. Yet he had most certainly crossed a dreadful open space to get where he was. His confusion and bewilderment increased with dangerous rapidity. Panic was not far away.

He was no longer on an omnibus route. A rare taxi crawled past occasionally, a whitish patch at the window indicating an anxious human face; now and again came a van or cart, the driver holding a lantern as he led the stumbling horse. These comforted him, rare though they were. But it was the figures that drew his attention most. He was quite sure they were real. They were human beings like himself.

For all that, he decided he might as well be positive on the point. He tried one accordingly—a big man who rose suddenly before him out of the very earth.

"Can you give me the trail to Morley Place?" he asked.

But his question was drowned by the other's simultaneous inquiry in a voice much louder than his own.

"I say, is this right for the Tube station, d'you know? I'm utterly lost. I want South Ken."

And by the time O'Reilly had pointed the direction whence he himself had just come, the man was gone again, obliterated, swallowed up, not so much as his footsteps audible, almost as if—it seemed again—he never had been there at all.

This left an acute unpleasantness in him, a sense of bewilderment greater than before. He waited five minutes, not daring to move a step, then tried another figure, a woman this time who, luckily, knew the immediate neighbourhood intimately. She gave him elaborate instructions in the kindest possible way, then vanished with

incredible swiftness and ease into the sea of gloom beyond. The instantaneous way she vanished was disheart-
ening, upsetting; it was so uncannily abrupt and sudden.
Yet she comforted him. Morley Place, according to her
version, was not two hundred yards from where he stood.
He felt his way forward, step by step, using his cane, crossing a giddy open space kicking the kerb with each boot
alternately, coughing and choking all the time as he did so.

"They were real, I guess, anyway," he said aloud.
"They were both real enough all right. And it may lift a
bit soon!" He was making a great effort to hold himself in hand. He was already fighting, that is. He realized
this perfectly. The only point was—the reality of the
figures. "It may lift now any minute," he repeated
louder. In spite of the cold, his skin was sweating pro-
fusely.

But, of course, it did not lift. The figures, too, became
fewer. No carts were audible. He had followed the
woman's directions carefully, but now found himself in
some by-way, evidently, where pedestrians at the best of
times were rare. There was dull silence all about him.
His foot lost the kerb, his cane swept the empty air,
striking nothing solid, and panic rose upon him with its
shuddering, icy grip. He was alone, he knew himself
alone, worse still—he was in another open space.

It took him fifteen minutes to cross that open space,
most of the way upon his hands and knees, oblivious of
the icy slime that stained his trousers, froze his fingers,
intent only upon feeling solid support against his back
and spine again. It was an endless period. The moment
of collapse was close, the shriek already rising in his throat,
the shaking of the whole body uncontrollable, when—his
outstretched fingers struck a friendly kerb, and he saw
a glimmering patch of diffused radiance overhead. With a
great, quick effort he stood upright, and an instant later
his stick rattled along an area railing. He leaned against
it, breathless, panting, his heart beating painfully while

the street lamp gave him the further comfort of its feeble
gleam, the actual flame, however, invisible. He looked this
way and that; the pavement was deserted. He was en-
gulfed in the dark silence of the fog.

But Morley Place, he knew, must be very close by
now. He thought of the friendly little V.A.D. he had
known in France, of a warm bright fire, a cup of tea and
a cigarette. One more effort, he reflected, and all these
would be his. He pluckily groped his way forward again,
crawling slowly by the area railings. If things got really
bad again, he would ring a bell and ask for help, much
as he shrank from the idea. Provided he had no more
open spaces to cross, provided he saw no more figures
emerging and vanishing like creatures born of the fog and
dwelling within it as within their native element—it was
the figures he now dreaded more than anything else, more
even than the loneliness—provided the panic sense——

A faint darkening of the fog beneath the next lamp
caught his eye and made him start. He stopped. It was
not a figure this time, it was the shadow of the pole
grotesquely magnified. No, it moved. It moved towards
him. A flame of fire followed by ice flowed through him.
It was a figure—close against his face. It was a woman.

The doctor's advice came suddenly back to him, the
counsel that had cured him of a hundred phantoms:

"Do not ignore them. Treat them as real. Speak and
go with them. You will soon prove their unreality then.
And they will leave you. . . ."

He made a brave, tremendous effort. He was shaking.
One hand clutched the damp and icy area railing.

"Lost your way like myself, haven't you, ma'am?" he
said in a voice that trembled. "Do you know where we
are at all? Morley Place *I'm* looking for——"

He stopped dead. The woman moved nearer and for
the first time he saw her face clearly. Its ghastly pallor,
the bright, frightened eyes that stared with a kind of
dazed bewilderment into his own, the beauty above all,

arrested his speech midway. The woman was young, her
tall figure wrapped in a dark fur coat.

"Can I help you?" he asked impulsively, forgetting his
own terror for the moment. He was more than startled.
Her air of distress and pain stirred a peculiar anguish in
him. For a moment she made no answer, thrusting her
white face closer as if examining him, so close, indeed,
that he controlled with difficulty his instinct to shrink back
a little.

"Where am I?" she asked at length, searching his eyes
intently. "I'm lost—I've lost myself. I can't find my
way back." Her voice was low, a curious wailing in it
that touched his pity oddly. He felt his own distress
merging in one that was greater.

"Same here," he replied more confidently. "I'm terrified of being alone, too. I've had shell-shock, you know.
Let's go together. We'll find a way together——"

"Who are you!" the woman murmured, still staring
at him with her big bright eyes, their distress, however,
no whit lessened. She gazed at him as though aware suddenly of his presence.

He told her briefly. "And I'm going to tea with a
V.A.D. friend in Morley Place. What's your address? Do
you know the name of the street?"

She appeared not to hear him, or not to understand
exactly; it was as if she was not listening again.

"I came out so suddenly, so unexpectedly," he heard
the low voice with pain in every syllable; "I can't find my
home again. Just when I was expecting him too——"
She looked about her with a distraught expression that
made O'Reilly long to carry her in his arms to safety
then and there. "He may be there now—waiting for
me at this very moment—and I can't get back." And
so sad was her voice that only by an effort did O'Reilly
prevent himself putting out his hand to touch her. More
and more he forgot himself in his desire to help her. Her
beauty, the wonder of her strange bright eyes in the

pallid face, made an immense appeal. He became calmer.
This woman was real enough. He asked again the address,
the street and number, the distance she thought it was.
"Have you any idea of the direction, ma'am, any idea at
all? We'll go together and——"

She suddenly cut him short. She turned her head as
if to listen, so that he saw her profile a moment, the outline
of the slender neck, a glimpse of jewels just below the fur.

"Hark! I hear him calling! I remember . . . !"
And she was gone from his side into the swirling fog.

Without an instant's hesitation O'Reilly followed her,
not only because he wished to help, but because he dared
not be left alone. The presence of this strange, lost woman
comforted him; he must not lose sight of her, whatever
happened. He had to run, she went so rapidly, ever
just in front, moving with confidence and certainty, turning right and left, crossing the street, but never stopping,
never hesitating, her companion always at her heels in
breathless haste, and with a growing terror that he might
lose her any minute. The way she found her direction
through the dense fog was marvellous enough, but
O'Reilly's only thought was to keep her in sight, lest
his own panic redescend upon him with its inevitable collapse in the dark and lonely street. It was a wild and
panting pursuit, and he kept her in view with difficulty,
a dim fleeting outline always a few yards ahead of him.
She did not once turn her head, she uttered no sound, no
cry; she hurried forward with unfaltering instinct. Nor
did the chase occur to him once as singular; she was his
safety, and that was all he realized.

One thing, however, he remembered afterwards, though
at the actual time he no more than registered the detail,
paying no attention to it—a definite perfume she left upon
he atmosphere, one, moreover, that he knew, although he
could not find its name as he ran. It was associated
vaguely, for him, with something unpleasant, something
disagreeable. He connected it with misery and pain. It

gave him a feeling of uneasiness. More than that he did
not notice at the moment, nor could he remember—he
certainly did not try—where he had known this particular
scent before.

Then suddenly the woman stopped, opened a gate and
passed into a small private garden—so suddenly that
O'Reilly, close upon her heels, only just avoided tumbling
into her. "You've found it?" he cried. "May I come in
a moment with you? Perhaps you'll let me telephone to
the doctor."

She turned instantly. Her face close against his own,
was livid.

"Doctor!" she repeated in an awful whisper. The word
meant terror to her. O'Reilly stood amazed. For a second
or two neither of them moved. The woman seemed petrified.

"Dr. Henry, you know," he stammered, finding his
tongue again. "I'm in his care. He's in Harley Street."

Her face cleared as suddenly as it had darkened, though
the original expression of bewilderment and pain still
hung in her great eyes. But the terror left them, as
though she suddenly forgot some association that had revived it.

"My home," she murmured. "My home is somewhere
here. I'm near it. I must get back—in time—for him.
I must. He's coming to me." And with these extraordinary words she turned, walked up the narrow path, and
stood upon the porch of a two-storey house before her
companion had recovered from his astonishment sufficiently
to move or utter a syllable in reply. The front door, he
saw, was ajar. It had been left open.

For five seconds, perhaps for ten, he hesitated; it was
the fear that the door would close and shut him out that
brought the decision to his will and muscles. He ran up
the steps and followed the woman into a dark hall where
she had already preceded him, and amid whose blackness
she now had finally vanished. He closed the door, not

knowing exactly why he did so, and knew at once by an instinctive feeling that the house he now found himself in with this unknown woman was empty and unoccupied. In a house, however, he felt safe. It was the open streets that were his danger. He stood waiting, listening a moment before he spoke; and he heard the woman moving down the passage from door to door, repeating to herself in her low voice of unhappy wailing some words he could not understand:

"Where is it? Oh, where is it? I must get back. . . ."

O'Reilly then found himself abruptly stricken with dumbness, as though, with these strange words, a haunting terror came up and breathed against him in the darkness.

"Is she after all a figure?" ran in letters of fire across his numbed brain. "Is she unreal—or real?"

Seeking relief in action of some kind, he put out a hand automatically, feeling along the wall for an electric switch, and though he found it by some miraculous chance, no answering glow responded to the click.

And the woman's voice from the darkness: "Ah! Ah! At last I've found it. I'm home again—at last . . . !" He heard a door open and close upstairs. He was on the ground-floor now—alone. Complete silence followed.

In the conflict of various emotions—fear for himself lest his panic should return, fear for the woman who had led him into this empty house and now deserted him upon some mysterious errand of her own that made him think of madness—in this conflict that held him a moment spellbound, there was a yet bigger ingredient demanding instant explanation, but an explanation that he could not find. Was the woman real or was she unreal? Was she a human being or a "figure"? The horror of doubt obsessed him with an acute uneasiness that betrayed itself in a return of that unwelcome inner trembling he knew was dangerous.

What saved him from a *crise* that must have had most dangerous results for his mind and nervous system gen-

erally, seems to have been the outstanding fact that he
felt more for the woman than for himself. His sympathy
and pity had been deeply moved; her voice, her beauty,
her anguish and bewilderment, all uncommon, inexplicable, mysterious, formed together a claim that drove self
into the background. Added to this was the detail that
she had left him, gone to another floor without a word,
and now, behind a closed door in a room upstairs, found
herself face to face at last with the unknown object of
her frantic search—with "it," whatever "it" might be. Real
or unreal, figure or human being, the overmastering impulse of his being was that he must go to her.

It was this clear impulse that gave him decision and
energy to do what he then did. He struck a match, he
found a stump of candle, he made his way by means
of this flickering light along the passage and up the
carpetless stairs. He moved cautiously, stealthily,
though not knowing why he did so. The house, he now
saw, was indeed untenanted; dust-sheets covered the piled-
up furniture; he glimpsed through doors ajar, pictures
were screened upon the walls, brackets draped to look like
hooded heads. He went on slowly, steadily, moving on
tiptoe as though conscious of being watched, noting the
well of darkness in the hall below, the grotesque shadows
that his movements cast on walls and ceiling. The silence
was unpleasant, yet, remembering that the woman was
"expecting" someone, he did not wish it broken. He
reached the landing and stood still. Closed doors on both
sides of a corridor met his sight, as he shaded the candle
to examine the scene. Behind which of these doors, he
asked himself, was the woman, figure or human being,
now alone with "it"?

There was nothing to guide him, but an instinct that
he must not delay sent him forward again upon his search.
He tried a door on the right—an empty room, with the
furniture hidden by dust-sheets, and the mattress rolled
up on the bed. He tried a second door, leaving the first

one open behind him, and it was, similarly, an empty bed-room. Coming out into the corridor again he stood a moment waiting, then called aloud in a low voice that yet woke echoes unpleasantly in the hall below: "Where are you? I want to help—which room are you in?"

There was no answer; he was almost glad he heard no sound, for he knew quite well that he was waiting really for another sound—the steps of him who was "expected." And the idea of meeting with this unknown third sent a shudder through him, as though related to an interview he dreaded with his whole heart, and must at all costs avoid. Waiting another moment or two, he noted that his candle-stump was burning low, then crossed the landing with a feeling, at once of hesitation and determination, towards a door opposite to him. He opened it; he did not halt on the threshold. Holding the candle at arm's length, he went boldly in.

And instantly his nostrils told him he was right at last, for a whiff of the strange perfume, though this time much stronger than before, greeted him, sending a new quiver along his nerves. He knew now why it was associated with unpleasantness, with pain, with misery, for he recognized it—the odour of a hospital. In this room a powerful anæsthetic had been used—and recently.

Simultaneously with smell, sight brought its message too. On the large double bed behind the door on his right lay, to his amazement, the woman in the dark fur coat. He saw the jewels on the slender neck; but the eyes he did not see, for they were closed—closed, too, he grasped at once, in death. The body lay stretched at full length, quite motionless. He approached. A dark thin streak that came from the parted lips and passed downwards over the chin, losing itself then in the fur collar, was a trickle of blood. It was hardly dry. It glistened.

Strange it was perhaps that, while imaginary fears had the power to paralyse him, mind and body, this sight of something real had the effect of restoring confidence. The

sight of blood and death, amid conditions often ghastly
and even monstrous, was no new thing to him. He went
up quietly, and with steady hand he felt the woman's cheek,
the warmth of recent life still in its softness. The final cold
had not yet mastered this empty form whose beauty, in its
perfect stillness, had taken on the new strange sweetness
of an unearthly bloom. Pallid, silent, untenanted, it lay
before him, lit by the flicker of his guttering candle. He
lifted the fur coat to feel for the unbeating heart. A
couple of hours ago at most, he judged, this heart was
working busily, the breath came through those parted lips,
the eyes were shining in full beauty. His hand encountered a hard knob—the head of a long steel hat-pin driven
through the heart up to its hilt.

He knew then which was the figure—which was the
real and which the unreal. He knew also what had been
meant by "it."

But before he could think or reflect what action he
must take, before he could straighten himself even from
his bent position over the body on the bed, there sounded
through the empty house below the loud clang of the front
door being closed. And instantly rushed over him that
other fear he had so long forgotten—fear for himself.
The panic of his own shaken nerves descended with irresistible onslaught. He turned, extinguishing the candle
in the violent trembling of his hand, and tore headlong
from the room.

The following ten minutes seemed a nightmare in
which he was not master of himself and knew not exactly
what he did. All he realized was that steps already
sounded on the stairs, coming quickly nearer. The flicker
of an electric torch played on the banisters, whose shadows
ran swiftly sideways along the wall as the hand that held
the light ascended. He thought in a frenzied second of
police, of his presence in the house, of the murdered
woman. It was a sinister combination. Whatever happened, he must escape without being so much as even

seen. His heart raced madly. He darted across the landing into the room opposite, whose door he had luckily left open. And by some incredible chance, apparently, he was neither seen nor heard by the man who, a moment later, reached the landing, entered the room where the body of the woman lay, and closed the door carefully behind him.

Shaking, scarcely daring to breathe lest his breath be audible, O'Reilly, in the grip of his own personal terror, remnant of his uncured shock of war, had no thought of what duty might demand or not demand of him. He thought only of himself. He realized one clear issue— that he must get out of the house without being heard or seen. Who the new-comer was he did not know, beyond an uncanny assurance that it was *not* him whom the woman had "expected," but the murderer himself, and that it was the murderer, in his turn, who was expecting this third person. In that room with death at his elbow, a death he had himself brought about but an hour or two ago, the murderer now hid in waiting for his second victim. And the door was closed.

Yet any minute it might open again, cutting off retreat.

O'Reilly crept out, stole across the landing, reached the head of the stairs, and began, with the utmost caution, the perilous descent. Each time the bare boards creaked beneath his weight, no matter how stealthily this weight was adjusted, his heart missed a beat. He tested each step before he pressed upon it, distributing as much of his weight as he dared upon the banisters. It was a little more than half-way down that, to his horror, his foot caught in a projecting carpet tack; he slipped on the polished wood, and only saved himself from falling headlong by a wild clutch at the railing, making an uproar that seemed to him like the explosion of a hand-grenade in the forgotten trenches. His nerves gave way then, and panic seized him. In the silence that followed the resounding echoes he heard the bedroom door opening on the floor above.

Concealment was now useless. It was impossible, too. He took the last flight of stairs in a series of leaps, four steps at a time, reached the hall, flew across it, and opened the front door, just as his pursuer, electric torch in hand, covered half the stairs behind him. Slamming the door, he plunged headlong into the welcome, all-obscuring fog outside.

The fog had now no terrors for him, he welcomed its concealing mantle; nor did it matter in which direction he ran so long as he put distance between him and the house of death. The pursuer had, of course, not followed him into the street. He crossed open spaces without a tremor. He ran in a circle nevertheless, though without being aware he did so. No people were about, no single groping shadow passed him; no boom of traffic reached his ears, when he paused for breath at length against an area railing. Then for the first time he made the discovery that he had no hat. He remembered now. In examining the body, partly out of respect, partly perhaps unconsciously, he had taken it off and laid it—on the very bed.

It was there, a tell-tale bit of damning evidence, in the house of death. And a series of probable consequences flashed through his mind like lightning. It was a new hat fortunately; more fortunate still, he had not yet written name or initials in it; but the maker's mark was there for all to read, and the police would go immediately to the shop where he had bought it only two days before. Would the shop-people remember his appearance? Would his visit, the date, the conversation be recalled? He thought it was unlikely; he resembled dozens of men; he had no outstanding peculiarity. He tried to think, but his mind was confused and troubled, his heart was beating dreadfully, he felt desperately ill. He sought vainly for some story to account for his being out in the fog and far from home without a hat. No single idea presented itself.

He clung to the icy railings, hardly able to keep upright, collapse very near—when suddenly a figure emerged from the fog, paused a moment to stare at him, put out a hand and caught him, and then spoke:

"You're ill, my dear sir," said a man's kindly voice. "Can I be of any assistance? Come, let me help you." He had seen at once that it was not a case of drunkenness. "Come, take my arm, won't you? I'm a physician. Luckily, too, you are just outside my very house. Come in." And he half dragged, half pushed O'Reilly, now bordering on collapse, up the steps and opened the door with his latch-key.

"Felt ill suddenly—lost in the fog . . . terrified, but be all right soon, thanks awfully——" the Canadian stammered his gratitude, but already feeling better. He sank into a chair in the hall, while the other put down a paper parcel he had been carrying, and led him presently into a comfortable room; a fire burned brightly; the electric lamps were pleasantly shaded; a decanter of whisky and a siphon stood on a small table beside a big arm-chair; and before O'Reilly could find another word to say the other had poured him out a glass and bade him sip it slowly, without troubling to talk till he felt better.

"That will revive you. Better drink it slowly. You should never have been out a night like this. If you've far to go, better let me put you up——"

"Very kind, very kind, indeed," mumbled O'Reilly, recovering rapidly in the comfort of a presence he already liked and felt even drawn to.

"No trouble at all," returned the doctor. "I've been at the front, you know. I can see what your trouble is—shell-shock, I'll be bound."

The Canadian, much impressed by the other's quick diagnosis, noted also his tact and kindness. He had made no reference to the absence of a hat, for instance.

"Quite true," he said. "I'm with Dr. Henry, in Harley Street," and he added a few words about his case. The whisky worked its effect, he revived more and more, feeling better every minute. The other handed him a cigarette; they began to talk about his symptoms and recovery; confidence returned in a measure, though he still felt badly frightened. The doctor's manner and personality did much to help, for there was strength and gentleness in the face, though the features showed unusual determination, softened occasionally by a sudden hint as of suffering in the bright, compelling eyes. It was the face, thought O'Reilly, of a man who had seen much and probably been through hell, but of a man who was simple, good, sincere. Yet not a man to trifle with; behind his gentleness lay something very stern. This effect of character and personality woke the other's respect in additioin to his gratitude. His sympathy was stirred.

"You encourage me to make another guess," the man was saying, after a successful reading of the impromptu patient's state, "that you have had, namely, a severe shock quite recently, and"—he hesitated for the merest fraction of a second—"that it would be a relief to you," he went on, the skilful suggestion in the voice unnoticed by his companion, "it would be wise as well, if you could unburden yourself to—someone—who would understand." He looked at O'Reilly with a kindly and very pleasant smile. "Am I not right, perhaps?" he asked in his gentle tone.

"Someone who would understand," repeated the Canadian. "That's my trouble exactly. You've hit it. It's all so incredible."

The other smiled. "The more incredible," he suggested, "the greater your need for expression. Suppression, as you may know, is dangerous in cases like this. You think you have hidden it, but it bides its time and comes up later, causing a lot of trouble. Confession, you know"—he emphasized the word—"confession is good for the soul!"

"You're dead right," agreed the other.

"Now if you can, bring yourself to tell it to someone who will listen and believe—to myself, for instance. I am a doctor, familiar with such things. I shall regard all you say as a professional confidence, of course; and, as we are strangers, my belief or disbelief is of no particular consequence. I may tell you in advance of your story, however—I think I can promise it—that I shall believe all you have to say."

O'Reilly told his story without more ado, for the suggestion of the skilled physician had found easy soil to work in. During the recital his host's eyes never once left his own. He moved no single muscle of his body. His interest seemed intense.

"A bit tall, isn't it?" said the Canadian, when his tale was finished. "And the question is——" he continued with a threat of volubility which the other checked instantly.

"Strange, yes, but incredible, no," the doctor interrupted. "I see no reason to disbelieve a single detail of what you have just told me. Things equally remarkable, equally incredible, happen in all large towns, as I know from personal experience. I could give you instances." He paused a moment, but his companion, staring into his eyes with interest and curiosity, made no comment. "Some years ago, in fact," continued the other, "I knew of a very similar case—strangely similar."

"Really! I should be immensely interested——"

"So similar that it seems almost a coincidence. *You* may find it hard, in your turn, to credit it." He paused again, while O'Reilly sat forward in his chair to listen. "Yes," pursued the doctor slowly, "I think everyone connected with it is now dead. There is no reason why I should not tell it, for one confidence deserves another, you know. It happened during the Boer War—as long ago as that," he added with emphasis. "It is really a very commonplace story in one way, though very dreadful in

another, but a man yho has served at the front will under·
stand and—I'm sure—will sympathize."

"I'm sure of that," offered the other readily.

"A colleague of mine, now dead, as I mentioned—a
surgeon, with a big practice, married a young and charming girl. They lived happily together for several years.
His wealth made her very comfortable. His consulting-
room, I must tell you, was some distance from his house
—just as this might be—so that she was never bothered
with any of his cases. Then came the war. Like many
others, though much over age, he volunteered. He gave
up his lucrative practice and went to South Africa. His
income, of course, stopped; the big house was closed; his
wife found her life of enjoyment considerably curtailed.
This she considered a great hardship, it seems. She felt
a bitter grievance against him. Devoid of imagination,
without any power of sacrifice, a selfish type, she was
yet a beautiful, attractive woman—and young. The inevitable lover came upon the scene to console her. They
planned to run away together. He was rich. Japan they
thought would suit them. Only, by some ill luck, the
husband got wind of it and arrived in London just in the
nick of time."

"Well rid of her," put in O'Reilly, "*I* think."

The doctor waited a moment. He sipped his glass.
Then his eyes fixed upon his companion's face somewhat
sternly.

"Well rid of her, yes," he continued, "only he determined to make that riddance final. He decided to kill
her—and her lover. You see, he loved her."

O'Reilly made no comment. In his own country this
method with a faithless woman was not unknown. His
interest was very concentrated. But he was thinking, too,
as he listened, thinking hard.

"He planned the time and place with care," resumed
the other in a lower voice, as though he might possibly
be overheard. "They met, he knew, in the big house, now

closed, the house where he and his young wife had passed such happy years during their prosperity. The plan failed, however, in an important detail—the woman came at the appointed hour, but without her lover. She found death waiting for her—it was a painless death. Then her lover, who was to arrive half an hour later, did not come at all. The door had been left open for him purposely. The house was dark, its rooms shut up, deserted; there was no caretaker even. It was a foggy night, just like this."

"And the other?" asked O'Reilly in a failing voice. "The lover——"

"A man did come in," the doctor went on calmly, "but it was not the lover. It was a stranger."

"A stranger?" the other whispered. "And the surgeon—where was he all this time?"

"Waiting outside to see him enter—concealed in the fog. He saw the man go in. Five minutes later he followed, meaning to complete his vengeance, his act of justice, whatever you like to call it. But the man who had come in was a stranger—he came in by chance—just as you might have done—to shelter from the fog—or——"

O'Reilly, though with a great effort, rose abruptly to his feet. He had an appalling feeling that the man facing him was mad. He had a keen desire to get outside, fog or no fog, to leave this room, to escape from the calm accents of this insistent voice. The effect of the whisky was still in his blood. He felt no lack of confidence. But words came to him with difficulty.

"I think I'd better be pushing off now, doctor," he said clumsily. "But I feel I must thank you very much for all your kindness and help." He turned and looked hard into the keen eyes facing him. "Your friend," he asked in a whisper, "the surgeon—I hope—I mean, was he ever caught?"

"No," was the grave reply, the doctor standing up in front of him, "he was never caught."

O'Reilly waited a moment before he made another re-

mark. "Well," he said at length, but in a louder tone
than before, "I think—I'm glad." He went to the door
without shaking hands.

"You have no hat," mentioned the voice behind him.
"If you'll wait a moment I'll get you one of mine. You
need not trouble to return it." And the doctor passed him,
going into the hall. There was a sound of tearing paper,
O'Reilly left the house a moment later with a hat upon his
head, but it was not till he reached the Tube station half
an hour afterwards that he realized it was his own.

XIV

THE LANE THAT RAN EAST AND WEST

I

THE curving strip of lane, fading into invisibility east and west, had always symbolized life to her. In some minds life pictures itself a straight line, uphill, downhill, flat, as the case may be; in hers it had been, since childhood, this sweep of country lane that ran past her cottage door. In thick white summer dust, she invariably visualized it, blue and yellow flowers along its untidy banks of green. It flowed, it glided, sometimes it rushed. Without a sound it ran along past the nut trees and the branches where honeysuckle and wild roses shone. With every year now its silent speed increased.

From either end she imagined, as a child, that she looked over into outer space—from the eastern end into the infinity before birth, from the western into the infinity that follows death. It was to her of real importance.

From the veranda the entire stretch was visible, not more than five hundred yards at most; from the platform in her mind, whence she viewed existence, she saw her own life, similarly, as a white curve of flowering lane, arising she knew not whence, gliding whither she could not tell. At eighteen she had paraphrased the quatrain with a smile upon her red lips, her chin tilted, her strong grey eyes rather wistful with yearning—

> *Into this little lane, and why not knowing,*
> *Nor whence, like water willy-nilly flowing,*
> *And out again—like dust along the waste,*
> *I know not whither, willy-nilly blowing.*

At thirty she now repeated it, the smile still there, but the lips not quite so red, the chin a trifle firmer, the grey eyes stronger, clearer, but charged with a more wistful and a deeper yearning.

It was her turn of mind, imaginative, introspective, querulous perhaps, that made the bit of running lane significant. Food with the butcher's and baker's carts came to her from its eastern, its arriving end, as she called it; news with the postman, adventure with rare callers. Youth, hope, excitement, all these came from the sunrise. Thence came likewise spring and summer, flowers, butterflies, the swallows. The fairies, in her childhood, had come that way too, their silver feet and gossamer wings brightening the summer dawns; and it was but a year ago that Dick Messenger, his car stirring a cloud of thick white dust, had also come into her life from the space beyond the sunrise.

She sat thinking about him now—how he had suddenly appeared out of nothing that warm June morning, asked her permission about some engineering business on the neighbouring big estate over the hill, given her a dog-rose and a bit of fern-leaf, and eventually gone away with her promise when he left. Out of the eastern end he appeared; into the western end he vanished.

For there was this departing end as well, where the lane curved out of sight into the space behind the yellow sunset. In this direction went all that left her life. Her parents, each in turn, had taken that way to the churchyard. Spring, summer, the fading butterflies, the restless swallows, all left her round that western curve. Later the fairies followed them, her dreams one by one, the vanishing years as well—and now her youth, swifter, ever swifter, into the region where the sun dipped nightly among pale rising stars, leaving her brief strip of life colder, more and more unlit.

Just beyond this end she imagined shadows.

She saw Dick's car whirling towards her, whirling away again, making for distant Mexico, where his treasure

lay. In the interval he had found that treasure and realized it. He was now coming back again. He had landed
in England yesterday.

Seated in her deck-chair on the veranda, she watched
the sun sink to the level of the hazel trees. The last
swallows already flashed their dark wings against the fading gold. Over that western end to-morrow or the next
day, amid a cloud of whirling white dust, would emerge,
again out of nothingness, the noisy car that brought Dick
Messenger back to her, back from the Mexican expedition
that ensured his great new riches, back into her heart and
life. In the other direction she would depart a week or so
later, her life in his keeping, and his in hers . . . and the
feet of their children, in due course, would run up and
down the mysterious lane in search of flowers, butterflies,
excitement, in search of life.

She wondered . . . and as the light faded her wondering grew deeper. Questions that had lain dormant for
twelve months became audible suddenly. Would Dick be
satisfied with this humble cottage which meant so much
to her that she felt she could never, never leave it? Would
not his money, his new position, demand palaces elsewhere? He was ambitious. Could his ambitions set an
altar of sacrifice to his love? And she—could she, on the
other hand, walk happy and satisfied along the western
curve, leaving her lane finally behind her, lost, untravelled,
forgotten? Could she face this sacrifice for him? Was
he, in a word, *the* man whose appearance out of the sunrise she had been watching and waiting for all these hurrying, swift years?

She wondered. Now that the decisive moment was so
near, unhappy doubts assailed her. Her wondering grew
deeper, spread, enveloped, penetrated her being like a
gathering darkness. And the sun sank lower, dusk crept
along the hedgerows, the flowers closed their little burning
eyes. Shadows passed hand in hand along the familiar
bend that was so short, so soon travelled over and left be-

hind that a mistake must ruin all its sweetest joy. To
wander down it with a companion to whom its flowers, its
butterflies, its shadows brought no full message, must turn
it chill, dark, lonely, colourless. . . . Her thoughts slipped
on thus into a soft inner reverie born of that scented
twilight hour of honeysuckle and wild roses, born too of
her deep self-questioning, of wonder, of yearning unsatisfied.

The lane, meanwhile, produced its customary few
figures, moving homewards through the dusk. She knew
them well, these familiar figures of the countryside, had
known them from childhood onwards—labourers, hedgers,
ditchers and the like, with whom now, even in her reverie,
she exchanged the usual friendly greetings across the
wicket-gate. This time, however, she gave but her mind
to them, her heart absorbed with its own personal and immediate problem.

Melancey had come and gone; old Averill, carrying his
hedger's sickle-knife, had followed; and she was vaguely
looking for Hezekiah Purdy, bent with years and rheuma-
tism, his tea-pail always rattling, his shuffling feet making
a sorry dust, when the figure she did not quite recognize
came into view, emerging unexpectedly from the sunride
end. Was it Purdy? Yes—no—yet, if not, who was it?
Of course it must be Purdy. Yet while the others, being
homeward bound, came naturally from west to east, with
this new figure it was otherwise, so that he was half-way
down the curve before she fully realized him. Out of the
eastern end the man drew nearer, a stranger therefore;
out of the unknown regions where the sun rose, and where
no shadows were, he moved towards her down the deserted
lane, perhaps a trespasser, an intruder possibly, but certainly an unfamiliar figure.

Without particular attention or interest, she watched
him drift nearer down her little semi-private lane of
dream, passing leisurely from east to west, the mere fact
that he was there establishing an intimacy that remained

at first unsuspected. It was her eye that watched him,
not her mind. What was he doing here, where going,
whither come, she wondered vaguely, the lane both his
background and his starting-point? A little by-way, after
all, this haunted lane. The real world, she knew, swept
down the big high-road beyond, unconscious of the humble
folk its unimportant tributary served. Suddenly the burden of the years assailed her. Had she, then, missed life
by living here?

Then, with a little shock, her heart contracted as she
became aware of two eyes fixed upon her in the dusk.
The stranger had already reached the wicket-gate and now
stood leaning against it, staring at her over its spiked
wooden top. It was certainly not old Purdy. The blood
rushed back into her heart again as she returned the gaze.
He was watching her with a curious intentness, with an
odd sense of authority almost, with something that persuaded her instantly of a definite purpose in his being
there. He was waiting for her—expecting her to come
down and speak with him, as she had spoken with the
others. Of this, her little habit, he made use, she felt.
Shyly, half-nervously, she left her deck-chair and went
slowly down the short gravel path between the flowers,
noticing meanwhile that his clothes were ragged, his hair
unkempt, his face worn and ravaged as by want and suffering, yet that his eyes were curiously young. His eyes,
indeed, were full brown smiling eyes, and it was the surprise of his youth that impressed her chiefly. That he
could be tramp or trespasser left her. She felt no fear.

She wished him "Good evening" in her calm, quiet
voice, adding with sympathy, "And who are you, I wonder? You want to ask me something?" It flashed across
her that his shabby clothing was somehow a disguise. Over
his shoulder hung a faded sack. "I can do something for
you?" she pursued inquiringly, as was her kindly custom.
"If you are hungry, thirsty, or——"

It was the expression of vigour leaping into the deep

eyes that stopped her. "If you need clothes," she had been going to add. She was not frightened, but suddenly she paused, gripped by a wonder she could not understand.

And his first words justified her wonder. "*I* have something for you," he said, his voice faint, a kind of stillness in it as though it came through distance. Also, though this she did not notice, it was an educated voice, and it was the absence of surprise that made this detail too natural to claim attention. She had expected it. "Something to give you. I have brought it for you," the man concluded.

"Yes," she replied, aware, again without comprehension, that her courage and her patience were both summoned to support her. "Yes," she repeated more faintly, as though this was all natural, inevitable, expected. She saw that the sack was now lifted from his shoulder and that his hand plunged into it, as it hung apparently loose and empty against the gate. His eyes, however, never for one instant left her own. Alarm, she was able to remind herself, she did not feel. She only recognized that this ragged figure laid something upon her spirit she could not fathom, yet was compelled to face.

His next words startled her. She drew, if unconsciously, upon her courage:

"A dream."

The voice was deep, yet still with the faintness as of distance in it. His hand, she saw, was moving slowly from the empty sack. A strange attraction, mingled with pity, with yearning too, stirred deeply in her. The face, it seemed, turned soft, the eyes glowed with some inner fire of feeling. Her heart now beat unevenly.

"Something—to—sell to me," she faltered, aware that his glowing eyes upon her made her tremble. The same instant she was ashamed of the words, knowing they were uttered by a portion of her that resisted, and this was not the language he deserved.

He smiled, and she knew her resistance a vain make-believe he pierced too easily, though he let it pass in silence.

"There is, I mean, a price—for every dream," she tried to save herself, conscious delightfully that her heart was smiling in return.

The dusk enveloped them, the corncrakes were calling from the fields, the scent of honeysuckle and wild roses lay round her in a warm wave of air, yet at the same time she felt as if her naked soul stood side by side with this figure in the infinitude of space beyond the sunrise end. The golden stars hung calm and motionless above them. "That price"—his answer fell like a summons she had actually expected—"you pay to another, not to me." The voice grew fainter, farther away, dropping through empty space behind her. "All dreams are but a single dream. You pay that price to——"

Her interruption slipped spontaneously from her lips, its inevitable truth a prophecy:

"To myself!"

He smiled again, but this time he did not answer. His hand, instead, now moved across the gate towards her.

And before she quite realized what had happened, she was holding a little object he had passed across to her. She had taken it, obeying, it seemed, an inner compulsion and authority which were inevitable, fore-ordained. Lowering her face she examined it in the dusk—a small green leaf of fern—fingered it with tender caution as it lay in her palm, gazed for some seconds closely at the tiny thing. . . . When she looked up again the stranger, the seller of dreams, as she now imagined him, had moved some yards away from the gate, and was moving still, a leisurely quiet tread that stirred no dust, a shadowy outline soft with dusk and starlight, moving towards the sunrise end, whence he had first appeared.

Her heart gave a sudden leap, as once again the burden of the years assailed her. Her words seemed driven out:

"Who are you? Before you go—your name! What is your name?"

His voice, now faint with distance as he melted from sight against the dark fringe of hazel trees, reached her but indistinctly, though its meaning was somehow clear:

"The dream," she heard like a breath of wind against her ear, "shall bring its own name with it. I wait . . ." Both sound and figure trailed off into the unknown space beyond the eastern end, and, leaning against the wicket-gate as usual, the white dust settling about his heavy boots, the tea-pail but just ceased from rattling, was—old Purdy.

Unless the mind can fix the reality of an event in the actual instant of its happening, judgment soon dwindles into a confusion between memory and argument. Five minutes later, when old Purdy had gone has way again, she found herself already wondering, reflecting, question-ing. Yearning had perhaps conjured with emotion to fashion both voice and figure out of imagination, out of this perfumed dusk, out of the troubled heart's desire. Confusion in time had further helped to metamorphose old Purdy into some legendary shape that had stolen upon her mood of reverie from the shadows of her beloved lane. . . . Yet the dream she had accepted from a stranger hand, a little fern leaf, remained at any rate to shape a delightful certainty her brain might criticize while her heart believed. The fern leaf assuredly was real. A fairy gift! Those who eat of this fern-seed, she remembered as she sank into sleep that night, shall see the fairies! And, indeed, a few hours later she walked in dream along the familiar curve between the hedges, her own childhood tak-ing her by the hand as she played with the flowers, the butterflies, the glad swallows beckoning while they flashed. Without the smallest sense of surprise or unexpectedness, too, she met at the eastern end—two figures. They stood, as she with her childhood stood, hand in hand, the seller of dreams and her lover, waiting since time began, she realized, waiting with some great unuttered question on their lips. Neither addressed her, neither spoke a word. Dick looked at her, ambition, hard and restless, shining in his eyes; in the eyes of the other—dark, gentle, piercing, but extraordinarily young for all the ragged hair about the face the shabby clothes, the ravaged and unkempt appearance—a brightness as of the coming dawn.

A choice, she understood, was offered to her; there was a decision she must make. She realized, as though some great wind blew it into her from outer space, another, a new standard to which her judgment must inevitably conform, or admit the purpose of her life evaded finally. The same moment she knew what her decision was. No hesitation touched her. Calm, yet trembling, her courage and her patience faced the decision and accepted it. The hands then instantly fell apart, unclasped. One figure turned and vanished down the lane towards the departing end, but with the other, now hand in hand, she rose floating, gliding without effort, a strange bliss in her heart, to meet the sunrise.

"He has awakened . . . so he cannot stay," she heard, like a breath of wind that whispered into her ear. "I, who bring you this dream—I wait."

She did not wake at once when the dream was ended, but slept on long beyond her accustomed hour, missing thereby Melancey, Averill, old Purdy as they passed the wicket-gate in the early hours. She woke, however, with a new clear knowledge of herself, of her mind and heart, to all of which in simple truth to her own soul she must conform. The fern-seed she placed in a locket attached to a fine gold chain about her neck. During the long, lonely, expectant yet unsatisfied years that followed she wore it day and night.

2

She had the curious feeling that she remained young. Others grew older, but not she. She watched her con-

temporaries slowly give the signs, while she herself held
stationary.   Even those younger than herself went past
her, growing older in the ordinary way, whereas her heart,
her mind, even her appearance, she felt certain, hardly
aged at all.   In a room full of people she felt pity often
as she read the signs in their faces knowing her own un-
changed.   Their eyes were burning out, but hers burned
on.   It was neither vanity nor delusion, but an inner conviction she could not alter.

The age she held to was the year she had received the
fern-seed from old Purdy, or rather, from an imaginary
figure her reverie had set momentarily in old Purdy's
place.   That figure of her reverie, the dream that followed,
the subsequent confession to Dick Messenger, meeting his
own half-way—these marked the year when she stopped
growing older.   To that year she seemed chained, gazing
into the sunrise end—waiting, ever waiting.

Whether in her absent-minded reverie she had actually
plucked the bit of fern herself, or whether, after all, old
Purdy had handed it to her, was not a point that troubled
her.   It was in her locket about her neck still, day and
night.   The seller of dreams was an established imaginative reality in her life.   Her heart assured her she would
meet him again one day.   She waited.   It was very curious,
it was rather pathetic.   Men came and went, she saw her
chances pass; her answer was invariably "No."

The break came suddenly, and with devastating effect.
As she was dressing carefully for the party, full of excited anticipation like some young girl still, she saw
looking out upon her from the long mirror a face of plain
middle-age.   A blackness rose about her.   It seemed the
mirror shattered.   The long, long dream, at any rate, fell
in a thousand broken pieces at her feet.   It was perhaps
the ball dress, perhaps the flowers in her hair; it may have
been the low-cut gown that betrayed the neck and throat,
or the one brilliant jewel that proved her eyes now dimmed
beside it—but most probably it was the tell-tale hands,

whose ageing no artifice ever can conceal. The middle-aged woman, at any rate, rushed from the glass and claimed her.

It was a long time, too, before the signs of tears had been carefully obliterated again, and the battle with herself—to go or not to go—was decided by clear courage. She would not send a hurried excuse of illness, but would take the place where she now belonged. She saw herself, a fading figure, more than half-way now towards the sunset end, within sight even of the shadowed emptiness that lay beyond the sun's dipping edge. She had lingered overlong, expecting a dream to confirm a dream; she had been oblivious of the truth that the lane went rushing just the same. It was now too late. The speed increased. She had waited, waited for nothing. The seller of dreams was a myth. No man could need her as she now was.

Yet the chief ingredient in her decision was, oddly enough, itself a sign of youth. A party, a ball, is ever an adventure. Fate, with her destined eyes aglow, may be bidden too, waiting among the throng, waiting for that very one who hesitates whether to go or not to go. Who knows what the evening may bring forth? It was this anticipation, faintly beckoning, its voice the merest echo of her shadowy youth, that tipped the scales between an evening of sleepless regrets at home and hours of neglected loneliness, watching the young fulfil the happy night. This and her courage weighed the balance down against the afflicting weariness of her sudden disillusion.

Therefore she went, her aunt, in whose house she was a visitor, accompanying her. They arrived late, walking under the awning alone into the great mansion. Music, flowers, lovely dresses, and bright happy faces filled the air about them. The dancing feet, the flashing eyes, the swing of the music, the throng of graceful figures expressed one word—pleasure. Pleasure, of course, meant youth. Beneath the calm summer stars youth realized itself prodigally, reckless of years to follow. Under the same calm stars, some fifty miles away in Kent, her stretch of de-

serted lane flowed peacefully, never pausing, passing relent-
lessly out into unknown space beyond the edge of the
world. A girl and a middle-aged woman bravely watched
both scenes.

"Dreadfully overcrowded," remarked her prosaic aunt.
"When I was a young thing there was more taste—always
room to dance, at any rate."

"It is a rabble rather," replied the middle-aged woman,
while the girl added, "but I enjoy it." She had enjoyed
one duty-dance with an elderly man to whom her aunt had
introduced her. She now sat watching the rabble whirl
and laugh. Her friend, behind unabashed lorgnettes,
made occasional comments.

"There's Mabel. Look at her frock, will you—the·
naked back. The way he holds her, too!"

She looked at Mabel Messenger, exactly her own age,
wife of the successful engineer, yet bearing herself almost
like a girl.

"*He's* away in Mexico, as usual," went on her aunt,
"with somebody else, also as usual."

"I don't envy her," mentioned the middle-aged woman,
while the girl added, "but she did well for herself, anyhow."

"It's a mistake to wait too long," was a suggestion
she did not comment on.

The host's brother came up and carried off her aunt.
She was left alone. An old gentleman dropped into the
vacated chair. Only in the centre of the brilliantly lit
room was there dancing now; people stood and talked in
animated throngs, every seat along the walls, every chair
and sofa in alcove corners occupied. The landing outside
the great flung doors was packed; some, going on elsewhere, were already leaving, but others arriving late still
poured up the staircase. Her loneliness remained unnoticed; with many other women, similarly stationed behind the whirling, moving dancers, she sat looking on,

an artificial smile of enjoyment upon her face, but the eyes empty and unlit.

Two pictures she watched simultaneously—the gay ballroom and the lane that ran east and west.

Midnight was past and supper over, though she had not noticed it. Her aunt had disappeared finally, it seemed. The two pictures filled her mind, absorbed her. What she was feeling was not clear, for there was confusion in her between the two scenes somewhere—as though the brilliant ballroom lay set against the dark background of the lane beneath the quiet stars. The contrast struck her. How calm and lovely the night lane seemed against this feverish gaiety, this heat, this artificial perfume, these exaggerated clothes. Like a small, rapid cinema-picture the dazzling ballroom passed along the dark throat of the deserted lane. A patch of light, alive with whirling animalculæ, it shone a moment against the velvet background of the midnight country-side. It grew smaller and smaller. It vanished over the edge of the departing end. It was gone.

Night and the stars enveloped her, and her eyes became accustomed to the change, so that she saw the sandy strip of lane, the hazel bushes, the dim outline of the cottage. Her naked soul, it seemed again, stood facing an infinitude. Yet the scent of roses, of dew-soaked grass came to her. A blackbird was whistling in the hedge. The eastern end showed itself now more plainly. The tops of the trees defined themselves. There came a glimmer in the sky, an early swallow flashed past against a streak of pale sweet gold. Old Purdy, his tea-pail faintly rattling, a stir of thick white dust about his feet, came slowly round the curve. It was the sunrise.

A deep, passionate thrill ran through her body from head to feet. There was a clap beside her—in the air it seemed—as though the wings of the early swallow had flashed past her very ear, or the approaching sunrise called aloud. She turned her head—along the brightening lane, but also across the gay ballroom. Old Purdy, straightening up his bent shoulders, was gazing over the wicket-gate into her eyes.

Something quivered. A shimmer ran fluttering before her sight. She trembled. Over the crowd of intervening heads, as over the spiked top of the little gate, a man was gazing at her.

Old Purdy, however, did not fade, nor did his outline wholly pass. There was this confusion between two pictures. Yet this man who gazed at her was in the London ballroom. He was so tall and straight. The same moment her aunt's face appeared below his shoulder, only just visible, and he turned his head, but did not turn his eyes, to listen to her. Both looked her way; they moved, threading their way towards her. It meant an introduction coming. He had asked for it.

She did not catch his name, so quickly, yet so easily and naturally the little formalities were managed, and she was dancing. The same sweet, dim confusion was about her. His touch, his voice, his eyes combined extraordinarily in a sense of complete possession to which she yielded utterly. The two pictures, moreover, still held their place. Behind the glaring lights ran the pale sweet gold of a country dawn; woven like a silver thread among the strings she heard the blackbirds whistling; in the stale, heated air lay the subtle freshness of a summer sunrise. Their dancing feet bore them along in a flowing motion that curved from east to west.

They danced without speaking; one rhythm took them; like a single person they glided over the smooth, perfect floor, and, more and more to her, it was as if the floor flowed with them, bearing them along. Such dancing she had never known. The strange sweetness of the confusion that half-entranced her increased—almost as though she lay upon her partner's arms and that he bore her through the air. Both the sense of weight and the touch of her feet on solid ground were gone delightfully. The London room grew hazy, too; the other figures faded; the ceiling, half transparent, let through a filtering glimmer of the dawn. Her thoughts—surely he shared them with her—went out floating beneath this brightening sky. There was a sound of wakening birds, a smell of flowers.

They had danced perhaps five minutes when both stopped abruptly as with one accord.

"Shall we sit it out—if you've no objection?" he suggested in the very instant that the same thought occurred to her. "The conservatory, among the flowers," he added, leading her to the corner among scented blooms and plants, exactly as she herself desired. There were leaves and ferns about them in the warm air. The light was dim. A streak of gold in the sky showed through the glass. But for one other couple they were alone.

"I have something to say to you," he began. "You must have thought it curious—I've been staring at you so. The whole evening I've been watching you."

"I—hadn't noticed," she said truthfully, her voice, as it were, not quite her own. "I've not been dancing—only once, that is."

But her heart was dancing as she said it. For the first time she became aware of her partner more distinctly—of his deep, resonant voice, his soldierly tall figure, his deferential, almost protective manner. She turned suddenly and looked into his face. The clear, rather penetrating eyes reminded her of someone she had known.

At the same instant he used her thought, turning it in his own direction. "I can't remember, for the life of me," he said quietly, "where I have seen you before. Your face is familiar to me, oddly familiar—years ago—in my first youth somewhere."

It was as though he broke something to her gently—something he was sure of and knew positively, that yet might shock and startle her.

The blood rushed from her heart as she quickly turned her gaze away. The wave of deep feeling that rose with a sensation of glowing warmth troubled her voice. "I find in you, too, a faint resemblance to—someone I have met," she murmured. Without meaning it she let slip the added words, "when I was a girl."

She felt him start, but he saved the situation, making it ordinary again by obtaining her permission to smoke, then slowly lighting his cigarette before he spoke.

"You must forgive me," he put in with a smile, "but your name, when you were kind enough to let me be introduced, escaped me. I did not catch it."

She told him her surname, but he asked in his persuasive yet somehow masterful way for the Christian name as well. He turned round instantly as she gave it, staring hard at her with meaning, with an examining intentness, with open curiosity. There was a question on his lips, but she interrupted, delaying it by a question of her own. Without looking at him she knew and feared his question. Her voice just concealed a trembling that was in her throat.

"My aunt," she agreed lightly, "is incorrigible. Do you know I didn't catch yours either? Oh—I meant your surname," she added, confusion gaining upon her when he mentioned his first name only.

He became suddenly more earnest, his voice deepened, his whole manner took on the guise of deliberate intention backed by some profound emotion that he could no longer hide. The music, which had momentarily ceased, began again, and a couple, who had been sitting out diagonally across from them, rose and went out. They were now quite alone. The sky was brighter.

"I must tell you," he went on in a way that compelled her to look up and meet his intent gaze. "You really must allow me. I feel sure somehow you'll understand. At any rate," he added like a boy, "you won't laugh."

She believes she gave the permission and assurance. Memory fails her a little here, for as she returned his gaze, it seemed a curious change came stealing over him, yet at

first so imperceptibly, so vaguely, that she could not say
when it began, nor how it happened.

"Yes," she murmured, "please——" The change defined itself. She stopped dead.

"I know now where I've seen you before. I remember."
His voice vibrated like a wind in big trees. It enveloped
her.

"Yes," she repeated in a whisper, for the hammering
of her heart made both a louder tone or further words
impossible. She knew not what he was going to say, yet
at the same time she knew with accuracy. Her eyes gazed
helplessly into his. The change absorbed her. Within his
outline she watched another outline grow. Behind the im-
maculate evening clothes a ragged, unkempt figure rose.
A worn, ravaged face with young burning eyes peered
through his own. "Please, please," she whispered again
very faintly. He took her hand in his.

His voice came from very far away, yet drawing nearer,
and the scene about them faded, vanished. The lane that
curved east and west now stretched behind him, and she
sat gazing towards the sunrise end, as years ago when the
girl passed into the woman first.

"I knew—a friend of yours—Dick Messenger," he was
saying in this distant voice that yet was close beside her,
"knew him at school, at Cambridge, and later in Mexico.
We worked in the same mines together, only he was con-
tractor and I was—in difficulties. That made no difference. He—he told me about a girl—of his love and admiration, an admiration that remained, but a love that had
already faded."

She saw only the ragged outline within the well-
groomed figure of the man who spoke. The young eyes
that gazed so piercingly into hers belonged to him, the
seller of her dream of years before. It was to this ragged
stranger in her lane she made her answer:

"I, too, now remember," she said softly. "Please go
on."

"He gave me his confidence, asking me where his duty lay, and I told him that the real love comes once only; it knows no doubt, no fading. I told him this——"

"We both discovered it in time," she said to herself, so low it was scarcely audible, yet not resisting as he laid his other hand upon the one he already held.

"I also told him there was only one true dream," the voice continued, the inner face drawing nearer to the outer that contained it. "I asked him, and he told me—everything. I knew all about this girl. Her picture, too, he showed me."

The voice broke off. The flood of love and pity, of sympathy and understanding that rose in her like a power long suppressed, threatened tears, yet happy, yearning tears like those of a girl, which only the quick, strong pressure of his hands prevented.

"The—little painting—yes, I know it," she faltered.

"It saved me," he said simply. "It changed my life. From that moment I began—living decently again—living for an ideal." Without knowing that she did so, the pressure of her hand upon his own came instantly. "He—he gave it to me," the voice went on, "to keep. He said he could neither keep it himself nor destroy it. It was the day before he sailed. I remember it as yesterday. I said I must give him something in return, or it would cut friendship. But I had nothing in the world to give. We were in the hills. I picked a leaf of fern instead. 'Fernseed,' I told him, 'it will make you see the fairies and find your true dream.' I remember his laugh to this day—a sad, uneasy laugh. 'I shall give it to her,' he told me, 'when I give her my difficult explanation.' But I said, 'Give it with my love, and tell her that I wait.' He looked at me with surprise, incredulous. Then he said slowly, 'Why not? If—if only you hadn't let yourself go to pieces like this!'"

An immensity of clear emotion she could not understand passed over her in a wave. Involuntarily she moved closer against him. With her eyes unflinchingly upon his own, she whispered: "You were hungry, thirsty, you had no clothes. . . . You waited!"

"You're reading my thoughts, as I knew one day you would." It seemed as if their minds, their bodies too, were one, as he said the words. "You, too—you waited." His voice was low.

There came a glow between them as of hidden fire; their faces shone; there was a brightening as of dawn upon their skins, within their eyes, lighting their very hair. Out of this happy sky his voice floated to her with the blackbird's song:

"And that night I dreamed of you. I dreamed I met you in an English country lane."

"We did," she murmured, as though it were quite natural.

"I dreamed I gave you the fern leaf—across a wicket-gate—and in front of a little house that was our home. In my dream—I handed to you—a dream——"

"You did." And as she whispered it the two figures merged into one before her very eyes. "See," she added softly, "I have it still. It is in my locket at this moment, for I have worn it day and night through all these years of waiting." She began fumbling at her chain.

He smiled. "Such things," he said gently, "are beyond me rather. I have found you. That's all that matters. That"—he smiled again—"is real at any rate."

"A vision," she murmured, half to herself and half to him, "I can understand. A dream, though wonderful, is a dream. But the little fern you gave me," drawing the fine gold chain from her bosom, "the actual leaf I have worn all these years in my locket!"

He smiled as she held the locket out to him, her fingers feeling for the little spring. He shook his head, but so slightly she did not notice it.

"I will prove it to you," she said. "I must. Look!" she cried, as with trembling hand she pressed the hidden catch. "There! There!"

With heads close together they bent over. The tiny lid flew open. And as he took her for one quick instant in his arms the sun flashed his first golden shaft upon them, covering them with light, But her exclamation of incredudous surprise he smothered with a kiss. For inside the little locket there lay—nothing. It was quite empty.

XV

"VENGEANCE IS MINE"

1

A N active, vigorous man in Holy orders, yet compelled by heart trouble to resign a living in Kent
before full middle age, he had found suitable work with
the Red Cross in France; and it rather pleased a strain of
innocent vanity in him that Rouen, whence he derived
his Norman blood, should be the scene of his activities.

He was a gentle-minded soul, a man deeply read and
thoughtful, but goodness perhaps his out-standing quality,
believing no evil of others. He had been slow, for instance,
at first to credit the German atrocities, until the evidence
had compelled him to face the appalling facts. With acceptance, then, he had experienced a revulsion which other
gentle minds have probably also experienced—a burning
desire, namely, that the perpetrators should be fitly punished.

This primitive instinct of revenge—he called it a lust
—he sternly repressed; it involved a descent to lower levels
of conduct irreconcilable with the progress of the race he
so passionately believed in. Revenge pertained to savage
days. But, though he hid away the instinct in his heart,
afraid of its clamour and persistency, it revived from
time to time, as fresh horrors made it bleed anew. It
remained alive, unsatisfied; while, with its analysis, his
mind strove unconsciously. That an intellectual nation
should deliberately include frightfulness as a chief item
in its creed perplexed him horribly; it seemed to him

conscious spiritual evil openly affirmed. Some genuine
worship of Odin, Wotan, Moloch lay still embedded in
the German outlook, and beneath the veneer of their pre-
tentious culture. He often wondered, too, what effect the
recognition of these horrors must have upon gentle minds
in other men, and especially upon imaginative minds.
How did they deal with the fact that this appalling thing
existed in human nature in the twentieth century? Its
survival, indeed, caused his belief in civilization as a whole
to waver. Was progress, his pet ideal and cherished
faith, after all a mockery? Had human nature not advanced . . . ?

His work in the great hospitals and convalescent camps
beyond the town was tiring; he found little time for recre-
ation, much less for rest; a light dinner and bed by ten
o'clock was the usual way of spending his evenings. He
had no social intercourse, for everyone else was as busy as
himself. The enforced solitude, not quite wholesome, was
unavoidable. He found no outlet for his thoughts. First-
hand acquaintance with suffering, physical and mental, was
no new thing to him, but this close familiarity, day by day,
with maimed and broken humanity preyed considerably on
his mind, while the fortitude and cheerfulness shown by
the victims deepened the impression of respectful, yearning
wonder made upon him. They were so young, so fine and
careless, these lads whom the German lust for power had
robbed of limbs, and eyes, of mind, of life itself. The sense
of horror grew in him with cumulative but unrelieved
effect.

With the lengthening of the days in February, and
especially when March saw the welcome change to summer
time, the natural desire for open air asserted itself. Instead
of retiring early to his dingy bedroom, he would stroll out
after dinner through the ancient streets. When the air
was not too chilly, he would prolong these outings, starting
at sunset and coming home beneath the bright mysterious
stars. He knew at length every turn and winding of the

old-world alleys, every gable, every tower and spire, from
the *Vieux Marché*, where Joan of Arc was burnt, to the
busy quays, thronged now with soldiers from half a dozen
countries. He wandered on past grey gateways of crum-
bling stone that marked the former banks of the old tidal
river. An English army, five centuries ago, had camped
here among reeds and swamps, besieging the Norman capital, where now they brought in supplies of men and material upon modern docks, a mighty invasion of a very different kind. Imaginative reflection was his constant mood.

But it was the haunted streets that touched him most,
stirring some chord his ancestry had planted in him. The
forest of spires thronged the air with strange stone flowers,
silvered by moonlight as though white fire streamed from
branch and petal; the old church towers soared; the cathedral touched the stars. After dark the modern note, para-
mount in the daylight, seemed hushed; with sunset it
underwent a definite night-change. Although the darkened
streets kept alive in him the menace of fire and death, the
crowding soldiers, dipped to the face in shadow, seemed
somehow negligible; the leaning roofs and gables hid them
in a purple sea of mist that blurred their modern garb,
steel weapons, and the like. Shadows themselves, they entered the being of the town; their feet moved silently; there
was a hush and murmur; the brooding buildings absorbed
them easily.

Ancient and modern, that is, unable successfully to
mingle, let fall grotesque, incongruous shadows on his
thoughts. The spirit of mediæval days stole over him,
exercising its inevitable sway upon a temperament already
predisposed to welcome it. Witchcraft and wonder, pagan
superstition and speculation, combined with an ancestral
tendency to weave a spell, half of acceptance, half of
shrinking, about his imaginative soul in which poetry and
logic seemed otherwise fairly balanced. Too weary for
critical judgment to discern clear outlines, his mind, during these magical twilight walks, became the playground of

opposing forces, some power of dreaming, it seems, too
easily in the ascendant. The soul of ancient Rouen, stealing beside his footsteps in the dusk, put forth a shadowy
hand and touched him.

This shadowy spell he denied as far as in him lay,
though the resistance offered by reason to instinct lacked
true driving power. The dice were loaded otherwise in
such a soul. His own blood harked back unconsciously to
the days when men were tortured, broken on the wheel,
walled up alive, and burnt for small offences. This
shadowy hand stirred faint ancestral memories in him,
part instinct, part desire. The next step, by which he saw
a similar attitude flowering full blown in the German
frightfulness, was too easily made to be rejected. The
German horrors made him believe that this ignorant
cruelty of olden days threatened the world now in a modern,
organized shape that proved its survival in the human
heart. Shuddering, he fought against the natural desire
for adequate punishment, but forgot that repressed emotions sooner or later must assert themselves. Essentially
irrepressible, they may force an outlet in distorted fashion.
He hardly recognized, perhaps, their actual claim, yet it
was audible occasionally. For, owing to his loneliness, the
natural outlet, in talk and intercourse, was denied.

Then, with the softer winds, he yearned for country
air. The sweet spring days had come; morning and evening were divine; above the town the orchards were in
bloom. Birds blew their tiny bugles on the hills. The
midday sun began to burn.

It was the time of the final violence, when the German
hordes flung like driven cattle against the Western line
where free men fought for liberty. Fate hovered dreadfully in the balance that spring of 1918; Amiens was
threatened, and if Amiens fell, Rouen must be evacuated.
The town, already full, became now over-full. On his
way home one evening he passed the station, crowded
with homeless new arrivals. "Got the wind up, it seems,

in Amiens!" cried a cheery voice, as an officer he knew
went by him hurriedly. And as he heard it the mood of
the spring became of a sudden uppermost. He reached
a decision. The German horror came abruptly closer. This
further overcrowding of the narrow streets was more than
he could face.

It was a small, personal decision merely, but he *must*
get out among woods and fields, among flowers and wholesome, growing things, taste simple, innocent life again.
The following evening he would pack his haversack with
food and tramp the four miles to the great *Forêt Verte*—
delicious name!—and spend the night with trees and stars,
breathing his full of sweetness, calm and peace. He was too
accustomed to the thunder of the guns to be disturbed by
it. The song of a thrush, the whistle of a blackbird, would
easily drown that. He made his plan accordingly.

The next two nights, however, a warm soft rain was
falling; only on the third evening could he put his little
plan into execution. Anticipatory enjoyment, meanwhile,
lightened his heart; he did his daily work more compe-
tently, the spell of the ancient city weakened somewhat.
The shadowy hand withdrew.

2

Meanwhile, a curious adventure intervened.

His good and simple heart, disciplined these many
years in the way a man should walk, received upon its imaginative side, a stimulus that, in his case, amounted to a
shock. That a strange and comely woman should make
eyes at him disturbed his equilibrium considerably; that
he should enjoy the attack, though without at first re-
sponding openly—even without full comprehension of its
meaning—disturbed it even more. It was, moreover, no
ordinary attack.

He saw her first the night after his decision when, in
a mood of disappointment due to the rain, he came down

to his lonely dinner. The room, he saw, was crowded with
new arrivals, from Amiens, doubtless, where they had "the
wind up." The wealthier civilians had fled for safety to
Rouen. These interested and, in a measure, stimulated
him. He looked at them sympathetically, wondering what
dear home-life they had so hurriedly relinquished at the
near thunder of the enemy guns, and, in so doing, he
noticed, sitting alone at a small table just in front of his
own—yet with her back to him—a woman.

She drew his attention instantly. The first glance
told him that she was young and well-to-do; the second,
that she was unusual. What precisely made her unusual
he could not say, although he at once began to study her
intently. Dignity, atmosphere, personality, he perceived
beyond all question. She sat there with an air. The becoming little hat with its challenging feather slightly
tilted, the set of the shoulders, the neat waist and slender
outline; possibly, too, the hair about the neck, and the faint
perfume that was wafted towards him as the serving girl
swept past, combined in the persuasion. Yet he felt it as
more than a persuasion. She attracted him with a subtle
vehemence he had never felt before. The instant he set
eyes upon her his blood ran faster. The thought rose passionately in him, almost the words that phrased it: "I
wish I knew her."

This sudden flash of response his whole being certainly
gave—to the back of an unknown woman. It was both vehement and instinctive. He lay stress upon its instinctive
character; he was aware of it before reason told him why.
That it was "in response" he also noted, for although he
had not seen her face and she assuredly had made no sign,
he felt that attraction which involves also invitation. So
vehement, moreover, was this response in him that he felt
shy and ashamed the same instant, for it almost seemed he
had expressed his thought in audible words. He flushed,
and the flush ran through his body; he was conscious of
heated blood as in a youth of twenty-five, and when a man

past forty knows this touch of fever he may also know, though he may not recognize it, that the danger signal which means possible abandon has been lit. Moreover, as though to prove his instinct justified, it was at this very instant that the woman turned and stared at him deliberately. She looked into his eyes, and he looked into hers. He knew a moment's keen distress, a sharpest possible discomfort, that after all he *had* expressed his desire audibly. Yet, though he blushed, he did not lower his eyes. The embarrassment passed instantly, replaced by a thrill of strangest pleasure and satisfaction. He knew a tinge of inexplicable dismay as well. He felt for a second helpless before what seemed a challenge in her eyes. The eyes were too compelling. They mastered him.

In order to meet his gaze she had to make a full turn in her chair, for her table was placed directly in front of his own. She did so without concealment. It was no mere attempt to see what lay behind by making a half-turn and pretending to look elsewhere; no corner of the eye business; but a full, straight, direct, significant stare. She looked into his soul as though she called him, he looked into hers as though he answered. Sitting there like a statue, motionless, without a bow, without a smile, he returned her intense regard unflinchingly and yet unwillingly. He made no sign. He shivered again. . . . It was perhaps ten seconds before she turned away with an air as if she had delivered her message and received his answer, but in those ten seconds a series of singular ideas crowded his mind, leaving an impression that ten years could never efface. The face and eyes produced a kind of intoxication in him. There was almost recognition, as though she said: "Ah, there you are! I was waiting; you'll have to come, of course. You must!" And just before she turned away she smiled.

He felt confused and helpless.

The face he described as unusual; familiar, too, as with the atmosphere of some long forgotten dream, and if beauty perhaps was absent, character and individuality were supreme. Implacable resolution was stamped upon the features, which yet were sweet and womanly, stirring an emotion in him that he could not name and certainly did not recognize. The eyes, slanting a little upwards, were full of fire, the mouth voluptuous but very firm, the chin and jaw most delicately modelled, yet with a masculine strength that told of inflexible resolve. The resolution, as a whole, was the most relentless he had ever seen upon a human countenance. It dominated him. "How vain to resist the will," he thought, "that lies behind!" He was conscious of enslavement; she conveyed a message that he must obey, admitting compliance with her unknown purpose.

That some extraordinary wordless exchange was registered thus between them seemed very clear; and it was just at this moment, as if to signify her satisfaction, that she smiled. At his feeling of willing compliance with some purpose in her mind, the smile appeared. It was faint, so faint indeed that the eyes betrayed it rather than the mouth and lips; but it was there; he saw it and he thrilled again to this added touch of wonder and enchantment. Yet, strangest of all, he maintains that with the smile there fluttered over the resolute face a sudden arresting tenderness, as though some wild flower lit a granite surface with its melting loveliness. He was aware in the clear strong eyes of unshed tears, of sympathy, of self-sacrifice he called maternal, of clinging love. It was this tenderness, as of a soft and gracious mother, and this implacable resolution, as of a stern, relentless man, that left upon his receptive soul the strange impression of sweetness yet of domination.

The brief ten seconds were over. She turned away as deliberatelly as she had turned to look. He found himself trembling with confused emotions he could not disentangle, could not even name; for, with the subtle intoxication of compliance in his soul lay also a vigorous protest that included refusal, even a violent refusal given with horror.

This unknown woman, without actual speech or definite gesture, had lit a flame in him that linked on far away and out of sight with the magic of the ancient city's mediæval spell. Both, he decided, were undesirable, both to be resisted.

He was quite decided about this. She pertained to forgotten yet unburied things, her modern aspect a mere disguise, a disguise that some deep unsatisfied instinct in him pierced with ease.

He found himself equally decided, too, upon another thing which, in spite of his momentary confusion, stood out clearly: the magic of the city, the enchantment of the woman, both attacked a constitutional weakness in his blood, a line of least resistance. It wore no physical aspect, breathed no hint of ordinary romance; the mere male and female, moral or immoral touch was wholly absent; yet passion lurked there, tumultuous if hidden, and a tract of consciousness, long untravelled, was lit by sudden ominous flares. His character, his temperament, his calling in life as a former clergyman and now a Red Cross worker, being what they were, he stood on the brink of an adventure not dangerous alone but containing a challenge of fundamental kind that involved his very soul.

No further thrill, however, awaited him immediately. He left his table before she did, having intercepted no slightest hint of desired acquaintanceship or intercourse. He, naturally, made no advances; she, equally, made no smallest sign. Her face remained hidden, he caught no flash of eyes, no gesture, no hint of possible invitation. He went upstairs to his dingy room, and in due course fell asleep. The next day he saw her not, her place in the dining-room was empty; but in the late evening of the following day, as the soft spring sunshine found him prepared for his postponed expedition, he met her suddenly on the stairs. He was going down with haversack and in walking kit to an early dinner, when he saw her coming up; she was perhaps a dozen steps below him; they must

meet. A wave of confused, embarrassed pleasure swept
him. He realized that this was no chance meeting. She
meant to speak to him.

Violent attraction and an equally violent repulsion
seized him. There was no escape, nor, had escape been
possible, would he have attempted it. He went down four
steps, she mounted four towards him; then he took one
and she took one. They met. For a moment they stood
level, while he shrank against the wall to let her pass. He
had the feeling that but for the support of that wall he
must have lost his balance and fallen into her, for the
sunlight from the landing window caught her face and lit
it, and she was younger, he saw, than he had thought, and
far more comely. Her atmosphere enveloped him, the
sense of attraction and repulsion became intense. She
moved past him with the slightest possible bow of recognition; then, having passed, she turned.

She stood a little higher than himself, a step at most,
and she thus looked down at him. Her eyes blazed into
his. She smiled, and he was aware again of the domination and the sweetness. The perfume of her near presence
drowned him; his head swam. "We count upon you,"
she said in a low firm voice, as though giving a command;
"I know . . . we may. We do." And, before he knew
what he was saying, trembling a little between deep pleasure and a contrary impulse that sought to choke the utterance, he heard his own voice answering. "You can count
upon me. . . ." And she was already half-way up the
next flight of stairs ere he could move a muscle, or attempt
to thread a meaning into the singular exchange.

Yet meaning, he well knew, there was.

She was gone; her footsteps overhead had died away.
He stood there trembling like a boy of twenty, yet also
like a man of forty in whom fires, long dreaded, now blazed
sullenly. She had opened the furnace door, the draught
rushed through. He felt again the old unwelcome spell;
he saw the twisted streets 'mid leaning gables and shadowy

towers of a day forgotten; he neard the ominous murmurs
of a crowd that thirsted for wheel and scaffold and fire;
and, aware of vengeance, sweet and terrible, aware, too,
that he welcomed it, his heart was troubled and afraid.

In a brief second the impression came and went; following it swiftly, the sweetness of the woman swept him:
he forgot his shrinking in a rush of wild delicious pleasure.
The intoxication in him deepened. She had recognized
him! She had bowed and even smiled; she had spoken,
assuming familiarity, intimacy, including him in her secret
purposes! It was this sweet intimacy cleverly injected,
that overcame the repulsion he acknowledged, winning
complete obedience to the unknown meaning of her words.
This meaning, for the moment, lay in darkness; yet it
was a portion of his own self, he felt, that concealed it
of set purpose. He kept it hid, he looked deliberately another way; for, if he faced it with full recognition, he knew
that he must resist it to the death. He allowed himself
to ask vague questions—then let her dominating spell con-
fuse the answers so that he did not hear them. The challenge to his soul, that is, he evaded.

What is commonly called sex lay only slightly in his
troubled emotions; her purpose had nothing that kept
step with chance acquaintanceship. There lay meaning,
indeed, in her smile and voice, but these were no hand-
maids to a vulgar intrigue in a foreign hotel. Her will
breathed cleaner air; her purpose aimed at some graver,
mightier climax than the mere subjection of an elderly
victim like himself. That will, that purpose, he felt certain, were implacable as death, the resolve in those bold
eyes was not a common one. For, in some strange way,
he divined the strong maternity in her; the maternal instinct was deeply, even predominantly, involved; he felt
positive that a divine tenderness, deeply outraged, was a
chief ingredient too. In some way, then, she needed him,
yet not she alone, for the pronoun "we" was used, and
there were others with her; in some way, equally, a part

of him was already her and their accomplice, an unresisting slave, a willing co-conspirator.

He knew one other thing, and it was this that he kept concealed so carefully from himself. His recognition of it was sub-conscious possibly, but for that very reason true: her purpose was consistent with the satisfaction at last of a deep instinct in him that clamoured to know gratification. It was for these odd, mingled reasons that he stood trembling when she left him on the stairs, and finally went down to his hurried meal with a heart that knew wonder, anticipation, and delight, but also dread.

3

The table in front of him remained unoccupied; his dinner finished, he went out hastily.

As he passed through the crowded streets, his chief desire was to be quickly free of the old muffled buildings and airless alleys with their clinging atmosphere of other days. He longed for the sweet taste of the heights, the smells of the forest whither he was bound. This *Forêt Verte,* he knew, rolled for leagues towards the north, empty of houses as of human beings; it was the home of deer and birds and rabbits, of wild boar too. There would be spring flowers among the brushwood, anemones, celandine, oxslip, daffodils. The vapours of the town oppressed him, the warm and heavy moisture stifled; he wanted space and the sight of clean simple things that would stimulate his mind with lighter thoughts.

He soon passed the Rampe, skirted the ugly villas of modern Bihorel and, rising now with every step, entered the *Route Neuve.* He went unduly fast; he was already above the Cathedral spire; below him the Seine meandered round the chalky hills, laden with war-barges, and across a dip, still pink in the afterglow, rose the blunt Down of Bonsecours with its anti-aircraft batteries. Poetry and violent fact crashed everywhere; he longed to top the hill and leave these unhappy reminders of death behind him. In front the sweet woods already beckoned through the twilight. He hastened. Yet while he deliberately fixed his imagination on promised peace and beauty, an undercurrent ran sullenly in his mind, busy with quite other thoughts. The unknown woman and her singular words, the following mystery of the ancient city, the soft beating wonder of the two together, these worked their incalculable magic persistently about him. Repression merely added to their power. His mind was a prey to some shadowy, remote anxiety that, intangible, invisible, yet knocked with ghostly fingers upon some door of ancient memory. . . . He watched the moon rise above the eastern ridge, in the west the afterglow of sunset still hung red. But these did not hold his attention as they normally must have done. Attention seemed elsewhere. The undercurrent bore him down a siding, into a backwater, as it were, that clamoured for discharge.

He thought suddenly, then, of weather, what he called "German weather"—that combination of natural conditions which so oddly favoured the enemy always. It had often occurred to him as strange; on sea and land, mist, rain and wind, the fog and drying sun worked ever on *their* side. The coincidence was odd, to say the least. And now this glimpse of rising moon and sunset sky reminded him unpleasantly of the subject. Legends of pagan weather-gods passed through his mind like hurrying shadows. These shadows multiplied, changed form, vanished and returned. They came and went with incoherence, a straggling stream, rushing from one point to another, manœuvring for position, but all unled, unguided by his will. The physical exercise filled his brain with blood, and thought danced undirected, picture upon picture driving by, so that soon he slipped from German weather and pagan gods to the witchcraft of past centuries, of its alleged association with the natural powers of the elements, and thus, eventually, to his cherished beliefs that humanity had advanced.

Such remnants of primitive days were grotesque superstition, of course. But had humanity advanced? Had the individual progressed after all? Civilization, was it not the merest artificial growth? And the old perplexity rushed through his mind again—the German barbarity and blood-lust, the savagery, the undoubted sadic impulses, the frightfulness taught with cool calculation by their highest minds, approved by their professors, endorsed by their clergy, applauded by their women even—all the unwelcome, undesired thoughts came flocking back upon him, escorted by the trooping shadows. They lay, these questions, still unsolved within him; it was the undercurrent, flowing more swiftly now, that bore them to the surface. It had acquired momentum; it was leading somewhere.

They were a thoughtful, intellectual race, these Germans; their music, literature, philosophy, their science— how reconcile the opposing qualities? He had read that their herd-instinct was unusually developed, though betraying the characteristics of a low wild savage type—the lupine. It might be true. Fear and danger wakened this collective instinct into terrific activity, making them blind and humourless; they fought best, like wolves, in contact; they howled and whined and boasted loudly all together to inspire terror; their Hymn of Hate was but an elaboration of the wolf's fierce bark, giving them herd-courage; and a savage discipline was necessary to their lupine type.

These reflections thronged his mind as the blood coursed in his veins with the rapid climbing; yet one and all, the beauty of the evening, the magic of the hidden town, the thoughts of German horror, German weather, German gods, all these, even the odd detail that they revived a pagan practice by hammering nails into effigies and idols—all led finally to one blazing centre that nothing could dislodge nor anything conceal; a woman's voice and eyes. To these he knew quite well, was due the undesired intensification of the very mood, the very emotions, the very thoughts he had come out on purpose to escape.

"It is the night of the vernal equinox," occurred to him suddenly, sharp as a whispered voice beside him. He had no notion whence the idea was born. It had no particular meaning, so far as he remembered.

"It had *then* . . ." said the voice imperiously, rising, it seemed, directly out of the under-current in his soul.

It startled him. He increased his pace. He walked very quickly, whistling softly as he went.

The dusk had fallen when at length he topped the long, slow hill, and left the last of the atrocious straggling villas well behind him. The ancient city lay far below in murky haze and smoke, but tinged now with the silver of the growing moon.

4

He stood now on the open plateau. He was on the heights at last.

The night air met him freshly in the face, so that he forgot the fatigue of the long climb uphill, taken too fast somewhat for his years. He drew a deep draught into his lungs and stepped out briskly.

Far in the upper sky light flaky clouds raced through the reddened air, but the wind kept to these higher strata, and the world about him lay very still. Few lights showed in the farms and cottages, for this was the direct route of the Gothas, and nothing that could help the German hawks to find the river was visible.

His mind cleared pleasantly; this keen sweet air held no mystery; he put his best foot foremost, whistling still, but a little more loudly than before. Among the orchards he saw the daisies glimmer. Also, he heard the guns, a thudding concussion in the direction of the coveted Amiens, where, some sixty miles as the crow flies, they roared their terror into the calm evening skies. He cursed the sound, in the town below it was not audible. Thought jumped then to the men who fired them, and so to the prisoners who worked on the roads outside the hospitals and camps he visited daily. He passed them every morning and night, and the N.C.O. invariably saluted his Red Cross uniform, a salute he returned, when he could not avoid it, with embarrassment.

One man in particular stood out clearly in this memory; he had exchanged glances with him, noted the expression of his face, the number of his gang printed on coat and trousers—"82." The fellow had somehow managed to establish a relationship; he would look up and smile or frown; if the news, from his point of view, was good, he smiled; if it was bad, he scowled; once, insolently enough— when the Germans had taken Albert, Péronne, Bapaume —he grinned.

Something about the sullen, close-cropped face, typically Prussian, made the other shudder. It was the visage of an animal, neither evil nor malignant, even good-natured sometimes when it smiled, yet of an animal that could be fierce with the lust of happiness, ferocious with delight. The sullen savagery of a human wolf lay in it somewhere. He pictured its owner impervious to shame, to normal human instinct as civilized people know these. Doubtless he read his own feelings into it. He could imagine the man doing anything and everything, regarding chivalry and sporting instinct as proof of fear or weakness. He could picture this member of the wolf-pack killing a woman or a child, mutilating, cutting off little hands even, with the conscientious conviction that it was right and sensible to destroy *any* individual of an enemy tribe. It was, to him, an atrocious and inhuman face.

It now cropped up with unpleasant vividness, as he listened to the distant guns and thought of Amiens with its back against the wall, its inhabitants flying——

Ah! Amiens . . . ! He again saw the woman staring into his obedient eyes across the narrow space between

the tables. He smelt the delicious perfume of her dress
and person on the stairs. He heard her commanding voice,
her very words: "We count on you. . . . I know we
can . . . we do." And her background was of twisted
streets, dark alley-ways and leaning gables. . . .

He hurried, whistling loudly an air that he invented
suddenly, using his stick like a golf club at every loose
stone his feet encountered, making as much noise as possible. He told himself he was a parson and a Red Cross
worker. He looked up and saw that the stars were out.
The pace made him warm, and he shifted his haversack
to the other shoulder. The moon, he observed, now cast
his shadow for a long distance on the sandy road.

After another mile, while the air grew sharper and
twilight surrendered finally to the moon, the road began to
curve and dip, the cottages lay farther out in the dim
fields, the farms and barns occurred at longer intervals. A
dog barked now and again; he saw cows lying down for
the night beneath shadowy fruit-trees. And then the scent
in the air changed slightly, and a darkening of the near
horizon warned him that the forest had come close.

This was an event. Its influence breathed already a
new perfume; the shadows from its myriad trees stole out
and touched him. Ten minutes later he reached its actual
frontier cutting across the plateau like a line of sentries
at attention. He slowed down a little. Here, within sight
and touch of his long-desired objective, he hesitated. It
stretched, he knew from the map, for many leagues to the
north, uninhabited, lonely, the home of peace and silence;
there were flowers there, and cool sweet spaces where the
moonlight fell. Yet here, within scent and touch of it,
he slowed down a moment to draw breath. A forest on the
map is one thing; visible before the eyes when night has
fallen, it is another. It is real.

The wind, not noticeable hitherto, now murmured towards him from the serried trees that seemed to manu-
facture darkness out of nothing. This murmur hummed

about him. It enveloped him. Piercing it, another sound that was not the guns just reached him, but so distant that he hardly noticed it. He looked back. Dusk suddenly merged in night. He stopped.

"How practical the French are, he said to himself—aloud—as he looked at the road running straight as a ruled line into the heart of the trees. "They waste no energy, no space, no time. Admirable!"

It pierced the forest like a lance, tapering to a faint point in the misty distance. The trees ate its undeviating straightness as though they would smother it from sight, as though its rigid outline marred their mystery. He admired the practical makers of the road, yet sided, too, with the poetry of the trees. He stood there staring, waiting, dawdling. . . . About him, save for this murmur of the wind, was silence. Nothing living stirred. The world lay extraordinarily still. That other distant sound had died away.

He lit his pipe, glad that the match blew out and the damp tobacco needed several matches before the pipe drew properly. His puttees hurt him a little, he stooped to loosen them. His haversack swung round in front as he straightened up again, he shifted it laboriously to the other shoulder. A tiny stone in his right boot caused irritation. Its removal took a considerable time, for he had to sit down, and a log was not at once forthcoming. Moreover, the laces gave him trouble, and his fingers had grown thick with heat and the knots were difficult to tie. . . .

"There!" He said it aloud, standing up again. "Now at last, I'm ready!" Then added a mild imprecation, for his pipe had gone out while he stooped over the recalcitrant boot, and it had to be lighted once again. "Ah!" he gasped finally with a sigh as, facing the forest for the third time, he shuffled his tunic straight, altered his haversack once more, changed his stick from the right hand to the left—and faced the foolish truth without further pretence.

He mopped his forehead carefully, as though at the same time trying to mop away from his mind a faint anxiety, a very faint uneasiness, that gathered there. Was someone standing near him? Had somebody come close? He listened intently. It was the blood singing in his ears, of course, that curious distant noise. For, truth to tell, the loneliness bit just below the surface of what he found enjoyable. It seemed to him that somebody was coming, someone he could not see, so that he looked back over his shoulder once again, glanced quickly right and left, then peered down the long opening cut through the woods in front—when there came suddenly a roar and a blaze of dazzling light from behind, so instantaneously that he barely had time to obey the instinct of self-preservation and step aside. He actually leapt. Pressed against the hedge, he saw a motor-car rush past him like a whirlwind, flooding the sandy road with fire; a second followed it; and, to his complete amazement, then, a third.

They were powerful, private cars, so-called. This struck him instantly. Two other things he noticed, as they dived down the throat of the long white road—they showed no tail-lights. This made him wonder. And, secondly, the drivers, clearly seen, were women. They were not even in uniform—which made him wonder even more. The occupants, too, were women. He caught the outline of toque and feather—or was it flowers?—against the closed windows in the moonlight as the procession rushed past him.

He felt bewildered and astonished. Private motors were rare, and military regulations exceedingly strict; the danger of spies dressed in French uniform was constant; cars armed with machine guns, he knew, patrolled the countryside in all directions. Shaken and alarmed, he thought of favoured persons fleeing stealthily by night, of treachery, disguise and swift surprise; he thought of various things as he stood peering down the road for ten minutes after all sight and sound of the cars had died away. But no solution of the mystery occurred to him.

Down the white throat the motors vanished. His pipe had gone out; he lit it, and puffed furiously.

His thoughts, at any rate, took temporarily a new direction now. The road was not as lonely as he had imagined. A natural reaction set in at once, and this proof of practical, modern life banished the shadows from his mind effectually. He started off once more, oblivious of his former hesitation. He even felt a trifle shamed and foolish, pretending that the vanished mood had not existed. The tobacco had been damp. His boot had really hurt him.

Yet bewilderment and surprise stayed with him. The swiftness of the incident was disconcerting; the cars arrived and vanished with such extraordinary rapidity; their noisy irruption into this peaceful spot seemed incongruous; they roared, blazed, rushed and disappeared; silence resumed its former sway.

But the silence persisted, whereas the noise was gone.

This touch of the incongruous remained with him as he now went ever deeper into the heart of the quiet forest. This odd incongruity of dreams remained.

5

The keen air stole from the woods, cooling his body and his mind; anemones gleamed faintly among the brushwood, lit by the pallid moonlight. There were beauty, calm and silence, the slow breathing of the earth beneath the comforting sweet stars. War, in this haunt of ancient peace, seemed an incredible anachronism. His thoughts turned to gentle happy hopes of a day when the lion and the lamb would yet lie down together, and a little child would lead them without fear. His soul dwelt with peaceful longings and calm desires.

He walked on steadily, until the inflexible straightness of the endless road began to afflict him, and he longed for a turning to the right or left. He looked eagerly about

him for a woodland path. Time mattered little; he could
wait for the sunrise and walk home "beneath the young
grey dawn"; he had food and matches, he could light a
fire, and sleep—— No!—after all, he would not light a
fire, perhaps; he might be accused of signalling to hostile
aircraft, or a *garde forestière* might catch him. He would
not bother with a fire. The night was warm, he could enjoy himself and pass the time quite happily without artificial heat; probably he would need no sleep at all. . . .
And just then he noticed an opening on his right, where a
seductive pathway led in among the trees. The moon, now
higher in the sky, lit this woodland trail enticingly; it
seemed the very opening he had looked for, and with a
thrill of pleasure he at once turned down it, leaving the
ugly road behind him with relief.

The sound of his footsteps hushed instantly on the
leaves and moss; the silence became noticeable; an unusual
stillness followed; it seemed that something in his mind
was also hushed. His feet moved stealthily, as though
anxious to conceal his presence from surprise. His steps
dragged purposely; their rustling through the thick dead
leaves, perhaps, was pleasant to him. He was not sure.

The path opened presently into a clearing where the
moonlight made a pool of silver, the surrounding brushwood fell away; and in the centre a gigantic outline rose.
It was, he saw, a beech tree that dwarfed the surrounding
forest by its grandeur. Its bulk loomed very splendid
against the sky, a faint rustle just audible in its myriad
tiny leaves. Dipped in the moonlight, it had such majesty
of proportion, such symmetry, that he stopped in admiration. It was, he saw, a multiple tree, five stems springing
with attempted spirals out of an enormous trunk; it was
immense; it had a presence, the space framed it to per-
fection. The clearing, evidently, was a favourite resting
place for summer picknickers, a playground, probably, for
city children on holiday afternoons; woodcutters, too, had
been here recently, for he noticed piled brushwood ready

to be carted. It indicated admirably, he felt, the limits of his night expedition. Here he would rest awhile, eat his late supper, sleep perhaps round a small— No! again—a fire he need *not* make; a spark might easily set the woods ablaze, it was against both forest and military regulations. This idea of a fire, otherwise so natural, was distasteful, even repugnant, to him. He wondered a little why it recurred. He noticed this time, moreover, something unpleasant connected with the suggestion of a fire, something that made him shrink; almost a ghostly dread lay hidden in it.

This startled him. A dozen excellent reasons, supplied by his brain, warned him that a fire was unwise; but the true reason, supplied by another part of him, concealed itself with care, as though afraid that reason might detect its nature and fix the label on. Disliking this reminder of his earlier mood, he moved forward into the clearing, swinging his stick aggressively and whistling. He approached the tree, where a dozen thick roots dipped into the earth. Admiring, looking up and down, he paced slowly round its prodigious girth, then stood absolutely still. His heart stopped abruptly, his blood became congealed. He saw something that filled him with a sudden emptiness of terror. On this western side the shadow lay very black; it was between the thick limbs, half stem, half root, where the dark hollows gave easy hiding-places, that he was positive he detected movement. A portion of the trunk had moved.

He stood stock still and stared—not three feet from the trunk—when there came a second movement. Concealed in the shadows there crouched a living form. The movement defined itself immediately. Half reclining, half standing, a living being pressed itself close against the tree, yet fitting so neatly into the wide scooped hollows, that it was scarcely distinguishable from its ebony background. But for the chance movement he must have passed it undetected. Equally, his outstretched fingers might have touched it. The blood rushed from his heart, as he saw this second movement.

Detaching itself from the obscure background, the figure rose and stood before him. It swayed a little, then stepped out into the patch of moonlight on his left. Three feet lay between them. The figure then bent over. A pallid face with burning eyes thrust forward and peered straight into his own.

The human being was a woman. The same instant he recognized the eyes that had stared him out of countenance in the dining-room two nights ago. He was petrified. She stared him out of countenance now.

And, as she did so, the under-current he had tried to ignore so long swept to the surface in a tumultuous flood, obliterating his normal self. Something elaborately built up in his soul by years of artificial training collapsed like a house of cards, and he knew himself undone.

"They've got me . . . !" flashed dreadfully through his mind. It was, again, like a message delivered in a dream where the significance of acts performed and language uttered, concealed at the moment, is revealed much later only.

"After all—they've got me . . . !"

6

The dialogue that followed seemed strange to him only when looking back upon it. The element of surprise again was negligible if not wholly absent, but the incongruity of dreams, almost of nightmare, became more marked. Though the affair was unlikely, it was far from incredible. So completely were this man and woman involved in some purpose common to them both that their talk, their meeting, their instinctive sympathy at the time seemed natural. The same stream bore them irresistibly towards the same far sea. Only, as yet, this common purpose remained concealed. Nor could he define the violent emotions that troubled him. Their exact description was in him, but so deep that he could not draw it up. Moonlight lay upon his thought, merging clear outlines.

Divided against himself, the cleavage left no authoritative self in control; his desire to take an immediate decision resulted in a confused struggle, where shame and pleasure, attraction and revulsion mingled painfully. Incongruous details tumbled helter-skelter about his mind: for no obvious reason, he remembered again his Red Cross uniform, his former holy calling, his nationality too; he was a servant of mercy, a teacher of the love of God; he was an English gentleman. Against which rose other details, as in opposition, holding just beyond the reach of words, yet rising, he recognized well enough, from the bed-rock of the human animal, whereon a few centuries have imposed the thin crust of refinement men call civilization. He was aware of joy and loathing.

In the first few seconds he knew the clash of a dreadful fundamental struggle, while the spell of this woman's strange enchantment poured over him, seeking the reconciliation he himself could not achieve. Yet the reconciliation *she* sought meant victory or defeat; no compromise lay in it. Something imperious emanating from her already dominated the warring elements towards a coherent whole. He stood before her, quivering with emotions he dared not name. Her great womanhood he recognized, acknowledging obedience to her undisclosed intentions. And this idea of coming surrender terrified him. Whence came, too, that queenly touch about her that made him feel he should have sunk upon his knees?

The conflict resulted in a curious compromise. He raised his hand; he saluted; he found very ordinary words.

"You passed me only a short time ago," he stammered, "in the motors. There were others with you——"

"Knowing that you would find us and come after. We count on your presence and your willing help." Her voice was firm as with unalterable conviction. It was persuasive

too. He nodded, as though acquiescence seemed the only
course.

"We need your sympathy; we must have your power
too."

He bowed again. "My power!" Something exulted
in him. But he murmured only. It was natural, he felt;
he gave consent without a question.

Strange words he both understood and did not understand. Her voice, low and silvery, was that of a gentle,
cultured woman, but command rang through it with a
clang of metal, terrible behind the sweetness. She moved
a little closer, standing erect before him in the moonlight,
her figure borrowing something of the great tree's majesty
behind her. It was incongruous, this gentle and yet sinister air she wore. Whence came, in this calm peaceful
spot, the suggestion of a wild and savage background to
her? Why were there tumult and oppression in his heart,
pain, horror, tenderness and mercy, mixed beyond disen-
tanglement? Why did he think already, but helplessly,
of escape, yet at the same time burn to stay? Whence
came again, too, a certain queenly touch he felt in her?

"The gods have brought you," broke across his turmoil
in a half whisper whose breath almost touched his face.
"You belong to us."

The deeps rose in him. Seduced by the sweetness and
the power, the warring divisions in his being drew together. His under-self more and more obtained the mastery she willed. Then something in the French she used
flickered across his mind with a faint reminder of normal
things again.

"Belgian——" he began, and then stopped short, as
her instant rejoinder broke in upon his halting speech and
petrified him. In her voice sang that triumphant tenderness that only the feminine powers of the Universe may
compass: it seemed the sky sang with her, the mating
birds, wild flowers, the south wind and the running
streams. All these, even the silver birches, lent their fluid,

feminine undertones to the two pregnant words with which she interrupted him and completed his own unfinished sentence:

"—— and mother."

With the dreadful calm of an absolute assurance, she stood and watched him.

His understanding already showed signs of clearing. She stretched her hands out with a passionate appeal, a yearning gesture, the eloquence of which should explain all that remained unspoken. He saw their grace and symmetry, exquisite in the moonlight, then watched them fold together in an attitude of prayer. Beautiful mother hands they were; hands made to smooth the pillows of the world, to comfort, bless, caress, hands that little children everywhere must lean upon and love—perfect symbol of protective, self-forgetful motherhood.

This tenderness he noted; he noted next—the strength. In the folded hands he divined the expression of another great world-power, fulfilling the implacable resolution of the mouth and eyes. He was aware of relentless purpose, more—of merciless revenge, as by a protective motherhood outraged beyond endurance. Moreover, the gesture held appeal; these hands, so close that their actual perfume reached him, sought his own in help. The power in himself as man, as male, as father—this was required of him in the fulfillment of the unknown purpose to which this woman summoned him. His understanding cleared still more.

The couple faced one another, staring fixedly beneath the giant beech that overarched them. In the dark of his eyes, he knew, lay growing terror. He shivered, and the shiver passed down his spine, making his whole body tremble. There stirred in him an excitement he loathed, yet welcomed, as the primitive male in him, answering the summons, reared up with instinctive, dreadful glee to shatter the bars that civilization had so confidently set upon its freedom. A primal emotion of his under-being, ancient lust that had too long gone hungry and unfed, leaped towards some possible satisfaction. It was incredible; it was, of course, a dream. But judgment wavered; increasing terror ate his will away. Violence and sweetness, relief and degradation, fought in his soul, as he trembled before a power that now slowly mastered him. This glee and loathing formed their ghastly partnership. He could have strangled the woman where she stood. Equally, he could have knelt and kissed her feet.

The vehemence of the conflict paralysed him.

"A mother's hands . . ." he murmured at length, the words escaping like bubbles that rose to the surface of a seething cauldron and then burst.

And the woman smiled as though she read his mind and saw his little trembling. The smile crept down from the eyes towards the mouth; he saw her lips part slightly; he saw her teeth.

But her reply once more transfixed him. Two syllables she uttered in a voice of iron:

"Louvain."

The sound acted upon him like a Word of Power in some Eastern fairy tale. It knit the present to a past that he now recognized could never die. Humanity had *not* advanced. The hidden source of his secret joy began to glow. For this woman focused in him passions that life had hitherto denied, pretending they were atrophied, and the primitive male, the naked savage rose up, with glee in its lustful eyes and blood upon its lips. Acquired civilization, a pitiful mockery, split through its thin veneer and fled.

"Belgian . . . Louvain . . . Mother . . ." he whispered, yet astonished at the volume of sound that now left his mouth. His voice had a sudden fullness. It seemed a cave-man roared the words.

She touched his hand, and he knew a sudden intensification of life within him; immense energy poured through his veins; à mediæval spirit used his eyes; great pagan instincts strained and urged against his heart, against his very muscles. He longed for action.

And he cried aloud: "I am with you, with you to the end!"

Her spell had vivified beyond all possible resistance that primitive consciousness which is ever the bed-rock of the human animal.

A racial memory, inset against the forest scenery, flashed suddenly through the depths laid bare. Below a sinking moon dark figures flew in streaming lines and groups; tormented cries went down the wind; he saw torn, blasted trees that swayed and rocked; there was a leaping fire, a gleaming knife, an altar. He saw a sacrifice.

It flashed away and vanished. In its place the woman stood, with shining eyes fixed on his face, one arm outstretched, one hand upon his flesh. She shifted slightly, and her cloak swung open. He saw clinging skins wound closely about her figure; leaves, flowers and trailing green hung from her shoulders, fluttering down the lines of her triumphant physical beauty. There was a perfume of wild roses, incense, ivy bloom, whose subtle intoxication drowned his senses. He saw a sparkling girdle round the waist, a knife thrust through it tight against the hip. And his secret joy, the glee, the pleasure of some unlawful and unholy lust leaped through his blood towards the abandonment of satisfaction.

The moon revealed a glimpse, no more. An instant he saw her thus, half savage and half sweet, symbol of primitive justice entering the present through the door of vanished centuries.

The cloak swung back again, the outstretched hand withdrew, but from a world he knew had altered.

To-day sank out of sight. The moon shone pale with terror and delight on Yesterday.

7

Across this altered world a faint new sound now reached his ears, as though a human wail of anguished terror trembled and changed into the cry of some captured helpless animal. He thought of a wolf apart from the comfort of its pack, savage yet abject. The despair of a last appeal was in the sound. It floated past, it died away. The woman moved closer suddenly.

"All is prepared," she said, in the same low, silvery voice; "we must not tarry. The equinox is come, the tide of power flows. The sacrifice is here; we hold him fast. We only awaited you." Her shining eyes were raised to his. "Your soul is with us now?" she whispered.

"My soul is with you."

"And midnight," she continued, "is at hand. We use, of course, their methods. Henceforth the gods—their old-world gods—shall work on our side. They demand a sacrifice, and justice has provided one."

His understanding cleared still more then; the last veil of confusion was drawing from his mind. The old, old names went thundering through his consciousness—Odin, Wotan, Moloch—accessible ever to invocation and worship of the rightful kind. It seemed as natural as though he read in his pulpit the prayer for rain, or gave out the hymn for those at sea. That was merely an empty form, whereas this was real. Sea, storm and earthquake, all natural activities, lay under the direction of those elemental powers called the gods. Names changed, the principle remained.

"Their weather shall be ours," he cried, with sudden passion, as a memory of unhallowed usages he had thought erased from life burned in him; while, stranger still, resentment stirred—revolt—against the system, against the very diety he had worshipped hitherto. For these had never once interfered to help the cause of right; their feebleness was now laid bare before his eyes. And a two-

fold lust rose in him. "Vengeance is ours!" he cried in
a louder voice, through which this sudden loathing of the
cross poured hatred. "Vengeance and justice! Now bind
the victim! Bring on the sacrifice!"

"He is already bound." And as the woman moved
a little, the curious erection behind her caught his eye—
the piled brushwood he had imagined was the work of
woodmen, picnickers, or playing children. He realized its
true meaning.

It now delighted and appalled him. Awe deepened in
him, a wind of ice passed over him. Civilization made one
more fluttering effort. He gasped, he shivered; he tried
to speak. But no words came. A thin cry, as of a frightened child, escaped him.

"It is the only way," the woman whispered softly. "We
steal from them the power of their own deities." Her head
flung back with a marvellous gesture of grace and power;
she stood before him a figure of perfect womanhood, gentle
and tender, yet at the same time alive and cruel with the
passions of an ignorant and savage past. Her folded hands
were clasped, her face turned heavenwards. "I am a
mother," she added, with amazing passion, her eyes glisten-
ing in the moonlight with unshed tears. "We all"—she
glanced towards the forest, her voice rising to a wild and
poignant cry—"all, all of us are mothers!"

It was then the final clearing of his understanding
happened, and he realized his own part in what would
follow. Yet before the realization he felt himself not
merely ineffective, but powerless. The struggling forces
in him were so evenly matched that paralysis of the will
resulted. His dry lips contrived merely a few words of
confused and feeble protest.

"Me!" he faltered. "My help——?"

"Justice," she answered; and though softly uttered, it
was as though the mediæval towers clanged their bells.
That secret, ghastly joy again rose in him; admiration,
wonder, desire followed instantly. A fugitive memory of

Joan of Arc flashed by, as with armoured wings, upon the moonlight. Some power similarly heroic, some purpose similarly inflexible, emanated from this woman, the savour of whose physical enchantment, whose very breath, rose to his brain like incense. Again he shuddered. The spasm of secret pleasure shocked him. He sighed. He felt alert, yet stunned.

Her words went down the wind between them:

"You are so weak, you English," he heard her terrible whisper, "so nobly forgiving, so fine, yet so forgetful. You refuse the weapon *they* place within your hands." Her face thrust closer, the great eyes blazed upon him. "If we would save the children"—the voice rose and fell like wind —"we must worship where they worship, we must sacrifice to their savage deities. . . ."

The stream of her words flowed over him with this nightmare magic that seemed natural, without surprise. He listened, he trembled, and again he sighed. Yet in his blood there was sudden roaring.

". . . Louvain . . . the hands of little children . . . we have the proof," he heard, oddly intermingled with another set of words that clamoured vainly in his brain for utterance; "the diary in his own handwriting, his gloating pleasure . . . the little, innocent hands. . . ."

"Justice is mine!" rang through some fading region of his now fainting soul, but found no audible utterance.

". . . Mist, rain and wind . . . the gods of German Weather. . . . We all . . . are mothers. . . ."

"I will repay," came forth in actual words, yet so low he hardly heard the sound. But the woman heard.

"*We!*" she cried fiercely, "*we* will repay!" . .

"God!" The voice seemed torn from his throat. "Oh God—*my* God!"

"*Our* gods," she said steadily in that tone of iron, "are near. The sacrifice is ready. And *you*—servant of mercy, priest of a younger deity, and English—you bring the power that makes it effectual. The circuit is complete."

It was perhaps the tears in her appealing eyes, perhaps it was her words, her voice, the wonder of her presence; all combined possibly in the spell that finally then struck down his will as with a single blow that paralysed his last resistance. The monstrous, half-legendary spirit of a primitive day recaptured him completely; he yielded to the spell of this tender, cruel woman, mother and avenging angel, whom horror and suffering had flung back upon the practices of uncivilized centuries. A common desire, a common lust and purpose, degraded both of them. They understood one another. Dropping back into a gulf of savage worship that set up idols in the place of God, they prayed to Odin and his awful crew. . . .

It was again the touch of her hand that galvanized him. She raised him; he had been kneeling in slavish wonder and admiration at her feet. He leaped to do the bidding, however terrible, of this woman who was priestess, queen indeed, of a long-forgotten orgy.

"Vengeance at last!" he cried, in an exultant voice that no longer frightened him. "Now light the fire! Bring on the sacrifice!"

There was a rustling among the nearer branches, the forest stirred; the leaves of last year brushed against advancing feet. Yet before he could turn to see, before even the last words had wholly left his lips, the woman, whose hand still touched his fingers, suddenly tossed her cloak aside, and flinging her bare arms about his neck, drew him with impetuous passion towards her face and kissed him, as with delighted fury of exultant passion, full upon the mouth. Her body, in its clinging skins, pressed close against his own; her heat poured into him. She held him fiercely, savagely, and her burning kiss consumed his modern soul away with the fire of a primal day.

"The gods have given you to us," she cried, releasing him. "Your soul is ours!"

She turned—they turned together—to look for one upon whose last hour the moon now shed her horrid silver.

8

This silvery moonlight fell upon the scene.

Incongruously he remembered the flowers that soon would know the cuckoo's call; the soft mysterious stars shone down; the woods lay silent underneath the sky.

An amazing fantasy of dream shot here and there. "I am a man, an Englishman, a padre!" ran twisting through his mind, as though *she* whispered them to emphasize the ghastly contrast of reality. A memory of his own Kentish village with its Sunday school fled past, his dream cf the Lion and the Lamb close after it. He saw children playing on the green. . . . He saw their happy little hands. . . .

Justice, punishment, revenge—he could not disentangle them. No longer did he wish to. The tide of violence was at his lips, quenching an ancient thirst. He drank. It seemed he could drink forever. These tender pictures only sweetened horror. That kiss had burned his modern soul away.

The woman waved her hand; there swept from the underbrush a score of figures dressed like herself in skins, with leaves and flowers entwined among their flying hair. He was surrounded in a moment. Upon each face he noted the same tenderness and terrible resolve that their commander wore. They pressed about him, dancing with enchanting grace, yet with full-blooded abandon, across the chequered light and shadow. It was the brimming energy of their movements that swept him off his feet, waking the desire for fierce rhythmical expression. His own muscles leaped and ached; for this energy, it seemed, poured into him from the tossing arms and legs, the shimmering bodies whence hair and skins flung loose, setting the very air awhirl. It flowed over into inanimate objects even, so that the trees waved their branches although no wind stirred— hair, skins and hands, rushing leaves and flying fingers touched his face, his neck, his arms and shoulders, catch-

ing him away into this orgy of an ancient, sacrificial ritual.
Faces with shining eyes peered into his, then sped away;
grew in a cloud upon the moonlight; sank back in
shadow; reappeared, touched him, whispered, vanished.
Silvery limbs gleamed everywhere. Chanting rose in a
wave, to fall away again into forest rustlings; there were
smiles that flashed, then fainted into moonlight, red lips
and gleaming teeth that shone, then faded out. The secret
glade, picked from the heart of the forest by the moon,
became a torrent of tumultuous life, a whirlpool of passionate emotions Time had not killed.

But it was the eyes that mastered him, for in their
yearning, mating so incongruously with the savage grace
—in the eyes shone ever tears. He was aware of gentle
women, of womanhood, of accumulated feminine power
that nothing could withstand, but of feminine power in
majesty, its essential protective tenderness roused, as by
tribal instinct, into a collective fury of implacable revenge.
He was, above all, aware of motherhood—of mothers. And
the man, the male, the father in him rose like a storm to
meet it.

From the torrent of voices certain sentences emerged;
sometimes chanted, sometimes driven into his whirling
mind as though big whispers thrust them down his ears.
"You are with us to the end," he caught. "We have the
proof. And punishment is ours!"

It merged in wind, others took its place:

"We hold him fast. The old gods wait and listen."

The body of rushing whispers flowed like a storm-wind
past.

A lovely face, fluttering close against his own, paused
an instant, and starry eyes gazed into his with a passion
of gratitude, dimming a moment their stern fury with a
mother's tenderness: "For the little ones . . . it is necessary, it is the only way. . . . Our own children. . . ."
The face went out in a gust of blackness, as the chorus rose
with a new note of awe and reverence, and a score of

throats uttered in unison a single cry: "The raven! The White Horses! His signs! Great Odin hears!"

He saw the great dark bird flap slowly across the clearing, and melt against the shadow of the giant beech; he heard its hoarse, croaking note; the crowds of heads bowed low before its passage. The White Horses he did not see; only a sound as of considerable masses of air regularly displaced was audible far overhead. But the veiled light, as though great thunder-clouds had risen, he saw distinctly. The sky above the clearing where he stood, panting and dishevelled, was blocked by a mass that owned unusual outline. These clouds now topped the forest, hiding the moon and stars. The flowers went out like nightlights blown. The wind rose slowly, then with sudden violence. There was a roaring in the tree-tops. The branches tossed and shook.

"The White Horses!" cried the voices, in a frenzy of adoration. "He is here!"

It came swiftly, this collective mass; it was both apt and terrible. There was an immense footstep. It was there.

Then panic seized him, he felt an answering tumult in himself, the Past surged through him like a sea at flood. Some inner sight, peering across the wreckage of To-day, perceived an outline that in its size dwarfed mountains, a pair of monstrous shoulders, a face that rolled through a full quarter of the heavens. Above the ruin of civilization, now fulfilled in the microcosm of his own being, the menacing shadow of a forgotten deity peered down upon the earth, yet upon one detail of it chiefly—the human group that had been wildly dancing, but that now chanted in solemn conclave about a forest altar.

For some minutes a dead silence reigned; the pouring winds left emptiness in which no leaf stirred; there was a hush, a stillness that could be felt. The kneeling figures stretched forth a level sea of arms towards the altar; from the lowered heads the hair hung down in torrents, against which the naked flesh shone white; the skins upon the rows of backs gleamed yellow. The obscurity deepened overhead. It was the time of adoration. He knelt as well, arms similarly outstretched, while the lust of vengeance burned within him.

Then came, across the stillness, the stirring of big wings, a rustling as the great bird settled in the higher branches of the beech. The ominous note broke through the silence; and with one accord the shining backs were straightened. The company rose, swayed, parting into groups and lines. Two score voices resumed the solemn chant. The throng of pallid faces passed to and fro like great fire-flies that shone and vanished. He, too, heard his own voice in unison, while his feet, as with instinctive knowledge, trod the same measure that the others trod.

Out of this tumult and clearly audible above the chorus and the rustling feet rang out suddenly, in a sweetly fluting tone, the leader's voice:

"The Fire! But first the hands!"

A rush of figures set instantly towards a thicket where the underbrush stood densest. Skins, trailing flowers, bare waving arms and tossing hair swept past on a burst of perfume. It was as though the trees themselves sped by. And the torrent of voices shook the very air in answer:

"The Fire! But first—the hands!"

Across this roaring volume pierced then, once again, that wailing sound which seemed both human and non-human—the anguished cry as of some lonely wolf in metamorphosis, apart from the collective safety of the pack, abjectly terrified, feeling the teeth of the final trap, and knowing the helpless feet within the steel. There was a crash of rending boughs and tearing branches. There was a tumult in the thicket, though of brief duration—then silence.

He stood watching, listening, overmastered by a diabolical sensation of expectancy he knew to be atrocious. Turning in the direction of the cry, his straining eyes seemed filled with blood; in his temples the pulses throbbed and hammered audibly. The next second he stiffened into a stone-like rigidity, as a figure, struggling violently yet half collapsed, was borne hurriedly past by a score of eager arms that swept it towards the beech tree, and then proceeded to fasten it in an upright position against the trunk. It was a man bound tight with thongs, adorned with leaves and flowers and trailing green. The face was hidden, for the head sagged forward on the breast, but he saw the arms forced flat against the giant trunk, held helpless beyond all possible escape; he saw the knife, poised and aimed by slender, graceful fingers above the victim's wrists laid bare; he saw the—hands.

"An eye for an eye," he heard, "a tooth for a tooth!" It rose in awful chorus. Yet this time, although the words roared close about him, they seemed farther away, as if wind brought them through the crowding trees from far off.

"Light the fire! Prepare the sacrifice!" came on a following wind; and, while strange distance held the voices as before, a new faint sound now audible was very close. There was a crackling. Some ten feet beyond the tree a column of thick smoke rose in the air; he was aware of heat not meant for modern purposes; of yellow light that was not the light of stars.

The figure writhed, and the face swung suddenly sideways. Glaring with panic hopelessness past the judge and past the hanging knife, the eyes found his own. There was a pause of perhaps five seconds, but in these five seconds centuries rolled by. The priest of To-day looked down into the well of time. For five hundred years he gazed into those twin eyeballs, glazed with the abject terror of a last appeal. They recognized one another.

The centuries dragged appallingly. The drama of civilization, in a sluggish stream, went slowly by, halting, meandering, losing itself, then reappearing. Sharpest pains, as of a thousand knives, accompanied its dreadful, endless lethargy. Its million hesitations made him suffer a million deaths of agony. Terror, despair and anger, all futile and without effect upon its progress, destroyed a thousand times his soul, which yet some hope—a towering, indestructible hope—a thousand times renewed. This despair and hope alternately broke his being, ever to fashion it anew. His torture seemed not of this world. Yet hope survived. The sluggish stream moved onward, forward. . . .

There came an instant of sharpest, dislocating torture. The yellow light grew slightly brighter. He saw the eyelids flicker.

It was at this moment he realized abruptly that he stood alone, apart from the others, unnoticed apparently, perhaps forgotten; his feet held steady; his voice no longer sang. And at this discovery a quivering shock ran through his being, as though the will were suddenly loosened into a new activity, yet an activity that halted between two terrifying alternatives.

It was as though the flicker of those eyelids loosed a spring.

Two instincts, clashing in his being, fought furiously for the mastery. One, ancient as this sacrifice, savage as the legendary figure brooding in the heavens above him, battled fiercely with another, acquired more recently in human evolution, that had not yet crystallized into permanence. He saw a child, playing in a Kentish orchard with toys and flowers the little innocent hands made living . . . he saw a lowly manger, figures kneeling round it, and one star shining overhead in piercing and prophetic beauty.

Thought was impossible; he saw these symbols only, as the two contrary instincts, alternately hidden and revealed, fought for permanent possession of his soul. Each strove to dominate him; it seemed that violent blows were struck that wounded physically; he was bruised, he ached, he gasped for breath; his body swayed, held upright only, it seemed, by the awful appeal in the fixed and staring eyes.

The challenge had come at last to final action; the conqueror, he well knew, would remain an integral portion of his character, his soul.

It was the old, old battle, waged eternally in every human heart, in every tribe, in every race, in every period, the essential principle indeed, behind the great world-war. In the stress and confusion of the fight, as the eyes of the victim, savage in victory, abject in defeat—the appealing eyes of that animal face against the tree stared with their awful blaze into his own, this flashed clearly over him. It was the battle between might and right, between love and hate, forgiveness and vengeance, Christ and the Devil. He heard the menacing thunder of "an eye for an eye, a tooth for a tooth," then above its angry volume rose suddenly another small silvery voice that pierced with sweetness:—"Vengeance is mine, I will repay . . ." sang through him as with unimaginable hope.

Something became incandescent in him then. He realized a singular merging of powers in absolute opposition to each other. It was as though they harmonized. Yet it was through this small, silvery voice the apparent magic came. The words, of course, were his own in memory, but they rose from his modern soul, now reawakening. . . . He started painfully. He noted again that he stood apart, alone, perhaps forgotten of the others. The woman, leading a dancing throng about the blazing brushwood, was far from him. Her mind, too sure of his compliance, had momentarily left him. The chain was weakened. The circuit knew a break.

But this sudden realization was not of spontaneous origin. His heart had not produced it of its own accord. The unholy tumult of the orgy held him too slavishly in its awful sway for the tiny point of his modern soul to have pierced it thus unaided. The light flashed to him from an outside, natural source of simple loveliness—the singing of a bird. From the distance, faint and exquisite, there had reached him the silvery notes of a happy thrush,

awake in the night, and telling its joy over and over again
to itself. The innocent beauty of its song came through
the forest and fell into his soul. . . .

The eyes, he became aware, had shifted, focusing now
upon an object nearer to them. The knife was moving.
There was a convulsive wriggle of the body, the head
dropped loosely forward, no cry was audible. But, at the
same moment, the inner battle ceased and an unexpected
climax came. Did the soul of the bully faint with
fear? Did the spirit leave him at the actual touch
of earthly vengeance? The watcher never knew. In that
appalling moment when the knife was about to begin the
mission that the fire would complete, the roar of inner
battle ended abruptly, and that small silvery voice drew
the words of invincible power from his reawakening soul.
"Ye do it also unto me . . ." pealed o'er the forest.

He reeled. He acted instantaneously. Yet before he
had dashed the knife from the hand of the executioner,
scattered the pile of blazing wood, plunged through the
astonished worshippers with a violence of strength that
amazed even himself; before he had torn the thongs apart
and loosened the fainting victim from the tree; before
he had uttered a single word or cry, though it seemed to
him he roared with a voice of thousands—he witnessed a
sight that came surely from the Heaven of his earliest
childhood days, from that Heaven whose God is love and
whose forgiveness was taught him at his mother's knee.

With superhuman rapidity it passed before him and
was gone. Yet it was no earthly figure that emerged from
the forest, ran with this incredible swiftness past the
startled throng, and reached the tree. He saw the shape;
the same instant it was there; wrapped in light, as though
a flame from the sacrificial fire flashed past him over the
ground. It was of an incandescent brightness, yet bright-
est of all were the little outstretched hands. These were
of purest gold, of a brilliance incredibly shining.

It was no earthly child that stretched forth these arms

of generous forgiveness and took the bewildered prisoner by the hand just as the knife descended and touched the helpless wrists. The thongs were already loosened, and the victim, fallen to his knees, looked wildly this way and that for a way of possible escape, when the shining hands were laid upon his own. The murderer rose. Another instant and the throng must have been upon him, tearing him limb from limb. But the radiant little face looked down into his own; she raised him to his feet; with superhuman swiftness she led him through the infuriated concourse as though he had become invisible, guiding him safely past the furies into the cover of the trees. Close before his eyes, this happened; he saw the waft of golden brilliance, he heard the final gulp of it, as wind took the dazzling of its fiery appearance into space. They were gone. . . .

9

He stood watching the disappearing motor-cars, wondering uneasily who the occupants were and what their business, whither and why did they hurry so swiftly through the night? He was still trying to light his pipe, but the damp tobacco would not burn.

The air stole out of the forest, cooling his body and his mind; he saw the anemones gleam; there was only peace and calm about him, the earth lay waiting for the sweet, mysterious stars. The moon was higher; he looked up; a late bird sang. Three strips of cloud, spaced far apart, were the footsteps of the South Wind, as she flew to bring more birds from Africa. His thoughts turned to gentle, happy hopes of a day when the lion and the lamb should lie down together, and a little child should lead them. War, in this haunt of ancient peace, seemed an incredible anachronism.

He did not go farther; he did not enter the forest; he turned back along the quiet road he had come, ate his food on a farmer's gate, and over a pipe sat dreaming of his sure belief that humanity had advanced. He went home to his hotel soon after midnight. He slept well, and next day walked back the four miles from the hospitals, instead of using the car. Another hospital searcher walked with him. They discussed the news.

"The weather's better anyhow," said his companion. "In our favour at last!"

"That's something," he agreed, as they passed a gang of prisoners and crossed the road to avoid saluting.

"Been another escape, I hear," the other mentioned. "He won't get far. How on earth do they manage it? The M.O. had a yarn that he was helped by a motor-car. I wonder what they'll do to him."

"Oh, nothing much. Bread and water and extra work, I suppose?"

The other laughed. "I'm not so sure," he said lightly. "Humanity hasn't advanced very much in that kind of thing."

A fugitive memory flashed for an instant through the other's brain as he listened. He had an odd feeling for a second that he had heard this conversation before somewhere. A ghostly sense of familiarity brushed his mind, then vanished. At dinner that night the table in front of him was unoccupied. He did not, however, notice that it was unoccupied.

THE END